When Forever Isn't

SUZANNE PRIGOHZY

ISBN: 0692746390
ISBN-13: 978-0692746394

DEDICATION

To my grandmother who weathered the storms.

Change is a law of nature.
Some shudder in its shadow; others see sunshine in its promise.
---Suzanne Prigohzy

ACKNOWLEDGMENTS

The author wishes to acknowledge the generous support and relentless encouragement given by:

Steve Prigohzy, Fritzie Manuel, George Tittle, Margaret Spencer, Martha Rogers, Janet Benton, Daniel Fraley, Paul Fraley, Leslie Graitcer, Barbara Stein, David Aiken, Heide Fraley

CHAPTER 1

BLANCHE – MAY 1946

Holstein cows grazed on the rolling pastures. Weathered barns leaned under the burden of time. Alongside quaint farmhouses, clotheslines strained under the weight of drying coveralls. Flapping in the morning breeze, they bore witness that families still worked the Tennessee soil.

When my brother slowed the black Ford sedan, only then did I turn my eyes from the scene slipping past my window. Once familiar, it now seemed foreign. Owen brought the car to a stop at the foot of the gravel drive, switched off the motor and secured the handbrake.

"You needn't come," I protested. "I'd prefer some time to walk about in my thoughts. You understand." My visits back to my home place were few but always required a stop here.

"Blanche, don't you worry. I don't plan to chaperone my sister while she visits the family cemetery."

His impish grin faded from his clean-shaven face and I couldn't help but notice how we both had aged. Owen was a handsome man, even now. Graying temples and prominent jawline had graced him with an air of sophistication that didn't go unnoticed, especially when he was wearing that three-piece gray suit. I didn't think the years had been as kind to me even if my chestnut-hued crown had been spared the gray intruders. As for my figure, it had been more of a battle, but what could I expect at my age when most everything sagged.

"Of late, it seems the final resting place of our people has become a destination for courting couples," he said, interrupting my thoughts. "You may be a mature woman of fifty-two, but your big brother will feel better if he walks you to the entrance. Want to be certain you're the only one keeping Mama and Papa's company. My first appointment is at ten, so I'm in no rush."

We closed the car doors and the cheerful breeze ushered us up the narrow, rutted driveway toward the top of the wooded knoll. A four-minute stroll, we kept company with our own thoughts. Only the padding of our shoes on the loose gravel and chastising blue jays in over-hanging oaks disturbed the serenity. Yes, I had often made this trek over the years, too often behind the casket of a loved one.

At the crest of the hill, Owen pushed against the rusty gate surrounding the grassy expanse. It creaked its protest but yielded passage. Owen stepped aside to wave me in.

Chuckling as I slipped through, I said, "Looks to me we're the only ones here, at least above ground. I turned to find my tall brother still outside the gate faced in the opposite direction with arms folded, unmoving, lost in the vista beyond. Sensing his mood, I returned to his side and reached my arm around his waist. In the near distance, Watts Bar Lake stretched in all directions, like fingers from the hand of the nearby Tennessee River. At the bottom of the hill on the far side, the lazy waters could be heard lapping the shore as if seeking to claim more ground. The expansive body of water seemed the master of the landscape, the focal point for an exquisite painting, testimony to the hand of the Divine. But we knew better. It was testimony to something far less pleasing.

"It's hard to fathom that it's gone, isn't it?" I mused.

"Yes, it is, sister," he spoke softly, without diverting his eyes. "A lot of newspaper ink was spilled to convince us President Roosevelt's plan was good...'ushering the South into the modern age with the promise of abundant electricity.'"

Detecting his sarcasm, I noted a subtle sadness slip across his features. His blue eyes gazed ahead, but his mind's eye was elsewhere.

"Yep, that's exactly how it was delivered," he said. "I recall thinking how fine a promise it was—what it would mean to our fair town. Never thought they'd build an electricity-generating dam that would destroy Rhea Springs right along with our home place...all under the colorful banner of progress."

Owen showed no interest in abandoning his reflections. What could ease my brother's lingering bitterness…or mine, albeit for an entirely different set of reasons? He lost his home place in 1941. Sadly, it was wrenched from me well before the waters rose.

The strengthening sun showered its cheer onto the lake's mirror surface, reflecting the cotton strips that drifted overhead. Surrounding oaks had donned their verdant green and rustled their pleasure in the clean morning air. On one side of the watery expanse, a forest of hardwoods crowded a ridge and spilled down to the shore; while on the other, well-tended fields showcased soybean crops and growing corn. Only a dark line of railroad track disturbed the fields' perfect squares, tracing its way diagonally like a ribbon of iron as far as the eye could see.

"A visitor here would never suspect what lay under that lake," Owen murmured. "Generations of our family called it home."

"Great Grandfather Wasson would twist in his grave," I added, "if he knew all that remains is this cemetery." Kind of ironic. Desolation had come to Rhea Springs. The community and its dwellings had disappeared under the waters of the Tennessee. But maybe its ruin helped drown my pain and disappointment…covering it over, making it easier to forget.

Owen sighed, "A great loss for us all."

I wondered.

"I've got to get along, Sister," he said, checking his wristwatch.

After a quick hug, he headed off.

"I'll fetch you at the lunch hour," he called over his shoulder, waving as he hastened. "Looks like you won't be bothered by the living." His words lingered as he disappeared down the drive.

"I'll be fine, Owen," I called after him.

I slipped through the open gate and strolled across the grass toward the ebony granite monument. Everything was tended, no ragged weeds skirting the headstones or trash strewn by those uninvited visitors my brother mentioned. My visits had been few over the half-decade since Rhea Springs had been swallowed up, but I was pleased this place still appeared cared for.

Nearing the rectangular stone taller than the others, I admired its carved leaf roping and sloping lines, a work of art likened to an ornate altar. My emotions stirred and awakened memories, memories as vivid as yesterday's conversations. I closed my eyes and the breeze caressed my face when the clarion call of a resting robin interrupted. Did I detect a hint of fresh cut hay somewhere? I filled my lungs and exhaled. The quiet was delicious and calming, and I heard myself sigh. "Papa, Mama, would you be proud if you knew how it has turned out for me?"

The smooth stone face offered only names and engraved dates, June 20, 1907 and September 11, 1936 and its inscription, "Blessed are the dead which die in the Lord, saith the Spirit, that they may rest from their labours; and their works do follow them." Feeling a lump swell in my throat, I turned away to meander among the other gravestones. Unlike Mama and Papa's, they resembled large mushrooms sprouted from the earth and were aged with lichen and moss and leaned in unexpected directions. I felt an aching urge to right them, to secure them anew. Many had stood here a century or more and bore testimony to our family's long history in this county. The cemetery reminded me of a tarnished crown sitting atop this hill.

After an hour and without realizing, I had circled back to the fenced boundary near the gate. No wonder. The feelings conjured here, the memories resurrected, caused time to cease. I clutched the rusty bars and scanned the lake's domain.

When I was a child, my town was right out there. "Over there was Grandfather's three-story, white-columned hotel," I pointed and mumbled---under my breath---to the invisible presence of all buried behind me. "It welcomed hundreds every summer."

The hotel was the County's bustling hub that drew months-long guests from far-flung places like Atlanta and Cincinnati, cities in Kentucky, even New Orleans. My young summers were spent buzzing about the place. What child could resist---recreation of every kind, musical concerts and dances and outdoor plays, and wayfaring strangers I was curious to watch, with accents different from mine, but who were always kind to me, the resort owner's granddaughter.

"Papa's wood-framed general store stood just up Muddy Creek Road past the livery stable," I heard myself say. "It was a gathering spot for locals, as much as the hotel was for visitors."

The store's broad front porch was lined with rocking chairs for those who wanted to tarry after completing business inside. And our churches—more than a few—welcomed folks weekly, and my school was housed in one. I remember clearly the old water bucket and ladle inside the door where I waited my turn after recess.

Neighborliness was nothing out of the ordinary. The town was strong and proud, even if it was small with more wide-open space than side-by-side shops down its main street. But it was also a place where everyone knew his neighbor's business.

In the distance, the faint doleful whistle of a train returned my vision to the quiet lake rather than my hometown. The long lonely call brought Charlie Reynolds to mind. A train like that had taken the young Negro man far away. I wondered what had become of him since our days in Rhea Springs when we huddled to talk about books in the shadow of the hotel or the behind the stable where he worked, always looking over our shoulders? I dare say Charlie would not remember the place as I, and not without reason.

CHAPTER 2

BLANCHE - 1903

"Lu—cinda…..Lu—cinnnda! Graaa-cey! Breakfast!" My voice rattled the stillness, shouting their names over the whitewashed fence. Almost hidden by the pale morning mist, my cow and lamb lingered among Papa's heifers in the distant pasture. Stretching, I wiped the night from my eyes and mounted the railing for a better vantage. At the far end of the field, the sun was peeking over the old weathered-gray barn. When I filled my nose with the lingering scent of sweet, fresh-cut hay, I knew another picture-perfect June day in Rhea Springs was mine for the having.

Jumping down, I took the bucket of feed corn at my feet and banged the fence post, yelling again. Lucinda lifted her lazy head and meandered in my direction, her big ole milk sack swaying to and fro. Gracey trailed behind. What a sight—my fuzzy, not-so-white lamb prancing in the shadow of the lumbering, fawn-colored cow. In spite of her constant bleating, Gracey thought she *was* a cow and never left the company of the others. Gifts from Papa on my ninth birthday to teach me responsibility, he had said. I mustn't forget to milk Lucinda later if I can't sweet talk Bertie into doing it.

"Blanche! Come on," my big sister Gay summoned, like a schoolmarm in the kitchen doorway of our two-story clapboard house. She called again before I could get a word out. "Leave the bucket by the fence. Your oatmeal is turning to stone. Bertie said to pop into the springhouse on your way and bring a block of butter. She's baking later."

"I'm com-m-m-ing!" I skipped to the corner of the yard where the small fieldstone building squatted over a spring of water near the sprawling oak that Papa said had been growing there since the Cherokees hunted on this land.

When I pushed open the wood door, the familiar whoosh of chilled air welcomed me. On summer afternoons, I'd often find my way here to cool off a spell. The two-foot thick walls and cool spring water bubbling inside guaranteed the dim room would keep our milk and butter fresh. Sneaking sips of cold milk in secret, feeling it slip down my parched throat on a hot day was the best.

The screen door slapped at my heels as I scurried with wrapped butter in hand to my seat at the kitchen table. My chair faced the sink where Bertie, the family cook and housekeeper, was busy working, perched on a stepstool with her back to me humming her Negro spirituals. I couldn't help but grin whenever I watched her, with that white apron pulled snug about her full hips, swaying in time to her rendition of "Gospel Train's A'Coming." Short and stout, she mounted the stepstool like a throne and the kitchen was her kingdom. Above the sink, multiple shelves were crowded with glass quarts of red beets, string beans, yellow crookneck squash and fruit from Rhea Springs' orchards, evidence of her and Mama's labors to keep the Wasson family well fed. This morning she was scrubbing carrots plucked from our garden, no doubt working on the next meal while the heat of the day was still tolerable.

When my sister slid the bowl of oatmeal in front of me and sat down to hers, I bit my lip to keep from laughing at the disapproval she also served up, with pursed lips and furrowed brow. At fifteen years, Gay tried to lord over me like she was Mama's equal, as if she had something to do with being the firstborn. With shiny, chestnut-colored hair pulled tight in a proper bun at the back of her head and wearing a freshly ironed skirt to show off her tall willowy figure, my sister looked as if she'd just stepped out of a McCall's Magazine. Unlike me, I loved nothing better than to wear coveralls and braids in my shoulder-length brown hair, figuring there was yet plenty of time to grow up.

With my first bite, I noticed my brother across the table draining his glass of milk. Owen raised his dark eyebrows over the glass rim to note my arrival. I thought it odd to see him on a Saturday with his unruly brown hair combed into submission and fourteen-year-old face cleaner than on any Sunday morning.

"Where are you going all gussied up?" I asked, wrinkling my nose. "It's Saturday."

"Remember, feather brain? My summer job starts today."

Owen promptly reminded me—with a haughty air—that he'd be driving the hotel's white surrey behind a team of white steeds to the train station four miles up the road to gather arriving guests. Having landed his first official position at Grandfather's hotel, he was quick to point out it was a pearl of a job. Unlike his friends who'd be working out in the heat on family farms, he'd be sitting in the shade of the surrey's fringed canopy having pleasant conversation with fascinating people from faraway places.

I couldn't argue that his duties wouldn't be fun. I loved going to the Spring City train station to watch the excitement—handsome couples pouring out of coach cars, the women with frilly parasols shielding themselves from the bright sun, gentlemen in their Sunday best, sporting Panama straw hats bought for the occasion, and happy children chattering as they hopped off idling trains. In a way, I envied my brother's new job but didn't let on.

"Oh, yeah, I forgot." Taking another bite of oatmeal, I considered my own plans for the day and then asked no one in particular, "Where's Mama?"

Bertie turned her red kerchief-wrapped head in my direction, her apple-butter brown face already dewy with moisture. "She's upstairs, sugar baby. Fixing to go to the stable and...."

Before Bertie could finish, Gay chimed in without looking up from her oatmeal, "And Mama said you're to finish your chores before you leave the house—and not to ask about riding your pony unless someone else supervises because she'll be busy exercising her own horse."

"I'm off," Owen pronounced, pushing away from the table, double-checking his white shirt for crumbs and paying no attention to the yammer of his sisters.

Without turning from her task, Bertie called out, "Wipe that milk mustache from your lip, Mister Owen." She chuckled under her breath because he always sported one when leaving the table. She had no need to look.

Owen brushed his shirtsleeve across his mouth and trotted for the front door, black tie in hand. "See you later," he called, the slamming door signaling his departure.

Gay ate in silence and watched Bertie work, paying no attention to me. After scraping my bowl for the last bite, I carried my dishes to the sink for Bertie to wash and shot her a smile that she returned.

"Where's my butter, Miss Blanche?" She silently scolded with an upside down grin and aside look.

Dashing to the table, I snatched the paper-wrapped block and returned it to her outstretched hand before scampering up the stairs.

Bertie called after me, "Be sure to pick up your room before you leave out."

Whizzing about the bedroom, I flung the sheets across the mussed feather bed and set my china head doll with the pursed pink lips atop my pillow. Once my bedclothes were stuffed into the chest-of-drawers, I grabbed my book off the bed table and hesitated at the door to determine if my room would pass inspection before hurdling down the stairs. Out the front door, I made a beeline for the hotel just across the dirt road.

Owen would remember his first summer position at the hotel, but the first dance of the season was going to be a special one for me too. I was gonna be Black Sam's personal assistant.

Sam Reynolds was Papa's most able colored worker and was given the nickname because of his dark skin—as dark as a walnut shell. Married to Bertie, he had worked at the Rhea Springs Hotel for longer than I'd been in the world. In my summer boredom, I wiled away many an afternoon shadowing the tall but lean, square-shouldered man as he carried out his duties around the hotel. One of late had especially interested me.

The hotel was not electrified. Open windows allowed the sought-after cross breezes in summer, but the cavernous dining hall used for dances heated up like a cook stove by late afternoon despite the hundred-year-old oak trees that circled the place. To solve the problem, Grandfather ordered from a Philadelphia furnishings company a giant ceiling fan, one that delivered a cooling stir of air as well as an exotic flare with its broad wood blades as long as I was tall. Single-handedly, Sam managed to hang it from a hefty ceiling beam. Took him all day, rigging the fan with a rope that snaked unnoticed along the beam through multiple pulleys and out a hole in the wall into the kitchen. Sam would station himself at that end and pull the knotted rope for the duration of every dance, every summer Saturday night. The pulley system was his idea, and he took great pride in its efficiency. With the heat stirred up by so many couples showing off the latest dance steps, Black Sam said many would faint without his constant service behind the wall.

After the fan was installed, I had pestered him like a circling gnat until he gave in and agreed to make me his special helper for tonight's dance. I would help out with the "fan rope". But keeping Black Sam's promise a secret was a must. Papa would surely say it wasn't proper for a hotel owner's granddaughter to do the work of the hired help, but I had a mind of my own and reasoned no harm would come of it. No one would notice me with Sam in the corner pulling on that knotted hemp rope.

With the upcoming evening still on my mind, I reached the rear of the hotel and found it hopping with workers racing the day, no doubt transforming the enormous dining room into a dance destination. Papa would have ordered the wood-planked floors oiled and buffed. Sam and the kitchen help would be placing refreshment tables along the walls, draping them with starched linens. Armloads of summer flowers had been picked from the hotel gardens and were being paraded into the kitchen just ahead of me, destined for crystal vases to crown the tables. With so many people scurrying about, I didn't see the boy coming until it was too late.

"Oh, my!" Knocked off balance and against the building, I caught a glimpse of the brown hands that latched onto my forearm to stop my fall.

"Sorry, Miss Blanche. I didn't see you a'tall. You all right?"

The thin boy with smooth brown skin scooped my book from the dirt and handed it to me. He reeked of animal manure, and his eyes grew large when silence and a wrinkled nose was my first reaction. Then I said, "Yes, I'm all right. Thanks," and wiped off my book. "Do I know you?"

About my age and a head taller with woolly black hair, he nodded as he dropped his eyes and brushed stray straw from his worn coveralls. "Yessum. I's Sam Reynold's boy," he muttered.

"Oh yeah. Your ma brought you along to our house sometimes? Years back? I vaguely remember chasing you and the chickens around the yard while she was hanging laundry. That's you?"

"Yessum."

Remembering my manners, I asked, "Are you all right?" His high forehead, almond-shaped eyes and dark skin made him a smaller copy of his pa. The boy was obviously nervous. He looked up to answer, but his eyes darted in every direction as if expecting the unexpected.

"Yessum. Can I go? I should get on."

I nodded and he rushed off, dodging others who were rounding the back of the building. I shrugged and joined the others. Once inside, I scooted around kitchen counters piled with fresh-picked produce searching for Papa, but to no avail. Then out of nowhere, I was snared in a net of strong arms.

"Papa! Morning! I didn't see you."

Papa and Grandfather stood with two stout women dressed in white and wearing cooks' caps. The women's brows damp with perspiration wrinkled into rows like scrub boards, irritated by my interruption. The room was abuzz with activity, but the two waited, albeit impatiently, as Papa and Grandfather turned attention to me.

"Of course you didn't see me the way you were roaring through here," Papa said. "Is there a fire?" He knuckled my head and ruffled my bangs.

Peering out the door as if looking for a posse, Grandfather stroked his white beard. "Or maybe the U.S. Deputy Marshall is after you?" He winked at Papa.

"Oh, stop, both of you! Today is Saturday." I informed them— as if they didn't know—that Uncle Jack came to town only on Sundays for church and it would be rare to see him otherwise.

Uncle Jack and Aunt Cinny Thompson lived on a farm six miles south where they raised cows and sheep. Uncle Jack was also the county's sworn-in U.S. Deputy Marshal, although he confessed he seldom had cause to pin on his star. Rhea County was mostly sprawling farms, meadows and orchards. The exception was Walden Ridge, on the county's west side about five miles from the hotel. Its forest, dotted with dogwoods and carpeted with ferns along meandering streams, drew the likes of picnickers not moonshiners. Papa said the last remaining stills were hidden in the remotest places that even Uncle Jack left unvisited. And with few cows ever reported missing from surrounding farms, I couldn't imagine Uncle Jack anywhere around the hotel today.

Papa and Grandfather finished their instructions to the waiting women, while Papa kept his love-hold on me. The cooks returned to work and Grandfather strolled off, but not before patting my head. I then spilled my plan to Papa in a gush of words. "Can I ride Beauty today? Mama's gone to the stable and said I'd have to ask you. That's why I was running—to find you. She's putting Marshall through his paces and said she couldn't watch me. Can I, Papa, can I?"

I held my breath as he planted both hands on my shoulders and gently lifted my chin with his finger. Arching one bushy eyebrow over his twinkling eyes, he declared, "Blanche Louella Wasson, can't you see how busy I am getting this place ready? I don't have time to watch you ride." He paused and then his brown mustache twitched as the corners of his mouth turned up, giving me hope. "Now...if Black Sam can snatch a free minute or two," he pondered aloud, "maybe he could lead Beauty over here and supervise while you ride around the grounds. Guests might enjoy seeing our finest young horsewoman in action."

"You know Mama is the county's best," I protested, but puffed with pride to hear Papa compare me to her.

He smiled knowingly and informed me that Sam was around the side of the building splitting wood and if I asked sweetly, he'd probably help. He knuckled my head and dismissed me. "Now, get along." Mumbling that work called, he headed to the far side of the noisy kitchen.

It was no surprise Grandfather had enlisted Papa to help run the hotel during the summer months. Papa was organized and efficient— Johnny on the spot, Grandfather would say. But as the youngest Wasson, I was free to follow my own whims and that suited me. Today, I needn't have brought my book along to read. I'd be riding instead. Taking a shortcut through the banquet hall toward the hotel's front doors, I heard my cousins' voices echoing across the room, "Blanche, Blanche...over here."

Whenever kinfolk arrived, Grandfather personally escorted them to the hotel from the train station. He made quite the impression driving the fringe-covered surrey, ever bit the likeness of Wild Bill Cody with untamed white hair, beard and mustache. When I begged to go along yesterday, he consented, even handing me the reins as we bounced along the country road. On our return trip with teenage cousins Nancy and Sarah, they chattered non-stop.

"Great-uncle, is the Chautauqua Circuit sending really interesting speakers this summer, ones you'd recommend?"

"Well, I think they all are." Grandfather twisted around to wink at Sarah and then instructed after they unpacked to check their bedside table for a printed list of amusements. Grandfather was proud as punch the hotel was now an official Chautauqua Circuit site.

Papa had penned many a letter to the New York State headquarters seeking that designation. Through Chautauqua, education and entertainment was brought to rural America; and according to Papa, even President Theodore Roosevelt championed it. Now, more visitors than ever were coming to Rhea Springs to hear noted preachers, scientists, and statesmen. And the concerts—classical to bluegrass—were just as popular. Papa favored political speakers who talked about women's suffrage, building a New South or the like. I fancied the plays, with gaily-costumed actors that drew young and old alike. My cousins never missed out on any of it. To hear them tell, no destination in the South was more glamorous than the Rhea Springs Resort Hotel.

"Over here," my cousins called again, waving me over. Across the dining hall, they sat at a small linen-draped table topped with a Mason jar of fresh-cut daisies. Sarah and Nancy's crisp white blouses were as bright as the tablecloth between them. How prim and proper they looked, their well-groomed brown tresses spilling onto their shoulders, shimmering in the light that streamed through the tall windows behind them.

"Hello," I said, nearing. "I'm on my way to find Sam—our hired help—so he can fetch my pony," I explained self-consciously, giving reason for wearing brown coveralls and floral shirt that Mama allowed only when I rode. "You can take a turn too, if you want. She's gentle."

"Here," Nancy patted the empty chair next to her. "Sit a spell. Want a biscuit? Here's jam...sorghum. I can't eat another bite."

"No thanks—I've eaten." The girls seemed to pay no attention to my coveralls.

Sarah declined my invitation, explaining that Owen had invited them to go boating on the hotel's new man-made lake. "Is it really true it took every man in Rhea Springs to form it?"

"Yes, it's true," I said with pride. "They sloughed off part of the Piney, but not before digging out the full size of the lake, three acres

13

worth. It took dozens of plows and a hundred men before water could be channeled in." Both girls' eyes grew large as their tea saucers with my description, and both chorused disbelief.

"Why don't you join us?" Nancy suggested. "Owen has promised a basket picnic lunch that the kitchen assembles—fried chicken, deviled eggs, all the fixin's."

"Thanks, but Owen wouldn't cotton to my tagging along." Seeing a chance to escape, I said, "Guess I'd better get along." I waved goodbye and turned to leave, as they called after me to come up to their room before the dance to see their ball gowns. I answered that I'd try.

Once outside, I broke into a run, hollering for Sam before I rounded the side of the building. I found him swinging an axe just as Papa had said, splitting the wood with such force that chips flew high into the air with every blow.

"Sam, Sam—Papa said when you finish here, could you go to the stable and saddle up Beauty and bring her over? He said I could ride around here for a while if you'd watch me."

Sam quieted his axe and pulled a tattered rag from his coverall pocket to mop his glistening brown neck and forehead. He appeared to welcome an excuse to rest as he stretched his back.

"Well, Miss Blanche, don't I get a 'good morning Sam' before you start barking orders?" He leaned on the axe handle and his show of pearly teeth signaled his good humor.

Blushing, I blurted, "I'm sorry Sam, but Papa said that he couldn't, and that maybe you could, and Mama can't because she's riding her horse…."

"Whoa—slow down Miss Energy. All right, if you want to ride, lend me a hand and pile this wood into that wheelbarrow behind you. A heap of cooking is going on today. Every stick is needed to keep those cook stoves stoked. The sooner this gets done, the sooner you'll be prancing about on Beauty."

I shot Sam a grateful smile and gathered an armful of wood.

CHAPTER 3

BLANCHE

Bertie had placed a clean pressed cloth on the supper table before leaving for the day, but now it was cluttered with dirty plates and half-empty serving bowls. Sister Gay had excused herself and was upstairs primping. Owen sat, eating in silence next to me in his own world. Papa, across from Mama, was quietly recounting the ins and outs of his hectic day as my gaze drifted to the nearby open window and across the wagon road. On the hotel grounds, glass lanterns dangled from ropes in the trees, like icicles dripping from their branches. The sun was resting low, washing everything in shades of pale yellow, while shadows stretched longer, predicting the magic of glowing lamps when darkness eventually settled in.

As many townspeople as hotel guests would soon gather for the first dance. Shopkeepers and farmers wearing their Sunday best will have turned into princes. Ladies will have traded their aprons for shiny taffeta and ruffles, with starched petticoats that rustle like dry leaves when they step through the hotel's welcoming double doors to join hotel guests.

It was like living in a storybook on summer Saturday nights, and I dreamed of being "Juliet" one day—wearing a shimmering gown that brushed the floor when waltzing with my Romeo. I fancied the dress but wasn't yet sure about the boy part. I was already changed into my favorite white-sashed chambray frock—the blue one matching my eyes and the skirt trimmed in rickrack. Bertie had polished my black Sunday shoes, and my shoulder-length brown hair shimmered from the earlier brushing Mama had insisted on.

"Mama...Mama," I spoke up.

Mama's face clouded and she scolded me. "Blanche, what have I told you about interrupting when your father and I are talking?"

"Sorry. Guess I was daydreaming."

Mama's face softened. "Well, you have our undivided attention. Go ahead."

"Sarah and Nancy invited me to their room tonight to see their gowns. I can go, can't I?" I glanced Papa's way, and then back to Mama.

"I know it's summertime," Mama said, "but there's church tomorrow, and it's not proper for a young lady your age to keep late hours."

Mama and I both looked to Papa, who nodded his consent, and then Mama added, "I want you home after five dance numbers. You're to be in bed by ten."

"I'll be home before then, I promise."

Sam would be disappointed I couldn't stay longer to help him out, but I didn't have any say-so in the matter.

"Walk over with your papa. I'm not attending," Mama said. "He and your grandfather are overseeing the festivities." Before turning attention back to Papa, she added, "Finish your milk before you leave out."

When the talk lulled, my brother glanced across to Papa and said out of nowhere, "Those rowboats Mr. Gonce built handle great. I took the cousins out this afternoon. Think I impressed them with my rowing. Their skinny fourteen-year old cousin is quite the Navy man." Owen grinned like a cat that had finally caught the mouse, and flexed his arm for me to see.

"Oh, you're escorting the older ladies?" Papa teased, and winked at me. "And on your first day on the job you're taking the afternoon off?"

Owen blushed. "Grandfather said no guests were expected on the afternoon train, so he thought I should show Sarah and Nancy the hotel's new amenities. Besides, they're cousins and only a few years older."

"Just having some fun with you. So, the boats handle well?"

"Easy to balance. No problem a'tall," Owen said. "And in the red, white and blue colors, they look swell out on the water."

"I wasn't convinced," Papa recalled, "when your grandfather came up with that grand scheme for a boating lake. It was a whale of a job, wasn't it?" Papa removed the cloth napkin from his shirt closure and pushed his chair back from the table. "Couldn't have pulled it off without you and darn near every able-bodied man—and every plow—in the county."

"It's gonna pay off, isn't it?" Owen asked.

"I think so. It's in all the newspaper advertisements now. There's more to Rhea Springs than just mineral water, correct?"

"That's right," Owen said.

Papa asked if he was headed to the dance, but Owen shook his head, complaining of sore arms. I figured he was still bashful over the prospect of asking girls to dance. Papa pulled out his pocket watch, looked at it and then at me, motioning as he stood up that it was time to leave.

When we stepped out the front door to cross the road hand-in-hand, dust was already kicking up from arriving wagons of party-going couples. They turned onto the horseshoe drive in front of the hotel like a parade. Papa and I waved, as I giggled with excitement. With me in my favorite dress and Papa all dressed up and wearing his new leather suspenders Mama had given him, I pretended I was on the arm of Romeo.

"Papa, the place is beautiful!"

"Do you like my idea for the lanterns in the big oaks?" Papa swung his arms open in introduction as we neared. "It took Sam and me the better part of the afternoon to hang all twenty-three. It'll be pure magic when darkness settles in, don't you think? We strung cedar branches along the rafters in the banquet area too. It'll smell like Christmas." And with that said, he gave me a quick hug.

When we reached the veranda that wrapped the hotel like a circular skirt, the fragrance of evergreens welcomed us through its open double doors. Once inside, we stood peering into the grand hall where the happy throng of the elegantly dressed was swelling by the minute. In addition to the hotel's guests, it appeared half the town had turned out. Papa patted my head in dismissal, saying he needed to get cracking. I watched him disappear into the crowd and then headed up the steps taking two at a time toward the guest rooms.

"Sarah, Nancy. It's me, Blanche," I called through the door of Room 304 as I knocked. The door cracked and then swung wide. Nancy stepped back from the open door to twirl around in her buttercup yellow gown. Her auburn hair was piled on her head in a loose knot, small ringlets escaping like tiny waterfalls that glimmered in the light of the room's oil lamps.

"What do you think, Blanche?" Looking down, she smoothed the chiffon bodice. "Mother fashioned it—hand sewed the yellow rose appliqués on the skirt. Spent a month of evenings bent over this dress."

"You and Sarah will be the most glamorous girls on the dance floor," I said, walking into the room.

Sarah sat at the dressing table across the room with her back to me, the mirror framing her beauty. Her burgundy-colored gown had a frilled scoop neckline that showed off her buttermilk complexion. She was pulling back her long brunette hair with a studded flower-shaped barrette.

Finding a perch on the bed, I sat cross-legged so I could watch without getting in the way. Self-consciously I twirled one of the two braids framing my face. Mama complained I always did that. She'd braid them so my shoulder-length hair wouldn't get in the way, but tonight the braids only pointed to my young years. Hoping to sound grown up, I asked, "Did Papa tell you the Tuskegee Band and Glee Club are coming the first part of August?"

Nancy walked to the bedside table and picked up the small printed card. "Yes, he did. It's listed here on the menu of activities. We're lucky to be staying until late August. After hearing Booker T. Washington speak at the hotel last summer, we wouldn't miss watching his students perform."

"Uncle Chapman and your grandfather are brave to bring controversial topics to the fore," Nancy said. "Mr. Washington raises the dander of many our people in the South."

"Folks don't cotton to change, but Southern progress demands it," I said, trying to sound smart and quoting—but not understanding—the import of what Papa often said.

They nodded.

"I think we're ready to make our entrance," Sarah said, as she rose from the bench at the dressing table, glancing one last time in the mirror. "Let's be off."

I trailed my cousins down the stairs, and Sarah offered a dismissive wink as the two strolled through the arched doorway into the hall turned ballroom and disappeared into the milling crowd that buzzed with conversation as a waltz played on.

Standing by the registration counter and peering in, I felt the music take me under its spell and I swayed along with it. Couples briskly circled the dance floor like the revolving fan overhead, and only then did I remember Sam Reynold's promise. Scanning the crowd and seeing no sign of Papa, I darted out the front doors and around the empty veranda toward the rear of the building, my Sunday shoes clacking wildly on the planks. The growing glow of lanterns in the last light of day sent a chill down my back and speeded my steps. When I opened the screen door to the kitchen, I saw Sam resting on his tall stool in the far corner of the busy room, methodically tugging the rope that operated the giant fan on the other side of the wall.

"Sam, I'm here. Can I pull the rope now?" I called out, hurrying to his side. When I reached for the rope, he gently elbowed my hands away.

"Blanche, wait a minute. Hold your horses. You've got to pull slow and steady…like this," Sam instructed as he demonstrated. With his shirtsleeves rolled high, the muscles under his dark skin rippled with each tug of the rope. "You can't jerk it or the fan will sway and clatter. Then you and me both will be in a heap of trouble. And you have to keep pulling 'cause it'll get hot in there, really quick, if you stop."

"I understand. I can do it," I said confidently as he stood to hand me the rope.

"You better stand so you can get more muscle into your pulling. This ain't no easy job."

Sam pushed the stool aside and we both stood silent and listening, my tugging at the rope with purpose while Sam enjoyed the rest. With an expressionless stare, he leaned against the wall—having left the room in spirit to some distant place. It had no doubt been a long day. When the waltz ended and the music shifted into a lively tune that set our toes to tapping, his tired dark eyes returned to mine and we both grinned, guessing the newest dance sensation, the Turkey Trot, was underway in the next room.

Minutes later the kitchen's back door flew open, banging the near cupboards. Out of the darkness, a wild-eyed boy appeared, his chocolate skin shining from the beaded sweat on his panic-etched face. Spotting Sam, he ran our way and then I recognized him, the boy who had knocked me over earlier in the day.

With the whites of his eyes on full display, he gasped, "Pa, you gotta come quick—It's Ma—She's hurtin' real bad—holding herself." He struggled to find words as he sucked in air. "She's down on the kitchen floor. She said to come fetch you."

"What happened?" Sam asked, his face clouding over.

"Don't know. I was playing with Ruby on the porch while Ma was cleaning up after supper. She yelled for me, but it wasn't like usual when she's calling me to do a chore. She sounded scared. I ran in and found her in a heap in front of the cook stove."

"Was there blood?" Sam asked as he turned toward the door pushing Charlie ahead of him. In the same breath as the question, he called to me over his shoulder that he was sorry but had to go and he'd trust me to carry on the fanning.

"No, Pa, I didn't see no blood," the frightened boy answered as the screen door slammed behind them and they disappeared into the night.

The drama in my corner had been drowned out by the frenzy of cooks barking orders, the rattle of refreshment trays shuffled in and out of the kitchen for refills. Sam and his son had been invisible to everyone but me, and I was dazed by it all.

Well, it *was* Sam's son Charlie who'd run into me this morning. Hadn't seen him in forever, I thought, but now twice in one day...

It was minutes before I realized the fan had gone idle. With trembling hands, I pulled at the rope. I had been confident that I could handle the fan, but without Sam? I tugged it as he had shown me, but my mind was jumping about like a wild horse in a small corral. I worried about people fainting from heat in the next room. I worried more about Bertie. What if she was sick enough to die? But Charlie hadn't said anything about her feeling sickly. What if she cut herself real bad, maybe with a butcher knife? Charlie said she was in the kitchen. But he didn't see blood. Maybe those scary men in white hooded robes had ridden by on horses and scared her so bad her heart stopped? I'd heard Mama and Papa whispering about such happenings in places where colored folk lived.

Yes, I remembered once after a Sunday family meal we children had drifted out to the front porch to play. I'd gone back inside for my jump rope and overheard Mama and Papa's quiet talk as they lingered at the table. Ku Klux Klan robes—secretly sewed by a group of women up in the Smithfield attic. Why? To frighten colored people into what was considered proper behavior.

I had stayed out of sight—no one knew I was eavesdropping. Mama had been clearly upset. Papa tried to calm her, saying the Klan hadn't been active around there in a long spell and the talk was all rumor. He pointed out that not many small towns shared one of their church houses with their colored folk and that demonstrated most people around Rhea Springs weren't closed-minded. But what he said next made my stomach churn—that there had been no lynchings in our county, unlike other places he'd read about. I couldn't imagine.

Mama said, "Is that supposed to make me feel better, Chapman, that scaring the devil out of people isn't so bad as long as we don't hang anybody from a hickory limb?"

"No," Papa answered calmly. "I'm saying that some folks get fearful without real cause, and if sewing sheets together makes them feel safer, then let them. That's not hurting anyone."

That didn't satisfy Mama one bit. I heard her chair drag across the floor when she pushed away from the table and then the loud clatter of dishes as she cleared them to the sink. She mumbled aloud that cowards hiding under sheets would come to no good, and innocent people would be hurt.

Maybe Mama had been right and the Klan had wanted to make Sam and Bertie an example to scare others. But they were decent folks and hadn't done anything mean or disrespectful.

I was still thinking on what had happened when my cramping arms and the finale of crashing cymbals in the next room jolted me back. The crowd was clapping wildly. Then it hit me. How many songs had been played? I promised Mama I'd be home after five. With no sign of Sam and not an inkling of the time, goose bumps rose on my arms and chills spilled down my back. It all turned to dread when the banquet hall door swung open and both Papa and Mama appeared with faces full of worry.

"Blanche Louella Wasson," Papa started in, as they neared. "Where have you been? And why are you back here of all places? Why aren't you home where you belong at this hour?"

Mama stood beside him glaring, in total agreement, with one hand on her hip that always spelled trouble.

"Papa, Mama, I'm sorry. I forgot the time. You see, I promised Black Sam I would help him with the fanning—and something bad happened—and he had to leave because his son came running. Said his ma was hurt…"

Papa's expression immediately changed. "What happened? An accident?" His questions brimmed with concern and his brow furrowed.

"I don't know. Maybe. I don't think he said."

Papa turned to Mama with a puzzled look.

"Heaven knows—you better check into it," she said. "See if Sam needs our help."

Turning to me again, Papa asked, "How long ago did he leave? Where *is* Bertie?"

"Charlie said his ma was at home on their kitchen floor. I'm not sure how long they've been gone—maybe twenty minutes?"

Turning back to Mama, Papa said, "I'll find Father and we'll get right out to Sam's."

Papa patted my head and said, "I'm going to have to buy you a pocket watch, daughter." He shot me a forgiving smile and left the kitchen to weave through the partygoers to find Grandfather, no doubt somewhere in the crowded room hobnobbing with guests.

Papa needed Grandfather to go along. Grandfather was a doctor as well as hotel owner. He didn't practice medicine anymore because he was old, he had once told me with an impish grin. Other doctors in town could do the job just fine. But whenever any of us Wasson children took sick, he was still the one to doctor us.

Unlike Papa, Mama's concern for Bertie did not change her disapproval of my behavior. She led me out the back door, and the fan rope was left dangling. As we walked across the hotel grounds, the brightly glowing lanterns now easily lit the way but not a word passed between us. Like her hand on my shoulder guiding me, I felt the silence.

At least our two-story house was welcoming. With its covered porch across the front of the house trimmed with gingerbread latticework and fancy carved columns, the curtains in its open windows fluttered their hello in the stirring night air. Only the towering grandfather clock in the entry hall signaled my transgression as we entered. Saluting us with eleven gongs, the mahogany cabinet stood tall like a disapproving sentry. Mama called up the stairs to

Owen to dress and skedaddle over to the hotel to lend a hand with the fan. Mama absently directed me to bed with a pointed finger.

Once in my room, I heard Owen coming out of his and hurrying down the stairs, asking Mama what was the matter. Relieved that I didn't have to answer to Owen, I walked to the window to pull the curtains and noticed then that the night sky had rearranged itself. Gathering clouds had chased away the stars and the shadows cast from the glowing lanterns had turned menacing rather than inviting. Faint sounds of music and laughter floated in from the direction of the hotel. I changed into my nightdress, wondering how all could be having a grand time when something horrible had surely happened to Sam's family. Climbing into bed, I clutched my doll close, nestled into the feather mattress and pulled the sheet over my head. It would be a long night—and I guessed it would be for Sam, Bertie, Charlie and Ruby as well.

CHAPTER 4

CHARLIE

Pa and I raced toward home and Ma in the rickety buckboard. He did his best to settle me, but I could tell by his fast talk and rapid-fire questions that he was as scared as me. Our empty wagon rattled and bounced and clanged as it slammed over the ruts and dry mud holes and the horses heaved for air. Seemed everthing and everbody was stirred up, and the darkness that swallowed us on the deserted road only made it worse.

"Charlie, what did you do with your sister—where is she?" Pa asked as he slapped the reins again to the backs of the team.

"I took her to Grandma Sulley's house. Ma told me to, before I lit out."

"Was she crying when you left her? You know Ruby squalls up a storm when something scares her."

"No, she didn't know nothing. When Ma called out from the kitchen and I ran inside, Ruby follered me. But Ma saw her and changed her talk—made it calm-like."

"Good…that's good," Pa's voice trailed.

"Yeah, when I took Ruby over to Grandma Sulley's, she thought we was going to visit."

Pa looked out after his little girl. Nearly three, she was the apple of his eye. When Ruby put them pudgy brown hands on both sides of Pa's cheeks and kissed his nose, he turned softer than Ma's bread dough. She had him in her back pocket for sure. I was special to Pa, too. But at eleven and the only son, he expected more from me—as man of the house when he wasn't around, to take care of things, and help Ma. But Ruby, he protected her like a rarified butterfly in the hollow of his hand.

The thirty-minute ride home took forever. Like wading through dark swamp waters with a pack of dogs at our heels, no matter how hard Pa pushed the horses or how fast they raced down the dirt road in the pitch black, it seemed like hours before I smelled the waters of Piney Creek and saw on the horizon the dark outline of the dozen or so huddled little houses. As we got closer, I could see a dim glow coming from our place, and the door stood wide open. I must've left it that way when Ruby and I lit out earlier.

As soon as Pa brought the horses to a stop, he threw the reins to me and jumped from the wagon. He hit the ground running, his shabby shoes slapping the packed earth as he headed to the wood porch. He disappeared inside and the night fell silent. Not a sound came from the house, and I couldn't bear to think what that meant.

After tying the reins to the gatepost, I trailed after Pa and reached the doorway in time to see him carry Ma from the kitchen to the bedroom. "Is she breathing?" I called out in a loud whisper, fearing the worst.

I was surprised when Ma answered in a hushed voice, "Well, of course I's breathin'. What'd you expect?"

I wanted to laugh out loud I was so relieved. Not knowing what to say, I looked down at my scuffed shoes and mumbled, "Ma, I was worried. It was so quiet when we got here."

Ma offered a weak smile as Pa lowered her to the bed. "Charlie, I was waitin' for you and your pa...and praying a bit. That don't call for a ruckus, now does it?"

"No, Ma. You gonna be all right?"

"I hope my Maker ain't done with me yet." Then she closed her eyes and fell silent. It was clear she didn't wanna talk. Maybe she was tuckered.

I glanced across the room into the kitchen where I'd left her hours before. There in the middle of the floor was a puddle big enough to make the hair on the back of my neck rise up. Dark red, twice the size of a pie tin, dribbles of it trailing across the wood planks into the bedroom, probably from when Pa carried her to bed.

Ma laid still, her eyes closed. Pa gently removed her worn shoes and pulled the thin sheet over her stained skirt and apron. Sweat beaded on her brow, and Pa's face was pinched with worry. Ma didn't say nothing more.

It was hard to take my eyes off her, but when I traced again that trail of blood, fear climbed up into my throat. Pa must'uv seen me staring because he said, "Charlie, how 'bout you cleaning up in there and then get over and see about Ruby."

Wanting to help and be a man and all, I did as Pa ordered but I swallowed hard when I stepped around the pool of blood. Searching for a bucket, I found one in the kitchen corner and filled it at the well out back. By the time I returned, water sloshing in my over-full pail, Pa and Ma was whispering in the other room but I couldn't make out their words. I dumped the water on the wood planks and washed it with rags the best I could. Bloody water seeped through the slats to the ground beneath. It took another trip to the well for a fresh pail to finish the job and turn the kitchen back to normal. Then I called over my shoulder to Pa as I headed out the back door, "I'm done here— going to get Ruby. I'll be right back."

"Wait a minute," Pa called after me.

I stood in the shadows and when he appeared at the backdoor, he looked over his shoulder toward the bedroom before telling me quiet-like to stay with Ruby at Grandma Sulley's until he fetched us.

He didn't see my face fall. "Can't I come back here to help?"

Pa frowned and growled, "You can help the most, Charlie, by staying with your sister. I'm guessing she's sleeping. But if she's crying or scared, it's better you keep her there. Ruby wouldn't understand anything she'd see here; probably would wanna crawl into bed with her ma. Now you stay with her at Grandma's, like I said." Then he turned away to go see after Ma.

Slinging the empty bucket and bloody rags aside, I made my way to the front of the house. The night was as black as tar, but I knew the place like the back of my hand. Had lived my whole eleven years here. At our fence gate, I stood by the wagon and peered into the dark till I could see clear to walk past the twelve other narrow clapboard houses toward the dim glow at the far end, coming from Grandma Sulley's place. The only thing stirring was my footsteps, the busy legs of crickets, and the squeak of Grandma Sulley's rusty screen door when I pulled it open.

There in the front room on the tired sofa sprouting cotton in spots was Ruby, fast asleep and cuddled on Grandma's lap. An oil lamp flickered low on the fireplace mantel as shadows danced on the dim walls of the bare room. I tiptoed in. Whispering, I told Grandma that Pa had sent me to check on my sister.

"Tell me how your ma is," she whispered back, pointing me to the worn cushion next to her.

Taking a seat, I reported that Pa was looking after Ma, and Ma herself had swore everything was going to be all right. Ma hadn't said that, but I figured I had to act brave and put the best face on the situation. Grandma patted my shoulder and forced a smile, but then bit her lower lip like she wasn't so sure. She commenced to tell me that Ruby hadn't been no trouble. She'd dropped off to sleep after hearing her favorite lullabies and drinking a cup of goat's milk. With that said, Grandma and me sat in the stillness watching Ruby sleep.

It wasn't until creaking footsteps on the rickety porch woke me that I figured I'd dropped off. Grandma Sulley had too. By the time I got from the sofa to the screen door, wiping sleep from my eyes, a white man in a fancy shirt, suspenders, and a black bow tie was knocking. It took a few seconds before I could make out Mister Wasson's face. But where was Pa? Was I dreaming? What was Mister Wasson doing out in our part of the county? Trembling inside, I stood dead still, staring up into that serious white face.

Through the screen, the man said, "Your pa asked me to fetch you and Ruby. I'm Mister Wasson. Your ma works for me." He pulled open the screen door so I could see him clear. "You recognize me, don't you, Charlie?"

"How's Ma?" was the only words to find their way out of my mouth.

His gaze shifted across the room to Grandma Sulley and Ruby. He quieted his voice and looked back at me. "Don't worry. My father is a physician and he's looking after her. He's an excellent doctor—takes care of my whole family. You can rest easy, Charlie. She's going to be up and cooking your vittles again in no time."

"She ain't going to die?" I asked, my voice cracking, giving away how scared I was.

"Oh, no. She'll be just fine."

Mister Wasson looked over at Grandma again and said, "I'm sorry to be barging in on you at this late hour. I'm Chapman Wasson.

Bertie Reynolds works for me. Sam is my father's and my handy-man at the Rhea Springs Hotel…in town. We got word that Bertie had been hurt, so we rode out to see if we could help."

"Yes sir," she said, her eyebrows knitting together in suspicion. "Thank you for comin'. If you can help Bertie, all of us 'round here will be as grateful as Sam. No finer folks than Sam and Bertie Reynolds. Yessir, that's the truth."

"You have no argument from me," Mister Wasson answered. "Sam and Bertie have been with us for years." He pulled his pocket watch from his trouser pocket and checked the time. Frowning, he said again, "Come on, Charlie. Your pa needs you. It's been a long night for everyone." He glanced Ruby's way and asked, "You want me to carry your little sister?"

I headed for the couch before the words left my mouth. "No sir, I will." Grandma Sulley offered up the sleeping bundle. Ruby was a limp brown doll, settling her head on my shoulder when I clutched her close.

Grandma gave a polite smile to Mister Wasson but didn't move from her seat. I'd wager she was as surprised as me to see a light-skinned man walking into her house in the middle of the night. Didn't matter that Ma or Pa worked for him. It was just plain odd to see white folk out here in the Bend. And if they was, it was usually for no good reason.

Grandma had long since gotten too old and crippled to venture far. Doubt she knew anything about the Rhea Springs Hotel, exceptin' it was for out-of-town white folks. Her days was filled with tending little'uns at her place. She was not a real grandma, at least not mine. But she was like kinfolk to all that lived along Piney Creek in the Bend who needed her help whilst they was off in the fields or working in town. Ever young'un called the small stooped, white-haired woman Grandma, including me.

"Goodnight, Grandma," I whispered before turning toward the door with my sister. So little and so light, Ruby was like a stuffed teddy bear in my arms. She turned her head on my shoulder, and her stubby pigtails brushed against my cheek. As she settled herself again, I spied part of a dried milk mustache still clinging to her lip. She never opened her eyes.

Mister Wasson held the torn screen door open and we headed into what was left of the night. I held my peace as we walked. Only the call of tree frogs from the nearby creek broke the silence. I didn't know what to say to grownups, especially white ones. Instead, I gave Ruby a gentle hug and whispered to her—and to myself—that everthing was gonna be all right. Mister Wasson followed silently behind.

When we reached the house, I crossed the sagging porch, pulled open the door with my free hand and headed to the bedroom, holding my breath. I could see Ma sitting in bed, wide-awake. When she saw me with Ruby, her face lit up. Pa stood next to her bed and his face said it all, his words sealing it. "Your ma has been in good hands tonight, Charlie," he stated, like it was gospel truth and gave the white-haired man standing at the foot of the bed a grateful smile. "She's gonna be just fine directly, thanks to Doctor Wasson here. Ain't that so, Doc?"

"Your ma will be fine," Doctor Wasson said to me. "All I did was help out Mother Nature a bit. Bed rest is what's called for now, so you two have to make sure she follows doctor's orders." Doctor Wasson looked down at Ma and winked. She returned a bashful smile.

Ma was in her pink cotton nightdress and the bed sheet was neatly folded across her bosom. This time I didn't see blood nowhere.

From behind me, Mister Wasson spoke up, "Well, are we done here, Dr. Wasson?"

"I do think so, son," his father said, sounding tired but satisfied. "I believe these folks would like us out of here so they can join that little girl in getting some rest. Won't be long before the roosters will be bringing up the sun."

Doctor Wasson picked up his black bag, and Pa followed the two men to the front door, thanking them over and over.

I carried Ruby to the corner of the room and lowered her onto our mattress on the floor. It rustled as the dried cornhusk stuffing gave under her weight. As I pulled the sheet over her small body, she settled in, still fast asleep.

Ma motioned me to her bedside with the same finger she often scolded me with, but I wasn't expecting none of that tonight. When I stood over her and my fingers pushed aside the dark strands of woolly hair that she always kept hidden under her head kerchief, I felt grateful. I leaned down and kissed her shiny forehead. Her brown eyes were soft as she smiled and pulled me to sit beside her. She looked peaceful, almost angel-like.

"Charlie, I'm real proud of you."

"Why, Ma? I ain't done nothing."

"Oh, but you did. You kept your head when I was in deep trouble and needed help. You got Ruby safe to Grandma Sulley's without scaring her. And you got your Pa back here in no time."

"Ah, that was easy. I'm just glad you's all right."

"Me, too."

"Ma?"

"Yes, Charlie?" Ma waited, closing her eyes.

"You ought'a leave off that kerchief. You look purtier without it."

With her eyes shut, a smile drifted across her round face, and she whispered, "Thank you, Charlie. You wouldn't remember, but years back the Wassons brought that bright red kerchief to me after their trip to Chattanooga. The mister said it would make his hired help stand out from the rest."

"Ma, you stand out, but not because of no kerchief."

Her words stirred up my feelings. Ma could work circles around anybody in Rhea Springs and she kept the Wasson place spit-shined like a new pair of Sunday shoes. He didn't need to give her no red kerchief. But tonight wasn't the time to point that out and be told I was disrespecting Mister Wasson.

When the oil lamps were later snuffed and Pa and I climbed into our beds, only a few hours was left until first light. The house sat quiet. In the darkness, I laid on the cornhusk mattress listening to the steady breathing of my sister next to me. I could hear Ma and Pa on the other side of the room when they shifted on their bed and its wood and rope frame complained with its usual groans.

I should'a stayed quiet, but I couldn't help myself. I talked out into the darkness. "Ma, are you sure you're gonna be all right? There was blood on the kitchen floor and on your clothes too."

Pa whispered back, but his voice was hard, "Charlie, you ask too many questions. Didn't the doctor say she was?"

"Yes, Pa, but…. Never mind. Goodnight."

Ma whispered, "Sweet dreams, Charlie. We're all fine and together and that's what counts, isn't it?"

"Yes ma'am."

Yes, we was, but I couldn't turn off my thinkin'. Why all the blood? They wasn't telling me. I had no choice but to take Ma and Pa's word.

According to Pa, Mister Wasson's father was doctoring as far back as the Civil War. Operated at field hospitals near the battlefields and dug out more Minie' balls from soldiers' bodies than he could keep count of. Pa said his worst job was sawing off Rebs' arms and legs that was shot up bad, but I think Pa found some odd pleasure in describing it, just so he could watch me squirm. When the war was over, Doctor Wasson had come back to Rhea Springs and bought the hotel. He kept looking after sick folk, but the hotel took more and more of his time until he got too old to keep up with both.

Didn't matter to me how long the silver-haired man with matching beard and mustache had been doctoring. I didn't cotton to the idea of his putting his hands on Ma. It didn't seem to bother Pa. He was gushing "thank you" in all directions when the men left.

I'd wager Grandma Sulley would see it my way, seeing the suspicion all over her wrinkled face when Mister Wasson came through her door. I'd heard her say many times that folks like us gotta be careful around white crackers, even when they was kindly. "You's only as interesting as you is useful," she'd said.

Her ma and pa had lived out hard lives on a two thousand acre peanut plantation in South Georgia. They was slaves. When Grandma Sulley started growing up purty, her owners sold her off for a sizeable sum. She ended up a house servant for a rich family in Chattanooga—a better lot than her folks, but terrible she got taken away from them. When the Emancipation Proclamation paper got signed, she hightailed it out of Chattanooga faster than a horse spooked by lightning. Went back to Georgia to find her folks, but they had died and she didn't know. Eventually she found herself a sharecropping husband who poured out his life tilling fields for other men. He died a few years back—just plain wore out, to hear her tell. With all Grandma Sulley had seen over her many years on God's green earth, she swore white folks—with few exceptions—were only interested in us colored folk when we served their purposes. They'd chew us up and then spit us out when they's through. Yep, that's what she said.

Shifting myself on the mattress again, I couldn't stop thinkin'. I reckoned Ma and Pa wouldn't agree with Grandma. They'd worked for the Wassons since before I was born, Ma at the Chapman Wasson house and Pa at the hotel. Pa said the Wassons was broad-hearted, even if they was white. Why, a few years back Mister Wasson offered us a few acres to clear and till, at the far end of his land. Said the soil wasn't no good for strawberries and he didn't want to take on any other farming than his strawberry crops. Anyhow, Pa didn't have to pay for using their land. Mister Wasson's only requirement was that we drop off a few bushels of corn at their kitchen door at harvest time. Pa and me managed that field easy, even with me working at the hotel stable and Pa at the hotel. Pa said someday I'd most likely be sharecropping and working a five-acre patch of ground was good practice. I had a few years yet to think on that.

With my body and mind plumb wore out, I finally fell asleep listening to Ruby's heavy breathing next to me.

CHAPTER 5

BLANCHE

When the rooster's rowdy call woke me, Papa had already left for the white-framed Methodist church. Needed to speak to the preacher, Mama said when I made my way down to the kitchen and asked. She glanced in the direction of the stairs and called impatiently for Gay while pointing me to the breakfast table. "Get yourself something to eat," she urged. "Be quick about it. We shouldn't be late." Mama moved to the steps and called again, just as the grandfather clock echoed behind her.

A pitcher of milk and loaf of sliced bread waited on the table, ready for butter and honey. As usual, Bertie had baked on Friday. And there was ambrosia that Owen had brought home after the dance. But I wasn't hungry; my stomach still churned with thoughts of last night.

Twenty minutes later Owen returned from the livery stable with the family's black surrey, just as Mama had ordered. Standing at the foot of the steps, she called Gay and me to get ourselves out the door. I finished my milk and left the dirty glass along with my worries, and scooted past Mama out to the surrey before my sister.

As we traveled the mile up the dusty road toward the church house, clopping hooves and the distant welcome of church bells were the only sounds stirring the morning air. No one said a word, not like most Sundays when the chatter in our surrey was as lively as the birds greeting the day. Mama sat next to Owen who was handling the horses, and Gay, next to me on the bench behind, was searching through her small brocade purse. I could hold my tongue no longer, so I raised my voice. "Mama, when did Papa get home last night?"

"In the wee hours," Mama replied without turning.

"How is Bertie?"

"Not now, Blanche," she said, offering a dismissive smile in my direction. "Bertie is going to be fine. We'll talk about it later." Mama was far more interested in Owen's properly managing the team than in my questions. I sighed. Patience was not my strong suit, but at least my failings were no longer on Mama's mind.

Turning attention to Gay, I wondered what she was looking for in that purse? She was stirring its contents like Bertie stirs a pot on the stove. Bored with no conversation to listen to, I asked innocently, "Are you playing at today's service?"

Gay looked up and snapped, "Of course, I am, silly." Then she went back to searching her purse.

My sister had been picked as the church organist after last year's arrival of a proper church organ, a grand instrument that had caused quite a stir in Rhea Springs. The church elders, Papa being one of them, had agreed that music added to the beauty and dignity of worship. But others disagreed, claiming no one ever professed religion with an organ bellowing like a cow. Old hymns sung in the old fashioned way, right alongside old-fashioned religion—that was God's way, they argued. When the organ was delivered, some left our Methodist congregation and joined the Baptist church south of town. I could not imagine the Good Lord turning up a nose at my sister's heavenly playing.

"Owen, ease up," Mama instructed, and the surrey shifted into a smoother ride. "Not so tight on their mouths."

Papa was usually at the reins on Sundays with Mama next to him. The Wasson family coming up the road to the Methodist church at this hour was as predictable as the sunrise, and not because of my sister's duties on the organ. In our family, Sunday school was as important as the worship service. But I didn't mind. We children had Father Cash as our teacher. To hear Mama tell, he had preached to the Cherokees and early pioneers—when my great grandfather Edward Wasson had settled in the area and it was Indian Territory. In my book, that made Father Cash as old as the hills. He always wore a worn brown leather jacket with long fringes along the arms and a bolo tie. He sat right in front of the preacher during worship, because he couldn't hear so good. In cold weather, even indoors, he donned an enormous fur cap with long earflaps—like Uncle Jack's coon dog's ears—pulled down over his wiry gray eyebrows. What an unforgettable sight he was—a weathered prune of a face encircled by brown bear fur.

During the Sunday school hour, Father Cash belted out Indian songs with gusto and acted out real-life bear stories, always ending in how God delivered him. With us children sitting around him on the floor, our eyes swelled as round as silver dollars when he spun his tales. He was the reason I didn't kick up dust about attending every Sunday. But it didn't matter. I was going whether I liked it or not.

"Whoa," Owen, called sternly as he pulled the horses to a halt in front of the church house.

Like every Sunday, I was first out of the surrey. My sister, having closed her purse, huffed at me as I scrambled across her feet. "See you all later," I called over my shoulder as I headed to my class on the upper floor of the building.

An hour later folks began filling the benches for worship on the first floor. When my class was dismissed, I scurried down to take my place between Mama and Papa in the middle of the third row, right where we sat every Sunday for as long as I could remember. Owen took his place next to Papa, and Gay was already settled at the organ.

Soon the preacher strolled down the aisle between the two sections to the front of the murmuring congregation and stood quietly. He was Papa's age, tall and thin with long arms. His black suit, shiny from age and use, gave him a stern appearance that scared me a little, especially when he delivered a sermon with a bellowing voice and gesturing arms.

At the moment, his arms were quiet at his side, his worn Bible in one hand, as he scanned the congregation. When his eyes fell on me and he nodded, I gulped and dropped my eyes. But he was motioning to Papa, who rose from his seat and cleared his throat. Smoothing his dark brown hair with one hand and double-checking that his suit jacket was properly buttoned with the other, he stepped into the aisle to join the preacher. I swelled with pride. The murmuring crowd quieted and I could have heard a pin drop.

My papa had the respect of the whole county and with good reason. According to Mama, he was always fair in his dealings both at his mercantile store and gristmill and extended credit to townspeople and farm families if they ran short on funds between harvests. He never turned anyone away.

Standing before the crowd of a hundred or so townspeople and visiting hotel guests as well, Papa announced, "Last night my father and I were called to a health emergency at Sam and Bertie Reynolds' place out on the Bend. As most of you know, the Reynolds have been with the Wasson family since our Gay was born. Dr. Wasson and I rode over to see how we could help. Out of respect for their privacy, I'll only say that Bertie did suffer a mishap but should be back on her feet in a week or so. For now, however, she's on complete bed rest and can't attend to the needs of the family. As is always the case with our fellowship, we knew some of you might want to show charity by sending food for Sam's family. If you'd like to help, please my missus after the service. We'll be taking meals over, starting tomorrow."

The worship service that followed droned on as my constant wiggling attested. I wanted to know in the worst way what had happened to Bertie. But it wasn't until bedtime prayers that I learned the facts—a lesson about medicine and the "birds and bees."

***

Sitting at my bedside, Mama explained that Bertie had had a baby growing inside her, but something went wrong. The doctoring word was a "fetus" but it had no life when it came out. She assured me it was God's way of not letting a baby be born when its body couldn't work right.

"Mama," I began, sitting up in bed, ready to share my own knowledge. "When the moon is full the stork leaves a baby under the growing cabbages in the field for the new parents to find."

"And who told you that?"

"Friends…at school."

"Blanche, they are—shall I say—misinformed," Mama said with merriment in her voice.

She patted my head, and I thought she might laugh. Instead, Mama put on a serious face. "These are matters that children have no need to fret over. I wanted you to understand so you wouldn't be afraid for Bertie."

She then said—the corners of her mouth turning up—that none of her children, including me, had emerged from a cabbage patch under a full moon and that was all I needed to know for now.

***

The next afternoon as I returned from playing with Gracey in the field, I spied Papa and Owen making repeated trips to our wagon with full baskets covered with red-checkered cloths.

"What are you doing?" I called, coming through the fence gate. Owen ignored me, but Papa heard.

"I'm fixin' to take dinner over to Sam and Bertie's," he said.

Bored, I asked, "Can I go?"

Rather than giving me a "yes" or "no," he answered that it was a long ride to the Bend. I'd never been out to where colored folks lived, but I didn't have anything better to do. "Please, Papa?"

Papa hesitated, but when he climbed up on the wagon, he patted the bench next to him. "Get on up here, or I'm leaving without you."

The back corner of the wagon was crowded with baskets of food. The aromas filled my nose as I settled next to Papa: fried chicken, probably fresh-baked biscuits, potato salad, and green beans that had most likely simmered for hours with fatback for added flavor. Papa said one church family had brought cobblers—a blackberry and a peach. Nothing was sweeter than peaches from our county's orchards. And in summer, loaded blackberry bushes along the fence lines were always begging to be picked. When cobblers came from the oven with juice bubbling up between the golden lattice pastry strips...well, that would bring healing to any body.

Owen emerged from the kitchen again to wedge a melon between the baskets and then signaled to Papa. With a flick of the reins, we were off. The wagon rolled along Muddy Creek Road past neighbors' houses and turned at Old Stage Road. Before long, the open fields stretched as far as I could see with crops growing here and yon. The world loomed large in the quiet of the unfamiliar landscape.

After awhile, Papa broke the silence. "The fields look like a big quilt."

I gazed into the distance and back at him, cocking my head with a silent question.

"Don't you see?" Papa explained, as he pointed. "The corn field over there, the strawberry fields way out there, and the soybeans there? Enormous square patches of color and texture. Mother Nature's giant quilt, don't you think?"

"Sure enough," I said. "I see now." We both grinned, and the vast countryside then seemed a little friendlier.

The Old Stage Road ran along the fence lines, and we rolled on until we reached a road angling right. It followed alongside Piney Creek, deep and lazy at that point, a dark ribbon of green. Later, a dozen or so clustered shanties appeared on the horizon. When we drew closer, I could see they were nothing like the houses around home. The small rickety structures leaned one way or another, with sun-bleached board sidings that hadn't felt a paintbrush in forever. When we reached the second house, Papa reined in the horses and brought the wagon to a stop. Sam's place offered a tiny covered porch that provided little shade for the two windows on each side of the door. The once-white house was narrow but deep—from front to back—and one level. Papa called it a shotgun house, saying if you shot a gun through the front door, it would narry hit a wall before going straight out the back door. No trees or grass surrounded the place, just packed earth with a few lonely chickens corralled between a wobbly picket fence at the road's edge and the house. They pecked lazily in the heat, searching for worms or seed. A solitary rose bush full of red buds next to the porch was the only color around. All the houses up the road were lined up like soldiers, shoulder to shoulder. Could have spit from one front porch to the next, and all appeared deserted.

"Papa, may I stay in the wagon? I don't want to go inside. Anyhow, I wouldn't know what to say to Sam's family." That wasn't the reason. The surroundings were strange, I didn't really know Sam's children, and I felt better where I sat.

Papa studied my face, smiled knowingly, and then said he'd pass along my get-well wishes to Bertie. He patted my knee before climbing down to gather baskets from the back. When Papa was halfway to the house, the door opened and Sam appeared, looking surprised to see him and what he had in hand. I couldn't make out their talk, but Sam waved in my direction. I returned the greeting and settled in to wait.

The scenery was lonely with every porch sitting empty and no one in sight. Then I heard something—coming from the far end of the row of houses. On closer inspection, I spotted a white-haired colored woman sitting on a porch step with a passel of toddlers playing at her feet like chicks around a mother hen. None of them wore anything but a diaper, and their happy squeals drifted my way.

In minutes, Papa was back to the wagon for the remaining baskets. "You all right?" he asked, as he tucked the melon under one arm and reached for the last basket.

"Yes, Papa, I'm fine," I said, returning my gaze to the old woman and the little ones.

He disappeared inside the house and minutes later returned with a look of satisfaction.

"How is Bertie?" I asked, as he climbed onto the wagon bench.

"She's feeling better. All smiles. So was Charlie and his sister when they got a whiff of what I brought through the door."

Papa fell silent as he turned the wagon and headed toward home, but I was thinking a lot. Finally, I asked, "Why do Sam and Bertie live so far out—over here along the Bend? And where are the people? I didn't see anyone stirring."

"You didn't see folks because they're all working—out in the fields and the women folk in the homes back in town. And they live out here…" Papa hesitated, and then explained, "This is where most of our Negros live. There's another area on the back side of Walden Ridge, over there," he pointed in the distance, "where the Hickeys, Ray and Smith families live, too. You remember Uncle Eli and Aunt America Caline, don't you—your grandfather hired them last summer for a spell when he needed some extra help? They live up there." Papa paused, but then added, "People like to be around their own, just as you like living close to your grandfather. Why, there's a whole section at the far end of town where families from up North live— the Livermores, the Gonces. Mr. Gonce is the boat-maker who built our rowboats. Remember?"

"But living way out here…they're so far from town. Where does Sam's son go to school?" Before Papa could reply, I added, "Do colored children even go to school?" I had never thought about it before, ever.

Papa held his peace, the clip clop of the horses' hooves the only answer. He absently fiddled with his mustache and then took off his hat to scratch his head. Then he said, "I hear Oliver Lyons has set up a Negro school in his barn. Colored children can attend there. I asked

Sam if he'd send Charlie, and he told me he was thinking on it, but hadn't decided."

"What's Sam need to think on? That's a swell thing Mr. Lyons is doing."

Papa nodded and said, "Sam needs Charlie working at the stable in the summer when the hotel is busy and he wants his help plowing and planting in the spring. Maybe in the winter months he could go. To be honest, he isn't sure what his son might get from school. Sam's family isn't blessed with books, like you, my little book worm." Papa gave me a wink.

After thinking on it a spell, I asked, "Wasn't it Mr. Booker T. Washington at the Chautauqua meeting last summer at the hotel who talked about that…that Negros needed schooling? Isn't that what he said? Remember?"

"What a memory. You were actually listening?" Papa teased. His face grew serious. "Blanche, it takes everybody working—doing their part—to grow a town. Everyone has his place. Our farms take a lot of work to keep them producing that good food you find on your table everyday. Most farmers around here couldn't manage without folks like Sam and Bertie to pitch in. Their labors are important."

"But you and Mama tell me all the time that I should study hard and learn all I can from my teachers—not just reading and writing—but my other subjects too. And my education will mean a better life as well as make me a better person. What about Charlie, if he doesn't go to school?"

Papa was quiet, thinking over his words, before he said, "Times are changing, Blanche. Sam's boy will be a strapping young man before long. Maybe the new railroads coming across the South will bring jobs offering more than a hardscrabble life. And, yes, to read and write could make it better. But Charlie's pa needs his pitching in to help his own family out. He can't see how reading and writing will make any difference."

"Do you think Charlie could ever live in a house like ours? I mean…his place is tiny! With that speck of a covered front porch and no trees around the place like ours, whew-wee, I bet it gets hotter than a firecracker inside."

Papa eyed me as I prattled on. His face softened as I fretted over a Negro boy's future, a Negro boy I hardly knew.

"Who knows what's in store for Charlie," he said, when I paused for a breath. "I don't have a crystal ball."

Papa's voice altered. He was growing impatient. "If colored children learn what you do," he said, "I don't know what difference that'll make to their future. Whether they could live in bigger houses…? I don't know…."

Shifting his weight on the buckboard bench, he wiped the sweat from his brow and concluded, "Blanche, it's just the way it is."

Papa snapped the reins over the team and looked straight ahead, signaling the conversation's end. I didn't ask anything else, and silence traveled with us the rest of the way home.

***

Two days later as I sat on the front steps of the hotel looking over the new book Papa had ordered for me, I heard slowed footsteps nearby. Twisting around, I found Charlie trying to sneak a peek.

"Whatcha reading?" he asked timidly.

I held up the book with the funny tin man and scarecrow dancing hand-in-hand on its cover. "*The Wonderful Wizard of Oz*," I answered. Remembering what Papa had said—about his not going to school or having books, I quipped, "You know how to read?"

"Of course I do," Charlie snapped, and his curious expression turned irritation.

I didn't mean to embarrass him, but I wasn't convinced. Mustering my courage, I asked if he'd like to borrow a book sometime. Charlie thrust his hands deep into his coverall pockets, drew his shoulders up to his ears before they fell back and he walked away.

Charlie kept turning up around the hotel over the next few days, usually in the shadow of his pa, helping him out with one task or another. Maybe the Good Lord was trying to tell me something, so I determined to take action. That very night I searched high and low in my bedroom for my first readers, ones that Sam's son might decipher. I carried two to the hotel the next day, hoping to spy him. I was lucky. While I swung in a hammock tied between two trees on the front plaza, Charlie rounded the building. He was headed off in the direction of the stable. I called out and ran to catch up. When I showed him the books and offered them as a loan, his eyes darted all

41

around to see who might be watching, like someone would think he was stealing them if he took them in hand.

"Why you wanting to give me your books?" he asked.

"I'm not giving them to you, Charlie. It's a loan. You seemed interested in my book the other day and I thought I'd be neighborly and share. You don't have to borrow them if you don't want."

But he did. He tucked the books under his shirt and ran off, muttering "thanks" over his shoulder. I smiled to myself, guessing these might not be the only ones, given his reaction.

By bedtime, my conscience had gotten the best of me. I had not shared any of my doings with Papa or Mama. Wasn't certain how they'd react. After prayers with Mama, I mumbled that I needed to confess something. She didn't hear that from me often, so she tilted her head looking puzzled. Still sitting on my bed, she called downstairs for Papa to come.

They patiently listened to my list of reasons why I should share my old books with Charlie, reasons I'd written earlier on a piece of paper so I could keep my mind straight when I told them. Then I confessed I had already loaned him two. They didn't speak until I finished, folded up my list, and looked up into their faces. Instead of scolding me, they offered faint praise, but also a solemn warning.

"Blanche, it's a generous thing you've done," Papa said. "I'm proud of you." But his brief smile faded and that gave me immediate worry. "If Charlie wants to borrow your books, you have our permission, but not everyone will appreciate your actions. We should keep this plan to ourselves, within our family. Some folks still have strong feelings about colored children and book learning. I've heard petty talk around the county about Mr. Lyons opening his barn to school colored children. You and I talked about that the other day. Remember? I'm sorry to say it's brought a fair share of disapproval."

Mama looked up at Papa from my bedside and added, "Don't you think you should speak to Charlie's pa when you get the chance? It's important that Sam be agreeable."

Papa nodded. Mama leaned over, kissed my forehead, before rising to snuff out the lamp. "We don't want Sam thinking that Charlie's done something improper," she said. "He'd skin him alive if he did."

I had not thought about that. And after Mama went downstairs, I lay in the dark staring at the ceiling wondering where Charlie had taken my books.

CHAPTER 6

CHARLIE

Miss Blanche wasn't like them other white girls. Different from her big sister. Friskier. Didn't know what to make of her up and giving me her primer books. I wasn't gonna tell her I couldn't read good. Almost a man at eleven years, I figured I should be reading more than my name and sentences like "See the boy run." Times was changin' whether Pa thought so or not. Nope, I never saw much of Miss Blanche other than when I was helping Pa out on special jobs at the hotel—when he needed my added muscle. Pa said she played around the hotel lots in the summer. Followed her papa—or my pa—like a shadow some days. He figured she treated the place like her playground because of all the recreation offered the guests there.

What I couldn't figure was why she was paying me any mind, even if we was close in age. It all started that Saturday night when Ma took sick and those Wasson fellers showed up and then two days later Miss Blanche's papa brought food baskets to our house. When I heard the wagon roll up, I peeked out and seen Mister Wasson and Miss Blanche. She didn't come in. Just sat on that wagon staring around like she was spooked. If anybody should have been spooked, it was me. Seeing white folk in the Bend was a rare happening, and now it had come to pass twice in one week.

That very week Miss Blanche turned her attention on me. Mister Waterhouse, my boss man who ran the livery stable, had sent me to the hotel with a message for Mister Wasson. Having delivered it, I had left the building when I heard Miss Blanche calling out after somebody. Turned out, it was me. I had no idea that peeking over Miss Blanche's shoulder days before was gonna stir things up. Ma had always warned me that "curiosity killed the cat."

***

Not knowing what to make of having honest-to-goodness books, and a white girl's to boot, I had run like a scared cat back to the stable with them jostling under my shirt. I was scared all right, but excited too. Now that I had them, what was I gonna do with them? Just inside the stable, I opened the creaking door to the tack room just as Mister Waterhouse's voice boomed from a stall somewheres toward the other end.

"Charlie, is that you?"

"Yessir, it's me." I froze. "Sorry, I was so long," I yelled into the air. "Mister Wasson was gone to his gristmill, and I had to wait." But that was just half of the story.

"Get back to work," Waterhouse ordered. "Those stalls ain't gonna clean theirselves."

Mister Waterhouse didn't take to slacking off. In summertime the place bustled with carriages full of white folk rolling in from far off places. Work was never done, not in the two years I'd been working there.

"Yessir. Want me to start in on those harnesses after lunch?" I called back to the faceless deep voice and slipped inside the tack room to tuck the books under the hay bale that I sat on when I cleaned leather tack.

"Nah," he called back. "Couple of carriages are scheduled to come in this afternoon. I'll need you to cool the horses down and put them away."

"Yessir," I said real loud as I stepped back out into the hall's dim light.

With Miss Blanche's books well hidden, I snatched the nearby pitchfork and wheelbarrow and headed to the stall left half-cleaned earlier. With Mister Waterhouse's whistling a tune, I guessed he didn't hear my loud sigh of relief.

By high noon, I'd finished the stall cleaning and my belly growled like I hadn't filled it with that big hunk of cornbread and butter before dawn. I stuck my head out of the stall to spot Mister

Waterhouse with his back to me. The hulk of a man was hammering a shoe onto the hoof of a sorrel mare tied off in the middle of the wide hallway. "Mister Waterhouse, can I get some grub now? My belly's talking."

"Sure, but don't take long. Gotta finish up them stalls before the carriages come in."

"Yessir. I'll be out back in my usual spot."

Mister Waterhouse was good that way—to always give me time to eat. Said I was a growing boy and knowed it took a lot to fill my long hollow legs. I'd go behind the stable with my lunch can and sit with my back against the spreading hickory tree and watch the horses graze in the paddock while I ate. But today I'd have a book on my lap. Mister Waterhouse would never notice. Always fooling with a horse, he said he had no time to eat.

I went to the tack room for my lunch can and grabbed the smaller book from under the hay bale. Slipping it under my shirt, I hustled past Mister Waterhouse as he hunched over the horse's hoof, filing away at it with a rasp. He paid me no mind. Out back, I settled under the shade tree and sucked in the fresh air, glad to free of the manure smell.

With the unopened book on my lap, a little white boy and girl stared up from its cover. I carefully opened it, having never had a honest-to-goodness book in my hands before. Each crisp, smooth page held one bright red alphabet letter, a colored picture of something that started with that letter, and the word printed in black underneath. I took a bite of my biscuit and ham, brushing away the crumbs that fell to the page. "'A', I mumbled aloud with my mouth full. I admired the picture of the shiny red apple in a white boy's hand and spelled out a-p-p-l-e printed underneath. "That spells ap-ple," I concluded. I sounded out the sentence at the bottom of the page, paying close attention to the letters of each word. "The b-oy ate the red ap-ple." Smiling to myself, I turned the page—and then the next, and the next. Before I knowed it, I was at the end.

That was easy. I swelled up like a toad. Closing the first book I'd ever read, I stared across the paddock and into the distance. Now what was I gonna do with them? Couldn't take them home. Pa would shoot me if he knowed I had Miss Blanche's books. Wouldn't matter if she loaned them or not. Besides, with the family sleeping in one room, where was I gonna read? Ruby would give me away if she saw them. Having never seen a book in her three years, she'd squeal like a baby pig if she got hold of one and seen them pictures. I had to think of something.

"Boy, are you working today or not?" Mr. Waterhouse boomed.

He had stuck his head around the corner of the barn, and the veins bulged in his muscular brown neck so I knowed he wasn't joshing. With my hand still on the book, I slipped it from my lap and slid it under my legs.

"I told you we have a heap to get done today, boy," his look and stern tone turned my belly to jelly. Had he seen the book? He didn't say and had already disappeared inside the barn.

"Yessir, Mister Waterhouse, I'm comin'!" I called after him and jumped to my feet.

The whole afternoon while I pulled off harnesses and washed down sweaty horses, I was calculating how to find reading time. Except for Sundays, ever day was a workday, and ever one was long. When Ma, Pa and I left out in the mornings, dropping Ruby off with Grandma Sulley, the sun was just peeking above the fields, scattering the darkness. We'd leave out so early that the rattle of the old buckboard and our lard cans—filled with biscuit and ham for lunch—would wake the sleeping chickens. And getting home most times after dark made finding a time or place to read near impossible.

Sundays was different. Colored folks around Rhea Springs had services at the two-storied Methodist church house after the white folks finished. By the time our wagon rolled home afterward, the sun would be dropping behind the trees. After supper—when the day was cooling, Pa would pull out his fiddle and sit on our porch picking tunes. That most always brought neighbors around to listen and join in. Slipping away to read would be hard then, too.

By day's end, I hadn't figured what to do. With the horses fed and put up for the night, the books would be safe for now in the tack room under the hay bale. "So long, Mister Waterhouse," I shouted as I ran out the open barn doors, guessing he was back in a stall still working.

I didn't see the three white boys crouched in a circle on the ground as I rounded the corner of the stable. I tripped over one and fell plumb in the middle of them. Cat-eye marbles scattered everwhere.

"Hey, nigger. What're you doing?" they shouted, looking as surprised as me as we all scrambled to our feet.

"I didn't see you," I said, stepping back when I saw their faces.

I'd seen those crackers before. Mister Waterhouse caught them throwing rocks at the horses in the back paddock and had chased them off more than once. Troublemakers he'd called them. Said he reckoned they was town boys with too much summertime on their hands.

Sizing them up, I saw quick they was bigger than me—and older. Two had dirty yeller hair. The other's tangled mop was the color of carrots pulled from the garden. They wore ragged coveralls, without shirts. And their skin was so smudged with grime I wasn't sure whether they was white or not. Lined up side by side, they gave me the once over. I could see in their narrowing eyes that I was in trouble. Meanness spread across the biggest one's face. He was a head taller than his pals and built like a barrel. Looking through the stringy yeller hair hanging over his eyes, he grinned and scratched his head like he was thinking on how he was gonna hurt me.

"Like I said, I didn't see ya," I said. "I wasn't trying to mess up your game."

Folding his arms across his chest, the big feller barked, "Well then, you'll be obliged to pick up them marbles and redraw our shooting circle. Now!"

I recalled Pa saying it was sometimes smarter to walk away and live to fight another day. So without another word, I leaned over to pick up the scattered marbles. When I did, somebody shoved me to the ground. With my face in the dirt, their kicking commenced. Even without shoes, the blows knocked the breath out of me, and I tried to cover myself.

"Look, he's rolling around like a catfish flung on the creek bank," a deep voice shouted and then snickered.

A quieter voice said, "Ease up. Somebody's gonna hear."

The kicking stopped, but not until a final one was delivered to my ribs with a powerful thud.

The voice that had sounded the warning, said, "You'll have a hard time finding them marbles if you's wallering in the dirt. Here, let me help you." A dirty hand appeared before my face as I lay there, feeling pain like a knife was in my side. Scared to take the hand, scared not to, I managed to sit up and the boy with orange hair took my arm and pulled me to my feet. With a few cat-eyes still in my fist and my ribs feeling like they was busted, I wasn't sure I could lean over to find the rest.

"Hey, what's going on?" Mister Waterhouse boomed as he appeared from inside the barn. Snatching the barrel-chested feller by the arm, he growled, "I said, what's going on here?"

"Your boy was stealing our marbles," the big feller protested. The other yeller-headed boy shot his buddy a questioning look, but then chimed in, "Yeah, that's right!" and then spat to the side the juice from his tobacco chaw.

Mister Waterhouse turned to me. "Charlie?"

"No! I fell over them when I ran out of the stable—I wasn't stealing nobody's marbles," I gasped, my ribs throbbing.

"What's he got in his hand, then?" the accusing feller asked, pointing to my fist.

Opening it for Mister Waterhouse to see, I said, "I was picking them up like they told me to."

Mister Waterhouse glared at the three young toughs and said, "Take your marbles and get. Now!"

The boys jumped into action, scooping up the remaining marbles, and then motioned for me to drop what I was holding. I obliged. They grabbed the green marbles from the dirt and took off, yelling "niggers!" when they were out of reach.

"You all right, boy?" Mister Waterhouse asked, inspecting me as he brushed the dust off my clothes and picked straw out of my wooly hair.

"Yeah, I's all right. I better get on. Pa will be looking to get home. Thanks, Mister Waterhouse." He sent me away with a pat on my back and then turned into the stable shaking his head.

Pa didn't seem to notice nothing different when we left in the wagon and stopped off at the Wasson's to pick up the basket of vittles. I about told him what Miss Blanche Wasson had done that day, but then thought the better of it. Didn't tell him about the white boys neither, though my side pained ever time the wagon hit a dry gulley. I wasn't up to talking.

***

It was two weeks since Ma's troubles, and she complained the house was closing in on her, said she was feeling fine and was bored with staying in bed, taking charity. Pa and I stopped by Miss

Blanche's house late that day to pick up the last of the food baskets. Pa was inside longer than usual. When he walked around from the back of the Wasson house and put the food basket in the buckboard, he climbed up and took the reins without a word. His face had turned to stone.

After the town's houses faded from sight and the fields surrounded us so nobody but the robins could hear, Pa turned to me. "You wanna tell me something?" he growled between gritted teeth.

I had no book learning, but I could put two and two together. Too much time at the Wasson place, Pa talking with Mister Wasson most likely, then coming out looking like he'd been slapped.

"Shucks, Pa, I was gonna tell you, honest I was," I started. Then I waited, hoping he'd say something. Instead, his eyes narrowed into slits, so I decided I'd better keep on talking. "It wasn't my doing, Pa. That girl cornered me at the hotel when I was on an errand for Mister Waterhouse. You see, I'd seen her sitting on the hotel steps and she asked me if I liked books. I promise I wasn't dallying. I answered her questions and left, but a couple of days later she upped and give me two of her books to read. Said I could keep them as long as I wanted." I stopped, wondering what Pa would do next.

"It's shameful to have the boss tell me things about my own son that I should already know."

"But I said I was gonna—"

Out of nowhere Pa whacked me hard across my chest with the back of his forearm. The horses lurched.

"Whoa, Henry, whoa," Pa called out, grabbing the reins with both hands to settle them. He turned to me again, and I braced myself. "Boy, you listen to me," he started in. "You's been ragging me for months about going to that school over at Mister Gonce's barn this winter. And I told you I'd think on it." His talk went faster and faster, louder and louder. "Why'd you take it on yourself to go ahead and... I don't for the life of me know why you got it in your head that it's important. I ain't never had no school learning and neither did my pappy. No sir. Didn't have no books and didn't need them. I watch and listen and learn. Don't I work for the biggest business in Rhea Springs? And they depend on me—yes—depend on me!"

What I wanted to say—but knew better—was that he didn't have no choice but to work in a white man's business or else sharecrop another man's fields. Was nothing else around these parts for a colored man. When I growed up, I wanted more. Didn't know what yet, but maybe reading would help me figure that out.

"Charlie, you should'a told me. Yep, you should'a told me." Slowly shaking his head and the edge gone from his voice, he was saying it to hisself as much as to me.

"I'm sorry Pa. I really am. Like I said, Miss Blanche pushed them books on me." I hesitated and dropped my eyes, as I mumbled, "...but I wanted to try my hand at them. And I did—and figured out most of them words." I didn't want to sound too excited, so I stopped.

Pa didn't say nothing. In a few minutes, he started up again, matter-of-fact like. "Mister Wasson told me it was all right with him if Miss Blanche loaned you her books. He said it was somehow important to her. But we agreed this arrangement you and Miss Blanche has needs to stay quiet. I don't want you telling nobody outside our family, not Grandma Sulley, not Mister Waterhouse, nobody. You got that?"

"Yeah, Pa. Sure. No one will know."

"And that means you keep up with your chores around the house and at the stable. I don't want to hear from Mister Waterhouse that he's found you piled up in the corner of a stall with your nose in a book."

"Oh, no sir, Pa. I won't. He'll never see me with a book, just like you said, Pa."

As the wagon rumbled on, I turned my head away from Pa and stared out over the fields. My mouth eased into a grin, but Pa didn't see. Tomorrow I'd be bringing them books home.

CHAPTER 7

BLANCHE

Two long weeks after Bertie's accident, I awoke that Monday morning to the smell of bacon as it crackled and popped in the iron skillet downstairs. But it was snatches of a hummed gospel tune that sent my bed sheets flying and my feet to the floor. I dressed and hurried down to find Bertie and Mama standing at the kitchen sink filled with fresh collard greens. Bertie eyed me—like she always did— with that gap-toothed grin that lit up her cabbage-round face. All was back to normal.

Bertie never failed to ask about my day's plan, but on her first morning back, she wanted to talk about herself—and she bubbled over. "The Good Lord has made me whole, yes He has. Why, Mister Wasson's doctoring was by the Almighty's hand. And all them mouth-watering meals your church folk sent? Manna from heaven."

Like always, Bertie was sporting her faded red kerchief with the knotted tie in front that wrapped her head like a swaddled baby. She wore a clean white apron—hadn't been in the kitchen long enough to dirty it—and looked as fit as a fiddle. She appeared as happy to be back in the Wasson kitchen as we were to have her.

"Now enough about me. What about that County fair last week?" Bertie asked, motioning me to the table to sit and eat, while she and Mama lingered at the sink. "Sam come home saying everybody across three counties was headed to the fairgrounds. So crowded you couldn't stir 'em with a stick. Why don't you tell me all 'bout it."

Both she and Mama stood with folded arms like they were waiting for an official report, so I started in. "Best fair yet, Bertie! Did Mama tell you she won a blue ribbon showing Marshall?"

Mama was petite—little more than a head taller than me—and a natural beauty, but she could outride any man. I described to Bertie how her gelding's high stepping and Mama's perfect handling made that Porter horse that won last year—from over in Meig's County—look like a plow mare. "By the time the horses went through their paces, the whole grandstand was whooping and whistling Mama on."

Mama interrupted. "Blanche exaggerates, Bertie. But I must say it was satisfying to see Marshall regain his standing as the best in Rhea County. I knew with enough training his Kentucky pedigree would serve him well. Enough about me. Tell Bertie what else you saw. What about the big fair house? Remember, the sign above the entrance, 'The Country Home Exhibit'?"

"The furniture exhibit?"

"Yes, and the quilts," Mama added.

"Oh, yes. Patchwork quilts everywhere, hung from rafters there were so many. All the churches' quilting bees brought their best this year. In a rainbow colors, they were like flying kites overhead. And underneath were tables, chairs and carved rockers, and in every size. I tried them all, just like Goldilocks."

Bertie pointed to my untouched eggs and ham.

"And guess what?" I said after a hurried bite. "The Rockwood Brass Band played, marching around the grounds until the crowd following them swelled into the hundreds.

Bertie, did anyone tell you about the merry-go-round?" Since colored folks didn't come around the fair, I thought I should give her the lowdown. "Papa said the Chattanooga newspaper reported it coming to county fairs across the South." I described how the carved horses were fitted onto a platform of painted scenes and mirrors that caught the sunlight when it turned, using an engine same as runs the new-fangled horseless carriages.

"Well, did ya' ride, Miss Blanche?"

"Of course," I said, sticking out my chest like a peacock.

"I wish I could'a seen that," Bertie said, but her smile had faded as she leaned against the sink.

I'd worn her down with my talk, but she motioned me on.

"Yeah, I kept riding 'til my pennies ran out."

The grandfather clock gonged from the next room, and Mama said I'd prattled on long enough. She finished her instructions to Bertie and then turned to me.

"Finish your breakfast and then skedaddle up to your papa's store and bring home a sack of flour. Bertie will whip up our special pound cake and get it into the oven before the day heats up."

"So you's need to hurry," Bertie added, as she walked to her own special chair in the corner of the kitchen, taking opportunity for a momentary break. The earlier sparkle in her eyes had disappeared. Maybe my tales weren't that interesting. Or maybe she was still sickly. But I wasn't going to worry. Bertie was back—and that's all that mattered.

***

It was Saturday, and every household was preparing for what Mama called the after-meeting spread, a big picnic held quarterly on the Methodist church grounds. After Sunday worship services, the Baptists and Presbyterians gathered with us Methodists under a shady stand of trees next to our white-washed church house. Rows of boards were laid on sawhorses where families unpacked baskets of vittles, leaving not an inch of empty space before all was said and done. Ham from Grandfather's smokehouse, collard greens cooked to tender perfection brought by the preacher's wife, crunchy cucumber and tomato sandwiches with the bread edges cut off, Mrs. Gonce's chewy brownies. A river of vittles. Once the preacher gave thanks, folks descended on the feast like pigs to a trough. Sundays are intended to be a day of rest, but Mama always said the quarterly picnics were a fitting way to please the Almighty *and* His people.

With coins in hand to buy flour, I finished breakfast and was out the door. Hopping down the porch steps, I headed up Muddy Creek Road and was immediately greeted by the clanging sound of a blacksmith at his anvil. As I passed the hotel and approached the livery stable, I could see activity in the shed at its far side. Opening out to the road like a stage was a flaming forge, bellows and iron anvil that were instruments of magic whenever Mr. Waterhouse was at work there. Sparks flew when he wielded that mallet, like a mere toy, to pound the red-hot iron to his will. When I'd come along, he always thrilled me with his fireworks show.

54

George Waterhouse was a Negro of many talents, according to Grandfather who had hired him to oversee the hotel stable and serve as blacksmith. Grandfather said there wasn't a colored man in Rhea County who handled horses as expertly as he, and his blacksmithing talents weren't shabby either.

"Morning," I called out as I neared.

Suspending his rhythmic swing, he grabbed a nearby pair of iron tongs and slung the glowing horseshoe into a bucket of water. It hissed its protest. Wiping the sweat from his broad brown forehead with his arm that was the size of a ham from Papa's smokehouse, the gentle giant greeted me with a broad smile. "Well, Miss Blanche, morning to you. It's a fine day. Hear all them robins singing it's so? Where you off to?"

"Papa's store. Bertie needs a sack of flour so she can get a cake going for tomorrow's church spread, and Mama gave me two cents for the biggest pickle I can scoop out of the pickle barrel. I love them, don't you?"

"Yep, you can't beat a big, juicy one," Mr. Waterhouse said. "The fatter, the better! 'Fore you head off, come round the side of the stable here." He took off the mule-hide apron that protected him from flying sparks and motioned for me to follow. "I wanna show you what came rolling in yesterday from up Knoxville-way. Belongs to an Army-man. Charlie is washing the road dust off."

When we rounded the stable, I gasped at what stood before me. An ebony carriage sparkled in the light of the morning sun, and the flourish of silver trim along its two staffs was exquisite.

With drying rags in both hands, Charlie looked up from wiping the carriage and smiled broadly as if showing it off as his very own. Our eyes met, and in those seconds, our unspoken talk reassured me that our secret was safe.

"I do declare, that looks like a prince's carriage," I said, shifting attention back to Mr. Waterhouse. "All the way from Knoxville? That's a long way."

"Seventy miles. The man's daughter came along...a young gal."

"You know how long they're staying?"

"Don't rightly know. Maybe for the summer."

"His girl looked your age, Miss Blanche, but not nearly as purty."

Blushing, I didn't know how to answer so I said I needed to get on up the road. With a last glance at the storybook carriage and a wave to them both as I skipped off, my thoughts turned to Charlie and how he was coming along with my books. Time would tell, but I couldn't help but grin to myself that Sam and Bertie's son was going to be a reader, and I was the reason.

Back to my immediate task, I turned left off onto the road that led to Papa's store and slowed up at the Widow Peter's place. It was a frequent happening to find one of her grown twin daughters out on their covered veranda, sitting at a spinning wheel taller than me. It being the only house around with a spinning wheel on the porch, I loved stopping by. The sisters looked so much alike I sometimes mistook one for the other. Slim girls with auburn hair, always pulled away from their faces with hair combs, both had freckles crowding their cheeks. Mama said they were fraternal twins, not identical, but that didn't help me tell them apart. Cynthia was a head taller than Thelma, but if they were sitting, that was hard to determine. Cynthia's voice, however, always gave her away. It was sweet and high-pitched and Thelma's was not.

"Hey, Miss Cynthia." I waved cheerfully, hoping I'd identified the right sister.

"Morning, Blanche. Where are you off to on such a lovely Saturday morning?"

"To Papa's store for flour—and a pickle for me," I answered, relieved that I guessed right.

"Come up and sit a spell?" Miss Cynthia asked.

Cynthia's fingers were nimbly working at the big wheel that squeaked like a baby bird with every turn. The foot pedal propelled the wheel, and its constant motion magically spun the lambs-wool fiber into the yarn that would eventually end up on the carpet loom inside her house. The Peters' parlor housed a big one that wove sturdy, but colorful rugs that found places of honor in many of Rhea County's homes and were often sold to hotel guests as well who'd ship them back home.

"Mama will be turning out some of her lighter-than-air biscuits any minute now," Miss Cynthia announced. "Can you smell them? I'm sure she'd be pleased to bring you a sample, maybe with her famous homemade apple butter."

Mrs. Peters' apple butter won blue ribbons at the fair, and it was a picnic to sit on the Peters' covered porch, munch a biscuit and watch Miss Cynthia or Miss Thelma at the spinning wheel.

"I'd love to sit a spell," I said, taking a seat on the steps. Mama wouldn't mind. She always reminded me how important it was to be neighborly. To hear her tell, times had gotten hard after Mr. Peters was killed in a work accident at the Cincinnati Southern Railroad— back when I was little. Even with a widow's benefit, the family had turned to making rugs to keep life and limb together. Mama said a lot of loneliness filled that house, so maybe my unexpected visits helped.

Cynthia's mama must have heard us. In no time, she appeared to place a small tray of refreshments on my lap.

"Enjoy," she said, and patted me on the head.

"Thank you, Mrs. Peters," I called after her, as she disappeared back inside. Crumbs from the fresh-from-the-oven biscuits dropped like snowflakes as I popped them into my mouth. The apple butter added to my delight, and the sweating glass of cold lemonade washed it all down, to my great satisfaction.

After asking how Miss Cynthia's family was faring and what was new about town, I told her how happy our family was that Bertie was back to work. But then she said, "You never know with hired help…when they's taking advantage and lazing at home well beyond what's called for, all the while enjoying meals good folk have cooked for them."

"Not Bertie," I protested. "She was really bad off for a while."

Miss Cynthia was in her twenties, and she talked to me in a grownup kind of way. I liked that, but what she said about Bertie left me uncomfortable. So I said, after finishing my biscuit, "I've dallied too long. Guess I better get on." Laying the empty tray aside, I stuck my head inside the door to holler a thank you to Mrs. Peters.

Bertie was at home, probably madder than a wet hen by now, so I hurried my steps in the direction of Papa's store five minutes up the road. There was no mistaking the building with its dizzying array of signs in every shape and size nailed to the outside walls, telling all who came along what was sold inside: Gilbert's Tools and Nails, Wasson Flour & Cornmeal, Brooms and Mops by Wilson & Company, and more. The usual clutch of ole timers greeted me from its porch. They reminded me of crows on a fence rail, squawking as they watched the day pass.

Mr. Cassidy, the bald man sitting in one rocker, was the oldest elder in our Methodist church. His voice could still command the air, though he was a small man almost as broad as he was tall. His black suspenders stretched so tight over his bulging middle I thought they'd snap if he sneezed. Talking a mile a minute from the rocker next to him was Mr. Moody—tall and lank with wiry white hair that reminded me of Grandfather's. An officer back in the Tennessee Confederate Infantry, Mr. Moody relived battles with anyone who'd lend an ear. Leaning against the porch rail was Professor Tankersley, always dressed like he was coming from church in his starched white shirt and bolo tie, fingering the waxed tips of his gray mustache as he listened. Once a lawyer, he'd moved South from Toledo, Ohio after his wife's passing to live with his daughter and her family. He had recently taken to teaching history lessons at my school.

In a chorus of "Good morning, Miss Blanche," Professor Tankersley pulled open the squeaky screen door for me, taking a bow as I stepped onto the porch. After polite hellos all around, I went inside but saw no one. I called for Mr. Cobb, who had agreed to clerk the store during the summer so Papa would be free to help Grandfather at the hotel.

Standing there, the mercantile store smelled strange, like always. Was it the brine from the four-foot tall pickle barrel or the large stinky cheese rounds on the front counter where the silver cash register sat? Or maybe it was all of them mixed together. I peered down each of the three aisles, but I saw no one, only stacks of sardine tins, boxes of soda crackers, yard goods and millenary supplies. Down the third I spied the small tote bags of sugar and flour on one side, while large bulging burlap sacks of cornmeal and flour from Papa's gristmill lined the other. But no Mr. Cobb. I called out again. Silence. Then an abrupt "hello" boomed through an open door to the store's back room.

I jumped.

"Are you here to help out?" The tall lanky man with thinning black hair and wire-rimmed spectacles teased as he appeared in the doorway. Wiping his hands on his dirty shop apron, he said, "Thought I recognized your voice, Miss Blanche. Could use a helper behind the counter while I mark goods back here. A wagonload's just come over from the train station, and you know I ain't going to get help from those fellers out front," he said, motioning with a chastising finger in the direction of the porch.

"Sorry, Mr. Cobb, but Mama sent me for flour so Bertie can bake a pound cake. And I've got two pennies here for a pickle."

"You go right ahead. You know where everything is. Now don't fall into that barrel reaching for the perfect pickle," he said with a wink, and then removed the thick-lensed glasses that made his eyes look like an owl's. "Leave your money on the counter. I'm gonna finish up back here." He wiped his face with his shirtsleeve and resettled the spectacles on his nose before disappearing into the storeroom and leaving me to complete my task.

I ran almost the entire mile and a half back home. When I reached our front porch, Bertie was waiting inside the screen door, impatiently tapping her foot, her lips drawn tight. She was not in the least interested in my morning adventures. Stirring up that pound cake was all that was on her mind. I wondered how long she'd been peering out the door waiting for me.

Opening the screen, she said, "Better be glad I knows how to keep secrets, my Little Friend. Your mama would be after you with a switch if she knew how long you've dallied. And she's not gonna be any happier with me if that cake don't get baked before I leave out today."

"I'm sorry, Bertie."

She took the flour and muttered under her breath as she disappeared. Bertie was not to be reckoned with when she was riled.

I turned on my heels and skipped across the road to the hotel to round up my cousins. Maybe I could talk them into a game of checkers on the veranda. Or maybe I'd see that Army-man and his girl who'd arrived yesterday. I so hoped she was my age.

CHAPTER 8

BLANCHE

Mama and Papa thought spending time with Captain Jacques' daughter was a fine idea, seeing she was from a good family and all. Captain Jacques was a retired United States Army officer and owned a sizeable cattle ranch south of Knoxville. Papa repeated exactly what Mr. Waterhouse had said earlier in the day and that their stay would mostly likely run until summer's end.

"Imogene is a little older," Mama said at the dinner table that night, "but she needs a young friend to take her around, show her your favorite haunts. It'll keep her busy and not thinking so much about her mother's passing."

What Mama said next left me feeling bad for a girl I'd never met. Imogene's mama had drowned the year before in a wagon accident. Summer storms spawned terrible flooding all over, especially along the Tennessee River near their farm. Mrs. Jacques tried to cross a swollen feeder creek alone in their family buggy. It turned over in the swell and her body was not found for days.

A year after the accident, Captain Jacques decided a change of scenery would be the best medicine for their terrible sadness. He read about our Rhea Springs Resort Hotel in The Knoxville Sentinel newspaper and knew a family who had visited. When he wrote to the hotel and outlined his special circumstances, Papa had reassured him by return letter, even mentioning me as a suitable companion for his daughter.

Since most of the girls living nearby were not my age, the prospect of having my own special friend for the summer was exciting. I readily accepted Mama and Papa's assignment and couldn't wait until Captain Jacques and Imogene settled in.

Mid-morning the next day Papa introduced her and her father, as the four of us gathered in the hotel lobby. Papa suggested my taking Imogene to one of the town's famous springs, and I looked to her for a reaction. Smiling and nodding her agreement, she absently twisted one of her two long blonde braids that framed her freckled face. Right off, I knew I liked her, even if she was a head taller and two years older.

Leaving Papa and Captain Jacques behind with their grownup talk, we girls set off on our first adventure and headed across the hotel grounds. I started in telling Imogene about the famous springs, thinking it would break the ice. "The two big springs you've probably already seen—that one over there," I said, pointing to the other side of the gazebo, "and the one just down Muddy Creek Road. Did you notice when you came into town yesterday?"

"Yes. I wanted Father to stop the carriage so I could sample it. With that fancy four-column covering over the spot, I guessed it must be some special water. But Father was in too big a hurry to get to the hotel."

"Well, it's good for your health and can heal ailments; but the spring I want to show you today is a secret one. None of the hotel guests and not many around here know about it. The trail picks up behind my house. It's not far."

Imogene's face lit up as I motioned for her to follow. Crossing the road, we circled to the back of my house and through the fence gate into the pasture. "Arrowheads are all around here," I said, my shoe scuffing the ground as we followed the path, stepping around the cow patties. "My brother's collected sacks of arrowheads."

"Really? They are all around our farm too," Imogene offered.

"Papa says the Cherokees believed magical healing flowed from these springs. And when word got out, pioneer families started coming by the droves. My great-great-g-r-e-a-t-grandfather's family was one of the first."

Imogene didn't seem much impressed, so I tried something else. "I'm warning you before we get there, don't drink from the spring…that is, unless you like the taste of rotten eggs!" My new blonde friend didn't flinch but silently followed on.

The trail led us to an old stand of tulip poplar trees at the field's far end, near an embankment. Nearing, we heard the faint sound of moving water and then I pointed Imogene to the stream escaping its hiding place amidst a small rocky outcropping to form a sizeable pool sheltered by the stand of trees. Bobbing in the water like fishes at play were green melons. Imogene's eyes danced with surprise.

"You and your father will likely find slices of those melons on your supper plates tonight," I said. Papa has the hired help put the melons in the water to keep them cold…until the kitchen folk are ready for them."

Rolling up my sleeves, I fished one from the water and smashed the melon against a nearby jagged boulder. Sweet red juice splattered in all directions. More than a few seeds found their sticking place on our faces and on Imogene's blonde bangs, followed by our surprise and matching wide grins. We broke off hunks of the sweet melon and ate with relish, the juice trickling down our arms. We couldn't stop giggling. By the time the sun slipped behind the ridges to the west, Imogene and I were chattering nonstop. Our friendship was off to a great start.

By August, we were fast friends. Most nights after supper, we'd find one other and roam the hotel grounds, trapping winking fireflies in glass jars. Since Imogene liked reading, I happily shared my books; and she'd often take one back to her hotel room. Dog-day afternoons were spent playing beneath the shade trees until Bertie summoned us with sweating glasses of fresh-squeezed lemonade. On one sultry afternoon, Imogene and I were cooling off with our lemonade in my kitchen when we spied Papa's newspaper left open on the table. Bold headlines of the August 2, 1903 Rhea Springs Gazette read, "Tuskegee Band and Glee Club To Perform." We read on, testing our ability to sound out the hard words. I would never have guessed our friendship was soon to be tested as well.

***

"Blanche, you're going to hear a band and glee club on Sunday afternoon that I guarantee will set your toes to tapping," Papa promised over dinner that night, as the whole family was chirping at once over the announcement. "They're forty members strong, young men chosen for their vocal and instrumental talent. They're coming in on the train tomorrow afternoon—in their own special rail car."

"Really?" Owen and I asked simultaneously and then laughed.

"Can Imogene and I sit together at the concert?" I asked.

"Yes," Papa said, "and we'll invite Captain Jacques to join us."

***

Imogene and I perched on the hotel steps on Saturday afternoon watching workers scurry about, dressing the gazebo with streamers and bows and encircling it with long benches. Excitement was definitely in the air.

"The band will play a 'unique program with every jubilee and plantation melody demonstrating its historical meaning,'" I read, holding the event pamphlet that Papa had printed. "I'm not sure what that means, but with forty voices strong, along with banjos and saxophones and the like, it's bound to be splendid."

"Are they in Rhea Springs yet?" asked Imogene. "Where are they gonna stay?"

"They arrive today and will sleep in their train car. Papa said they have their very own and it's painted in their school colors. I overheard him telling Mama that they travel under Tuskegee rules and report daily to Mr. Washington."

Imogene looked at me like she knew something I didn't and then she said, "Well, Father told me the Tuskegee Institute is for training colored people for farming, blacksmithing, wagon making, and the like, and they should stick to that. Having all those young men roaming the countryside could be risky business."

What did she mean, "risky business"? They were chaperoned, Papa had said, and traveled together, so I didn't pay her comment much mind. "Papa says the school covers a thousand acres and teaches two thousand students. Can you imagine that?"

Imogene shrugged and said, "Not really."

We turned our attention back to the printed program—ten songs, some familiar, some not: an African melody entitled "Ethiopia"; a saxophone quartet doing "Sewanee River" and "Peter Go Ring Dem Bells." It was going to be a day to remember.

***

That sunny Sunday afternoon brought the usual August heat, but steady breezes off the river offered blessed relief. Townspeople and hotel guests alike gathered early, right after church, to secure the best seats. Uncle Jack and Aunt Cinny stayed on after services, citing that the event was "most unusual" and not to be missed. The Negro congregation had cancelled their afternoon services and many were gathered around the far fringes of the crowds. Latecomers were ringing those already seated, willing to stand to see what Chautauqua would inspire.

Papa had invited Captain Jacques and Imogene to be our family's special guests, so Sam had arranged chairs on the hotel veranda. A stone's throw away, the large white gingerbread-trimmed gazebo resembled a gift box, done up with trappings in purple and gold, Tuskegee's colors.

When Captain Jacques and Imogene appeared through the hotel's front doors, Papa and Mama greeted him with handshakes and polite hugs. Imogene and I exchanged smiles. Captain Jacques— a tall, slender man—stood with head held high and shoulders back, like a true military man. Imogene and I had donned our Sunday best, she in a dusty yellow gingham frock that matched her hair and I in my favorite blue one with the wide white collar that Bertie had ironed for the occasion. Mama had even added matching ribbons to my braids.

Owen and my sister chose to sit with our cousins closer to the gazebo, so our party of five took our places on the veranda with Imogene and I huddled together in anticipation.

"Where are they?" Imogene whispered. The gazebo platform stood empty, and the crowd was twisting in their seats looking for the performers.

"I don't know. I overheard Papa say they should start any minute."

Then over the noise of the crowd came a distinct rhythmic clacking from down the road. Rounding the corner from the far side of the stable, three Negro young men appeared in white trousers, navy blue coats and military caps. Aligned shoulder to shoulder, they were led by an older man with greying hair dressed in a similar uniform. Marching in step, the three were followed by three more carrying drums, loudly thumping the metal rims with their sticks, setting a tempo. Behind them were three trumpeters. Now in full view coming toward us was the Tuskegee Band and behind them, the Glee Club, forty members strong. The crowd fell silent.

Imogene and I swapped amazed grins. Would they all fit on the gazebo platform? Then I felt a tap on my shoulder. It was Charlie.

"Hey, Charlie. Isn't this fun? Where are your folks?"

"They's round the side. There." He pointed to the far end of the hotel where Sam was waving my way. Bertie, Sam and Charlie's little sister were among other colored folks peering around the building, all as excited as me.

Charlie dropped a small flour sack on my lap, but instead of flour, two small books fell out—one a primer, a Christmas gift from my first grade teacher, and a child's book of poems. Without another word, but wearing a mischievous grin, Charlie darted off in the direction of his family.

"What's that about?" asked Imogene, as she watched the Negro boy dash off.

"Oh, that's Charlie. His ma and pa work for my family. Bertie helps Mama at the house. She's made lemonade for us. Remember? And Sam, he works here at the hotel."

"Why's he giving you those?" she asked, looking quizzically at the books.

"I loan him my old ones to read from time to time," I said, only then recalling what Papa had warned. It was too late. Maybe it didn't matter. Imogene didn't live in Rhea Springs. However, her frown wasn't reassuring and the frosty stare that followed accused me of doing something terrible.

She cupped her hand to my ear and leaned in. "My father would never, ever permit me to give books to our workers."

A bit surprised, but not lowering my voice one whit, I said indignantly, "I'm not 'giving' them to Charlie. Dog-gone-it, I'm 'loaning' them."

I glanced Mama and Papa's way. They wouldn't be happy hearing I'd let the cat out of the bag. Nor would they approve of my tone with Imogene, but I wanted it known how strong I felt. But my folks were busy talking with Captain Jacques and paid us no attention.

"That doesn't matter," Imogene said quietly, like it was a shameful thing to talk about out loud. "Father says book learning is a waste when it comes to coloreds, that they need to do what they're good at, working the fields, harvesting crops and the like. They don't need book learning for that."

"Well, my papa says it takes everyone working together to rebuild the South, and that includes the Negro. Mr. Booker T. Washington was here last summer, and he gave a speech about how Negroes need different training so they can do more to make the South better...for everybody. Papa and I have talked about it and we think he's right. Besides, I just don't see anything bad about helping Charlie read, if he wants to."

Imogene stared at me, but then turned her eyes back to the gazebo. I'd upset her, so I changed the subject. "The program here says that Clark Smith is the bandmaster. Must be that old man in the fancy blue uniform with the brass buttons," I said, pointing in the direction of the leader with white hair. "See the medals on his chest? Wonder what they're for?"

Imogene shrugged her shoulders. She stared ahead but answered, "Well, I bet he didn't serve in the Army like my father. His medals were earned."

It was my turn to shrug, but I said nothing.

After the young men assembled in the gazebo, the bandmaster thanked the people of Rhea Springs for the invitation to perform, and without further ado turned to the choir and raised his baton.

Papa was right. The music and singing were like none I'd ever heard. I knew "Dixie" and "Sewanee River." Everyone else did too. With tapping feet, many sang right along with the choir. But the other music, no one knew. In the African song, "Ethiopia," powerful voices swelled in perfect harmony like an impending eruption of a mighty rumbling volcano. Everyone was spellbound and goose bumps ran down my arms.

When the performance ended, we all jumped to our feet in unanimous, resounding applause that did not cease until the band lifted their instruments to "High Old Time in Dixie." I glanced around to where Charlie was standing, and his grin was so wide I swear I could see every tooth.

After the concert, Imogene seemed herself again. Nothing more was said about Charlie. The Tuskegee group marched back in the direction from which they'd come. Imogene and I chased up the steps to the bandstand and for hours pretended to be a chorus of two, singing Dixie over and over again.

***

I learned two days later at breakfast that Captain Jacques and Imogene were leaving. Surprised that Imogene had said nothing to me, I peppered Papa with questions. He reported Captain Jacques had sought him out to thank him for our hospitality, but Papa was also surprised at the captain's decision to leave earlier than planned.

Hurriedly finishing my oatmeal, I ran to the stable in hopes of seeing Imogene. I found her and her father by their black carriage, waiting while Mr. Waterhouse made final checks to the horse's harnesses.

As I neared them, I thought I heard Captain Jacques saying to Mr. Waterhouse, "Boy, we need more coloreds like you up Knoxville way. You've taken fine care of my horse over these last two months. A man who knows his horseflesh is worth his weight in gold—nigger or no. Too many of ours have left—gone north looking for jobs."

Nothing but silence answered the captain. Mr. Waterhouse—his face flat and expressionless—checked the bridle at the horse's head, like he didn't hear.

After a minute, Captain Jacques raised his voice. "Boy, did you hear me? I was talking to you."

Dead silence again, and I slowed my steps, thinking I might be stepping into some unpleasantness. A deep voice answered, "Yessir, I heard you…and I have a name. It's George, George Waterhouse."

Just then, Imogene caught sight of me and ran my way. As she did, Mr. Waterhouse walked to the rear of the carriage and hefted two travel trunks aboard, secured them and returned to hold the horse's harness without looking at anyone.

The captain was distracted by Imogene's actions. He removed his hat as I neared, his hard expression softening as he offered a gentlemanly bow.

"Miss Blanche, you have been a fine companion for my Imogene. If ever your family gets to Knoxville, we'd be honored to have you drop by for a visit."

"Thank you kindly, Captain Jacques."

Imogene and I hugged a last time before the two climbed onto the carriage. Mr. Waterhouse stiffly held the horse's bridle until Captain Jacques took the reins. When the horse was turned north, Imogene waved as the carriage rumbled away.

Mr. Waterhouse cast a steely glance in their direction before walking toward the stable entrance. When I noticed his clinched fists,

I called after him, "Mr. Waterhouse, are you all right?" He did not stop, but answered resolutely over his shoulder, "I be fine, Miss Blanche. You go on home now." In the deep shadows of the stable, I thought I saw Charlie watching, staring.

***

I later learned from Papa that Captain Jacques had left a letter for him at the hotel that revealed the full truth about the early departure. The Tuskegee performance, though entertaining, had offended the captain's sensibilities about the changing role of Negros in a post-Civil War South. My loaning Charlie books and encouraging his reading only added to his discomfort. In leaving, Captain Jacques was protecting his daughter from influences he didn't want.

Papa calmly explained to me that we had done nothing wrong, and just like Captain Jacque, we should stand true to our convictions. He added that we shouldn't hold hard feelings toward good folk who saw things differently, but I wasn't satisfied with that thinking. Captain Jacque's convictions held people back, ours didn't. But I didn't challenge Papa. What left me the most sad was wondering if I'd ever see my summertime friend again.

CHAPTER 9

CHARLIE

Mister Waterhouse didn't take to much talking, so his walking by me without so much as a peep wasn't nothing unusual. But it was the look on his face when Captain Jacques and his girl left Rhea Springs that really ate at me. I knew I should'a kept my mouth shut. Pa would have said I should, but I couldn't help myself. I wondered aloud why he just took it from that man. When he spun around and narrowed his eyes, I knew my ears was gonna get pinned back.

"Well, Charlie, I could have busted his head open like a ripe watermelon."

And he could have with those powerful arms of his. I'd watched him hammer out red-hot iron as easy as Ma rolls out pie dough.

"Is that what you think I should'a done?" he asked, and walked into the harness room scowling, "...beat some manners into him? What good would that'a done except bring down the KKK on us?"

I leaned against the doorway and watched him straighten the bridles and harnesses on the wall hooks that didn't need no attention. He was keeping his hands moving to corral his anger. Under his breath, I he muttered, "Saying somethin' to that cracker would have cost my job. Doctor Wasson wouldn't allow his stable man to sass any hotel guest. No sirree."

Mister Waterhouse turned on his heels and pushed past me to head down the stable hallway. I trailed after, dogging him with questions that I should'a kept to myself. At the feed room door, he whirled around and glared at me. "I's been living in a white man's world longer than you, boy. You got a lot yet to learn. I wasn't much older than you when Doctor Wasson took me on here. Said he saw something special in me when I was fooling with the horses. A special instinct, he called it. Now, after twenty years of perfecting it, you think I's gonna throw that away because of an ignorant white cracker?"

His anger spewed out on me, but I spoke my mind anyhow. "You know a hundred times more about horses than anybody around here—and way more than that Captain Jacques, I'd wager."

"So? The man said hisself I was an expert. But his calling me 'boy' and 'nigger'? Most say it without no thought. I don't know…" Mister Waterhouse's voice trailed and then he looked me square in the face again and said, "Maybe when you's a man, respect will be yours for the having, no matter your skin color. But I wager that ain't gonna come soon or easy."

He turned and walked away. It was clear he was done talking. I mucked stalls the rest of the day thinking on what he'd said and wondering what Pa would have done. After supper that night, I learned.

***

Ma was washing dishes and Pa had pushed back his bench from the supper table and was riding Ruby on his knee. I'd been in the front room with my book but couldn't concentrate, so I walked back to the kitchen. Leaning against the doorframe, I told him about my day.

"What would you have done, Pa?"

"Pretty much the same as Waterhouse. By the time you get to our age, Charlie, more than a few white fools will have hurled names your way. A man has to pick his fights and be smart how he goes about it."

"But he should have called him out, demanded some respect," I complained, getting stirred up again.

"Waterhouse is respected around these parts. He's as good as any school-trained doctor with them animals. Knows things you can't learn in a book. Why, his know-how has saved more than a few lame animals from a bullet to the head, and he keeps that stable running like a fine machine. That's no small job when carriages are coming and going all summer. Of course, that's possible because he's got a strapping young feller like you helping him."

Pa wasn't gonna move me off the subject. Standing my ground, I said, "I don't understand why white people act like we's nothing to be noticed.

"For example?" Pa asked, turning his attention to Ruby, tickling her bare feet.

I had my answer ready. "When I'm over to the hotel on an errand and see white folks, I do what you taught me, Pa. I look down and step to the side to put space between us, but not a one looks my way. Just last week I rounded the corner of the building and accidentally bumped into a lady coming from the other way. I said, 'Excuse me, ma'am'. All she did was stare at me and examine her skirt like I'd dirtied her up."

"Charlie, knowing how many stalls you muck in a day, that don't surprise me one bit." Pa chuckled and pinched his nose and Ruby's at the same time. She laughed out loud and he did too.

"Maybe," I said, without smiling. "But when I walk down Muddy Creek Road and pass boys coming out of stores—and am spitting distance away—they don't see me. It's like I's invisible."

Pa's smile faded. "Things is changing, Charlie, but not nearly as fast as they ought'a. You know it wasn't that many years ago that white men owned people like us, but a man can't be another's property no more. It's the law of the land. Has been for some forty years now. I'm sorry to say most white folks are awful slow to line up their thinking with the law. When you own something, you do with it as you please. That's the way we's been thought about way too long. We made them rich—working their land, caring for their livestock and houses, even their families. The fact that we's 'human' didn't make us the same, not in their minds. Shoot, anyone whose skin ain't lily white could never be as smart, as upstanding, as good. Least, that's what they thought. Most still do."

"Sounds like you's agreeing with me, Pa."

"What I'm differing with you over is what to do about it," Pa said. "We gotta show them how smart we can be, how good we are to our own, how honest we are in our dealings, even with white folks. Now, if you're gonna beat them up..." Pa lifted both his fists and playfully boxed the air over Ruby's head. "Respect ain't gonna be what you get in return. If you outsmart them AND treat them like the Good Book says, then there's a chance."

"And what does the Bible say about outsmarting white folks?" I asked in what Pa knew was a sarcastic sass, but he pretended not to notice.

"'Do unto others as you'd have them do unto you,'" he answered matter-of-factly.

"I don't know." I made a face at Ruby before turning away and heading to the porch steps where the darkness had finally cooled the air and the crickets had commenced their usual chorus. I plopped down and thought over what Pa said. Outsmarting white folk just to be treated right? I stared into the night sky and got no answers from the stars that winked back.

***

It was two weeks before I saw Miss Blanche again. I was behind the stable under the big hickory, eating my lunch when she came skipping up the road. Seemed like whenever I saw her she was skipping somewhere and today it was in the direction of her Pa's general store. I'd about finished the last books she'd loaned me and was itching for more, so I whistled to catch her attention.

"Over here," I called out and stood to my feet.

When she spied me, she waved and walked over. "Hey, Charlie. What are you doing back here?"

"Eating my lunch and sneaking a read. I's about finished with this last one." I pointed to the open book at my feet next to my lard can. "It's the one about the rabbits."

"Oh, *Peter Rabbit?*" Miss Blanche asked.

"Yep, that's it."

"That's a new book, just published this year according to Papa. I wanted to get it to you as soon as I finished with it. I thought you'd like it, and your sister too, I'd wager."

"Yeah, Ruby loves the pictures. Now she looks to bring home every wild rabbit she spots out in the fields. And Lord help if Pa shoots one for supper."

Miss Blanche laughed.

Leaning over, I picked up the book and started flipping through the pages. "By the way, could you help me out with this one word?"

"Only one?" she teased. "Sure. Which one?"

"It's right here at the end of the story. Peter's ma doses him up with hot tea when he finally escapes Mr. McGregor's garden. But for the life of me, I can't figure what kind of tea. I tried to sound it out, but it still don't make any sense. Here it is."

I pointed to the word on the page and began spelling "c-h-a-m-o-m-i-l-e."

Miss Blanche grinned and said the word before I finished spelling it. Chamomile, she said, was a kind of herb tea, a special flavor.

"I's never heard of such," I said shaking my head. "And neither had Ma."

"Well, I've never had any of it myself," Blanche said, "but Mama says it helps one sleep if you drink it before bedtime."

"I guess it settled Peter's belly," I said. "Thanks for explaining."

"So you're ready for two more books?" Miss Blanche asked. "You've just about seen all my easy readers. I'll ask Papa to help me pick two harder ones. You're sure a fast learner, Charlie Reynolds."

I was plumb embarrassed and couldn't do nothing but scuff my shoe in the dirt.

With that said, she turned to leave, saying, "I'd better get on up the road. Your ma's got me on an errand to the store. How about I meet you tomorrow evening when you're finished work? Under this tree?"

"Sure, I'll be here," I promised, and sat down to finish lunch. As she walked away, I called after her, "I wanna talk to you about something else tomorrow, all right?"

Miss Blanche kinda cocked her head and her face puzzled, but she kept on up the road and called out "all right" and waved goodbye.

***

The next evening I was under the gnarly old tree behind the livery stable well before Miss Blanche showed up. Mister Waterhouse had already slid shut the stable's giant wood doors, closing down business for the day. September had brung shorter days and fewer guests, so workdays were shorter too.

Leaning against the tree to rest my tired bones and staring at the ground, I was thinking hard on how I was gonna bring up a sore subject to this white girl that had made a friend of me. What did she know about being treated like nothing? She was not only white, but the hotel owner's granddaughter. I wagered she'd never been called a "cracker" or "ghost" or the like. Probably never heard them words slung at white folks. Besides, even if she had, what could a nine-year-old do to set people straight?"

"Hey Charlie."

I looked up to see Miss Blanche standing in front of me.

"You trying to spook me?"

Instead of answering, she handed me two books.

"Thanks," I said, eyeing the colorful covers. *"The Wonderful Wizard of Oz?* Isn't that the one I saw you with awhile back?" I asked, examining it and the other book.

"Yes. You remembered," she said with surprise. "Papa thought it might be too difficult, but give it a try. Some great pictures in it. The second one is easier. Do you have the two you've finished?"

I stepped around the tree to fetch the hidden books. I'd left them after lunch so not to risk discovery at day's end when Mister Waterhouse was closing up. Too big a chance he might see me carrying them out of the barn. I handed them to Miss Blanche, but before she could turn to leave, I took hold of her arm and said, "Can I ask you something?"

She looked down at my hand and slowly pulled loose, but she waited. "Sure, what?" Blanche replied, but she wasn't smiling now.

"Let's walk over there," I said, pointing to the fence farther from the barn. "I don't want Mister Waterhouse to hear…or anyone else."

"Well, all right. Why are you acting so mysterious?"

"I don't want no one listening." I stuck the new books under my shirt and led the way. When we reached the fence, I stepped closer to her so I could talk low.

"All right, now what is it?" Miss Blanche asked, and the way she said it, I was about to change my mind. But I didn't know another white person even close to my age, so I pushed on.

"Remember when that Captain Jacques and his girl was leaving Rhea Springs?"

"Of course I do. Why?"

"Did you hear how he talked to Mister Waterhouse?"

"Well, I heard the captain talking to him as I walked up, but I don't remember exactly what. I do remember Mr. Waterhouse seemed bothered when they drove away."

"Bothered? He was madder than a wet hen. Miss Blanche, why'd that Captain Jacques need to treat Mister Waterhouse so poorly, talking to him the way he did? He didn't have to say nothing a'tall. When white folks come to the stable for their horses and carriages, they hardly talk to the help...excepting to take care of business. They don't pass the time of day with us."

"What I thought I heard was Captain Jacques complimenting Mr. Waterhouse's way with horses. Besides, if somebody's got reason to be angry, it's me. I'm the reason he upped and left...and took my friend with him."

"Huh?"

Then out of nowhere a woman's voice called from a distance, "Miss Blanche? Blanche Wasson, is that you?" The voice was a grownup's, a white woman's. We both turned toward the voice coming from the other side of the fence. Across the short field a young woman stood outside the back door of her house with hands firmly planted on her aproned hips.

"That's Miss Cynthia—Cynthia Peters," Miss Blanche whispered aside to me.

"Yes, it's me!" Miss Blanche hollered and waved in her direction.

Miss Cynthia answered back with rapid-fire questions, staring hard like she wasn't sure what she was interrupting. "Are you all right, Blanche? Who's that darkie with you? Is he bothering you?"

"I'm fine," Miss Blanche answered. "This is Charlie—Charlie Reynolds. His ma and pa work for my family. Uh...he was sent out to find me. I've been fooling with my pony all afternoon and guess I forgot the time. Papa was worried."

Miss Blanche went on with her yarn like it was the gospel truth. I about laughed out loud, but knew that wouldn't be the thing to do. Instead I stood looking down at my manure-crusted shoes and readjusted my dirty shirt over my books so they wouldn't slip out and cause a ruckus. Given what she just called me, she wouldn't need much excuse to stir up trouble.

"How are you doing, Cynthia? And your mother and sister?" Miss Blanche went on, turning full attention to the white lady. "It's been a while since I've stopped off to visit."

Miss Blanche went on with her talk like I wasn't there. She climbed the lower rail of the fence for a better vantage. "Would love to see the rugs you're working on now," she called out in a happy voice. "Maybe tomorrow afternoon?"

"You're welcome at our house any time, Blanche," the woman replied, her arms now casually folded over her waist. Miss Blanche waved goodbye, and the lady waved back before turning to go inside, peering a last time over her shoulder…at me, I figured. Miss Blanche hopped down from the fence and turned back to me. She picked up talking right where she left off. I was going to tease her about her fibbing to that lady, but decided agin it.

"Like I was saying," she started up with me again, "Captain Jacques left a letter for Papa." She dropped her eyes and hesitated. Then she looked me square in the face and said real fast, "Captain Jacque wrote that he thought it was a mistake that the hotel hosted a young Negro group from Tuskegee. Said things were gonna get out of hand if Southern folk weren't careful. On top of that, I made the mistake of telling Imogene I was loaning you books. Remember, you brought two back to me just before the performance, and she saw them. Told her father later, and he said I was wrong to share them, like you and I were friends or something."

Miss Blanche's words burned my ears, but she didn't have no way of knowing because my face didn't twitch one whit.

"He all but accused me of putting bad ideas into Imogene's head. Papa told me people like him are afraid of your kind and don't know what to expect now that Negroes have been given their freedom. He said bringing the Tuskegee Singers to Rhea Springs was an important first step to getting white people around here to think differently and it was opportunity for colored people to show they have talents and skills that can add to the Southern way of life."

"What does your papa mean 'to think different about my kind'?" I asked, looking down, hoping my face didn't show my feelings. I kicked the grass and braced for her answer.

"I don't know exactly," she said. "Maybe that Negroes can be just as smart as us? But Papa said I shouldn't judge the captain and Imogene harshly—that they are still good people."

"Good people? …Good because he treats his own good?" I mumbled, and then said matter-of-fact, "Folks need to think on what makes people 'good.'"

I couldn't stand it no longer, so I turned to walk away and leave Miss Blanche there before saying something I'd regret. She was a white girl. How could she begin to understand how it felt to be me.

"Charlie, where are you going?"

I knowed I'd better answer because I didn't want her stirred up at me. Getting those books was important. Determined to make my voice normal so not to let on I was mad, mad at all her kind, I answered over my shoulder, but without slowing my escape, "I's got to hurry, Miss Blanche, or Pa will leave out without me. Thanks again for the books. I'll take good care of them."

CHAPTER 10

BLANCHE

The seasons came and went, and the memories of my summer with Imogene faded. But my odd friendship with Charlie grew, maybe because the boy was always itching to get his hands on more books from the Wasson library. The exchanges happened often, and rambling on with Charlie about his reading in the shadow of the hotel broke up my all-too-frequent summer boredom. When he'd inquire, all bashful-like, about the ways of white folks he read about, I'd laugh out loud. Sounded like he was peering into other worlds on the pages of those books. His curiosity didn't bother me. But as the summer of 1907 commenced, I looked forward to more than leisure time for reading and talking with Charlie on the sly. I had begged for years to enter the Pony Exhibition at the county fair and had finally gotten the nod from Mama and Papa. The intensive training meant many more hours circling the oval rink in the paddock behind the stable than in turning the pages of my books.

***

On what promised to be a scorcher of a Saturday in July, Mama and I lit out for the stable after breakfast. It was best to ride while the air was still damp with dew and the sun had not yet climbed above the treetops.

My pinto horse-pony, Beauty, was waiting. A gift from my parents on my sixth birthday, I was still small enough at age thirteen to ride her despite Papa's teasing I was growing like a weed.

"Good morning, Mr. Waterhouse," Mama's voice echoed, as we stepped into the cool of the long stable.

Mr. Waterhouse appeared out of a stall to greet us. "Morning, Missus Wasson. Gonna be a hot one."

"No doubt. Blanche and I are out early to get ahead of the heat."

Mr. Waterhouse nodded agreement and said, "Miss Blanche, Charlie put Beauty out in the back lot for a little morning grazing. Marshall is in his usual stall, Missus Wasson. Anything else I can do for you?"

"No, thank you. Don't let us interrupt your work," Mama said, as we headed into the tack room to retrieve the bridles.

Loving the musky smell of conditioned leather, I inhaled deeply as I pulled Beauty's bridle from the wall peg. Down the dim hallway, I headed with a bounce in my step. Whistling was coming from an open stall toward the far end; and when I neared, I looked in to find Charlie slinging manure into a wheelbarrow with his pitchfork, all in time with his whistled tune.

"Uh-hmm. Hey Charlie."

He looked up and showed off that familiar toothy grin—like two rows of perfect white corn—just like his pa's. Charlie was favoring him more and more, I thought.

"Morning, Miss Blanche. I's already brushed out Beauty for you. Now that her winter coat has shed, she's showing off a purty sheen. Did Mister Waterhouse tell you I put her out back?"

"Sure did, Charlie. Thanks for grooming her."

"Happy to, Miss Blanche. Gets me out of these stalls for a spell," he said with a smile.

Charlie went back to mucking and whistling, so I cleared my throat. I wasn't done with him yet. He looked up, puzzled.

"Yessum?"

I reached into my pocket and pulled out a brown strip of leather with a small, open book imprinted on it. "Here, Charlie, I thought you might like this. It's a bookmark." Surprise lit up Charlie's sweaty face. When I stretched my arm out as far as I could across the manure-filled stall, he wiped a hand on his coveralls before reaching for it. He was speechless.

"I had several and thought you could use it with all that reading you're doing these days." I shot him a smile and as I turned to leave, I catch a glimpse of his examining his gift.

"This is swell. Thanks, Miss Blanche," his voice trailed after me.

Heading to the fenced paddock, I inhaled the scent of fresh-cut hay in the warming air and spun around in a circle of happiness, holding the bridle like a dance partner. Summertime was the best, and I was on my way to becoming an accomplished horsewoman like Mama.

Spotting Beauty under the shade of a tree, I whistled as I neared. She greeted me with a nicker and met me halfway. Carrots were usually stuffed in my pockets, but today I had forgotten them. Beauty had not. She nuzzled my side with her velvet nose in search of the prize. I slipped the bridle over her head as she nickered again. Laughing, I apologized, "Sorry, Beauty, I forgot…." But shouts interrupted—a loud commotion from the stable.

I heard Waterhouse holler amid the sounds of whinnies and stamping hooves, "Hey, what's going on?" Then, "Miz Wasson, Miz Wasson—Oh, my Lord!"

A hundred feet from the barn, I dropped Beauty's reins and ran toward the confusion in what seemed slow motion. The sun was bright, and its glare veiled the frenzy inside the low light of the stable. As I neared, Marshall bolted past me toward the open field, reins flailing in the air. It appeared Mr. Waterhouse was kneeling over something in the middle of the hallway with an overturned saddle nearby. When my eyes adjusted to the light, my heart seized. It was Mama. Dirtied with straw dust, she lay clutching her body like someone with severe cramps. When I neared, her contorted face and glazed stare of both shock and agony stopped me dead in my tracks.

Mr. Waterhouse's voice trembled, "Get your papa! Hurry, girl. Go! Your mama's been kicked!"

I was frozen. My legs would not move.

Charlie's commanding voice rang out from behind me. "I'll go, Blanche. Stay with your mama." He raced out of the stable and toward the hotel. In minutes he was back with Papa and Sam.

They carried Mama home to her bed. Our town's six doctors all gathered to her bedside. By noon, they were still unsure as to the full extent of Mama's internal injuries. She remained ashen and unresponsive. Moving her to a hospital—any hospital—was cause for grave concern. They decided against it. An urgent message was wired to a Chattanooga physician. As the shadows grew long at day's end, a messenger from the train station knocked at our door with an answer. A Chattanooga surgeon would arrive on the morning train.

Mama would be tended to at home. When I learned that, I sighed with great relief. Although I was not allowed in her room, I felt reassured knowing she was close. Papa remained at her bedside, attentive to her every moan. We children hovered around the house for the most part, keeping our own company, not knowing how to speak about what was happening. Mama had always been well and never suffered grave accidents. We were walking in a dream, a bad one, and fear ruled the day.

Silence blanketed the dark house that night, but I couldn't sleep. After tossing and turning for what seemed hours, I slipped from under my sheets and tiptoed toward Mama and Papa's room. Passing the closed doors of my sister and brother's rooms, I heard no sound. At the end of the hall, a thin band of light escaped from around the cracked door to my parents' room. I edged closer. The grandfather clock downstairs struck once. Peeking around the door, I saw Papa sitting in a chair, drawn close to Mama's bedside, his back to me. The table lamp's flame was low and his shadow loomed large against the opposite wall. Mama laid as still as death, eyes closed, but her breathing was steady. Her skin was pale, colorless like the sheets that covered her.

I couldn't see Papa's face, only his hands—strong, rugged hands—holding Mama's like they were delicate flowers and periodically stroking her slender fingers. Otherwise, he was silent and motionless. Would I be reassured if I could look into his face, into his eyes?

Lingering long, not able to pull myself away, I began to shiver. It was not cold in the house, but my trembling sent me back down the hall to my bed and the longest night ever.

Bertie had remained at the house, sleeping on a pallet downstairs that Owen had prepared for her in Papa's reading parlor. She had pleaded to help in whatever way she might be called upon. When the sun rose, she cooked breakfast, but no one ate. The minutes, ticking loud and slow from the direction of the grandfather clock, turned into hours as we all awaited a miracle.

Dr. Schwartz, the Chattanooga surgeon, finally arrived. Grandfather met his train in Spring City and rushed him to the house. When they came through the front door, the doctor's appearance alarmed me. A head taller than Grandfather with black hair and goatee, a black suit, hat and medical bag, he wore the gravest appearance. But as he stood quietly talking with Papa and Grandfather at the foot of the stairs, I clung to Papa's side listening, hoping. It was then I saw in his eyes kindness and concern. Surely he would help Mama.

The three men climbed the stairs and disappeared into Mama's room. I followed to linger outside my own bedroom, trying to make out their murmurs. After what seemed forever, the men stepped back into the hall. Seeing me out of the corner of his eye, Papa motioned for me to follow them downstairs and out to the porch. Gay and Owen were sitting in silence on the hanging swing, waiting to hear any encouraging news.

"Children, I want you to meet Dr. Schwartz," Papa said in a most formal voice, his face drawn and pale. "He's been extremely generous to drop everything and rush here. After thoroughly examining your mama and having discussed his findings with your grandfather and me, he advises that surgery be performed immediately to pinpoint the internal injuries and do whatever repairs are needed. The surgery will be performed here as it would be too dangerous to move her."

None of us children said a word. The pronouncement filled us with dread. I could not speak for Gay or Owen, but I feared any questions I might ask would bring answers I could not bear.

Papa struggled for words, and his voice quivered. "I want you three to walk over to the hotel…and wait until I send for you. Bertie will help out here with whatever the doctor needs. Grandfather and I will be right by your mama's side." He hesitated and then directed, "Now go along…and let's all be saying our prayers."

Gay and Owen silently rose from the swing, their faces like chiseled stone. I was frightened, having never seen Papa show that kind of emotion. Looking up into Grandfather's face for some hint of what was to come, I saw his eyes were flat and dull and offered no comfort.

Owen led the way across the road; Gay laid her hand on my shoulder and we followed. Nigh unto twenty years older than me, she was every bit an adult, too big to play with the little sister who climbed trees and played hopscotch. She occupied herself with church activities, with others her own age, and I didn't see much of her except at meal times and on Sundays. But today, on this terrible day, she seemed to draw near—even without words—and I found comfort in her closeness and the warmth of her hand.

At the hotel, we sat outside under a sprawling pin oak on the far side of the lawn. Owen carried porch chairs to its shade where we could see the house, where Mama was. We wanted to avoid guests who might unknowingly offer cheerful greetings about a lovely day that was anything but.

As noon approached, the morning breezes disappeared and the air grew as heavy as our hearts. Nothing stirred across the road; no one entered or left the house—not Grandfather, not Papa, not Bertie. Only silence, as we kept vigil watching and waiting. The afternoon heat brought gathering clouds, graying with each passing hour. I stared up, watching the shapes and color change, too frightened to ponder what might be changing across the way.

It was late afternoon when we spotted Grandfather, his head and shoulders drooped as he crossed the road in our direction. The long, seemingly unending day drew to a close as his caved-in voice spoke the unthinkable. She was gone. We were left without our mama, and Papa no longer had his cherished wife. The summer that was to have been my debut as a budding horsewoman under the tutelage of the most accomplished rider in the county was instead the summer we would lay her to eternal rest. We were all numb.

Four specially appointed ladies from church and a man from Spring City came to the house that night to prepare Mama's laying out. We children were sent up the road to Grandfather's house. Papa worried we would be upset by what we might see.

When Grandfather escorted us children home the next morning, the air was fresh with the smell of fields basking in the warming sun, having been bathed by the rains the night before. The road was spotted with puddles, but I hardly noticed. My sister's guiding hand led me around them and kept my feet dry.

Papa and Bertie were waiting at the door. Bertie lingered, silently wiping her eyes with her apron hem as Papa ushered us past her into the front parlor. In a simple black coffin, Mama lay dressed in her favorite robin-egg blue Sunday frock, her delicate hands folded across her bosom. The diamond on her ring finger, the one with which Papa had pledged his love years before, sparkled in the morning rays from the nearby window. Papa, Grandfather and Owen stood like statues watching over her. Only Gay's quiet sobs intruded on the silence. I felt nothing but a stone wall damming my heart from any release.

The days strung out in an unending blur. Mama's wake brought streams of mourners through our front door that had been draped with black cloth. Papa and Grandfather took the hand of everyone who passed through. Whispered words of kindness were offered, but none eased the dull pain in my chest.

The funeral was held at our Methodist church. It bulged with people crowding the benches, lining the walls, spilling out its doors as the church bell tolled the sad news across the countryside. Instead of my sister, Mrs. Peters sat at the organ, leading the gathering in "Amazing Grace," Mama's favorite. At that moment I recalled the mutterings of those that had opposed the organ's arrival years before but were now moved by its resonant tones. They were completely wrong. Its music did fill the air with God's presence and brought us all a measure of comfort, even as we wept.

Afterward, friends and townspeople waited to join the procession that would follow the wagon, shrouded in black and bearing Mama. We exited the church first; Papa guided Gay and me through the crowd. Owen and Grandfather followed. I felt the gazes of everyone, even as my eyes stared at my black shoes as I walked. When we neared the back, I looked up to see Mr. Cobb, our storekeeper, along the wall with his hat in hand, his red eyes appearing even larger and sadder through his thick spectacles. At the open door, Professor Tankersley reached out and touched my shoulder as I walked past. Once outside, I caught sight of Sam, Bertie and Charlie waiting to file in at the back of the stream of town folks that would soon walk to the cemetery on the hill.

The day was cloudy, but the heat did not release its grip. Walking that final mile, the world fell away except for the rattle of the wagon bearing its load. As my steps carried me forward, I could sense Mama kneeling by my bedside for evening prayers and kissing my forehead after saying amen. I could hear her instruction as I rode my pony around the paddock ring. I could see that laughter in her blue eyes when she reassured me the stork had not delivered me to a cabbage patch as a newborn. Only as we neared the cemetery and the horses leaned noisily into their harnesses to climb the hill did I become aware again of my place at the front of the column of mourners.

When we reached the gravesite, the makeshift hearse came to a halt near a hole that loomed dark and deep with dirt piled alongside. The pallbearers unloaded the coffin and carried it to the edge. I felt myself shudder. My family gathered near and the crowd encircled us. Standing at the head of the grave, our Methodist preacher pronounced a blessing and said a short prayer, and then it was over. People stirred momentarily, offering consolation but then dispersed. Our family was finally alone and we lingered.

When Papa said it was time, I felt his arm across my shoulders, and our family haltingly turned to leave. Outside the cemetery entrance, I glanced back and saw four men, Sam and Charlie among them, with ropes in hand lowering the wood box oh-so-slowly into the hole. With shirt collars open and shirtsleeves rolled up, their muscles strained to control its gradual descent. My chest seized.

"Blanche? Where are you going, Blanche?" Papa called after me.

I could not tear my eyes from the scene as I ran back to the graveside. "Sam, Charlie," I pleaded, when I stopped only feet from the mound of dirt ready to be returned to its rightful place. The ropes were lax—the coffin had come to rest at the bottom. Sam stepped toward me, blocking my view of the hole. I searched Sam's dark face and then Charlie's. "Please, please," I cried, "be careful with Mama."

Charlie's eyes brimmed with emotion. "Miss Blanche, you has our word. We'll take special care of everything here and pay your mama all our respect, won't we, Pa?"

"That's right, son," Sam answered. His face was more serious than I'd ever seen in all the years I'd known him. "Your mama is safe with us, Miss Blanche. You go along with your family now. We'll handle things here—Don't you worry your head none."

Papa had returned to my side. With his arm across my shoulders, he smiled weakly at Charlie and Sam before guiding me back to our waiting family. We descended the hill in silence—Papa on one side of me, Grandfather on the other, Gay and Owen ahead. I looked back a final time. Sam and two of the other men were already shoveling dirt. Charlie stood idle, leaning on his shovel, gazing in my direction.

***

It turned out Mama's horse had been stung by wasps just as she carried the saddle around his rump to the other side. Mr. Waterhouse later discovered the wasps' hole right in the middle of the stable's sawdust floor. The kick was instinctual, never intended for the mistress who had lovingly trained and ridden him for years.

Nevertheless, Marshall was soon sold to a Bledsoe County farmer. Papa could not bear to look upon the animal, and my interest in becoming an accomplished horsewoman was buried alongside Mama.

The grandfather clock in our house continued to mark the passage of time, but it angered me that it did. With each passing hour and day and week, I was that much more removed from the sound of Mama's voice, her presence, her touch.

Bertie arrived at the house each morning to cook breakfast, clean and prepare the evening meal, as always, but the place felt cavernous and desperately quiet. Supper was dreadful. Papa removed Mama's empty chair from the table, but to me, that only made matters worse. There was little conversation as we ate, staring at our plates, the only sound that of clicking utensils against the china as we speared one bite and then chewed another. Worst of all, Papa had all but disappeared even though he was still seated at the head of the table with his family around him.

We children went through the motions of daily life. Owen continued to work with Papa and Grandfather at the hotel and put in time at the general store as well, helping Mr. Cobb restock shelves and wait on customers. Invariably they asked after Papa and the family, earnestly expressing their sympathies. Owen told me he tried to be polite, but wanted only to shun the attention.

Gay appeared more devoted than ever to domestic duties. I saw her often huddled with Bertie in the kitchen, learning the ways in which Mama had run her household so efficiently. They both seemed to find comfort in talking over how Mama had done this or that.

I, on the other hand, was left to my own devices. With no interest either in riding my horse or discussing with Bertie how to can fresh-picked peaches, I often rowed one of the hotel boats across the lake to linger under low hanging tree boughs where the brown and white ducks gathered to escape the summer heat. There, listening to the water lap gently against the boat and watching bright blue dragonflies flit about, I could think about Mama and cry without anyone's notice. I not only missed her, I missed Papa as well. I was no longer his shining star. He didn't tease or brag on me as he once did. A light had gone out inside him, and I struggled to find my way in the darkness.

Weeks later—on a Sunday afternoon in August—I wandered into Papa's library and, with nothing to do, pulled from the bookshelf the black photograph album with the embossed design on its cover. Sitting on the loveseat, legs crossed under my dress, I turned the pages filled with images that carried me to another time. Loose newspaper clippings had been tucked among the pages. I held up one to read, a printed wedding announcement that named me as the flower girl at Aunt Adah Pearl's wedding in the summer of 1900. Mama and Papa had hosted a wedding luncheon at our home before the ceremony. How nervous I had been that I might drop food on my "dainty blue frock," as the newspaper had described my dress. Aunt Marian had sewn it especially for the occasion and mailed it from Chattanooga. I remembered Mama bragging that her six-year-old managed both a basket of white roses and a silver plate bearing the wedding rings the entire distance of the ceremony aisle without dropping either. Examining the photographs from that day, I admired how handsome Mama and Papa appeared standing together in their finery. Maybe if I kept staring at Mama in happier times, I could blot out the memory of her twisted body on the stable's dirt floor. Lost in thought, I didn't hear Papa's approaching footsteps.

"Blanche...here you are. I was looking for you." He took a seat opposite me and avoided looking at the open album. He had some pressing matter on his mind, I could tell.

I wasn't prepared for what Papa said next, that Mama's passing required that he consider what was best now for each of his children. Because Owen and Gay and I were of such varied ages, he said our needs required different responses. Papa went on to say that because I was almost fourteen and becoming a young lady, I needed the special guidance of proper women. He said that he had exchanged several letters with my grandparents in Paris, Kentucky. They were Mama's family, and because of the distance, I didn't know them well. He went on to describe a girl's finishing school outside Paris, Kentucky named Sayre Academy. My grandparents had already visited and talked with the administration about my attending. Papa was quick to reassure me that the boarding school offered all my favorite subjects, even art classes and a chance to learn a foreign language. My grandparents would visit on weekends and put me on the train home for the Christmas holidays and summers.

Papa spoke without pause. Once I fully understood his intent, I could scarcely breath and instead stared through tears at my trembling, folded hands on the album.

"But Papa, what about Gay and Owen?" I managed to ask without looking up.

"Owen is needed by your grandfather at the hotel and he will also assume more duties at the store and mill. Besides, he's finished with his schooling here this year. He's decided to wait awhile before going to university. Your sister Gay will take on more of the household responsibilities." Softening his tone, "Blanche, it's only for the school term. You'll come back home afterward, I promise. Someday you will understand the wisdom of my decision."

"But Papa, who will tend to my pet lamb and cow?" And who would see to Charlie's books and answer his questions? It didn't surprise me that my protests fell on deaf ears. Mama had often reminded me that children were to be seen, not heard. But Papa had decided my future without so much as a word with me beforehand. How could he?

CHAPTER 11

BLANCHE

Now a young woman of seventeen, again traveling the many miles home, I closed my copy of *Anne of Green Gables* and laid it on the empty seat beside me. The heat inside the train coach was sapping my energy, so I lowered the stubborn glass, hoping the rush of air would cool my damp neck. As the familiar countryside slid past the window, I remembered like it was yesterday staring at this landscape on my way to Sayre Academy three years ago. Smothered by dread and loneliness, I had clung to Papa's promises. Indeed, painting and sculpting had eventually become daily sustenance; and Shakespeare along with Emily Dickinson became loyal companions. And, as Papa had hoped, the proper etiquette of a young woman coming of age had become second nature.

Back home, my pets had been well looked after. Papa saw to that. He even stepped in to keep Charlie interested in reading, all without bringing unwanted attention, a concern he could never quite let go of. Papa wasn't enthusiastic about taking over as mentor, but he did so for me. With Chattanooga and Knoxville newspapers sent to Papa for advertising purposes, he passed them on to Charlie. Charlie was learning about a bigger world than Rhea Springs just as I was.

After hours of crossing pasturelands and tunneling through the mountains of Kentucky and Tennessee, I was ecstatic when the whistle finally sounded, longer and louder than the protest of the screeching iron wheels that signaled our approach to the Spring City Train Station. A porter stepped into the train car and bellowed what I had waited all day to hear. "Next stop, Spring City!"

Peering out the window, I spotted the Wasson men huddled on the platform talking and laughing. As the train rolled to a stop, I hurriedly gathered my things. When I reached the exit, I abandoned the etiquette of a proper young lady and hopped down the train's steps, my flailing skirt and petticoat almost tripping me. Racing through the idling train's cloud of steam and into the open arms of all three, I couldn't contain my excitement. "Owen, Papa, Grandfather!" The weariness of the long journey evaporated in their welcoming hugs. The white surrey with the fringe-covered top stood ready to ceremoniously carry us home. With Grandfather proudly driving, my happy chatter went unchecked.

Sister Gay must have heard the approaching surrey because she and Bertie were waiting on our gingerbread-trimmed porch as we neared. Watching them wipe their hands on mussed aprons, I was sure a welcome-home feast was in store. As soon as Grandfather brought the horses to a stop, I bounded from the surrey and up the steps into Gay's outstretched arms.

She kissed my cheek and recited Mama's favorite Mother Goose saying, "Home again, home again, jiggety jig. Let the summer begin!" Detecting the sweet scent of roses, I noted the nearby bushes full of red blossoms, ones that Mama had planted years back, maybe her special welcome-home bouquet.

As soon as Gay turned me loose, Bertie wrapped her arms around me. "Miss Blanche, Miss Blanche, you're home at last." With a broad smile and happy glint in her eyes, she put me at arm's length, looking me up one side and down the other before declaring, "My, my, what are they feeding you at that school? You are taller and purtier than ever."

I was flattered she noticed. With Bertie and Gay on each of my arms, we stepped inside to be greeted by savory aromas wafting from the kitchen. Even the grandfather clock heralding the six o'clock hour seemed to announce my homecoming.

After Owen and Papa unloaded my trunks, I trailed them up the creaking steps as they groaned under the cumbersome load, teasing me that I had brought home bricks. Giggling, I followed them into my bedroom and was immediately transfixed. Draped across the bed was a shimmering smoky-blue, floor-length gown, more beautiful than any I'd ever laid eyes on. My dear Aunt Marian had granted my wish.

Months before, amidst the doldrums of a gray winter and endless school days, I daydreamed of my summer homecoming and the dances that lit up the hotel on Saturday nights. I had presumed on Aunt Marian's kindness and written to ask if she might sew a gown for me. With crossed fingers and a prayer, I mailed the letter along with a newspaper clipping of a dress I had admired.

Her reply came weeks later, asking for my various measurements. I had waltzed about my dormitory room waving the letter high overhead. She was a magician at her foot-pedal sewing machine and I would not be disappointed. She promised the gown would be shipped to Rhea Springs—and there it was.

"Well, what do you think?" Gay questioned from behind, offering an approving nod when I turned around speechless.

The moment would be forever etched in my memory. It wasn't just the dusty blue damask dress that mimicked the color of my eyes or its sophisticated bell-shaped skirt that would compliment the figure I was now graced with, but I sensed Mama was probably smiling from somewhere, making her pronouncement, "My daughter is quite the young lady now."

I held the dress to my bosom in front of my wardrobe mirror and piled my hair atop my head with the other hand, curled brown tresses falling to frame my face. Even Owen and Papa whistled as they looked on. Now I was ready for the hotel's summer socials.

In the years since Mama's passing, Papa and Grandfather had redoubled efforts to bring celebrated chamber orchestras on a regular basis from as far away as New Orleans and Atlanta. In addition, Chautauqua was now offering some of the country's noted speakers—and most controversial. Carrie Nation, an activist in the temperance movement, had been a lecturer. And there was William Jennings Bryan, a theologian from nearby Dayton, Tennessee who was of late receiving acclaim from across the country for his "Prince of Peace" sermon in which he proclaimed that individual and group morality was the foundation for peace and equality.

Owen had teased Papa that he'd gone to great lengths to secure Mrs. Nation as a speaker because the number of saloons in our fair town had grown to five, which Papa had not been happy about. Rumor had it that Mrs. Nation had once taken matters into her own hands, literally emptying a big-city saloon by preaching temperance while simultaneously wielding an axe. The Rhea Springs establishments, however, were spared. Indeed, at age seventeen, I was less interested in hearing about the evils of alcohol than taking in the glamorous summer dances and concerts.

After a welcome-home supper fit for a queen, Bertie brought out her fresh-baked peach pie. "Just for you, Miss Blanche," she said, with great pride as she placed the flaky-crusted prize on the table, sliced and ready to serve. An hour later with empty dessert plates all around, we still lingered, laughing and catching up on life in Rhea Springs. It never changed in any great measure, but I had.

With each passing summer, I was less inclined to seek out old schoolmates. We hadn't much in common now. Stories of dormitory life grew stale over time especially when local girls knew nothing of that world, nor showed much interest. Rather, I savored the time with my family, reading alongside Papa or lazing on the porch on Sunday afternoons or competing with my brother at the hotel's new miniature golf course, laughing and regaling him with mischievous boarding school tales. I even enjoyed preparing meals alongside Gay and Bertie, knowing my three months at home were fleeting.

Always teasing whenever I saw him at the hotel, Sam was ever the same and Bertie, too. But not Charlie; he had grown up. When I was last home for Christmas, we had passed at the hotel.

"Charlie, how are you? I haven't seen you in a month of Sundays," I had said.

"Miss Blanche. Good to see you," he had replied in pleasant surprise. "You home for the holidays?"

Charlie's boyishness had disappeared along with his alto voice. A foot taller since I first left for boarding school, he had sprouted a mustache.

"Yes, three weeks home isn't nearly enough," I said.

Charlie turned his eyes to the ground and shifted his weight from one foot to the other. He hesitated and then brought his eyes to mine, and his deep voice morphed into a stiff formality. "Yes, ma'am, I reckon being away from your family is hard."

Now a strapping nineteen-year-old, he appeared cautious, not out of shyness, but rather some wordless boundary. A grown Negro man stood before me, no longer a boy asking for books. Turned out, Charlie had attended Mr. Lyon's school as long as it operated, and my father was faithfully passing along his already-read newspapers. To hear Papa tell, he'd taken to reading happenings from far and wide with even greater fervor than reading Papa's bound classics.

I felt a bit nostalgic for the boy who tucked books under his dingy shirt and ran, who was always anxious to get his hands on a fresh one, a more difficult one. That shared innocence had faded over time, but as Papa once said, 'It's just the way it is.' Though unspoken, I nevertheless felt a bond with Charlie because of those years of shared talk over stories we had both read and fancied. But whether that bond was still shared, I didn't know.

***

At the first dance of the summer, wearing my shimmering new gown and feeling exceptionally confident, I noted how many of the young men encircling the dance floor I'd known since childhood. Even with clean-shaven faces or shadows of growing mustaches and hair slicked into place, they were still the freckled-faced boys in coveralls I had beaten at hopscotch or outrun at church picnics. Then a tall, well-dressed stranger strolled with confidence across the room in my direction. Maybe a hotel guest, his penetrating dark eyes disarmed me as he neared. I nudged my sister standing next to me, only to see her catch his eye in recognition. Then she stepped away, saying she was going for a cup of punch, leaving me defenseless. It all unfolded so quickly that there was no time to gather my wits.

The gentleman's good looks were enough to make any girl take notice. With a strong chiseled jaw and groomed hair the color of a polished chestnut, he wore a dark brown suit that complimented his fit physique. It was obviously custom-made, no doubt from some big city tailor. Nothing like that could have come from around Rhea Springs. In the wake of his steady gaze, I nervously smoothed the bodice of my gown and took a deep breath.

"Miss Wasson, am I correct? Chapman Wasson's daughter?" he asked as he approached, and before I could answer, "Your father has spoken often of you, so I was certain I recognized you when you walked in. And I must say, your father didn't exaggerate." Embarrassed by his own forthrightness, he quickly added, "I'm sorry. My name is William Day. Friends call me Will." He offered a slight bow, his silver horsehead cufflinks catching the light in the room and my attention. There was a dignified air about him, and he was obviously some years older.

"Well, hello Mr. Day. Yes, I am Blanche Wasson. May I ask, what was the occasion of my father speaking with you—and about me?"

"I'm here visiting the Prescotts. They're cousins on my mother's side. I trained down from Winchester, Kentucky to discuss a possible business venture—opening a general mercantile business here."

"Oh, really? Papa owns the largest general store here, but I guess you knew that. Why would we need another?"

"Your town's growing by leaps and bounds, thanks in large part to your family's successful promotion of this resort. My father…and I…think another mercantile business could be accommodated. Our family owns two in Kentucky—Day Brothers and Company—and expanding the business into Tennessee, if the conditions are right, may be a good direction."

"And what does Papa think about that?" I asked, trying to ignore my jitters.

"It's possible the two stores might stock distinct, complementary inventories…" He stopped mid-sentence. "But this isn't a topic of conversation for a star-lit night." And then it was he who became a little tongue-tied, hesitating before asking, "Would you, instead, permit me a dance?"

I nodded and he offered his arm. With the musical ensemble already filling the room with a waltz, we glided across the floor, his hand on my waist and mine on his shoulder, hand in hand. With every step, I silently thanked God that ballroom dancing had been among my school subjects—even if my dance partners were girls. Our movements were in tandem and fluid. I was floating. When I looked up into his brown eyes, the crowd around us faded away.

Within the hour, Will Day was no longer a stranger. I found his company easy and supremely enjoyable—with no end to conversation when we were not circling the dance floor. Nor did Will show interest in leaving my company for another dance partner. Instead, he asked to hear the history of the hotel and my family's involvement and seemed totally absorbed in whatever I said. The fact that he was eight years my senior didn't seem to matter. Before I knew it, we were poking fun at our families' obsession with Thoroughbred horses and their pedigrees—apparently, a common

Kentucky-borne malady. I learned much about William Day and found it to my liking. An only son with two much older sisters, Will came from a long line of Kentuckians, just like Mama, earning him my immediate favor. His father and uncle co-owned three lumber mills supported by ten thousand acres of timber as well as farmland. They had built their own railroad in Kentucky, the Mountain Central, to transport timber and crops to towns across the region. Ten years earlier Will's father had started a wholesale grocery in Winchester, Kentucky and later bought out another wholesaler in Lexington. That's when he'd brought Will into the business, grooming him to carry on the family's myriad ventures.

As the evening wore on and was late, Will and I drifted out of the hotel in search of a breeze. We strolled onto the gazebo and into the shadows cast by a moon peeking through the surrounding trees. Our conversation ebbed as we admired the crystal specks sprinkled overhead.

"How long will you be in Rhea Springs?" I finally asked.

"Until tonight I would have said another week," Will remarked, his upward gaze unchanged. "Father is insistent that I talk with every business owner here. We need an accurate appraisal of the town's prospects for growth. Now that I'm meeting so many interesting people," he said, with a glance my way and what I thought was a smile, "...I may extend my stay...maybe until summer's end."

I squeezed the gazebo rail in a rush of excitement and was thankful he couldn't see my flushed cheeks. Will then asked if he might see me again.

"That would please me," I said, camouflaging my enthusiasm.

"I will see your father on Monday here at the hotel to discuss some business," Will said. "I'll speak with him then about calling on you. Will I see you and your family tomorrow at the Methodist church services? I'll be with my aunt and uncle."

"Certainly. I'll look forward to seeing you."

With a ceremonial bow, Will reached for my hand and quickly kissed it. Before I could react, he descended the gazebo steps and disappeared into the shadows.

The hour was late, and the musical instruments had gone silent. When I entered the hotel, Gay was idling among the thinning crowd. We soon bade everyone goodnight and strolled across the road arm-in-arm in non-stop chatter. What an evening it had been!

The house was quiet. Papa and Owen were at the hotel overseeing the cleanup. Happy to be home rather than walking into the clamor of a dormitory, I anticipated climbing into bed and mentally replaying Will Day's every word. I wondered what Papa thought of Mr. Day. Would he approve his calling on me? I smiled to myself as I pulled back the bed covers. It would be wise not to make a flap over William Day, no matter my enthusiasm, at least not yet.

Maybe Papa would be generous, given his own new attraction. He had fallen in love…with his new Victrola gramophone, the only one in the whole county, to hear him tell. He looked for any excuse to demonstrate how the invention worked—placement of a music cylinder on the contraption, stylus onto the cylinder, and a fervent crank of the handle to launch melodic sound into every corner of the house. His purchase had so energized his spirits, but we were worn down by his obsession. Even Bertie complained the constant playing interfered with her hymn singing.

With a silent vow to be discreet and give no hint of my attraction to Will Day, I gingerly stepped out of my gown and hung it on the mirrored wardrobe. Changing into my nightdress, I climbed onto my feather bed, sinking into its comfort. Pulling the sheet up to my chin, I circled my thoughts back to life at boarding school. On most weeknights in the hours before bedtime, we girls huddled over book assignments. But rather than work math problems or diagram sentences, we drifted to other topics and someone would pull out their book of romantic literature—like Jane Austen's *Sense and Sensibility*—to sneak a read. Before long, everyone within earshot would hear, "Listen to this girls…." Titillating excerpts read aloud detailing some romantic pursuit. Imagining the scenes, giggling girls dramatized being swept off their feet by the book's handsome hero.

I thought it was all silly and frivolous, nothing more than what it was…fiction. But now? After an evening in the company of Mr. Day, I was reconsidering. Giggling to myself, I was intrigued with the prospects but soon fell into blissful sleep.

CHAPTER 12

CHARLIE

Behind the row of look-alike clapboard houses on the long stretch of fallow field that separated them from Piney Creek, a Sunday shindig for us colored folk was underway ever bit as lively as the dance at the Rhea Springs Hotel the night before. It was even better from my way of looking at it. Laughter, music, and the hum of talk floated on the late afternoon air as neighbors and friends gathered. Along the creek bank, weeping willow trees offered shade. A lone hickory stretched two of its gnarled limbs over a pool of deep water, each dangling a long knotted rope that the young'uns could not resist. A passel of them took turns swinging off the bank to cannonball into the water, each one trying to out splash the other, whooping and hollering all the while. Ma said there were no happier sounds.

My sister Ruby had just turned eleven years old, but there was no taming her. Clinging to the rope like a vine wrapped around a fence post, she swung higher than everone, yelling for Ma to watch as she turned loose of the rope, her two long pigtails tied with yellow ribbons sailing through the air like black kite tails.

Not far away, a clutch of old codgers stayed cool under the shade of the trees as they made music. One with a banjo and the others with harmonicas formed a circle and fired off one tune after another, adding fancy trills and flourishes with fingers that still moved fast in spite of their years. If one didn't know the tune, he'd jump in with the rest, sounding it out the best he could on the fly. When they finished, they slapped each other's backs in self-congratulations. The gathering crowd—young'uns and old folks alike—couldn't resist their playing. With dancing in their feet, just about everbody within earshot joined the cakewalk, high-stepping and prancing around the picnic blankets urging more to join in.

With so many coming out to the shindig, it was no time before the pasture was turned into a giant patchwork quilt of tattered plaid blankets. Scattered across the field were three fire pits with flames licking high into the air. Women gathered around them with iron skillets, frying up cornmeal-battered catfish. Didn't matter it was hot as blazes standing over a fire on a summer afternoon. Crispy fried catfish—taken out of Piney's waters—was worth the sweat, and the cooks happily volunteered!

Neighbors was still gathering at five o'clock, strolling from their houses with piled-high baskets. Wagons of families had already rolled in from the colored settlement up on Walden Ridge—the Hickeys, the Smith family of eight, the Jenkins' brood, and others.

Pa told me to fetch some wood from our house and bring it to the fire pit he was tending. By the time I returned, he was greeting folks like a preacher on Sunday and carrying on with the women frying fish at his pit. I dropped the logs at his feet.

"Thank ya, son," he said, in an obvious good mood as he flung a log onto the flames.

He asked if I was ready for some finger-licking catfish. But I had something else on my mind. Standing next to him, I mumbled, "You didn't tell me Blanche Wasson was back home." I didn't want the cooks to overhear, but they was busy with their own gossip, so I went on. "When I saw her circling that dance floor last night in the arms of that tall feller, I hardly recognized her. Didn't know the man neither, never saw him around these parts."

"Yeah," Pa answered. "Bertie said she come home this summer looking more like her mama than ever." Pa talked on like he didn't care who heard. "Last night was the first I'd seen her since she trained home a few days back. Throw another log on, would'ya son? Gotta keep them skillets sizzling."

I did as he asked and stared into the fire, wondering aloud, "Who was that feller she was with?"

"Mister Wasson says he's from up Kentucky way. Looking to bring new business to the county. Has relatives here. Did you speak to Miss Blanche last night?"

"Nope. You know I was with you in the kitchen pulling that dang rope all evening. I got a glimpse when the kitchen help was trailing refreshments in and out of the hall. Didn't see her again until we was cleaning up after the dance. She came in looking around—for her sister, I guess. The two of them left arm in arm, carrying on like two chickens at feeding time with their chatter."

Pa slowly stirred the fire with his pitchfork, his eyes reflecting glints from the flames. "You young-uns do have a way of growing up." He glanced at me, now half a head taller than him. "You're almost as good looking as your pa," he said with a straight face and then laughed.

It was true. I favored Pa. A strong jaw like his and as muscled across my chest and arms, I beat him on occasion at arm wrestling.

Pa landed a fist to my arm and added, "And you read—and write—as good as any white child around these parts."

"Yeah, Pa," I said, and turned to walk away, rolling my eyes. He was down right embarrassing the way he gushed over his young'uns. Ma was no better. She'd brag to anybody who'd listen. Once heard her tell Grandma Sulley I was smart enough to be president of Tuskegee someday.

I skirted around the picnic squares and made my way toward the family blanket. Ma was there, having just unloaded our food basket. When she saw me, she called out and pointed toward the edge of the field up near the road. "Charlie, that's Uncle Eli and Aunt America coming." Their wagon was edging off onto the open field. "Skedaddle over and help 'em, will ya?"

I trotted across the ragged pasture toward the wagon carrying two rocking chairs. The two knowed how to plan. Too old to sit on the ground, they just up and brought their seats with them.

"Howdy, Aunt America, Uncle Eli," I called. "Let me help you with your things." I tied the team at a near fencepost and hurried around to lend a hand. The old couple looked more like twins than husband and wife, with their snow-white hair, faces as wrinkled as prunes, and bodies stooped and gnarled like two ancient trees, likely from years of working the fields.

Uncle Eli managed getting off the wagon by hisself, complaining all the while that he was down in his back. He nodded for me to take Aunt America's arm so I could ease her down. After she was safe on the ground, I pointed to our spot across the field. "We's over there." Ma was waving for their attention.

Uncle Eli reached under the wagon seat and pulled out a basket of vittles. A whiff of cornbread set my mouth to watering and I told them I was happy they was gonna be at our picnic spot. They both laughed. Uncle Eli took Aunt America's thin arm, carrying the basket in his spare hand, and they moved in Ma's direction, mapping out their steps so as not to stumble.

At the rear of the buckboard, I wrestled the two rockers to the ground. One under each arm, I slowly wove around the picnickers so as not to whack nobody. Happened by Amos and Geraldine Hickey—also from up on Walden. Mister Hickey looked a true mountain man with his curly beard as black and thick as the hair on his head. His missus was short and squat and always tight-lipped around other folks, a sour-looking woman. She kept her eyes to the ground most of the time, even at church. But today she was yakking with a young gal sitting next to her that I'd never seen before. And the gal was purty. I didn't remember their having no family.

"Howdy," I said, as I passed. They nodded a silent hello. About my age, the girl greeted me with the greenest eyes I'd ever seen. When she smiled, her cheeks swelled up like ripe peaches, the right one showing off a dimple. In a split second, my eyes took her in and I liked what I saw. Tall and lean, she sat lady-like with long legs tucked under a yeller gingham dress. Two long braids was wrapped around the crown of her head like a halo. In the late afternoon light, they looked the color of the dark red horses I'd groomed to a high sheen the day before. Mysterious—she was one mysterious-looking gal.

So busy staring, I forgot my feet and darn near fell over one of the rockers. Managing to stay upright, I turned my attention back to where I was going, away from the green-eyed beauty.

By the time I reached our picnic spot, Ma had already smothered my aunt and uncle with welcoming hugs. I put the rockers at the blanket's edge and helped the two settle in to watch the celebration unfold. Ma busied herself emptying their basket, adding their vittles to ours. The sun had lost its punch, and the breeze had tamed the afternoon to a tolerable feel, perfect weather for the first summer jig. Counting all the little ones running about, the crowd had swelled to over a hundred. Horseshoe pits were set up in the field and I could hear the fierce competition. Must'a been ten fellers crowded around one, so I knowed heavy betting was underway. The hootin' and hollerin' was ear splitting whenever a throw ringered the iron shoe on the post and hands was outstretched for pay-ups. Right there in the middle of the ruckus was Elijah Jenkins, a tall drink of a feller with extra long arms. He was the best horseshoe thrower in the county. Could make a ringer with his eyes closed. Lost a whole day's pay once when I thought Jeremiah Jones could out throw him. Pa said I learned two things that day: One, that gambling was sinful and God was showing me it didn't pay to go against the Good Book. And two, if I ever gambled again to put my money on Elijah Jenkins.

There was something for everbody at our shindigs. Across the way, long jump ropes was turning non-stop, swishing in time with the music. Boys and girls alike lined up waiting a turn. No gambling going on there. Grownups wandered among clutches of friends and relatives, catching up on gossip. The music was constant and the buzz of talk and shots of laughter grew louder and louder until the cooks with the iron skillets shouted, "Come and git it!" That stopped ever one in his tracks. Young and old alike grabbed a tin plate and headed to the nearest fire pit for some sizzling catfish. Given the crop of baskets everwhere, it was a sure thing a feast was about to be had: Fried chicken on ever plate right beside the catfish. Jars of cream-style corn from last summer's crop, pickled cucumbers and beets. Deviled eggs, my favorite, just the size for popping in my mouth. Hoecakes and bean salad, too.

With plates piled high, everbody dug in. But it wasn't twenty minutes before the young scamps was already headed back to the creek and jump ropes swished to contests of double-dutch jumpin' between double-whirling ropes.

Ruby had finished off her supper except for the hoecake she nibbled at. With her empty plate in the middle of her crossed legs, she started up. "Ma, can I go back now?" Sitting next to me wrapped in the big towel Ma had brought down from the house, she looked like a wet cat. There was no keeping Ruby away from water when there was fun to be had.

"Ruby, you wait a spell before wading back in. Your food's gotta settle. You don't want belly cramps."

"I can watch. Please?" she pleaded. "I won't get in. I promise."

"Make sure you don't..."

Before Ma got out another word, Ruby had sprung to her feet and tossed the damp towel on my head as she ran off.

Satisfied to stretch out and snatch some reading from the Chattanooga Times newspaper Mister Wasson had given me the day before, I folded it up small so as not to draw attention. Ever so often I looked in the direction of the Hickeys and that purty girl.

It wasn't long before Ruby showed up again with something cradled in her arms. Plopping onto the blanket next to Ma, she started begging before anybody knew what she was asking. "Ma, can I keep it? Can I? Ain't it cute? So soft and sweet. See, it don't even try to get away. Can I keep it?"

Ruby offered up a furry black kitten with a white patch on its chest and tip of its tail. It was cute, but I knew exactly what Ma was gonna say. Her face had already wrinkled into a frown.

"Ruby, we has too many cats hanging around the place now. We can't take in ever stray critter in the county. Not enough mice and scraps to go around."

"Oh, Ma." Ruby cuddled the kitten and it mewed softly.

"Don't 'oh ma' me. Take it back to where you found it. Mama cat's probably lookin' for it now."

Ruby protested, "I found it at the creek where we was swimming, next to a tree trunk. I didn't see no other cats." She held the kitten up for me to see, hoping I'd side with her. I didn't. I reached for the last deviled egg on the plate, stuffed it in my mouth and smiled her way.

She stroked the kitten on her lap, and I watched to see what she was gonna do. With disappointment on her face, she got to her feet and ambled away, cradling the kitten close. She glanced over her shoulder, frowned and stuck her tongue out at me.

The sun soon slipped below the distant ridge and the fires was giving out too. Pa got up from our blanket and stretched before stepping over me to go throw another log on the nearby fire and then headed across the field toward our house. Within minutes, he was back with his fiddle under his arm, a gift from Doctor Wasson who had himself had received it as payment for his doctoring. Pa had named it "Willie." Playing by ear, he picked out tunes ever night after supper and had gotten mighty good over time.

When the harmonica players saw him with Willie, they gathered around and in no time the bunch was harmonizing. Ever one within earshot clapped hands and joined in, singing "When the Saints Go Marching In." The music just kept a'comin. By the time we got to "Skip to My Lou, My Darlin," the dancing had commenced and I jumped to my feet and grabbed Ma up in my arms, swinging her around in front of Uncle Eli and Aunt America. She laughed and laughed, all the while protesting, "Turn me loose, boy! Now turn me loose." But I knowed she was loving ever minute and the old folks got a real kick cheering us on.

By the time darkness settled in and the half moon climbed high, everbody was tuckered. Glowing embers sent sparks into the night air and the instruments fell quiet. Spontaneous singing of the heart-felt hymn of hope filled right in, with others humming along: "Blessed assurance, Jesus is mine! Oh, what a foretaste of Glory divine! Heir of salvation, purchase of God..." So many harmonizing voices brought heaven down, knitting our people together.

Nobody wanted to leave, but finally folks stirred, gathering up blankets, empty baskets and plumb-wore-out young'uns. A rising sun on a back-to-work Monday would call soon.

"Charlie, go git Ruby, would ya?" Ma ordered. "She's probably with her chums." Ma was helping Uncle Eli and Aunt America gather their belongings. Pa had taken their rockers back to the wagon and returned to help them cross the field.

I headed toward the creek bank. "Ruby! Time to go home. Come on," I called in the direction of the tree with the ropes hanging idly from its limbs. Why was I always the one who had to fetch her? She was like a flea on a dog. You could never catch her. Ruby was nowhere among the trees and neither were her pals. It was deserted and black as pitch. The clustered trees blocked even the stingiest glimmer of the half moon overhead.

"Ruby! Let's go," I yelled louder, and picked my way along the slippery creek bank. Something sloshed in the water, and I strained to see in the direction of the sound. Didn't see nothing at first, but called Ruby's name again anyhow. No answer. I heard it again and moved farther along the bank, only to spot a dark form caught among the roots and boulders jutting into a little eddy. It bobbed in the water amidst the floating twigs and brush snagged there. My belly leaped. I couldn't get her name out of my mouth, so I stepped into the shallow black waters to get a closer look. I sent up a silent prayer and thanks be to God it was answered. A rotting log sloshed about, probably washed down the creek in the last hard rain. Now soaking wet up to my knees, I determined to wring my little sister's neck when she did show up.

I headed back in the direction of our picnic spot, thinkin' she might be with one of her friends. Along the way, I saw a neighbor boy crossing the field. "Caleb! You seen Ruby?"

"Nope, I seen her a while back—carrying around a kitten. Said she was gonna keep it. Didn't see her after that."

"If you do, tell her to git home, will ya?"

"Sure will, Charlie."

Something inside me said to double check back along the creek bank, so I did—inspected around ever tree trunk a fer distance. Nothing. I returned to the tree with the hanging ropes. I stood at its base looking into the water when something caught my eye. Laying on the bank close to my feet was a muddied yellow ribbon, like the ones Ruby had tied to her pigtails. My stomach twisted as I picked it up and gazed out over the dark, murky water, watching its slow, quiet movements. "Ruby!" I shouted again.

I ran to where our family had picnicked, but the blanket was gone and so was Ma and Pa. Thinking I heard Pa's voice in the distance, I hurried to the road just as he and Ma was waving at Uncle Eli's wagon disappearing into the night.

"Ma, Pa. Can't find Ruby. She ain't nowhere. I ran along the creek and found this near the ropes." I held out the soggy ribbon.

Ma took it from my hand. Her face flattened with fear as she stared at it. "Maybe it fell off when she was swinging on that rope," she said, trying to convince herself, but emotion was creeping into her words. "Was she wearing them when she came to eat?" Staring at me and Pa, Ma begged for a piece of hope. We couldn't remember.

"Charlie, tell me again what ground you covered," Pa asked. Before I could even answer, he added, "How far along the creek? What about her friends? Did you see any of them? What'd they say?"

I told Pa everwhere I'd searched.

Ma said, "I told her to take that kitten back to where she found it, and she said it was next to a tree trunk by the water. You looked there? It's blackness down among them trees."

"Yeah, Ma. Nobody's there. I yelled in ever direction."

Pa barked orders for Ma and me to spread out and ask any remaining folks in the field for help. He was going down along the creek. I said I'd go with him, but he was already headed into the darkness and yelled for me to do as he said.

"Ruby, Ruby." Within minutes her name was echoing from every direction across the field. There was no answer. When I passed Ma five minutes later, she said some of the neighbor men was gonna work their way along the creek banks on both sides and needed the torches. She told me to get the ones Pa kept stored under the porch. A can of kerosene was in the kitchen.

I found the five makeshift torches under the porch and then went into the kitchen. The moon offered little help inside the dark house. I squinted, but the kerosene can was nowhere to be seen—not in a corner, not around the cornmeal sacks under the counter or under the sink. Not next to the brooms and mop leaning against the wall neither. Maybe Pa had moved it, to put it somewhere safer, far away from the cook stove. I looked in the corners of the front room. Not there. Wouldn't be in the bedroom, but I'd look. I opened the closed door and scanned the room through the darkness. Not a can anywhere, but I caught sight of something in the far corner on top of the cornhusk mattress where Ruby and me slept.

I edged closer. There, fast asleep and curled into a ball was Ruby. A clear, sweet "meow" greeted me from a small furry form snuggled next to her neck—a purring black kitten with a white patch on its chest and tip of its tail.

CHAPTER 13

BLANCHE

As the summer days unfurled, sightings of Will and me together became the talk of the town—or at least that was the subject of the Methodist church ladies' circle, according to Papa's sources. "You overheard what?" I asked one Sunday afternoon as Papa and I shared the porch swing and a few leisure moments, just father and daughter.

He reassured me, saying, "Pay them no mind, Blanche. The old busybodies are victims of the summer heat and seeing "double." He chuckled and gave me a wink before rising to say he needed to walk over to the hotel. He left, and I found myself giggling at his revelations.

The truth was I *often* shared Will's company. We blended into the fabric of the hotel happenings: picnics on the grounds, music concerts, Chautauqua-sponsored speakers of all persuasions. In those happy hours, the interest and manners that Will showed as we talked and he listened set me perfectly at ease. Conversations moved seamlessly across topics. Papa had commented that Will was an astute and ambitious businessman, but I also discovered his interest in the arts and love of the printed word. That carried far more weight with me. Literature crept into our conversations, and I found he enjoyed Shakespeare as I did. When he came to the house to call, I often descended the steps from my room to find him in Papa's library turning pages of a book pulled from the crowded shelves. I soon learned Will seemed to enjoy sharing his knowledge on almost any subject.

***

Will suggested a buggy ride that Sunday afternoon after a chamber concert on the hotel's gazebo. It was a favorite pastime for young courting couples seeking solitude, and I was delighted by his invitation.

Back from the stable in no time with horse and buggy, he offered his hand and I climbed aboard. With a flick of the reins, we escaped the milling crowd and headed into the countryside. As cotton clouds drifted across the canvas of sky, robins soon greeted us from the trees alongside the road. The rolling fields, some carpeted with red clover, occupied a few grazing cows and horses in the cooling of a late afternoon. Oddly, the rhythmic clopping of the horse's hooves added to the serenity. My every sense was heightened. I'd never felt quite like this before.

Eventually Will broke the silence. "What did you think of the concert? That quintet for horn, violin, violas and cello was impressive, didn't you think? And the French horn...its clear mellow sound. Exquisite."

I nodded, gazing at his handsome features that radiated his enthusiasm. I was proud to be in Will Day's company. The talk of church busybodies didn't matter one whit.

"Second to the violin," I said, ready to offer an opinion, "the French horn is my favorite instrument. When I saw the program was entirely Mozart, I was thrilled. And you see, Mr. Day, I knew what to expect from a Mozart concert because of your recent music appreciation lesson." Will glanced aside to me and we both beamed.

"My dear Blanche," he said, jokingly adopting the tone of a professor, "Did you know that Wolfgang Amadeus Mozart was one of the most prolific classical composers in history? With over six hundred works in his short thirty-five years."

"Really, Professor Day? I didn't know that." I quizzically put my fingers to my chin and played along, masking amusement, and asked what else I should know about Mr. Mozart.

"Well, for one, he began composing when he was only four. He learned to write music before he learned to write words."

"Hmmm...I am impressed," I said chuckling, "with Mozart *and* your bottomless well of information."

Will shifted his attention to the landscape. Without a word, he turned the horse off the well-traveled road and headed the buggy across the open pasture toward a high knoll by way of a worn cow path. Other than a few staring Black Angus that paused from their grazing and lazily chewed their cuds, we were alone. As we bounced this way and that over the irregular terrain, Will offered no explanation for his detour. I felt a twinge of anxiety, but calmed myself with the assurance that I was in the company of a gentleman.

Then Will broke his silence. "Now, wait a minute...I've saved the best till last." He went on with his trivia, declaring that Mozart had composed "Ah vous dirai-je, Maman" which, when I tilted my head quizzically, he revealed was "Twinkle, Twinkle Little Star."

When we reached the crest of the hill, Will turned the buggy around and pulled the leather reins, bringing the horse to a standstill. Before us was a panorama of beauty: acres of growing corn and soybeans, square fields of strawberry plants and pastureland, with an endless smooth sky above that transported the aromas of a country summer and bathed it all in the yellow hues of late afternoon.

Not until I sensed his gaze did I turn to look into his soulful eyes. He brought his hand to my chin and gently brought us closer. A hint of a gentleman's cologne greeted me, and his lips slipped to mine in a kiss that lasted but seconds. His eyes lingered, looking into mine, expressing what would have made me blush if spoken. Great warmth filled me. We both returned our gaze to the rolling farmland and took in the changing reality between us. Momentarily and without a word, Will turned attention to the horse, slapping the reins to its rump. Only then was the spell broken. I had never been kissed before.

***

I was smitten with Will Day. At twenty-five-years of age, he was not only handsome but ambitious; that he thought I was beautiful and smart didn't hurt either. And Papa approved, I could tell. Mama's people attested to the Days' reputation, although they didn't know the family directly. All who had business dealings with Mr. Day in Kentucky held him in high esteem. Apparently his success had not changed his kindly nature and generosity of spirit. Papa always said you didn't have to look further than a man's family to get a reading of his character. He commented that Will had big shoes to fill if he followed in his father's footsteps.

From all I could tell, Will was an upright man, a church-going fellow, a patriotic Southerner like Papa and our family. But his idea of progress didn't involve a willingness to change much about his world. He seemed to long for the glory of a South of a yesterday year that predated him. I came to recognize that over time, but chose to ignore its warning.

***

One Sunday afternoon Will called on me, and in a desire to escape Papa's watchful eye, we decided on a stroll. I took his arm and we left the house in the direction of the lake. Not fifty paces down the road we heard the clop of animal hooves behind us and stepped aside to allow its passing and then I heard a familiar voice.

"Good day, Miss Blanche."

I turned to see Charlie Reynolds coming from the direction of the Methodist church, riding bareback on a muscular gray plow mule. Wearing his Sunday best—a shirt, no doubt ironed by Bertie, neatly buttoned, and trousers secured with red suspenders—he was a sight to see. I chuckled. Back in the day when I was passing books to him, Charlie wore only ragged coveralls and dingy shirts missing more buttons than not. Seemed odd to see him in trousers—without holes. His brown dusty feet dangled not far from the ground as his long legs hugged the sides of the sweaty mule.

"Well, hello Charlie," I replied, noting Will's puzzlement out of the corner of my eye. Charlie pulled the halter ropes, bringing the animal to a stop beside us.

"Yes, ma'am. It's good to have you back home again, Miss Blanche."

"I'm glad to be back, Charlie. Having your ma cooking my breakfast again is half of what 'home, sweet home' is all about."

"Yes, ma'am. Saw you at the hotel dance a few weeks back—I was helping Pa with the fanning out in the kitchen."

"You've taken over my job? Being your Pa's assistant at the fan was my first summer job—actually my only one and it was short lived." I laughed and glanced at Will, whose boredom was unmistakable. "I'll explain later," I said, as an aside to Will.

"I don't believe you've met Mr. Day?"

"No, ma'am."

"Well, Charlie, I'd like to introduce you to Mister William Day. He's here from Kentucky and is talking over some business dealings with Papa and other store owners in Rhea Springs."

Charlie tipped his floppy straw hat in Will's direction and offered his big toothy grin. But it disappeared when Will returned a stone-faced "hello" and a wordless nod to me to shorten the conversation. Easily noticed, Charlie excused himself and kicked his mule. "Let's get on, Sal."

When he was out of earshot, I reminded Will that Charlie was Sam and Bertie's son.

"Yes, I guessed he was, given how neighborly you were," Will said, with a shade of sarcasm.

Given Will's tone, I let the subject of Charlie slide, and we strolled on to the lake and out to the end of the long wooden dock that extended over the still water. Several couples in their various red, white and blue boats were drifting about. The shrubbery skirting the shoreline was draped with honeysuckle in full flower, and the sun's rays had released its sweet fragrance. I audibly sighed.

"When Papa sent me off to boarding school, I thought I might never get back here—to all of this beauty and contentment. This is my Eden, Will." Closing my eyes, I breathed in deeply the fragrance of home, and said, "You know...when Mama died, I was convinced it had been my fault somehow...and was sure Papa didn't love me in the same way afterward...and then he sent me off to school."

Will's smiling eyes were recognition of my emotion, but he replied, "Poppycock, Blanche. Your father is supremely proud of you..."

I interrupted, wanting to impress on him that I had come to more mature insights. "Now I know differently—that he wanted more for me—the best education, intelligent women as role models, rubbing shoulders with young ladies from the best families. I understand that...now."

"Yes, your papa had your best interests at heart and," Will said, starting again.

"And it's a chance few around here have," I said, finishing his sentence. Will realized I was not through, so he restrained himself. "Don't get me wrong," I said. "I don't turn up my nose at the schooling I received in Rhea Springs. My sister finished her education here. And Owen. He's now headed to the University of Kentucky."

"Really? That's good," Will said, absently peering into the water below, searching for fish.

"My teachers here were dedicated, without a doubt, but weren't trained as educators, not like those at Sayre Academy. Take Professor Tankersley, my civics instructor. He's from Ohio and his legal background qualifies him, I suspect, but there were no textbooks—or Mr. Moody, who loves teaching about the Civil War, but I'd dare say can't take his students back to the Revolutionary War period, and I doubt he knows anything about European history."

With no apparent reaction from Will, I wondered if he was listening. But when I paused, he turned his eyes from the water and said, "Well, that speaks to the quality of the instruction, I'd guess, but probably not the dedication." His gaze then appeared to re-focus on my appearance rather than my words.

I self-consciously checked the upsweep of my hair, fingering the bun, and replied, "Also, schooling in the countryside is cut short because of the harvesting season, as you know."

"There is something to be said for growing up in the shadow of the city," Will said. "I had no choice. Father determined I was to attend the private academy outside Louisville, just like he had, and then be off to Cumberland College in Virginia. I concede it did give me a head start."

"See there, you make my point. In your family, it was 'expected' that you would receive the best education. And that's fine, but what about us young ladies who want to learn what you took for granted? And, if we girls have less opportunity, what about colored youngsters? Out in the country, anyway, there's no chance whatsoever. Why, Sam's son Charlie only learned how to read a couple of years ago. I used to loan him my old books…."

"Really? The colored boy we just passed? Why did you do that?" he asked, and before I could answer, said, "Seems a waste of time. Don't need an education to pick strawberries or manage a plow."

"That's not the point, Will. He didn't even have a choice until Mr. Lyons, one of our townspeople, opened a colored school in his barn. But it closed down after a few winters. Colored families stopped sending their children—got scared off by rumors that white folk around here might see it as uppity. Stirring up trouble wasn't worth the risk, they imagined."

"Well, I'm not sure I'd argue that."

"Why? What's uppity about learning to read? It gives them tools to learn there's a world out there—beyond Rhea Springs."

"And experience nothing but frustration," Will said, frowning, "when there's little chance they'll find a better place in that world."

"What do you mean? Booker T. Washington himself said right here in Rhea Springs a few years back that if colored people are given the right education they can help build the South into a more prosperous place—for everyone. Isn't that what the South needs—to come back stronger than before the War? Are we happier to see colored folk flee to the North because of discontent?"

"Building a New South sounds good, but I'm not sure how it translates for Negroes," Will said. He took my hand and we turned to walk back, continuing our conversation.

"Well, we won't know if we don't give them an opportunity," I protested. "Everyone deserves a chance at a better life, wouldn't you agree?" With my every muscle tensed, I didn't care that I was preaching. My face must have betrayed me, because Will appeared amused, let go of my hand and hugged me to his side. I was taken aback. We were right out in the open; someone might see.

Then Will said, "I think that's what sets you apart from other young ladies I know, Blanche. You're fiery with idealism, and I find that attractive indeed."

I accepted his compliment without protest, but his dismissive wink and squeeze of my hand suggested he had not necessarily agreed with me.

As we neared home and the hotel, sporadic laughter of a crowd around the gazebo caught our attention. Will and I exchanged a look of surprise and turned onto the grounds to investigate.

"Yesterday a fella on a unicycle was peddling around the hotel," I said. "Had a sign on his back advertising a magic show."

We neared the crowd and caught sight of a man in black baggy pants and candy-apple red shirt just as he bowed and tipped his red and white-striped funnel hat, pulling out a white rabbit with long ears and pink eyes that he held high. After raucous clapping, he handed the rabbit to his assistant and held up both hands to quiet the crowd. Will and I turned to one another with amused grins and then back to the magician as he dramatically pulled his blue sequined suspenders off his shoulders. Out of his falling trousers flew four white doves in all directions, leaving only his long red shirttails for cover. Everyone cheered and clapped and we joined in.

By the time Will and I finally reached my porch steps, all signs of our disagreeable discussion had taken flight along with the doves. He politely offered his arm.

"Thank you, Will. Won't you linger a spell?" I asked, gesturing toward the double swing at the end of the porch. He nodded. As we settled there, I contemplated how to bring up Will's lack of manners toward Charlie when the front screen door opened and Papa appeared.

"I was wondering where you two had skedaddled," Papa inquired with feigned concern and puckish grin.

"We took a stroll to the lake. Such a lovely afternoon called for one, don't you think?" I smiled coyly at Papa.

Not in the least perturbed, he pulled up a porch chair. Conversation between the two men soon turned to business, and within minutes my presence was unnoticed. The porch swing creaked, adding to the drone of conversation as dusk settled in. Discussion of education and Charlie's right to learn would wait. I wondered if Papa would think to include Will in our supper plans at the hotel.

CHAPTER 14

CHARLIE

Ma called to me from the kitchen where she and Ruby were scurrying to put Sunday supper on the table. "Your pa and me has solved a mystery," she hollered. Laying aside my newspaper, I rolled off the sagging sofa and strolled back to the kitchen doorway. Leaning there, I yawned and stretched before asking, "What mystery, Ma?" Ruby was setting out the tin plates and forks on the wood table. She glanced at me with a rascal of a grin, but kept quiet—not her usual way. Ma stood at the cook stove with her back to me, stirring the pot of greens with purpose. Glancing over her shoulder, she said, "Charlie, call in your pa, will ya? Sounds like he's on the porch with his fiddle." She turned back to stirring.

"I thought you was going to tell me about some mystery," I complained. I turned my head in the direction of the front door and yelled, "Pa! Supper's ready!" Ma snorted her disapproval, saying she could'a done that.

Settling at the table, me and Pa on a bench on one side and Ma and Ruby on the other, Pa bowed his head to ask the Good Lord's blessing. After a chorus of "Amens," Ma spooned a mess of beans and turnip greens onto our plates and passed around the cornbread slabs. It got quiet with our eatin', but then she brought it up again.

"Like I was saying, Charlie, your pa and me figured out why you's been so keen on getting to church lately." Ma winked at Pa across the table. He didn't say nothing, but smothered a grin. "Until lately," she said, "you'd as likely slip off to fish with a friend and show up again at the church house ten minutes before the last amen and ease onto a back bench during the singing and shouting, figuring nobody'd notice. You thought you'd pulled the wool over our eyes."

Ruby giggled, eyeing me.

I gave my eleven-year old sister a look to kill, and she dropped her eyes to her plate to push the beans around with her fork.

"But that wasn't no real mystery," Ma went on. "Mysterious is what you's been up to the last few weeks. Your pa and me wondered why you was set on riding the mule to church and not going with us in the wagon. And you stayed later."

"Ma, I'm a man now—nineteen years old. Nothing wrong with me traveling on my own." I turned to Pa to back me. He just nodded his agreement. But that caged grin he wore was worrisome.

Ma went on. "Yep, you's been showing up at the church house way before time and lingering after in the crowd. Then you call out to us that you'll be on directly and for us to go on."

"So what?" I wasn't gonna say more than I had to.

"Well, like I said, it was a mystery—your warming to church-going like never before." Ma smirked. "But Aunt America solved it. She pulled me aside today after the preaching and asked what your pa and me thought about that new purty thing you's been staring at with cow eyes. Not knowing what she was talking about, I asked her to explain. She said a young filly is staying up on Walden with the Hickeys. They's her aunt and uncle. Said she had a falling out with her ma and left home on foot. Made her way here all the way from Alabama a month back. She rides down to church with the Hickeys most Sundays. I'd seen her, but didn't pay her no mind. But it appears you have."

I could feel myself tense with ever word she poked at me, but I held my peace.

"Aunt America says you's got competition. Fellers has been buzzing around her like bees to a hive, some even making visits up to Walden Ridge. You been one of them, Charlie?"

I could hold my tongue no longer. Out of my mouth spewed the words, "That's my business, not yours!" What Ma didn't know was that I'd been pondering the idea of calling on that gal but hadn't worked up the courage.

Pa pounded his fist on the table, rattling everthing. "Don't you sass your Ma!"

I scowled, but he didn't take my bait. So I pushed away from the table and left by way of the kitchen door, slamming it to make a point. Once outside, I broke into a run across the field to the Piney. Maneuvering my way along the creek bank through the trees and their bulging roots, I stumbled and cussed. By the time I got to my old fishing spot a mile upstream and plopped down on the bank, my mind was settling down. Taking a deep breath, I stared into the rippling green water and listened to its unchanged sounds. I had a lot to think on. With so many other fellers circling that gal, did I even have a chance? And what did I have to offer? A steady job, but stable work wasn't so impressive.

An hour or so later, the full moon was climbing into the darkened sky when I skipped one last rock across the water and stood to my feet. Making my way across the empty field up to the wagon road, I headed home along its rutted path, kicking the dirt along the way, still thinking.

The cicadas was already making a racket as the dark outline of the huddled houses took shape in the distance, each with a glow in a window from a burning lamp. As I got closer, I could hear the soft talk of folks lingering on their porches and front steps, visiting with one another in the shadows. The small fry giggled as they played tag and hide-and-seek. When I got to my house, Pa was sitting alone on the porch step.

"Where's Ma...and Ruby?" I asked, as I unlatched the squeaky gate.

"They's up the road visiting Grandma Sulley."

When I plopped beside him, our black and white kitten appeared out of nowhere looking for a lap to curl on. Except for the soft mews when I stroked her, Pa and I watched the moon in silence. After a bit, I asked, "Remember when you used to tell me there was a man up there?"

"Yep, I do. Have you spotted him lately?"

"Nope." In the quiet between us, I found my courage. "Pa, how did you know Ma was the one?"

"The one? What do you mean, boy?" he asked, without turning his head.

"You know—the one...the one you wanted to be with."

"Oh," Pa glanced at me and then returned his eyes to the moon. "Hmm…how did I know?" Pa scratched his head like he hadn't thought about that in a long spell. "Your ma was fifteen when we met. She and her ma had come up from Alabama after Bertie's pa died. Her ma was at loose ends—needed to be close to her sister, to her kin. But her ma had no use for me. I was older—lots older than Bertie. And being dark didn't help neither—too dark for the likes of her light-skinned baby girl. But that didn't slow me up. When I laid eyes on her…well, I just couldn't stop. And when I went to courting her, it didn't take no time a'tall to know."

"Really?" I asked.

"Sure enough. And the fact her ma wasn't keen on me just made me more determined." Silence hung heavy between us. Then Pa said, "I reckon I know why you's so curious." He never took his eyes off the moon, but said, "You's found yourself a gal—one that makes your head spin when she looks at you…the purtiest thing that ever walked God's earth…and when you talk to her, you can't get the right words out. You feel like one of them scarecrows in the field, with hay for brains. Am I right?"

"Yep, that about says it."

We sat in the darkness still staring at that big yeller circle overhead when I felt Pa's arm around me, and he tussled my hair like he did when I was a tadpole. Then he said, "Don't worry your head, son. You'll figure it out."

***

The next Sunday I did just what I'd been doing ever Sunday since the shindig three weeks back. I slung myself up on Sal and turned its head toward the church house in Rhea Springs. Wanted to beat the Hickeys there, so I left early. When the two-story building with its steeple came into view, a few white families were still socializing outside, after their own services. To avoid their stares, I rode to the far side where I could watch up the road without drawing notice.

Keeping my eyes pealed, I fidgeted. I passed the time thinking on what I'd say to Ida Mae. Timing was important, so I headed my mule around front when the white families was finally gone. Just as I tied Sal to the hitching post, their wagon rolled up but it stopped under the grove of hickories to the side of the building. "Darnn, why didn't he pull up front?" I whispered aloud. Nothing I could do about that now.

"Good day," I called out, and walked in their direction.

"Afternoon Charlie," Mister Hickey answered as he jumped from the buckboard.

"How is you doing, Miz Hickey, Miss Ida Mae?" I asked as easygoing as I could muster. "Here, let me help you down."

Miz Hickey didn't have much to say. She was a sour-faced woman and looked like she'd been sucking a persimmon. Mister Hickey was grinning out of that black beard of his, like he knew something I didn't. I helped Miz Hickey down and then Ida Mae scooted across the wagon bench toward me. Her auburn hair glistened in the sunshine and when she smiled, it satisfied like drinking lemonade on a hot day. Taking my hand, she stepped to the edge and I lowered her to the ground. She was light as a feather and smelled of fresh talcum powder. Finding my courage, I blurted the words I'd swallowed for two Sundays straight, "I'd be obliged to walk you in."

Ida Mae didn't hesitate. "Of course, Charlie. For that matter, would you like to sit with us? Aunt and Uncle don't mind." She glanced over her shoulder at them, but I saw their eyes was on me.

Ida Mae waited for my bent arm, and I stood as straight as an arrow as we started toward the open doors. If my feet touched the ground, I sure didn't notice. Ida Mae led me to where she and the Hickeys sat ever service, about half-way down, and we settled onto the bench. Her aunt and uncle took seats behind us. Ida Mae picked up a paper fan from the bench, left there after the white services, I reckoned, and began moving the air. Felt good on a June afternoon. Her skin was damp with heat but smooth as a brown feather. I couldn't take my eyes off her waving that fan. Then Mister Hickey cleared his throat real loud. He'd been watching. I jerked my head straight ahead and tried without much success to think about God.

Then Ida Mae started in. "Uncle Amos tells me your ma and pa work for that family who owns the big white hotel. You work there too?"

"Uh...I work at the hotel stable. I'm assistant to Mister Sam Waterhouse. He's taught me everthing there is to know about horses. Been there since I was knee high to a grasshopper." I dressed up the facts the best I could. It wasn't the gospel truth, but maybe God would forgive me if He was listening. Sure sounded better than telling I mucked stalls most days.

"Hmm...Is that so?" Ida Mae wasn't paying no attention to my answer. She was looking over her shoulder at the young bucks coming down the aisle. Each one turned his head as he passed, giving her a look. They nodded and held their hats to their chests polite-like. And she smiled back. Then Ma and Pa and Ruby came in, scouting out seats. I turned my head to escape notice. Sitting close to Ida Mae left me all jittery inside, a good feeling, but I didn't want to listen to Ma's yammering later.

Minutes later the service started. Ever Sunday was different. With no regular preacher, the gathering sang and waited for the Holy Ghost to come down. When someone felt the call, he'd go up and preach. Singing was the best part. The white church preacher said our congregation wasn't allowed to use the church organ, but we didn't need it. Ma was right; our harmonizing was heavenly. People's spirits soared when it commenced and praise filled the place.

Church went on longer that day, for which I was grateful. Maybe it was the Good Lord's way of smiling on the idea of Ida Mae and me. When church let out, it was late afternoon, but I was in no rush to head my mule back to Piney Creek. Miss Ida Mae sashayed out the church door on my arm, and I felt taller than any man there. When we joined the folks visiting outside with one another, the three who'd eyed her earlier circled us like foxes ready to raid the chicken coop. But Ida Mae didn't mind. She seemed pleased to be the center of their attention. Each one gushed on about how fine she looked. One feller asked if he could call on her...and done so right in front of me.

Before she could answer, Mister Hickey stepped over and said, "Excuse me, but Miss Ida Mae is leaving now...with me and her aunt." He motioned toward Miz Hickey who was sitting on the buckboard with an impatient frown.

I was relieved he chased the others off. Ida Mae let go of my arm and took her uncle's. They walked toward the wagon, but not without her looking back over her shoulder and giving—not just me—but all four of us a smile that would melt butter. She turned back to her uncle and left us standing with our hands in our pockets.

***

It took a week before I worked up the courage to ride my mule the long trek up Walden Ridge. After church and our supper meal back home, the afternoon was about spent, but summer kindly offered longer light and time for leisure. About six o'clock, Pa sauntered into the front room with a slab of buttered cornbread in his hand. I got up from the sofa and told him where I was headed. He took a big bite and gave me a knowing smile. I didn't have to explain nothing to Ma because she was nowhere to be found, Ruby neither. They was up the road visiting neighbors.

"It'll be dark before I git home," I called out, as I left through the back door to fetch Sal from the shed. As I walked him around to the road and was fixin' to climb on, I got an idea. Looking in ever direction to make sure Ma wasn't in sight, I tied the mule to the front fence and slipped across the yard to our lone rose bush—full of red velvet blooms. I broke off three branches full of sweet clusters, but not without bloodying my fingers on the thorns. Pulling a rag out of my trouser pocket, I wrapped it around the stems, thorns and all, and climbed onto my mule to rode off quick.

An hour later when the Hickey's cabin came into view, I spotted a muscled plow horse tied to a front hitching post. If the animal was theirs, it wouldn't be tied out there. Figuring it smart to wait and watch, I turned my mule into a nearby stand of trees. I busied myself fixing my bouquet for Ida Mae, cutting off the thorns from the stems with my knife. Then I used my rag to wrap the roses along with the Queen Ann's Lace and Goldenrod I'd picked along the way. It looked purty nice.

Directly, I heard the loud squeak of a door opening and looked up to see coming out of that cabin none other than Elijah Jenkins with a beat-up black Derby hat in hand, still in his Sunday clothes. Right behind him was Ida Mae. Standing there on the porch, he took her hand and offered a slight bow before turning to leave. Mounting his horse, Jenkins held his hat over his heart and winked at her before galloping off in the opposite direction. Ida Mae never stopped waving until he was out of sight.

Now what was I gonna do? Ride my mule over and knock on her door, another suitor the same day? She would compare everthing I'd say with that Elijah Jenkins. Even if he could beat everbody at horseshoes, he wasn't as good a "catch" as me. He was tall, but I was stronger. Why, his arms was no bigger around than broomsticks, and about as long. Besides, I'd ridden a long five miles to get here. I made up my mind. Laying the red, yeller and white bouquet aside, I resettled my shirt into my Sunday trousers, brushed the road dust off my pants and wiped my face with my shirtsleeve. There, I was ready.

Picking up the flowers, I swung myself onto the mule and trotted him to the cabin. I climbed the wood steps to the porch and faced the closed door. I sucked in my courage and knocked. When I heard footsteps, my belly leaped. The door creaked as it opened, and Mister Hickey filled the doorway. With folded arms across his broad chest, he stared straight through me. Didn't say nothing, and his face didn't move, or at least the part showing through his bushy black beard.

"Uh, afternoon Mister Hickey. I wonder if Miss Ida Mae might see clear to visit a spell. I've been up the road to see my Aunt America and Uncle Eli and thought to be neighborly while I was near. Is she busy?"

Mister Hickey didn't answer. Just turned his head and called back into the cabin, "Ida Mae. You got company again. It's Charlie...Charlie Reynolds."

He left me standing at the door without so much as an invite to step in. I thought to leave while the getting was good, but then Ida Mae appeared from a back room with that big smile and suggested we sit outside, since the sun was sinking and the air was cooling.

"Charlie, did I hear you say your aunt and uncle live around here?" she asked, as she pointed me to one of the two empty cane chairs on the porch. She took the other one and smoothed her yellow gingham dress as she settled herself.

Rather than follow her lead, I stepped in front of her and pulled the flowers from behind my back to present them. Ida Mae beamed and took them in hand.

"Oh my, Charlie Reynolds. How beautiful!" Taking a long whiff of the velvet roses, she exclaimed, "These surely smell sweeter than any store-bought perfume." And then she fingered the delicate Queen Ann's Lace. "Thank you, Charlie," she said, and laid the bouquet across her lap and waited for me to sit.

"My Aunt America and Uncle Eli moved up the road a few years back," I said. "Got too old for sharecropping. They get by with raising turkeys now, along with a little moonshining. I look in on them when I can 'cause they don't get off Walden much."

Maybe Ida Mae would favor me more, knowing I show respect for my elders. Pa said the gals saw that as a sign of strength in a man.

"Well, that's mighty nice of you to come this far," she said. "Even us going into Rhea Springs to church is a long ride, and you live thirty minutes beyond."

"Ah, I don't mind. Sometimes Uncle Eli needs help around the place. He ain't strong like he used to be." Ida Mae appeared agreeable to my dropping by, so I let her know she was partly the reason I'd come. "Besides, I kinda had stopping to see you on my mind. I wouldn't have brought along them flowers otherwise."

Ida Mae lifted the bouquet again to her nose. The silence hung long between us, so I thought to say, "Ida Mae, are you's thinking of staying in Rhea County…maybe for good?"

"I'm thinkin' on it. I came to visit my aunt and uncle because Ma and me wasn't getting along."

"Why not?" I asked, and then figured I'd stuck my nose where it didn't belong. But the words was already out.

Ida Mae whispered she didn't want to talk about it. Everthing on her face drooped and she lowered her gaze. Then she said, "If I stay, I's got to find work. I can't keep sponging off my kin."

"Would you like to work at the Rhea Springs Hotel?" I said without thinking. "My pa could put in a good word with his boss man. They's always needing maids, 'specially in the summertime."

Ida Mae turned to me like I was offering her a new store-bought dress. "That sounds a heap better than picking strawberries in the fields," she said. "There ain't nothing for me up here on Walden. I'd have to travel to town anyhow, even to take work as a picker on one of the farms farther out. Do you think your pa really could help?"

"I don't know why not. He and Ma has worked for the Wasson family for ages. The elder Doctor Wasson owns the hotel. I'll talk to Pa when I go home, if you want me to."

"Yes, I'd be mighty appreciative." The sparkle was back in her eyes, and she lifted the bouquet to her nose and gave me a smile that I'd surely dream about.

When I headed off Walden Ridge, the night closed in before I was a mile down the road. But I whistled the whole way in the dark thinking on how Pa could help out Ida Mae…and help me win her hand. I determined I was gonna be seeing a lot more of that gal.

CHAPTER 15

BLANCHE

As June drew to a close, Papa's workdays wore long as hotel workers labored to prepare for the most festive celebration of the summer—the Fourth of July. The anticipation of sharing the day with Will Day kept me awake at night. I imagined our gathering with the throngs of picnicking revelers on the hotel lawn, unfolding our blanket and spreading a feast Bertie would prepare for us. Political speeches and patriotic music played by the Spring City Band would carry on nonstop. The gazebo was already dressed in red-white-and-blue bunting for the occasion. There'd be sack races and pie-eating contests. An afternoon ball game behind the hotel would surely draw Will to take a turn at bat. At nightfall fireworks would light up the sky with colorful explosions—giving me excuse to clutch Will's arm in awe. I had been counting the days, crossing them off the calendar hanging on our kitchen wall.

***

Papa was never idle, especially on those days leading to July fourth, so I was a bit surprised to find him quietly talking with Bertie at the kitchen sink when I came down in search of breakfast. Handing me a glass of milk and pouring one for himself, he motioned me to the table. When we sat, he broke the news that Will had left on an early train going north.

"Blanche, I knew you'd be upset, so I wanted to tell you myself. Will came by the hotel last night while I was still there helping your grandfather. He told me he'd received a telegram from his father—no family crisis, you'll be relieved to hear—but it had something to do with business dealings that required his presence as well as his father's. He wanted to tell you personally, but it was intolerably late. He left this morning at dawn."

A thousand questions circled my head, but Papa had few answers. I was downcast. My first weeks home from school had been glorious, like none I'd experienced, but now I was filled with doubt. Was Will's reason for leaving just an excuse? Papa said Will didn't say when he'd return—had seemed somewhat vague about that. Did I disillusion Will in some way, to alter his esteem for me?

The days that followed were boring, nights eternal. I walked daily the dusty mile and a half to Papa's general store where the town's mail was delivered. No letter from Will. No telegram received at the train station either. When the fourth of July arrived, it felt like an insult. I spent the day in my bedroom and from my window saw and heard it all. Just as I had imagined, the hotel lawn was overflowing with gaily-dressed revelers, all wearing something red, white or blue. Children waved small American flags as they ran about, playing like frisky puppies. When darkness fell, the crowd whooped and clapped with every explosion and spiral of color shooting into the inky darkness while the band played patriotic tunes. The happy spectacle served only to anger me and afterward I did nothing but toss and turn all night.

Two more weeks. Silence. No amount of Papa or Gay's consoling helped. Even Owen's offer of excuses for Will's absence fell on deaf ears. I was thinking more often of Mama—wanting to talk to her, needing her advice.

It was a Saturday afternoon and I had settled myself on the loveseat in the library and opened the time-worn photo album that preserved Mama's memory and prevented her permanent escape. The house was quiet. All were busy elsewhere on the dreary, rainy afternoon that only encouraged my sour mood.

Leafing through the pages of photographs, examining every detail, my family came alive across the years: Mama and Papa in their wedding photos, handsome and not much older than me; later, each of us children as babies in white lace christening gowns; pictures of

Mama and Papa with my proud grandfather in front of his newly purchased hotel; Aunt Adah Pearl at her wedding not too many years ago. I touched each tenderly, finding solace in the musty memories held on its pages. Mama would never grow wrinkled with age nor her chestnut hair turn grey.

Staring at her face on the photograph, I felt a hand on my shoulder. I jumped and heard myself gasp as I turned. "Huh?!" A man stood over me. It was Will. "You scared the devil out of me," I exclaimed, feeling an involuntary smile emerge.

"Then maybe that's a good thing?" Will teased, offering cautious optimism.

My racing heart slowed, and when my mind caught up with what had just occurred, my smile vanished. I jerked away from Will's touch and turned to face him squarely. "What do you want?"

Stepping around the loveseat, Will took a seat next to me. I glared at him. He wasn't going to escape my displeasure, my hurt. In rapid fire, I demanded, "What happened to you? Where have you been? No proper goodbye, no real explanation?" Will tried to speak, but I didn't give him the chance as my questions peppered him. "You told Papa you would write, but you didn't. No letter—no telegram. How hard is a two-line telegram?" I fought back tears that I determined not to give him the satisfaction of seeing.

Will said nothing. He had not tried to interrupt my tirade. I slammed the album shut and it fell to the floor as I rose to leave. Will caught my hand.

"Blanche, please," he solicited quietly. "Let me explain."

I didn't want to comply; but, yes, I did.

"Just sit a minute," he said. "Please?"

Demonstrating my obstinacy with a feeble effort, I pulled my hand loose, but plopped down on the seat. Crossing my arms, I stared at the floor.

"Blanche, I'm not making excuses, honestly. When I arrived in Lexington, Father and Uncle Winston met me at the train station, and we were off by horseback to one of our lumber mills in the wilds of the Appalachian Mountains. Father had been negotiating to sell it and that required the presence and signatures of all owners, and I am one. He feared the agreement might fall through and he wanted to get there pronto in order to address any lingering issues. It was a full week before we returned to civilization."

"I don't suppose that Winchester—or Lexington—is without telegraph services," I sniped.

"Well, no," Will stammered, "but there was so much I had to attend to that I just didn't…"

"What?" I shot back. "You had so much to attend to? You couldn't get into town from the farm to send me word—any word? This is getting better by the minute," I said, as I stood again.

Will pulled me back. "I know—I know it sounds bad. But…"

"But what?" I asked, noting that my own voice was calming. Maybe I didn't care, I thought. Maybe this man wasn't who I thought he was after all. Maybe I'd be better off…

"Blanche, you're right. I should have made the time, but I was…. Well, just hear me out…please." Pausing, Will muttered to himself, "This isn't what I envisioned."

He turned to face me squarely and took both my hands. His face was ashen. Mine was flushed, I knew.

Will began, "Remember back in June when you and I met at the hotel dance?"

"Of course I remember," I answered flatly.

"Well, it wasn't the first time I'd met you. Not really. When I arrived in Rhea Springs—weeks prior to your homecoming—your papa and grandfather were the first businessmen on my list to see. When I met them, I liked them both immediately. And one of the reasons, in addition to their business savvy, was their obvious pride of family. I had supper at your home my first week here and had the best time bantering with your family around the table. Afterward, your papa, grandfather and I spent time right here in this room, talking business. But I also met you, in a way. After your father related the terrible tragedy you all experienced a few years back, he pulled out that very album," Will nodded toward the one at my feet, "and showed me pictures of you, the absent daughter that he was so proud of. He spoke of your love of horses and desire to show them like your mama, your interest in literature far beyond your years— mythology and Shakespeare. He bragged on your school reports with all those high marks. And then there were your school photographs… When I left that evening, my thoughts were not of business discussions but of you, Blanche, as silly as that may sound."

I said nothing, but felt my tense muscles relaxing.

"At that first dance in June," Will continued, "when you walked into that hall... All I can say is that love came with you, and took my heart away."

Tears welled in Will's eyes. Speechless, I waited.

After a long sigh, he said, "When that evening came to an end, I knew—even then, that soon. The time we've spent together over these past weeks has only confirmed it. When I talked with your papa the night before I left, I told him the business reasons for my travel, but I also told him of my feelings for you and my intentions. Blanche, I swore him to secrecy, but talking with him first was the proper thing to do, don't you agree?" Before I could answer, he went on. "And while I was with Father and Uncle Winston, I talked over my plans with them—and then with Mother later. I spent every moment of my time in Kentucky discussing my future—personal and business—and it all revolved around you. Every moment included you in some way, but there was so much to accomplish before I could get back here—to you—to ask you.... Blanche, will you marry me?"

Will's words echoed in my head.

He had entered my life like a whirlwind less than two months before, and I was flattered—no, enthralled—by the pursuit of this most handsome of men. And he was smart, and appeared to think I was too. Later, the excitement of that complicated emotion called love sent me soaring. Having never known its bliss, my world spun under its power. Yet, a whispered uncertainty tugged within. Was it real? Would it last? Then he was gone. Abandoned and lonely, I fell to depths I hadn't known since Mama's death. Now, with Will's four spoken words, those questions and my hurt were borne away. This man pledged his love. But where would it take me? Was I willing to find out?

I looked silently into his eyes and for a fraction of a second wondered what Mama would say. Then I heard myself speak. "Yes, Will. I will marry you. Yes, yes, yes." Tears trickled down my cheeks, but my smile and then Will's filled us both with unspeakable joy.

***

Our engagement was soon announced in the Rhea Springs Gazette. The news circulated even faster on the invisible small town wire service that Grandfather coined "over-the-back-fence news." Everywhere Will and I went—church, community gatherings, even my visits to the local millinery shop or Will's to the barber shop—brought enthusiastic well wishes, sometimes from people we didn't know. Considering myself a private person, the unexpected notoriety was off-putting, but Will took it all in stride, even saying it would be good for his new business. He said it was the best publicity one could ask for, joining ranks with one of the town's most prominent families, but I was left flat by his comment.

An afternoon wedding on October 12 was set. Will's family would train from Kentucky, as well as Mama's folks. Aunt Marian and Uncle Bill, along with my cousins, would make the trip from Chattanooga. October, off-season for the hotel, would afford ample lodging for out-of-town guests. A home wedding was my choice. I could not imagine it any other way. If Mama could not be there, I would at least be surrounded by her essence in the home she had made for me. Aunt Marian offered to sew my wedding dress and the white silk was promptly ordered from one of Chattanooga's finest fabric shops. Meanwhile Gay and I spent countless hours pouring over details. Grandfather Wasson would host an ante-nuptial wedding breakfast for the wedding party at his home on our wedding day before the afternoon ceremony. Papa insisted that the hotel dining room be reserved for a rehearsal dinner for wedding guests the night before. And, of course, our house would be transformed into a wedding sanctuary. My head swirled with what needed to be accomplished and I was so grateful for my sister's support. Bertie pitched in, offering to take charge of the breakfast cooking at Grandfather's place. Said she'd enlist Aunt America Caline to help since she'd spent time cooking in Grandfather's kitchen over the years and knew her way around the place.

***

Sundays with Will brought a breath of relief from the stress of wedding preparations. Late afternoons were perfect, as hotel guests drifted back to their rooms to dress for the evening meal and we had the deserted lake to ourselves. Only resident ducks remained as chaperones. On a mid-August Sunday afternoon, we relaxed in a canoe letting it drift on the water that mirrored pillowed clouds and hovering trees at its shallows. The retreating sun flung long shadows, and doves were roosting in the lush surroundings, cooing for others to join. Will's and my eyes met.

"I have to pinch myself," I declared, breaking the blissful silence and playfully pinching my arm. "Do you realize that in two months, I will be Mrs. William Blair Day, wife of the new mercantile store owner? And after the honeymoon, we'll return to our very own home, not even a mile from this spot. It's perfect."

"And we'll coo like these doves every evening as we rock away on our front porch," Will said with a wink, but his voice trailed like his mind had carried him some place else.

Maybe what I embraced as bliss, he greeted with some angst— this new life with its new responsibilities. Expanding the Day family business to Tennessee in buying out Papa's mercantile store and doubling its inventory was a calculated risk. Will knew its success was solely his to make. He'd also bought a perfect little white-framed cottage for us, and I was certain that had drained his savings. Then there was caring for a wife.

To quiet my musings, I took in the bouquet of honeysuckle and jasmine that blanketed the nearby bushes and relished the peace that surrounded us. This was our birch-bark canoe's maiden voyage, and I wouldn't diminish Will's enthusiasm. He had shipped the surprise by train from Lexington. Hand crafted and lightweight, it was a sleek vessel. Sensing his pride, I didn't comment how different it felt from Papa's rowboats—much harder to balance. I sat cautiously as he periodically corrected the canoe's drift.

When the sun had disappeared completely below the horizon, Will said, "Why don't you take us back?" and he offered me the paddle.

The canoe had glided beneath the branches of a maple leaning out from the shoreline. Just as he spoke, I caught sight of something falling—maybe a gnarled dead branch—from its leafy boughs. It struck the canoe with a thud behind where Will was sitting. In an instant, I saw it was no long, twisted stick but rather a writhing water snake.

My panic sent the canoe into mad gyrations and Will reacted. Amid my screams and our wild swinging arms to keep us balanced, the canoe flipped. I surfaced first. The snake was nowhere to be seen but neither was Will. I plunged under—reaching, groping—finding nothing with my searching fingers but water. Terror choked me, but I couldn't give in. My hand grazed a shoulder and my fingers grasped a hunk of shirt. I pulled desperately to reach the water's surface. Will's limp body was buoyed little by the water, and I struggled to keep his head up. My long skirt made staying afloat even more difficult. I shouted for help, twisting in the water to scan the shoreline. Even in my panic, I knew I couldn't keep him afloat long. The sudden roiling of the water nearby went unnoticed until two arms and then a dark brown head surfaced, grabbing Will's body away from me. It was Charlie.

"You all right, Blanche? Can you make it?"

"Yes. Help Will," I gasped, and we swam toward land.

When Charlie pulled Will's limp body onto the shore, I saw blood oozing from a gash on his head. Laying him out flat, Charlie straddled his body and began pumping his chest. In what seemed an eternity but was only seconds, water trickled from his mouth and then Will erupted in coughing, and I burst into tears.

"What happened?" Will moaned as he struggled to sit up, holding his head as the goose egg rose beneath the wound.

I sank to the ground and hugged the drenched man. "Oh, Will, I'm so, so sorry. A snake fell out of the branches onto the canoe— right behind you—and I almost jumped out of my skin. I turned us over. You hit your head on the canoe or a flying paddle."

Still bewildered, Will looked up at Charlie, "Who are you?"

"I'm Charlie. You know me, Mister Day." Charlie glanced at me. "You took a bad hit out there, and I heard Miss Blanche shoutin'."

"Charlie saved us, Will," Blanche interrupted. "I don't think I would have made it to shore if he hadn't come along."

"Yessir," Charlie explained. "I was heading over to tie up the rowboats for the night when I saw ya'll out in the water and that there canoe upside down."

"Where is it?" Will asked, as his eyes turned to the lake and he frantically scanned the water's surface. "The canoe—where is it?" He attempted to stand. Charlie and I each took an arm to help him find his footing. Immediately, Will jerked loose from Charlie's grasp. "I'm all right. Get your hands off me. I don't need your help." Charlie let go and stepped back, bewildered.

"Will, everything will be all right," I said trying to calm him as I offered Charlie a silent apology. "Charlie will get the canoe for us, won't you Charlie?"

"Why, yessum. I'll ask Pa to help me. First thing tomorrow morning we'll get her back to dry land. The lake ain't deep so we'll find her easy. Don't worry, Mister Day. We'll clean her up—she'll look as good as new."

Will again surveyed the lake. Seeing nothing, he muttered to me, "Let's get out of here." He leaned on me and I staggered under his weight as we made our way toward the hotel. I glanced back at Charlie over my shoulder and mouthed, "Thank you. I'm sorry." Charlie smiled weakly, looking perplexed.

Grandfather sutured Will's scalp. Six stitches closed the wound, but an invisible one seemed to fester. Out of sorts and moody, Will made sarcastic remarks about Charlie's heroic efforts whenever I recapped the accident to neighbors who jokingly asked if I had bopped Will. Whenever I questioned his attitude in private, it met with angry denials and usually resulted in a squabble and my hurt feelings. I talked to Grandfather about it, thinking the blow to Will's head had possibly done some mental damage, but he laughed and told me not to worry. Grandfather divulged that while he was stitching Will's head he had learned Will couldn't swim a lick, could hardly stay afloat, and was horrified to ponder the consequences if I had been the one knocked unconscious. But I still could not understand Will's resentment of Charlie. I decided it best to let the subject drop. Maybe understanding the minds of men—or at least Will's—was something that would require time.

CHAPTER 16

CHARLIE

I'd talked to Pa about finding Ida Mae work at the hotel, and he promised to talk to the elder Wasson when he saw the time was right. He'd never asked that big a favor before. In the meantime, Ida Mae grew more purty with each passing Sunday, and I counted the days on my fingers from one Lord's Day to the next. Visits to Walden Ridge didn't stop neither. Mister Hickey had grown used to my knocking on his door on Sunday evenings. Even smiled at me now and again. I think he kinda' took to the idea of a young man with a book under his arm, helping his niece learn her letters rather than filling her head with romantic nonsense. But I was accomplishing both. While Ida Mae and me sat out on his porch with our chairs pulled close and a book between us, the smell of her hair and skin and seeing the light dance in her eyes as I read gave me chill bumps and was the stuff of my dreams. When I told Miss Blanche about my reading to Ida Mae, she was kind to loan me several books that had been favorites of mine years back. I knew I was making headway with that beautiful gal in more ways than one. But a month later, everthing changed.

A Sunday basket supper was planned after services on the church grounds. As usual, Pa had asked permission on behalf of the congregation and Mister Wasson took it to the white church deacon board for a vote. It was allowed—with little dissent—and Mister Wasson told Pa not to worry.

The picnic would be the perfect time to corral Ida Mae with good news, and I would deliver it in a way she'd never forget. Having courted her awhile now, I was ready to make my intentions clear. With my news, I would be a shoe-in for Ida Mae turning her sole attention to me and turning out to pasture that Elijah Jenkins and those other fellers who still had ideas.

***

"Howdy Mister Hickey, Missus Hickey," I said, tipping my straw hat as the wagon pulled up to the church house that Sunday. I smiled up at Ida Mae and her eyes returned her good feelings. Offering my hand, I helped both ladies down, and like usual Ida Mae and me strolled inside with the mister and missus following.

We took our seat and waited while the others filed in. When Elijah Jenkins ambled down the aisle, Ida Mae turned her head away so as not to speak. I let out a little laugh, but Ida Mae didn't hear. Yep, Elijah Jenkins was gonna be history I figured, smiling to myself.

Coming out of the building two hours later, everyone scurried to their wagons to fetch their food baskets. Tables from the church were moved outside to form a long row under the nearby shade trees. Ida Mae and the other women busied themselves laying out the feast for the hungry crowd.

Spotting Pa passing the time with Mister Waterhouse, I ambled over. Surprised to see Pa's fiddle under his arm, I asked, "You brought Willie along. You gonna play?"

"Thought I would later," Pa said. "Tried to get Waterhouse here to join with his harmonica, but looks like I'll be playing solo."

"Wouldn't want to outshine you, Sam," Waterhouse joked, keeping a straight face.

"I didn't know you played, Mister Waterhouse," I said.

"You think shoeing horses is all I's good for?" he said, grinning.

I stumbled to apologize. All that was going through my head right then was what I was gonna say to Ida Mae. Not even the smell of fried chicken or sight of cakes and pies tempted. Shortly, a prayer was offered up so all hundred or so folks could hear. With the 'amen', everybody crowded in like flies to molasses. Laughter and talk filled the air, and Pa's fiddle music lifted it higher.

Ma and Ruby had gathered with Aunt America and Uncle Eli but I stood back from the crowd, watching Ida Mae talk and laugh with those near her in line. She was even purtier than the first time I saw her. Spotting her aunt and uncle on a blanket spread under one of the trees, she carried her full plate in their direction. I waited. Minutes later, Elijah Jenkins moseyed up alongside them. Too far away to hear their talk, I could see Ida Mae looking up at him, being polite as he talked with the three. Then she laughed and covered her mouth. Even Mister and Missus Hickey was chuckling like Jenkins was the afternoon entertainment.

A fire lit in me as I watched. Directly, Jenkins walked away, but not before giving Ida Mae a wink. And that's when I started pacing. I couldn't walk over there now, I thought, not with what was stirring inside me. My mouth would sure say something I'd regret. So to cool down, I walked around speaking to others, saying how good the vittles was. And I hadn't had a bite.

Finally, Ida Mae got up from her blanket and headed toward the food tables with her empty plate in hand. I made my move.

"Hey, Ida Mae," I said, joining her.

"Hello, Charlie. I wondered what happened to you. Didn't see you in line."

"Oh, I was talking with Pa." I couldn't wait another minute, so I reached for her free hand and said, "Ida Mae, can I talk with you...a few minutes...alone?"

When she tilted her head in question, I explained, "I have some good news, and I'd like to tell you without everbody listening."

With her hand in mine, I led her to the side of the church house where the horses and wagons was tied. Not the most romantic spot, but nobody would eavesdrop there. We wound our way between wagons and stopped when we was out of sight. Holding Ida Mae's hand, I turned to face her. With a questioning gaze, she waited. In the silence, I could hear Pa's fiddle playing and remembered his encouraging words. With sweaty hands and excitement in my throat, I managed to draw out the words with suspense. "I have good news for you. Like I promised awhile back, I asked Pa about finding you work at the Rhea Springs Hotel. He talked to the owners when he thought the time was right for the asking." Something like hope spread over her face and lifted her eyebrows in anticipation, but I let her wait a few seconds. Then I finished. "There's a job for you—as a room maid—if you want it. Pays seventy-five cents a day. You'd work six, maybe seven days a week."

When the words sunk in, Ida Mae jumped up and down like a happy pup. "Really, Charlie, really?"

"Yes, ma'am." My chest swelled with pride. "You can start next week if you want."

She dropped her empty tin plate, took me by both shoulders and kissed me square on the mouth. Then she blurted, "Thank you, Charlie. Thank you so much. This is somethin'. I can make my own money and buy my own things."

Don't know what got into me, but before I could think the better of it, I wrapped my arms around her and kissed her lips hard. They was warm, and so was her body against mine. I never wanted to let go. When I finally did and looked into her green eyes, I saw what I was feeling, all the way down to my toes.

But then something changed and I was looking into the eyes of a spooked rabbit.

Ida Mae said, "What all does a hotel maid do?"

Relieved, I said, "I don't know, but you'll do a fine job. Changing bed sheets and tidying up the rooms, I guess. Maybe washing—sheets and towels. Pa said that only honest women were hired for that job and he told Mister Wasson you was as honest as the day is long."

"But don't high-faluttin white folks stay there? I wouldn't know what to say or how to act." The more she talked, the more her face wrinkled and her eyes clouded with worry.

"Nobody's in the room when you clean, Ida Mae. They've gone for the day or checked out. Besides, you're finer—and purtier—than any white woman I ever saw stroll into that hotel. You hold your head high. They have nothing on you." I tried my darnedest, but Ida Mae dropped her head and shifted her weight. Her excitement had vanished.

Then she said slow and serious, "I'll talk to Uncle Amos and Aunt Geraldine. Uncle would have to bring me off Walden ever morning. That could be a problem."

"Well, if it is, you know I'd ride up to the Ridge everday and fetch you myself. Don't let that stand in your way."

It all started out like I planned. But now? Maybe Ida Mae just needed encouragement and a little time. Moving closer to her, I brought my finger under her chin and lifted it so her eyes met mine, and we lingered.

***

The next Sunday couldn't come fast enough. I wanted in the worst way to hear what Ida Mae had decided. I'd kept a keen eye out the stable doors toward the hotel all week long. But no Ida Mae. Maybe she needed time to convince her aunt and uncle.

When the Hickey wagon rolled into sight, my belly squeezed into a knot. Amos Hickey was driving the wagon and the missus sat next to him, like usual, but no Ida Mae. When Mister Hickey brought the horses to a stop, I hurried over.

"Good afternoon," I said, offering my help like usual. The missus stared at me and looked to her husband to do the talking.

"Afternoon to you, Mister Reynolds," Mister Hickey said, taking off his hat and scratching his head like he was uneasy. That was the first time he'd ever called me by my proper name.

I couldn't wait. "Mister Hickey, where's Ida Mae? Is she ailing?"

When he answered, the words echoed like they was sounding from the other end of a long, hollowed-out log. Ida Mae had left Walden Ridge. She had gone back to Alabama.

According to Mister Hickey, a letter had come in the post from Ida Mae's ma saying how much she missed her only daughter and wanted to set things right between them. Wrote she'd married a good man of late, and life was not nearly as hard. She promised home would be better if she returned.

"Her ma came for her?" I asked, my head busting with questions.

"No. She wrote that her and her husband would meet Ida Mae halfway, in Chattanooga…yesterday."

"Yesterday?" I gasped. "How'd she get to Chattanooga? That's seventy miles from here. You took her?"

If I had been thinking straight, I'd have knowed he didn't. They wouldn't be at church today. It's a long, hard wagon ride to Chattanooga and back.

Mister Hickey set a steady gaze on me and said without blinking, "Elijah Jenkins took her."

"Jenkins?" I asked, wondering all the while whether I heard right what the man said. He didn't answer. I wanted to jump up on that wagon and shake him. How could he have done that—let her ride off with that Jenkins feller.

"He volunteered," Mister Hickey finally said, staring back at me, "and I wasn't up to no long trip to Chattanooga." What he said next was the knife to my gut, that it was all "for the best."

I stood there dumb, looking up at the man. Guess he was feeling some guilt, because he slowly stroked his black beard and said Jenkins was at their house when he'd come from town with the letter for Ida Mae. Jenkins had offered on the spot to take her.

The life drained out of me. I turned my eyes to the ground and walked back to my mule. Mister Hickey called after me that Ida Mae had promised she would write. I rode home, tied up the mule, and walked down to Piney Creek to my fishing spot. Never had my world caved in like this. By the time the sun disappeared behind the hills, Ma and Pa had also heard the news.

CHAPTER 17

BLANCHE

October arrived, painting the Rhea County countryside in the warm, colorful hues of change. Everyone who saw me—at church or in the community—spoke of the beauty of the season as a perfect backdrop for my soon-to-be wedding. With every expression of congratulations and as the day edged closer, the butterflies that flitted about my heart only increased in number.

The Day family had just arrived from Kentucky and settled into their accommodations at the hotel. Mama's folks had arrived two days earlier. This night the families would share their first meal together. Papa, Gay and Owen had left for the hotel moments earlier, leaving me a snatch of time to relish the solitude, a rarity of late.

I slowly descended the stairs to follow after, and then paused in a wave of nostalgia. A whippoorwill's serenade floated through open windows and the curtains fluttered in the evening air as if conducting the bird's concert. Lulled by the familiar ticking of the grandfather clock, I closed my eyes. How would it feel to wake each morning and not be here, to miss breakfast cooking in the kitchen while Bertie hummed her gospel hymns? Instead, I would be preparing the morning meal for my husband and myself. With an anxious stir in my stomach, I opened my eyes to peer into Papa's library below. I would miss Sunday afternoons with him there, discussing his well-read classics or, of late, listening to music on his gramophone. But I reminded myself that my own home would soon be filled with books that Will and I cherished, and maybe orchestral music would warm it as well.

Papa's library, in advance of the wedding, had been transformed into a gift display. Every surface was covered: linens monogrammed handsomely with the blue initials W-D-B from my new relatives in Kentucky; a pink glass decanter and cordial glasses with tray sent by Aunt Marian and Uncle Bill; and from Uncle Jack and Aunt Cinny, "practical gifts" they called them—my first black iron skillet, muffin tins, rolling pin, and assorted pots. And there was the small mahogany chest that held the sterling silverware. Papa and Grandfather had ordered twelve settings from Philadelphia in the most exquisite pattern imaginable and the initial "D" had been inscribed on the handle of each. Will and I had gushed with surprise when we opened the gift while Papa and Grandfather looked on, beaming with pride. They later confessed that Aunt Marian had been the guiding hand in scouring catalogs for the perfect selection. Atop the piano in the corner of the room stood multiple pairs of brass candlesticks from well-wishing neighbors and hand-embroidered pillowcases stacked ten deep on the piano bench. Everywhere my eyes traveled were expressions of friendship from family and friends around Rhea Springs. On the floor lay one of the most meaningful— in hues of royal blue, maroon, gold, my favorite colors—a woven rug large enough to warm Will's and my new parlor floor and welcome guests in the grandest style. Mrs. Peters and Cynthia and Nancy reported they put all orders aside when they learned of my betrothal and dedicated their labors to the gift that was delivered yesterday. It would remind me always of my happy visits to the Peters' front porch.

I forced my thoughts back to the task at hand, to make the right impression on my future in-laws waiting across the way. Some would be easier than others. From the moment I met Will's people at the train station, I had felt warmly received by Mr. Day, a man obviously impressed with the bride his son had selected. Instead of a polite bow, his father had embraced me with a hug as warm as Papa's. It surprised me, actually. And Will's jovial Uncle Winston had been equally accepting. But with Mrs. Day, that reception was not to be. A small woman like Mama, but not a beauty, with a small hard chin and cheekbones one couldn't ignore, she was merely polite as she extended her ivory-gloved hand in greeting. In every encounter since, her piercing green eyes followed my every move. Was this young lady good enough for her only son? It seemed she had not decided, but I determined to win her favor with my charm and decorum.

Taking a deep breath, I gathered my courage for the evening ahead. Smoothing my skirt and rechecking the upsweep of my hair, I hurried out the front door.

When I entered the familiar hotel dining room, heads turned in my direction from the long elegantly set table at the far end. Thankfully, few other hotel guests were present.

Papa rose from the head of the table. With a welcoming hug, he gushed with every word of his formal introduction. "Here she is, the beautiful bride, Miss Blanche Louella Wasson."

I blushed when all clapped as if a princess had been announced. "Oh, Papa, please," I begged as a giggle escaped. "I'm sorry to be a little late, everyone."

The table, draped in white linen, was adorned by a vase of burgundy and gold mums and set with gold-rimmed white china. I searched out my place next to Will but saw he was seated next to his mother. His Uncle Winston, a handsome middle-aged man that bore a slight resemblance to Will, was seated at his other hand. The chair reserved for me was across the table from Will, with my brother and sister on either side. And Mama's folks were relegated to the far end.

"Who determined these seating arrangements?" I thought to myself—one family staring across the table at the other family, with the bride and groom sitting opposite one another? Mama would never have allowed this.

Will rose and hurried around to pull out my chair. I smiled weakly at him with questioning eyes, but he didn't seem to notice my misgivings. Neither did Papa.

Within minutes, wine glasses were filled and Papa rose to propose a celebratory toast. Crystal goblets were raised and well wishes were voiced in unison. I could not help but notice, however, Mrs. Day's more intense gaze from across the table. I inhaled and waited—for what, I wasn't certain.

"Blanche, you look especially lovely this evening," Mrs. Day began as we waited to be served. "You don't appear a nervous bride. All is under control, I presume?"

"Yes, ma'am," I answered, not certain where to go with conversation. "My sister has been my heroine these last months. She's kept me on track. You must come to the house tomorrow and see the gift display. Will and I have received so many lovely presents."

"I'd be delighted. And I'll bring along our gift. Tomorrow morning after breakfast, about ten o'clock?"

"That would be fine," I said, now dreading the coming day.

When she dismissed me by turning full attention to her son next to her, I whispered into Gay's ear, "Was this seating arrangement your idea?"

"No. As soon as we arrived, I went into the kitchen to check on things and by the time I got to the table, Grandfather had already seated the Days. It was too late to make changes."

"Oh, well," I said, in resignation. "We'll just have to make the best of it."

The table was abuzz with paired conversations, and even Grandmother and Grandfather Gay appeared happily engaged. Will kept his mother's attention for much of the meal, for which I was grateful. His periodic gaze in my direction was accompanied by a wink when our eyes met. Over dessert, I informed Mrs. Day of my recent efforts to can summer produce in anticipation of winter meals I would prepare for Will, hoping to win some approval. But I didn't tell her that I had been a poor student, according to Bertie, my canning instructor, who had frowned in disappointment when a third of the batch of jars had not properly sealed. After what seemed a long evening, it finally came to a close and no one was more relieved than I.

***

Our wedding day was a whirlwind of activity with happy faces everywhere. A formal breakfast at nine o'clock was served at Grandfather's home for the wedding party and out-of-town relatives. Bertie and America, under my sister's guidance, had transformed the dreary widower's parlor into a bright, verdant garden setting with flowers and greenery everywhere. Unfortunately, my nerves prevented much appreciation of the artistically presented breakfast covering the table laden with etched crystal and bone china.

As the morning edged closer to the bewitching hour, I scurried home and closeted myself in my bedroom. Aunt Marian was present to help me into the wedding gown she had sewn. After she fastened the last silk-covered button at my back, I turned for inspection. She stepped back, her blue eyes trailing every seam of the classic white gown, checking for non-existent imperfections. Finally, her handsome face that so reminded me of Mama broke into an approving smile that filled her cheeks with color and her eyes with sparkle.

"Oh, little sister," exclaimed Gay, who had popped into the room to check on progress. "You are exquisite beyond words. Aunt Marian," she declared, "I've long since realized that my tomboy sister had turned into a fine young lady, but your magic has transformed her into a fairy princess!"

Aunt Marian's agreement required no response. We three beamed. My sister blew me a kiss so as not to risk mussing my appearance and disappeared out the door again, calling over her shoulder that she had to get downstairs to check on last minute preparations. With the time nearing, Will, Owen, Papa and Grandfather were already welcoming friends and relatives, many bearing gifts to be added to the library display.

The Spring City Gazette society section would later detail the events of that glistening fall day with a perfect nip of cooled air:

"Spring City Gazette, Saturday, 12 October 1911: Day—Wasson. A beautiful home wedding was that of Miss Blanche Louella Wasson and Mr. William Blair Day, of Winchester, Kentucky, celebrated at the residence of the bride's father, Chapman Wasson, Rhea Springs, on Saturday, October 12. At 10 o'clock an ante-nuptial wedding breakfast was served the bridal party at the home of Dr. J.C. Wasson, grandfather of the bride. The room was beautifully decorated in the color motif of lavender and white with superb lavender chrysanthemums, smilax and ferns. Each of the seven breakfast courses was also garnished in the same color scheme. The marriage ceremony performed by Reverend Tobin at 1 p.m. took place in the parlor of the Chapman Wasson residence, tastefully decorated in the nuptial colors, green and white. The Mendelssohn wedding march, played by Miss Gay Wasson, announced the bridal party. The bride and groom came in together, and Lange's "Flower Song" was played during the taking of the vows. The bride was handsome in an artistic gown of white silk and beautiful bridal veil fastened with a pearl and diamond brooch, gift of the groom. She carried a shower bouquet of roses and maple leafed branches in shades of fall. In an adjoining room many splendid presents were displayed, attesting to the popularity of the bride and groom. At two o'clock genuine southern hospitality was dispensed to all the wedding guests at the elegant Rhea Spring Hotel ballroom. An elaborate meal in many courses was faultlessly served. Mr. and Mrs. William Day left that same day for an extended wedding journey to Cuba."

***

By the time the sun had retreated to the far side of Walden Ridge, Will and I were at the Spring City station, surrounded by a stir of well-wishers. The L&N passenger train belched white clouds anticipating an imminent departure. Owen and Uncle Jack hurried to hoist our trunks from the wagon onto the station cart for loading, and the clutch of friends and family was loud and celebratory as we awaited the boarding call.

Will's parents pressed in, as did my family. Gay, the big sister she'd always been, adjusted the cape to my travel outfit, but the tear that slipped down her cheek wasn't lost on me when we embraced. Papa shook Will's hand, hesitated and then gave him a bear hug. Turning to me, Papa held me at arm's length, his immense pride visible on his face. His grin spoke volumes as did mine in return. When he encircled me with his arms, the silent tears were unstoppable. I felt a tap on my shoulder and turned, wiping my wet cheeks with the lace handkerchief Aunt Marian had given.

My father-in-law stood waiting. "Don't I get a hug as well, Mrs. Day? he asked.

"Well, of course, Mr. Day." I said, smiling through tears.

"We'll discuss later what you should call me, now that we're family. Over dinner on your and Will's first visit back home to Kentucky?" he asked with an affection that was disarming.

Nodding, I gave him the biggest hug I could manage. I loved him already.

Mrs. Day, who had been standing next to him, stepped closer. "Come here." She took my hand and pulled me near. With a fleeting hug, she said she was pleased her son had taken me as his wife and then whispered into my ear her confidence that I would take good care of him.

"Mrs. Day, I'll do my best. I love him very much."

"Yes, I can see that, dear."

Then came the shout of the conductor—"all aboard"—and I was saved from further conversation. Will took my hand and we mounted the train's steps, waving to everyone gathered before disappearing inside.

In my eighteen years, the world had stretched no farther than two hundred miles north to Kentucky or the occasional family excursion seventy miles south to Chattanooga. A honeymoon trip to Jacksonville, Florida and on to Cuba by ship was an excursion to the ends of the earth. But I was ready. Will had cautioned the trip would be arduous, changing trains at Chattanooga and then Mobile, Alabama before traveling across the Florida panhandle to Jacksonville. Since the War, the rebuilding of Southern rail lines had been a priority, he had said, but passenger service still lagged.

Two hours into our trip the train eased into the Chattanooga, Tennessee Depot, and we transferred to one with Pullman service. Led to our compartment by the steward, he opened the narrow door with a glass panel to our five- by eight-foot compartment. A sofa-berth ran its length and would convert into our bed. A sliver of a table was attached to the wall below the train window and on it a tiny vase held a single red rose. Our first night together would be confined to this tiny space, and it troubled me that others would occupy sleeping quarters nearby, separated only by paper-thin walls.

At nine o'clock our train departed the Chattanooga station. Exhausted by that hour, Will and I welcomed the privacy of our compartment. I suggested we prepare our bed and that Will should walk to the dining car for a nightcap while I change into my nightclothes. Will explained that a porter would prepare our sleeping berth, and he pulled the wall cord to request service. Within minutes a smartly dressed Negro man arrived. While he prepared the bed, Will and I found the dining car. My new husband ordered a chilled glass of buttermilk, his favorite beverage.

After ten minutes and feeling an onset of nerves, I pondered, "Do you think the room is ready by now?"

"Probably," he said, and took a long sip from his glass, winking at me over its rim.

"I'm going to walk back."

"Wait a minute, and I'll walk with you." Will took another drink.

"Take your time. I want to change out of these clothes. I can find my way," I said, feigning confidence. Will relented, but not without a sly grin.

When I reached our compartment, the porter was gone and the pressed white sheets and fluffy pillows were inviting. Inside, I closed the door and pulled the curtain over its window. Glancing at the small mirror on the wall, I noticed my face was flushed. And Will wasn't even here yet. Pulling my valise from the overhead rack, I opened it to lift out the white nightgown—another gift from dear Aunt Marian. Exquisite with its delicate lace trim, the sheer silk brought an even brighter hue to my cheeks when I held it to my body. Double-checking the door curtain, I quickly changed, feeling more nervous than I had all day.

Fifteen minutes later there was a knock, and Will's voice relieved my alarm. The door opened and he stepped inside, his eyes capturing my visage in the muted light. He appeared transfixed, his eyes moving from my face to my bosom and beyond. I stood self-conscious before him but gratified that I had moved him so. As his eyes returned to mine, he took my hand and gently pulled me to himself, softly kissing my lips as his hands slowly traveled the curves of my body as if seeking to commit every one to memory. After a moment, he released me and began to remove his clothing. I slipped into the tiny bed to await him and when he joined me, his gentleness guided our passion into the night.

CHAPTER 18

BLANCHE

Two endless days of smothering heat and incessant rumbling of the train rendered us both grumpy and in an unpleasant frame of mind. I whined more than talked. "Will, I know you warned me, but will we ever see Jacksonville?" I knew his answer.

"Eventually," he said, staring out the open window next to him. "I guess passenger service in the South isn't the government's highest priority these days. A train should run a more direct southern route, not down through Alabama and then east."

Will took the occasion to ramble on about wealthy men like Carnegie and Rockefeller, their interest in the South laudable, but that they should have come to the aid of railroads instead of throwing money after institutions like Tuskegee.

I bristled at Will's arrogant tone so I proceeded to defend men I knew nothing of. "Well, it's theirs to give as they wish. Papa has shown me newspaper articles about Mr. Carnegie and the institutions he supports—libraries for the public, education and such. And the Rockefeller name is familiar, but I can't place it."

"Oil. You've never heard your papa talking about the Standard Oil Company?

"No, I don't think so."

"His refineries are powering the engines of Northern industry," Will began, like he was instructing a civics class. "Wealthy, powerful men determined to help rebuild the South, a business opportunity not to be missed."

I didn't care to argue the merits of Tuskegee nor passenger rail service. Staring out the window as his voice droned on about the world of business, my thoughts drifted to the bath I would savor at our destination. In boredom, I eventually fell asleep, my head propped against Will's shoulder. By the time the train rolled into Jacksonville and we climbed into the waiting carriage for the final leg to the Weeping Willow Inn, all I craved was sleep in the comfort of a bed, wrapped in my husband's arms.

***

Optimism returned as the morning sun streamed through our room's open windows, the sheer white curtains fluttering in the breeze like the wings of butterflies. Taking in the fragrance of the salty air as I roused, I wasn't certain where I was. Rolling over, I whispered to Will, "Honey, are you awake?" I nudged him. "Do you hear that noise? What is it? There it goes again."

Will stirred and stretched his arms into the air before pulling me into an embrace, "That's the ocean's waves pounding the beach," he whispered. "They never stop."

"I can't wait to see."

By the time we dressed and found our way to the inn's wrap-around white veranda, a hearty breakfast awaited at the tiny wrought-iron table for two. At the ten o'clock hour, we had the place to ourselves. A cluster of nearby willow trees offered cooling shade, their long wispy branches swaying like the skirts of hula dancers in the air currents. Our only company was the chatter of gaily-colored native birds nestled in the trees, urging us to linger beyond a second cup of tea.

Later, we strolled hand in hand beyond the trees, across the near-deserted beachside road, and onto a landscape of rolling sand dunes that leveled out before reaching the water—water that stretched across the landscape, in every direction. The sight left me breathless—blends of blues and greens as the ocean swelled and then rushed toward the beach. The wind blew my skirt and toyed with the strands of loose hair that I tried in vain to recapture. The white sands stretched as far as the eye could see, seeming to restrain the forceful onslaught of waves. I had never encountered anything so awe-inspiring.

We stepped onto a weathered boardwalk that led over dunes that sprouted wheat-like sea grasses. Overhead, seagulls screeched as they flew along the shoreline in search of food. At the end of the walkway, we descended to the smooth flat sand where we removed our shoes and carried them as we strolled the shallows, lifting our faces to the sun's caress and filling our lungs with the sea air. Relentless waves pummeled the white crystal sands before frothing in surrender around our feet. In utter amazement at the scene, I said to Will, "Let's stay on here. The Weeping Willow is lovely and I don't think we could improve upon this, do you?"

Will smiled and we lingered, bathing our senses in it all. With a sudden wind shift, Will grabbed his Panama hat before it could blow into the swirling surf.

"I would never tire of this magic," I said.

Will turned from the ocean's drama and looked long into my eyes, one hand vainly redirecting the tresses of my hair. He lifted my hand to his lips and said, "It is magical here, but you're the magic." His gaze was penetrating and my cheeks flushed.

"You are my Romeo," I replied, and then thought how childish I sounded. My confidence would grow in time, I promised myself.

"Always," he replied, not noticing my embarrassment, and we walked on, arm-in-arm.

After three days of bewitching sunsets and endless strolls along the water's edge, we were restored and ready to sail for Havana.

***

The ship eased out of Jacksonville's harbor, its chimneys billowing white steam into the morning blue with air horns signaling the departure. As we headed for open waters, I stood at the railing, realizing the port would soon slip entirely from view and we'd be surrounded by nothing but water and sky. Will seemed to have no reservations. In his enthusiasm, he took my hand and pulled me after him saying we should explore our floating hotel. Maybe the distractions would chase away my fantasies of doom, so I complied.

Leaving the first level promenade deck, we climbed the stairs to a higher deck that wrapped the second level. With splendid views of the fading land and dark waters that stretched to the horizon, Will pointed out the sturdy white lifeboats strapped to the ship's side. Knowing his swimming deficits, I wondered if he was reassuring himself or me.

As we wandered, we came across a formal dining room. Peeking through the glass double doors, the large deserted room was filled with white cloth-covered tables, already topped with small vases of fresh-cut flowers, just like the Rhea Springs Hotel. An ebony baby-grand piano sat in front of a wall of full-length windows that gave dinner guests uninterrupted views of the ocean and a sky that in a few hours would be filled with twinkling stars. Surveying the scene, Will and I looked at each other and exclaimed in unison, "This is where we'll spend our time," and we both laughed.

After a thorough exploration of our new lodging, we returned to our cabin to fetch reading materials with the anticipation of lounging on the deck for the remainder of the day. When Will unlocked the cabin door, a tiny dim room stared back. It offered little—two straight chairs and a petite round table opposite a small bed for two. The only amenity that spared our labeling it a "wardrobe closet" was the round porthole window that allowed meager light but provided a view if a nose was pressed to the glass. Thankful that only one night would be spent there, we found our books, Will locked the door behind us and we headed to the deck chairs.

***

That evening we returned to the ship's dining room dressed in the evening attire we'd packed for the occasion.

"Yes, Mr. and Mrs. Day," said the maître d'. "Right this way. Your table is by the windows, just as you requested, Mr. Day."

Will politely seated me and then took his place. The table was set with fine white china, gold etched and bearing the ship's insignia. Sterling silver utensils lined up like soldiers on both sides of the plates that reflected our excitement. The waiter filled our crystal-stemmed flutes with white wine and we toasted our life together. A meal of five courses followed, served while a handsome fellow in a tuxedo caressed the keys of the nearby piano, filling the room with the music of romance. We lingered long into the evening, afterward strolling the promenade decks, putting off as long as possible our cramped quarters as we wished upon the stars crowding the night sky.

The next morning we awoke to the long and heavy heave of the ship's foghorn, signaling our approach to Havana Harbor. When we disembarked, the hotel's horse-drawn carriage awaited. Although it didn't resemble our surrey from back home nor was a grandfatherly gentleman with silver hair at the reins, pangs of homesickness stirred nevertheless.

After a short ride, we were delivered to the Hotel Inglaterra in the heart of the city. The open-air carriage slowed in front of the neo-classical, three-storied structure, and a rush of excitement dispelled all longing for home. The driver, wearing a broad-brimmed straw hat, hopped from his perch and offered his arm. Descending the carriage steps, I was mesmerized as I stared up. Juliet balconies of wrought iron lace framed each set of French doors across the stone four-storied building, no doubt offering views of Havana and the harbor. When Will and I entered the expansive hotel lobby, its majestic walls greeted us with floor-to-ceiling tile mosaic scenery— artistic floral designs behind the registration desk, others of Spanish noblemen and women in bright tropical settings on other walls. No doubt, the hotel was one of the jewels of Spanish domination before Cuba's fight for independence. The grand chandelier was animated by electric lights. Tall windows welcoming the tropical sun illuminated crowning transoms of stained-glass depictions of palm trees and pineapples. Guests lounged in plush velvet seating areas, enjoying quiet conversation. If this was the lobby, I couldn't imagine our honeymoon suite. After checking in, we stepped into a small iron cage that lifted us to our third floor destination. It was in itself a brief adventure, having never ridden on such a contraption.

"Room 310—that's us," Will said, as the bellhop unlocked the door. Will tipped the man who disappeared to retrieve our travel trunks from the lobby.

"Are you going to carry me across the threshold?" I kidded, knowing he'd done so at each lodging since leaving Tennessee.

Without a word, he whisked me into his arms and through the doorway, kissing me as well. When I was returned to my feet, we both stood staring into the room: a carved four-poster bed regally draped with crimson silk covers; a colorful, intricate tapestry rug at our feet; a loveseat with Spanish brocade toss pillows; round table and chairs positioned in front of French doors opened to the faux balcony, filling the room with sea air.

"Look out there, Will," I pointed. Beyond the tops of the city's buildings was the harbor we had just departed. Below and across the street from the hotel was a spacious manicured Parque. Couples strolled its winding walkways enjoying bubbling stone fountains and tropical floral gardens, as tall palm trees cast artistic shadows.

As I admired the view, Will stepped away. A minute later he called, "Blanche, come here. You're not going to believe this." His voice echoed from an open doorway. When I crossed the room, my mouth fell open as I looked inside. "My goodness, what is this?"

Will laughed and said, "What does it look like? It's just for us!"

The suite had its own bathroom, unlike the hotel back home with a communal one on each floor. I giggled with delight. A claw-footed porcelain tub and all the other necessities sat on a white marble floor, sparkling under electric lights. Will demonstrated that piped-in water, hot and cold, was as near as a turn of the knobs, and he laughed as he did so. The place was fit for royalty.

After our trunks were delivered to the room, we changed and set out to explore. The day was young. The Parque was as breathtaking at ground level as from three stories up. We'd never seen palm trees, except on a printed page. Their peculiar tops reminded me of the feather dusters Bertie used. Around the palms, plantings boasted large rainbow-colored leaves—as if splattered with paint—bright bird-shaped flowers, drawing the interest of bees and butterflies. Every turn brought into view bubbling fountains topped with mythical life-size statues, surrounded by more tropical plants. Conversations hung in the air as we strolled, but we couldn't eavesdrop, because they were languages of other lands. Some flowed like honey, others were staccato and guttural. We listened at every opportunity, like children overhearing gossip.

That evening we dined at the Garden Room, one of the hotel's two restaurants. Aptly named, we stepped into the space to find tall potted ferns scattered throughout the grand room, some towering fifteen feet or more. Gleaming white paneled walls were the canvas for a painted garden mural of more exotic plants and colorful parrots that rivaled anything seen in the Parque that afternoon.

"Isn't this beautiful, Will?" I was as excited as a child at Christmas. Will nodded and took my hand. Escorted by a young man in a white suit to our reserved table, we were seated and presented menus. Opening them, we stared at unrecognizable words, exchanged puzzled looks and laughed out loud. Since food from the ocean was nonexistent in Tennessee or Kentucky, we dared to select shrimp in some unpronounceable preparation and waited with delight for our meal from the sea.

"Your entrée, senor and senora," the waiter announced in broken English as he set the plates before us.

"Will, this looks delicious and smells divine," I said, savoring the steam rising from the plate.

Will answered by piercing a shrimp and bringing it to his mouth, the delicate sauce dripping as he did. With sounds of satisfaction, he urged, "Tasting is even better. Go ahead."

Will was right. We cleaned our plates, as Mama always instructed, and only after eating a number of shrimp tails did we decide they'd be better left for the kitchen help to throw to the feral cats residing in the Parque.

Sated and relaxed from the sumptuous meal, we later departed the room, only to be greeted by frenzied musical rhythms of guitars, trumpets and drums from down the hotel hallway. We trailed the sounds to a ballroom where our eyes were first drawn to two grand chandeliers showering their light through crystal beads to an ebony dance floor. It was encircled by small tables of enthusiastic spectators. The light itself danced on the black shiny surface right along with uninhibited couples that moved their bodies in unimaginable ways, yet simpatico with the rhythms that filled the room. With exchanged nods, we slipped inside to watch. The tango was a far cry from a Tennessee waltz, but it was a suitable conclusion to a magical first day in Cuba.

***

Rising the next morning, we readied for an outing to the Plaza de Armas, one of the busiest marketplaces in Havana. After breakfast, a hotel carriage carried us along the city's busy thoroughfares. Shoulder-to-shoulder buildings stood at attention to watch us pass, all looking amazingly similar—in the baroque and neoclassical styles of Spain whose centuries-old presence had dictated the city's architecture. With archways and columns adorning the many historical buildings, the repetitions were anything but boring.

As the carriage ferried us along, we passed the occasional man strumming a guitar on a street corner and spied along the way a small impromptu gathering of three instrumentalists who had drawn lingering passersby as they played in a small plaza. Music, as it turned out, was the oxygen Havana breathed, not only in hotel ballrooms, but also along its quaint streets that laced in all directions and in plaza squares throughout the city.

"Will," I said as we passed, "we're a million miles from Rhea Springs, aren't we?"

"Yes, we are."

When we reached the Plaza, my eyes swelled at the size of the stirring throng. "I've never seen so many people in one place, not even our County fairs back home." My heart pounded almost as loud as the cacophony that greeted us. We stepped from the carriage to be swallowed by the milling crowds on the cobblestone expanse that stretched in every direction.

I clutched Will's hand and we wound through the mass of people. Wooden carts lined the square like rows of crops. Their wares were shaded from the unforgiving sun by makeshift burlap tarps hanging above them. Vendors hawked their goods to all within earshot. Jewelry of sorts, hung like brown icicles from cart railings— necklaces of beans and seedpods, bracelets from coconut shells, trinkets I could not identify and none I wanted. Cages filled with squawking poultry were stacked high on rickety tables awaiting selection. After purchase, the chicken's head was chopped off and legs tied together presumably for the trip back to a boiling pot in someone's kitchen. Children darted barefoot in and out of the throng, themselves like chickens on the loose.

The entire scene resembled a roiling pot: women in skirts of bright hues and white blouses, carrying baskets of colorful produce, bound for supper tables; peasants clothed in hopsack, buying and selling; men dressed like cowboys, many wearing ammunition belts across their chests. Most donned wide-brimmed straw sombreros. Tourists were easy to spot because of their more subdued dress, and all were taking in the sights and smells.

"Will, look at this," I said pointing to carts stacked with fruits of every shape and in a rainbow of colors, begging to be handled and sampled. "Oranges, grapefruit, coconuts, bananas. And look, what are those?" I picked up a lopsided oval fruit with a thick, but smooth greenish-orange skin.

"I think they're mangos," Will answered.

"Besides apples and peaches we grow back home, that's all I see. Maybe oranges at Christmas, if we're lucky. How 'bout you?"

"No mangos in Kentucky," Will said, bringing it to his nose.

As we strolled, mysterious aromas wafted about and our mouths watered. Will pulled me in the direction of a smiling, snaggle-toothed woman who waved at us like we were long-lost cousins.

"Let's see what she has," Will said, looking at me like a mischievous boy.

Standing next to a steaming cauldron, the stooped woman had pulled something out of it that she extended in her sun-weathered hands.

"She wants us to try it, don't you think?" Will said.

"It smells interesting, but I don't know," I said, hesitating.

"Come on, Blanche," Will urged, as we inspected the offering. "We'll hurt her feelings if we don't give it a try."

Whatever it was, it was packaged in a dried cornhusk, and some kind of ground meat inside was wrapped in a sort of cornmeal dough. A giant steaming black pot behind her was piled high with them. The woman beckoned us in Spanish with great animation, her enthusiasm the only translation needed to win us over.

Will held up two fingers and pulled from his pocket a fist of pesos. She took the money and handed us our purchases, each wrapped in brown paper. When we peeled back the cornhusks, our nostrils filled with the spicy aroma—spices I knew Bertie had never used or heard of. With each bite, sauce dripped onto our hands and clothes, but our wide eyes declared it tasty, despite the mess. We learned later that we had enjoyed our first tamales.

By the time we departed the market square at noon, we had in our possession two beautifully designed clay ollas with tile inlays in the same hues as our new parlor rug. One for our home and the other for Papa, they served no utilitarian purpose, but ours would sit atop our fireplace mantel to remind us of our first worldly journey together.

***

After our morning at the market and the remainder of the day poking around the hotel's neighborhood, we retired early after dinner. However, in the wee hours, I awoke to groans. Fear seized me, and I reached for Will but felt only crumpled bed sheets. In the muted light cast from the street lamps outside our French doors, I saw moving shadows in the bathroom.

"Will, is that you?" I called out. All I heard in return were groans. Grabbing my robe from the end of the bed, I slipped it on and tiptoed in the direction of the sound. Peering around the door, I saw nothing at first, but then as my eyes searched further, a headless body appeared on its knees over the toilet. There was a heave. My fuzzy brain focused enough to realize it was Will. When he lifted his head from the toilet to answer, his pallor was that of a ghost.

"Oh, Will, what's wrong?"

"I didn't want to disturb you," he moaned. "I think the tamales are to blame." He wretched again as his head disappeared into the bowl.

We spent the rest of the night on the bathroom floor. Bracing for the same fate, I somehow mercifully escaped. The next day was a quiet one and we didn't venture far from our accommodations. Lounging in the hotel lobby, we played checkers on inlaid board tables of tile and strolled in the Parque after a lunch of chicken broth especially prepared by the hotel restaurant for Will's recovering constitution. When we returned to our room that afternoon, we reclined on our regal bed to delight in the panorama beyond the open French doors. Before the sun slipped away, we were drawn to new intimacies in the flowering of our marriage, and we drifted into sleep that carried us to the morning.

CHAPTER 19

CHARLIE

A week after the Wasson-Day wedding, Rhea Springs was easing back to normal, but Pa's work hadn't slowed a whit. Apart from his usual chores at the hotel, he'd spent plenty of time putting Doctor Wasson's parlor in order following that pre-wedding breakfast. Furniture was returned to the proper places and extra chairs carted to the hotel along with the purty wedding plants and flowers for guests to enjoy. The other Mister Wasson had complained all week he needed his reading room back and all those gifts out of his way. So this morning Pa had me helping out—loading presents from Chapman Wasson's house onto a wagon to take down the road to the newlyweds' place.

Ma was cleaning Mister Wasson's library and supervising our work when she caught me dallying—scanning the books that lined the shelves, stroking the spines, running my fingers over the gold lettering. In the years Miss Blanche had supplied me with books, she had shared more than a few. After she went off to school, that sharing stopped and then all I got was her papa's already-read newspapers. But Pa said I should be grateful, that those papers talked about happenings in the real world, not a make-believe one.

"You ain't here for reading, son," Ma said, shooing me from the bookcases with her feather duster. I gathered another load of boxed gifts and trailed Pa to the wagon.

According to Ma, Miss Gay was already at the Day house down the road, waiting to direct where she wanted these things placed, and most likely she'd be as particular at this task as she was overseeing that wedding. When we pulled up in the loaded wagon, she was standing in the doorway.

I lugged the rug inside and began unrolling it in the parlor when Miss Gay said, "Charlie, pull that farther back from the fireplace." Her hands were on her hips like a field overseer. "If it's too close, a winter fire will spit sparks on that work of art."

"Yessum," I said, moving it like she ordered.

Pa came through the door with two fancy carved chairs under his arms. "Where you want these, Miss Gay?"

"Close to the window...over there," she said pointing. "Those were Mama's and I know Blanche wants them in a prominent spot."

After several more trips, Pa announced the wagon was empty.

"Thank you both for your help," Miss Gay said, leaning against the wall like she'd been doing the hauling.

"You want to ride back to your place with us?" Pa asked, noticing she looked tuckered.

"No, I'll finish tidying up here. It'll be weeks before the honeymooners return, but I'm anxious to get this done. Besides, it's a crisp fall day, and the trees in full color will make for a pleasant stroll home."

Pa and me climbed on the wagon and headed toward the hotel when, out of the blue, he said, "Looks like I'm gonna be taking a road trip and will have some time myself to admire the fall color."

Before I could ask, he explained, "Mister Wasson is sending me down to Chattanooga to fetch some brass bed stands and chests-of-drawers for the hotel. I'll need two wagons according to the mister." Pa hesitated and then added, "I asked him if I could call on you to drive the second one and he said 'sure.' Would you like to come along...see a big city where there's more stores than you can count on your fingers?"

I had never been anywhere, never mind Chattanooga, unless you counted where I'd gone in my mind when reading them books.

"Why doesn't Mister Wasson have them sent by train?" I asked. "According to Mr. Hickey, the wagon trip takes a full day."

Just the thought of the Hickeys and Ida Mae's leaving stirred up my belly like I'd eaten too many green apples. I'd be headed down the same dirt road that took her away.

"I think Mr. Wasson was afeared the furniture would be damaged with the loading and unloading by them railroad workers," Pa said. "He'd rather hold me responsible for a safe delivery, and it probably costs less, too."

After a pause, I heard myself say, "Yeah, Pa, I think I'd like to trail along."

***

Two mornings later we lit out before the roosters stirred. By the time we had harnessed the teams and headed the two empty wagons onto Stage Coach Road, the chill had hatched goose bumps along my arms. Glad that Pa had told me to wear my long-sleeve Sunday shirt and hat, I felt dressed up and even excited. Pa looked handsome, wearing the second-hand suit jacket Mister Wasson had given him. Sleeves was a tad short 'cause he arms was longer than his boss man's, but it was hardly noticeable.

As we traveled the dirt road, Pa leading the way in one wagon and me behind in the other, the morning fog stretched like a blanket across the honey-gold fields, but the advancing sun was already showing off the trees decked out in leaves of orange and red.

Ten miles out, Pa broke the silence, calling back over his shoulder. "Charlie, I hear tell Chattanooga has trolley cars running down the middle of the streets."

"You don't say?" I called ahead. "How many folks in Chattanooga?"

"I asked Mister Wasson that. According to him, more than forty thousand. How 'bout that? Says he gets his information from the Chattanooga newspapers, so he knows."

"Hmm," I mumbled, thinking I'd read about the numbers of folks coming out for KKK rallies in Chattanooga. Those were the numbers that got my attention. But I wasn't gonna let thoughts like that spoil my day. Instead I pondered how fine it was to be out from under Mister Waterhouse. With the steady clop of horses' hooves and occasional call of a meadowlark, my thoughts drifted to Ida Mae and the letter she'd promised. The hours passed in peaceful silence and when the sun reached straight overhead, we headed the wagons off the road near two spreading oak trees to take a rest and open our lunch tins.

Sitting with our backs to one of the trees, I was saying to Pa we hadn't passed a single soul all morning when the distant sound of pounding hooves stopped me mid-sentence. Two riders came over a rise in the road raising a cloud of dust. Rather than ignoring us and passing on, they stopped right in front of us. The men appeared surprised to come across two colored men alone at the side of the road in the middle of nowhere.

Pa cleared his throat and I knew he was feeling uncomfortable, just like me. He said nothing and kept his eyes trained on the strangers, not moving, waiting to see what would happen. The white men was Pa's age, but didn't act hostile. I sure hoped they was just curious.

"Where you coloreds going on such a purty day?" one of the men asked. "Don't you have fields to till or crops to pick? You know…make hay while the sun shines?" He removed his hat and shot a sarcastic grin to his sidekick. The other one said nothing, and they waited for Pa to answer.

"We's headed to Chattanooga," Pa explained, as he stood to his feet and reached into his jacket pocket. He pulled out a folded piece of paper, opened it and handed it up to the man. Glancing at the page and shifting uneasily in his saddle, the man handed it across to his friend and stared at us while he waited for him to read.

I didn't move a muscle. The eyes of the man reading moved across the page. When he finished, he folded and handed it down to Pa. Then he said to us both, "If I was you'uns, I'd be off the road before dark, letter or no letter." And with that, they pulled the horses' heads back toward the road and galloped north.

Pa sat down, pulled an apple from his lunch tin and shined it on his pants leg before saying, "I hope we don't have the luck of passing them two on the way back."

"What's on that there paper, Pa?"

"I don't know. Mister Wasson give it to me yesterday and said to carry it along, just in case."

Pa bit into his apple and handed me the robin-egg blue paper that was heavier than any book page I'd turned. "I reckon this is genuine linen stationary," I said, running my fingers over it. All Pa said was 'hmmph.'

I read the neat, back-slanted writing. "It says here that we work for Chapman Wasson of the Rhea Springs Resort Hotel and have been sent on a *leg-it-imate* business trip to Chattanooga to secure a shipment of furniture from Fowler Brothers Furniture Company and will bring it by wagon to Rhea Springs. Anyone reading this is asked to allow *un-en-cumbered* passage, whatever that means. That's basically all it says." I refolded the paper and handed it back. Pa stuffed it into his pocket and stood up.

"Let's get a move on," he said, tossing the apple core aside and gathering his lunch tin and mason jar of water. "The man's right. We don't need to be out here come nightfall."

"Where we gonna sleep tonight, Pa? In the wagons, outside town—way off the road, like them white men warned?"

"No, we's gonna sleep in a bed at a boarding house right on Ninth Street in downtown Chattanooga," Pa said with a grin that showed off practically all his white teeth, like he'd just revealed a special-held secret.

"A boarding house? For us?" I was flabbergasted. "You mean like the Rhea Springs Hotel?"

"Kind'a." With great pleasure, he shared the details he'd held secret. "The boarding house is for coloreds only and is located on Ninth Street. You see, Eighth Street down to the Tennessee Riverfront is white, but Ninth Street is all Negro-owned stores, including the boarding house." Untying his team, he climbed onto his wagon. "Come on," he said, grinning. "We's got a room waiting for us with indoor plumbing!"

Before I could get up from the ground, he had slapped the reins to the back of his team and was off down the road, putting distance between us. I slung my lunch bucket onto the wagon, jumped aboard and shook the leather reins. The horses lurched into action. I could hear Pa laughing over the jangling of his wagon as it headed south, kicking up a swirling dust cloud. I was gonna need a washroom and plenty of water by the end of the day.

***

Pulling the teams to the side of the road atop a ridge outside Chattanooga, we gawked as the sinking sun washing everthing in gold. Pa pointed to the dark green river snaking around the mountains beyond, skirting the edge of the town below. A long, wide wood bridge crossed over and the road led down the main street through town.

"I do declare," Pa said. "It's just as spectacular as I pictured in my head."

We both forgot how tuckered we was as we stared at the crisscrossing streets, with buildings all along them, and scattered church steeples that appeared to reach higher than the last. And beyond the town was houses, lots of them, all around.

"Pa, how's we gonna pay for a night at a boarding house? We don't have money for that, do we?"

"Can't I do something nice for my favorite son?"

"I'm your only son, Pa. And you shouldn't..."

"Before you go worrying I'm taking food off your Ma and sister's plates, let me put your mind to rest...Mister Wasson is footing this bill. Said our hauling the furniture north was a big job and he didn't want his help risking a night out along the road where scoundrels could take advantage."

"Do you know exactly where this boarding house is, since you've never been to Chattanooga neither?"

"Mister Wasson said to take that bridge over the river and follow the road through town until we come to Ninth Street at the far end. Turn left onto Ninth and we's there. So what do you say, boy? Let's get us a up-close look at Chattanooga, Tennessee."

In no time we was rolling along cobblestone streets so wide six wagons could travel it side by side. Men, women, carriages and horses were bustling in all directions. Never seen so many folks at one time, excepting the Rhea County fair. Since crossing the longest bridge I'd ever seen, I'd already counted twenty stores down one side of Market Street. Fixing to point that out to Pa whose wagon was ahead of mine, I heard over the noise on the street something likened to a cow calling after its calf. No, maybe it was a donkey braying. Pa turned in his seat to look back at me and pointed to the far side of the road. A crowd of men was gathered, admiring something resembling a shiny black carriage, but there wasn't no horse. The carriage let out that braying again and the crowd laughed, just as our horses did a jig in surprise. Our wagons kept rolling but we couldn't take our eyes off the scene.

We turned down Ninth Street and stopped in front of a red brick building as tall as the Rhea Springs Hotel. Pa announced, "We's here!"

I was busting with questions, but he said to wait on my wagon while he got us a room and found where to leave the wagons. Tying his team to the horse railing, he disappeared inside.

From where I sat, I could peer through the street-level windows of the place to see a room with tables occupied by colored men and women eating. Someone inside opened a window to let in the cool of the coming evening, and I heard the clatter of dishes and folks buzzing with talk. When I caught the smell of roasted meat, my belly commenced to growling.

After Pa and I left the wagons at the livery stable, we walked past store after store along the long boarded walk. Given it was the supper hour, shops was closing, but the area was still busy with colored men and women all dressed up and young'ins running about like loose chickens. I'd never seen so many of my own kind in one place. Passing a haberdashery, barbershop, dry goods store, general store, two saloons, and even a storefront with a sign that a doctor was there, I was speechless. So was Pa. With businesses owned and operated by men like us, it appeared Negro folks had their very own town.

By the time we found an empty table in the boarding house dining room and ordered plates of beef stew and cornbread, we both was talking over each other in the excitement of what we'd seen and heard.

"Pa, what was I seeing along the street—those tall wood poles branched out at the top? Looked like scalped trees with ropes connecting one to the other down the road."

Pa didn't answer, but pointed to the tin ceiling overhead and three hanging lights. After taking a swig of lemonade, he said, "Poles run the wires along the streets so businesses can use electric lights. Yeah, one of these days the Rhea Springs Hotel will have electricity," Pa predicted. "And then I won't be pulling that darn fan rope no more."

We both laughed.

"Carriages that run without horses and light that travels on wires," I said, rolling my eyes. "But the real miracle is living where doctors are Negro and store owners are too. This is a different world, Pa, a better one in my estimation."

"I reckon it is."

With our bellies filled and weariness in our bones, we climbed the stairs to our room and took advantage of the indoor plumbing at the end of the hall. Pa crawled into our sagging bed and his eyes was closed before I could turn off the light. Streetlights outside our window drew strange shadows on the room's faded flower wallpaper and its lone bed table and chair. The excitement of the day had helped keep my mind off Ida Mae. That was good.

My body ached from the day's journey, and I twisted and turned on the squeaking bed for the longest. Finally, I slipped from under the bed sheet and stood by the window, pulling aside the dingy curtains to peer down onto the street. Now almost midnight, it was empty except for the lively saloon across the way. Men were lingering outside talking and laughing. Piano music seeped through our closed window. I turned to see if Pa was stirring. He was not, so I opened my tote sack for the fresh shirt Ma had packed. After pulling on my trousers and grabbing my shoes, I tiptoed to the door and checked over my shoulder before heading out. I wouldn't be gone long.

On the street the piano melody was loud and carried along a woman's downhearted words. I crossed over and hesitated by the door. At the far end of the dim, smoke-filled room was a gal my age leaning against a black upright piano with a man hovered over its keys. From where I stood, she wasn't that purty, but her white dress showed off her young brown arms and shoulders and a shimmering head wrap with long black feathers bunched on one side made me believe she'd seen a lot more of the world than me. Her singing carried a deep sadness like she had lived the words she sang. The men slouched at the wood tables paid her little mind, more occupied with the cards in their hands and the brew in their glasses. When the young woman's last words fell on deaf ears, the piano quieted and she gave a slight bow before slipping away.

I ventured inside the stale-smelling room and found an empty table near the piano. As I sat, a woman wearing a tight red dress and matching shiny lipstick brushed past me just as the player-man brought his hands hard onto the keys, commanding everybody's attention.

"You fools," the tall shapely woman called out above the din, hand on her hip in disgust. The room fell silent. "You've just heard one of Chattanooga's rising talents, and you're too damn busy yammering at one another to listen. Now you give Miss Bessie Smith a proper applause. Come on back here girl and take a bow," she gestured to the younger woman standing in the shadows.

I was close enough to see her beaming face as she stepped to the piano and was greeted by raucous clapping and whistles from all the men, including me.

A tap on my shoulder sidetracked my attention to a light-skinned bar maid standing over me. In a tight black skirt and white blouse opened enough to invite inspection, she parted her full lips and hollered above the fray for my order. I pointed to the man at the next table and yelled, "I'll have what he's got." She turned on her heels and left, but soon set an over-full glass with a sudsy white head in front of me. I smiled, hoping she might take notice, but all I got was a bored stare. "Do you want me to start a tab?"

"Uh, no," I answered, disappointed.

"Beer's a nickel." She waited, but I panicked. Remembering the coins stuffed into my trouser pocket before leaving home, I dug into one and then the other before breathing a sigh of relief. Laying the coin on the table, I watched her scoop it up and disappear into the haze.

The woman in the tight red dress, alone now by the piano, launched into a song of love longed for and filled the room with her sultry sound. Watching the words pass over cherry lips as red as her dress, a chill woke my senses and I traced her curves, taking my time, relishing her brown velvet skin and a bosom that bulged from her dress.

Settling deep into my chair, I sipped at the brew that tasted nothing like the moonshine I'd had but twice, once when I helped Uncle Eli chase down three turkeys that had flown the coop and into the woods—for which he wanted to properly thank me—and the other, when I found a filled mason jar hidden in the shed behind the house. I figured Pa stashed it there for emergencies and my taking a little swig was all I could manage without raising suspicion. Moonshine kicked hard, much harder than this here in my glass. As I drank, the sudsy foam coated my mustache and the liquid felt smooth and cold going down. I liked it.

Wiping my mouth, I gave full attention to the appealing vision not twenty feet away. As she sang, her eyes fell on me and I offered a gestured smile and was surprised she returned it. After her final notes, she bowed and I clapped harder than the others who volunteered little attention. She looked to her piano man to begin anew and then turned to purr the words, training her gaze on me, as if to invite me…to what I wasn't certain. My eyes took in her body with its slow, purposeful movements, and the same feeling rushed through my veins that I felt when Ida Mae's warm lips had pressed against mine. Staring into the woman's deep-set eyes, I saw Ida Mae looking back. I blinked, looked into my empty glass and back again at the woman. Her eyes were brown, not green like Ida Mae's. But the draw was as strong as a roped calf being pulled into submission.

Startled, I pushed away from the table and stood up. My chair fell backward to the floor with a loud thud. With a fleeting glance at the purty vision calling with lilting voice and welcoming gestures, I escaped through the maze of tables out into the cool night air. Retracing my path across the deserted street, I breathlessly climbed the boarding house stairs to our room. By the time I slipped into bed next to Pa, my head had finally cleared and my thoughts returned to Ida Mae.

***

Next morning after buckwheat pancakes and buttery grits that rivaled Ma's, our wagons headed toward Fowler Brothers. The empty wagons rumbled over the Ninth Street cobblestones, and I took a long last look passing the saloon, doors now closed and locked. Shaking my head, I turned back to my team and minutes later turned onto Broad Street, joining as many wagons and carriages as yesterday. Rows of stores lined both sides of the wide street just like Market, and folks were crowding the boardwalks bordered by the stores. Hardie and Caudle Men's Store, Minnette's Candies, City Barbershop, a dry goods store—all with printed signs out front spelling out what was inside, and I easily read ever one.

When we arrived at the warehouse. Pa climbed down and delivered the order into the supervisor's hands. While workers loaded the wagons under Pa's watchful eye, a thought took hold of me. I hopped down from my wagon, calling to Pa that I would be back shortly. He stared after me like I'd lost my mind, but other Negro men walked Market and Broad Streets. I'd seen them yesterday and this morning, and I had no worries.

Walking back up the boardwalk along Broad Street, I spotted the shop I'd eyed when we passed. A store clerk was turning the sign on the door to "Open for Business." The first inside, I asked politely to see a kerchief from the display window.

"Which one?" the clerk asked, looking me over, I thought.

"The yeller one with the little flowers," I answered, double-checking the neatness of my shirt and suspenders.

"The one with rosebuds?" the man asked, reaching to fetch it from a clothesline with hanging merchandise.

"Yessir, that's the one," I said, as the clerk held it up.

"That'll be twenty cents," he said. "You have twenty cents?"

I pulled from my pocket the ten-cent pieces and proudly laid them on the counter. The clerk wrapped the kerchief in brown paper. "Thank you, sir," I said, slipping the package under my shirt. I popped into the shop next door, whose front window was filled with large glass containers on shelves, filled with hard candies of every color. At the counter, I asked the owner which ones cost two cents and she pointed to several.

"Which do children like best?"

"All of them," she answered flatly.

Pointing to the jar with shiny red balls the size of marbles, I asked for four. She counted them into a small paper bag and took my copper coins. The bag smelled like cherries and I stuffed it into my now-empty pocket.

Trotting back toward the warehouse and whistling in satisfaction, I was stopped in my tracks by a loud clanging bell. Down the middle of the cobblestone street behind me lumbered a green closed-in wagon on rails like a train car and it spilled over with men, women and children. Another contraption without horses, it powered along by a long pole above its roof touching wires that ran the length of the street. Watching it stop often to let folks on and off, I stared as it passed. But Pa was waiting, so I hurried on.

It was late morning when we re-crossed the bridge over the green Tennessee River with our wagons packed tight with new furniture. When we crested the ridge north of the city, we stopped for a final look. I'm sure Pa never expected to return, but I wondered aloud, "It's a strange new world down there, ain't it? A better one, in my view."

"Maybe, son, maybe," he answered. After some pause, we slapped the reins to our teams and the wagons lurched in the direction of home. "We's got to take it slow," Pa called back to me, "but we ain't stopping until we see the hotel."

Thinking on how the package under my shirt was gonna excite Ma, I settled in for the long haul, wondering as well if there might be a letter waiting for me when we arrived.

CHAPTER 20

BLANCHE

Within days, Cuba had disarmed us with its charm and allure: the colorful dress of its people in their serapes and wide-brimmed sombreros, cuisine that woke our taste buds with its mysterious flavors, stately churches and buildings that heralded the culture of historical colonizers. Any evening offered a dizzying array of entertainment choices: ballrooms filled with exotic dance, theatre houses rivaling those in Europe, and fine dining everywhere. Havana's pulse outpaced Rhea Springs even in its busiest of summers.

At our breakfast table several days into our stay, Will held up two Tacon Theatre tickets. I clapped and bounced in my chair with childish excitement. We both had been awed by the building's beauty while strolling the Parque our first day in Havana. Its carved stone exterior resembled a castle draped in lace. Now our first theatre performance amidst the Tacon's elegance was in the offing.

Donning our formal attire that evening, Will and I joined the throngs passing through the theatre's immense doors adorned with carvings and gold inlay. When we reached our seats on the second of three levels, we had a perfect view of the performance stage. In a state of wonder, we gawked at the gold- and silver-scrolled embellishments along the ceiling and walls—illuminated by electric lighting—that dazzled like diamonds in a crown. The interior alone was worth the price of admission. I confessed to Will that the only acting I had ever seen were small Chautauqua drama groups at Grandfather's hotel that would not hold a candle to what was ahead.

Ten minutes later the lights dimmed and the blue velvet curtains parted. Will and I were taken captive by the operatic voice of the fiery gypsy Carmen and a stage set that transported us to Spain where she seduced a naive soldier outside a cigarette factory. In the next acts, we watched a smitten Jose abandon his childhood sweetheart for Carmen and desert his military duty, but in the end lose her to a glamorous toreador. At the tragic death of the main character two hours later, the entire audience jumped to its feet in resounding applause. In the electric atmosphere, we all lingered, in no hurry to leave.

***

The next morning I posed an idea to Will as we dressed for the day, "What about our venturing beyond the city to see the sugarcane plantations? If we're going to 'see' Cuba, we should do the countryside as well."

Will nodded, "Hmm, sounds good."

After breakfast, Will was off to the lobby to secure a carriage before I could remove the napkin from my lap. His enthusiasm was contagious, so I hurried to our room for my hat and parasol.

Our carriage came with a driver who served as guide. We stepped into the open-air carriage and settled in for an adventure. As Havana's crowded streets and buildings slipped into the distance behind us, we were soon surrounded by rolling countryside and welcoming breezes, a landscape similar to that of home. Traveling farther west, the land flattened and we came upon fields of green towering plants in such density that a man could not walk through. The foliage resembled corn in its early stages of growth. The guide explained in broken English that the sugar was derived from the harvested stalks that were boiled. Farther down the dirt road, we came to a large clearing where dark-skinned field workers were swinging long machetes, hacking into the stand of plants and methodically felling stalks that stood taller than they. Stacked like cordwood, piles lay everywhere awaiting transport.

"I've read," Will said, "that United States companies own three-quarters of the Cuban sugar industry."

"Is that so?" I said absently, eyeing the native men and women working under the growing heat and thinking how similar it was to the life of Negroes back home. With the sun bearing down like the lash of a master, I pointed out to Will that the look of resignation on their perspiring faces retold the story of our South. He curtly replied that U.S. companies brought jobs to those people that they wouldn't otherwise have. I held my peace but kept a fixed gaze on the scene.

The guide pointed to the opposite side of the road and explained in halting English that the acres of waist-high, broad leafy plants were tobacco. Will and I exchanged knowing looks. We were well versed on the tobacco plant, a major crop in our world.

Will whispered into my ear, "Cuban tobacco has stiff competition with our Kentucky crops."

I whispered, "Well, your insistence on carrying Cuban cigars back home points out which you think is superior."

He stuck out his tongue, but grinned.

After the morning in the countryside, our driver returned us to the city along the streets of Havana's historic areas where grand buildings and churches of Spanish design had been built during the country's occupation. By the time the sun had slipped into the west, we had managed to explore several other city marketplaces and fancied the unique energy of each. We refrained, however, from eating anything that could not be identified, no matter how tempting. By the time we stepped from the carriage at day's end, we were ready for a proper meal and quiet evening.

On our eighth day in Cuba, we awoke with renewed energy and decided a walk to the Cathedral of Havana would be an ideal way to savor the surroundings. The church bordered Cathedral Square and not far from the hotel. Though the Square wasn't the city's largest, it was a popular tourist destination according to the hotel concierge.

As the caged elevator descended to the lobby, I mused that we had only two days left before returning to the States. I would miss the uninterrupted, relaxed time with my new husband. But Will seemed ready. Increasingly restive, he frequently wondered aloud how his mercantile store was faring in his absence. He was burdened by his father's expectations to continue managing the family businesses beyond Rhea Springs. In colorful, faraway Havana, we had lived a storybook existence uninterrupted by life's demands. Writing the opening chapter of our life together as Mr. and Mrs. William Blair Day, I didn't want it to end.

"What a lovely morning for a walk, don't you think, Mr. Day?" I said, glancing into the clear blue as we departed the hotel. Will offered his arm and we turned south. Browsing the store windows of the many three-storied buildings huddled along the cobble-stoned streets, we marveled at what the city offered with its myriad shops along cobblestone streets, a far cry from what we had back home.

Cuban cigar stores drew Will like a magnet, with open shop doors and unmistakable aromas. He had already purchased three boxes of the world-famous Bolivar cigars to take home for Papa, his father and uncle. Advertised as strong, powerful and robust, the disgusting things would send any proper lady running for air. My protest was loud and clear that I would not remain in the same room when he or Papa lit up, but that didn't deter him one bit.

When Will and I came upon The Peacock Room, aptly named given its windows stacked with bolts of gaily-colored fabrics, I couldn't resist. Will waited outside while I browsed the aisles of familiar cottons and ginghams, running my fingers over the bolts of smooth, shiny silks and nubby linen fabrics from Europe. Within fifteen minutes, four yards of silk—enough for two dresses—were cut and wrapped in brown paper, ready for passage in my travel trunks to Rhea Springs. Stepping from the shop with tied package in hand, I was already mentally framing a letter to Aunt Marian to ask if she would fashion a new Sunday dress for me.

Will took my hand and suggested, "We should skirt the square when we get closer…to avoid the crowds. I wager there's a side entrance to the Cathedral we can enter and then afterward leave by way of the Square."

"As long as you don't get us lost," I warned.

Will grinned with confidence and took my package. Tucking it under an arm, he guided us down the side streets, many narrow as alleys. The tall twin steeples of the church appeared in the distance, offering sneak peaks between the nearer structures like a game of hide-and-seek. It would be hard to lose our way, I guessed, but I didn't relish the dreary passageways that shut out the sun. We walked the cobblestone alleys passing few others. Roaming cats skittered in all directions at the sound of our approaching steps. I shuddered to think of the rodents that lurked and lifted my skirt even higher above my ankles and quickened my pace to keep up with Will.

After what seemed a long while, we turned a corner and the side of the enormous stone building was finally revealed, its bell towers reaching into the sky at the far end. We'd found the Cathedral of Havana.

"See, I told you I'd get us here," Will said in triumph.

Relieved to feel the sun's rays again and see people milling about the majestic structure, I conceded, "You managed to get us here all right. There, Will. There's a side entrance." Will led the way and when we entered the cavernous sanctuary, we gasped.

"Baroque architecture," Will whispered, pointing to its interior. We had been told the church was constructed in the eighteenth century during Spain's colonization. Colossal stone columns flanked each side of the altar area. Will pointed to a chandelier taller than he was that hung from the ceiling far above the center aisle. A cascading waterfall of candles hung in the air, all interconnected by a netting of brass chains supporting each candleholder and linking it to the next.

Recognizing the need to be reverent, I suppressed my giddiness and whispered, "Will, let's go to the front. I want a closer look at those columns." Taking his hand, I pulled him along the polished-stone aisle that I guessed had borne the footsteps of multitudes over the centuries.

At the front, we craned our heads to view the carved wood ceiling that formed the magnificent dome. "And these columns," I said, approaching the closest one. "I can't believe the size." Holding hands, we circled the column but could not reach around its girth. Near the altar, we could see its carved and beautifully grained wood, so polished that it reflected the candlelight in the muted light of the sanctuary. I whispered into Will's ear, "The tapestry on that altar must have come from a Spanish castle. Actually, given the musty smell in here, all the furnishings look like they came from a castle."

Will smiled and nodded.

We headed to a pew to sit, and only then saw that they had been intricately carved, giving them the appearance of an elegant lace drape.

Later, when we slipped from our seats, we noticed the many tourists and locals scattered across the expansive sanctuary quietly sitting, some praying. Walking toward the rear of the church, we noted above its massive wood entry doors round stained-glass windows directing the incoming sunlight, bringing to life the familiar Biblical scenes depicted on the glass. We were left in awe.

Will and I spent the rest of the afternoon exploring neighboring surroundings, drinking in the sights and sounds, storing it all for future fond remembrance. Only as the sun sank low in the distance did we notice our fatigue. What a day it had been!

"I think we should make our way back to the hotel if we're going to have dinner at a decent hour," Will said, pulling out his pocket watch to check.

"I am exhausted," I admitted.

"Let's take the most direct route. It'll save time and energy."

I guess my face clouded, because Will quickly added, "Don't worry. I've a good sense of direction. Got us to the church this morning, didn't I?"

"Yes, I guess."

Will scanned the street signs near us and then turned north. From the busier main boulevard, he veered right. In no time we were enmeshed in the back streets and alleyways again, hearing only the echoing sounds of our shoes striking the cobblestones as we sought our way. As the light dimmed, I knew Will was feeling uncomfortable in our surroundings because he quickened his pace and I pulled my skirt higher to keep up.

When we found ourselves in a dilapidated neighborhood with no storefronts, it was obvious we were far from the beaten track. Closed doors with faded and peeling paint and windows covered by shabby curtains stared back from all sides. Empty liquor bottles littered the alleyways, and our noses were insulted by the odors emitted from the dark and damp surroundings.

Will stopped abruptly.

"What is it, Will?"

"Nothing. I'm just getting my bearings."

"Are we lost?"

"Of course not."

He answered too quickly. Steering me across the alleyway, he guided us down another narrow street. Soon I heard faint sounds of horses and buggies in the distance and was relieved we were closer to a thoroughfare. But as we turned the corner, Will walked directly into something or someone leaning against an adobe wall.

"Excuse me." Will sought to right himself, grabbing a man's shoulder to steady him as he swayed to one side.

Reeking of whiskey, the man reacted in Spanish, slurring his speech as he jerked from Will's grasp. I shrank back, but that drew his attention. He sneered, exposing missing teeth. Fear clawed at me.

Will raised his voice—diverting the man's stare—and apologized again, this time in broken Spanish. But the drunkard's eyes shifted back to me and then lurched in my direction. Will lunged and grabbed his arm to fling him aside. But the man regained his balance and turned, drawing back a fist. It landed squarely on Will's jaw and sent him reeling. I screamed, and the man turned to me. A menacing grin spread across his dirty, stubble-covered face. But before he advanced, Will landed a fist to his head from behind. The man crumpled to the street. Will kicked him in the ribs and then straddled his body to pummel his face and head with a vengeance.

Was I in a dream, a nightmare? I heard screaming; it was mine. In what seemed like slow motion, I grabbed the back of Will's shirt collar to pull him off the now unconscious man. But Will kept pounding him, ignoring my pleas. He was in a rage. Even in the encroaching darkness, I could see blood smeared across the man's face, his nose askew and blood oozing from it.

When I could not stop him, I slumped to the cobblestones, sobbing uncontrollably. Only then did Will come to himself, crawl off the man's body and come to my side.

"Blanche, are you all right? Are you all right?" he kept repeating.

I couldn't stop crying but nodded yes. Will stroked my head with his bloodied hands trying to reassure me.

When we struggled to our feet and stared down at the unconscious man, I was relieved to see his chest rising and falling. "What are we going to do?" I asked, looking up into Will's face, his eye already red and swelling, his face streaked with grime.

"What we're going to do is get out of here," he said, checking the alleyway in both directions. "We don't want to be around if his drinking buddies show up. Come on."

With his arm on my shoulders for support, he motioned in the direction of the city sounds we'd heard earlier. Within minutes, we had reached the hotel and staggered through the entrance. Seeing our disheveled appearance, three men from behind the registration counter rushed to our aid. The police were summoned, and upon their arrival, Will gave a full report. One of the hotel staff translated, as the two policemen did not speak English. Unable to pinpoint exactly where we were accosted and given the exchange in Spanish between the policemen, Will and I imagined the report would be filed and nothing more would come of it. The bloodied man lying in the street would surely have been scooped up and taken home by now. I hoped my husband had not done irreparable damage. In any case, we would be leaving Cuba in less than forty-eight hours. The events of the day left much to ponder, especially my husband's extreme actions.

CHAPTER 21

BLANCHE

If our courtship was a whirlwind, the months that followed were a tornado. Indeed, ignorance was bliss on the fair morning that we eased out of Havana Harbor toward the open ocean. The rising sun reflected on the waters predicting a cheerful day. Relishing the brisk, salty air, I chose the promenade deck and settled onto my deckchair to read and nap. By lunchtime, I was tallying the days until we'd be back in Rhea Springs settling into our bungalow and sharing our recent adventures with family. Will spent much of the morning wandering the ship's decks, exchanging pleasantries with fellow travelers and crewmembers. Eventually he joined me and stood strumming his fingers at the deck railing.

"Why don't you sit and relax with a book, like me?" I asked, patting the deck chair next to mine.

Will smiled but declined. "I couldn't concentrate. My head is spinning with what I've got ahead of me once we're home."

Will's mercantile business had dominated conversation over the last few days. He worried the inventory would be low because of our long absence. Had Mr. Cobb managed the reorders? He fretted how best to advertise his new ownership, since it was a well-established fact that customer loyalties were to Papa as much as to the quality of goods that lined the shelves. Must be handled with real sensitivity, he said. And there was arranging the meeting with Mr. Lyons, the carpenter, to finalize plans for enlarging the store. That needed to be accomplished by spring planting in order to handle the additional hundred pound bags of corn and soy seed.

And, of course, there was Will's father and his ever-present expectations. No doubt, letters from Kentucky would be waiting, bringing him up-to-date on the family businesses and soliciting his involvement in one fashion or another. I imagined Will would likely unpack only to repack within the week and train north to answer his father's summons.

By bedtime both our moods had soured, and anticipating the cabin's cramped quarters only worsened matters. Our return trip to Tennessee by ship and then train would drag on for days. It would feel like weeks.

***

At long last, the train's screeching brakes announced its arrival at the Spring City depot. Peering out my window, I spotted Papa on the platform appearing relieved his wait was over. Grandfather sat in the fringed surrey nearby, managing the team of white horses that had been spooked by the train's cacophony of wheezes and hisses.

I descended the train steps as quickly as that young teen returning from boarding school, overjoyed to be home. Will followed, laden like a packhorse with bags and boxes from our trip. With hugs from Grandfather and Papa and smiles all around, our travel fatigue seemed to disappear.

Owen and Gay were notably missing from the entourage. Owen had opened a new chapter in my absence. Delaying school in the wake of Mama's death, he was finally off to the University of Kentucky. But at least my sister would be near and anxious to hear of our escapades.

"Where is Gay?" I asked, after our travel trunks had been loaded and we were well down Old Stage Road toward Rhea Springs.

"She's at home," Papa answered, without elaborating.

"Is she too busy to meet her sister at the station? Oh, I know. She and Bertie are cooking up a welcome-home feast, just like the good old days." I winked at Will.

Papa glanced in Grandfather's direction, with what appeared a furrowed brow. With Will and I sitting behind the two, Papa raised his voice above the clopping of the horses' hooves to answer over his shoulder, "Your sister has been unwell since the wedding. She

177

guessed she was just run down, overworked. You know how insistent she was to get every detail perfect for that wedding. She developed a bad cough that wouldn't go away, and it got us worried. And when the night sweats started...."

My weary mind couldn't follow where Papa's words were leading me. When he turned to face me and said he had accompanied her to Chattanooga to see a specialist and then related the doctor's findings, I was stunned. Gay had consumption—tuberculosis.

"Papa, why didn't you send word? I would have come home immediately—you know I would."

I turned to Will in disbelief, and his ashen face mirrored my shock.

"Blanche, there's nothing you could have done," Papa said. "And Gay insisted that we not. As she put it, she wasn't going to spoil your honeymoon over her silly cough."

Grandfather drove the surrey directly to Papa's. After an abbreviated meal without my sister at the table, Will followed Papa and Grandfather into the parlor. Behind closed doors, the three puffed on the Cuban cigars that Will had brought while I remained upstairs at Gay's bedside. Grandfather warned the disease was contagious, but nothing was going to keep me from her. Even in a weakened state, she pushed herself up on pillows and insisted I regale her with our Cuban escapades. My animated recollections of flamboyant dancing and mysterious foods and descriptions of magnificent Spanish edifices buoyed her spirit. She laughed herself into a coughing fit over our introduction to tamales and my midnight discovery of a headless man hovered over the toilet.

By the time the grandfather clock downstairs struck nine, Gay's energy had waned and I conceded it was time to leave. My sister needed her rest, and my exhaustion had returned. Grandfather drove Will and me the mile down the road to our picket-fenced cottage. I whispered to Will along the way that the night seemed especially dark without the light of the moon or stars. Maybe it was my mood. After helping to carry our travel trunks to the porch, Grandfather kissed my forehead and gave Will a pat on the back.

Standing at the door to our dark house, Will asked me to wait. He disappeared inside and lit an oil lamp in the parlor before returning. "I know it's been an upsetting day, Blanche," he said, "but to carry you over the threshold is a befitting way to begin our home life. Don't you agree?" Will's gentleness brought tears. I nodded and offered an appreciative smile as he lifted me and stepped through the doorway.

Within weeks, Papa and Grandfather had worked out arrangements for Gay to travel to a well-respected Arizona sanatorium, outside Phoenix, where she could benefit from rest, fresh air and a special diet. According to the Chattanooga specialist who had made the recommendation, other patients had fared well there.

When Grandfather drove the family to the train station that chilly November morning and my sister disappeared into the train car, it tore at my heart. Reassuring waves and thrown kisses—even Bertie and Sam who'd asked to come along—couldn't minimize the serious nature of what she faced. At least Papa was accompanying her and that brought some consolation.

Weeks later, Will and I trained to Kentucky to celebrate our first Thanksgiving together. We gathered around the Day's elaborate dining table set for a fine holiday celebration, an enormous roasted turkey at its center and all of the season's bounty on display. My husband's family—my family now—rejoiced in our presence, but it didn't feel much like Thanksgiving and I felt very much alone. Then came Christmas and a return trip to the Day's, but knowing Papa and Owen were with my sister in Arizona was more meaningful than any gift presented to me from under their tree.

After Papa returned home in January, I took the first opportunity to inquire after my sister's health. I riddled him with questions as we sat on the loveseat in his library but found little satisfaction in his answers. "Blanche, your sister is doing as well as can be expected," Papa reassured me.

"How does she look, Papa?"

"Well, she's lost some weight, but says the diet is not unpleasant and that the warm, persistent sunshine is welcome solace."

"When will she be coming home? What did the doctors say?"

"They don't know when she might come home, Blanche. They don't have a crystal ball," Papa said with an edge of impatience as he shifted his weight on the loveseat and then readjusted his tone. "Gay sends her love and said to tell you that she misses you, but that you should not worry. By the way, she said to remind you that you owe her a letter," he said with a smile, trying to lighten the conversation.

Relating the conversation to Will later, my frustration spilled over. Papa knew more than he was telling, I complained as I paced about our parlor. Sitting in his easy chair watching me, Will was upbeat with encouragement, but I resisted. On my knees that night at bedtime, I complained vociferously to God but got no answers from Him either.

By the time the yellow tulips along our picket fence welcomed spring, the Day household in Rhea Springs had settled into its own rhythm. When Will was home, averaging two weeks out of four, I'd awake with the chickens to prepare a hearty breakfast of fried eggs and ham, always served with his favored glass of buttermilk. Our time together in the quiet of the dawning day was important, before he rushed off to his store citing the need to open early so local farmers could buy supplies at convenient times. He coddled the business like it was his only child and only he knew what would make it thrive. I realized early on that Will's attention to business was his highest priority.

"Will, can't you linger a bit before you leave for the store?" I asked the morning after he'd returned from an extended trip to Kentucky. He had hurriedly eaten and was draining his glass as he rose from the table. "I've been away from the store three weeks and need time in the stockroom before we get busy."

He leaned down and kissed my head, as I sat at the table feeling pangs of disappointment. He seemed not to notice as he turned and disappeared out the back door. While I cleaned up the kitchen, I stewed over his dismissal and tried to ignore my hurt.

***

Filling my days with domestic duties, I was like a robin feathering her nest, arranging and re-arranging furniture looking for that perfect placement. The tiled vase from Havana found a home on the fireplace mantel, right where I'd imagined, its small shiny tiles mirroring the hues of our rug. In front of the fireplace, the cotton chintz couch and Will's overstuffed easy chair anchored the rug. This was Will's and my gathering spot on chilly evenings when he stoked the fire, turned up the oil lamp, and I cuddled under one of Mama's afghan covers on the couch. Settling into his easy chair, Will read aloud from a favored book until later when a hand stroking my cheek would rouse and head me off to bed. Home life was indeed to my liking.

With the arrival of spring, I noticed my skirts fitting more snugly and in late May learned I was with child. A Rhea Springs physician made the pronouncement, as Grandfather had long since retired as family doctor.

Departing the doctor's office, I hurried home...to its emptiness. Will was traveling and I'd been alone for weeks, but he would be home Saturday. Excited to share the news, I would have to wait. I couldn't tell Papa, not before Will. That wouldn't be proper. How I wished Gay was up the road. I'd swear her to secrecy, sit her down, and tell her everything.

I lingered in the middle of the parlor looking about, feeling a sense of satisfaction at the atmosphere I had created. Floor-to-ceiling bookcases on one wall were filled with our books. On the opposite wall above my curio table were four oil paintings, offering sweeping pastoral landscapes, two in hues of a vivid autumn and two depicting the summer countryside. Gifts to Mama from a Kentucky relative who had achieved notoriety for her artistic talent, they hung in her parlor and were objects of bragging to visitors. Papa had presented them to Will and me as "house warming" gifts, and I displayed them with equal pride. Perched on the mahogany curio table, bird figurines of glass caught the sunlight streaming through the nearby window and cast small rainbows of color around the room. Two carved rosewood chairs with gold velvet seat cushions flanked the table. Our home was a pleasing place, I thought. But Will was not there, and it felt especially empty on this day that had generated such glorious news.

Mulling the future, I wandered from room to room. Will had insisted on buying a two-bedroom cottage. He wanted a bedroom for his mother when she visited. Said the hotel was too impersonal. I disagreed. She, on the other hand, had not returned to Rhea Springs since the wedding. Weekly letters arrived instead, newsy ones sent to her son, offering only a closing line of greeting for me. Leaning against the doorframe and sizing up the spare room, I envisioned our child's belongings there, not my mother-in-law's.

Stepping across the tiny hallway into Will's and my bedroom, I wanted to determine the best placement for a crib. Yes, in the corner on my side of the bed. The baby could easily be lifted into the bed to nurse during the wee hours without disturbing my husband's rest.

The afternoon had grown warm and I felt sapped. Blaming my condition, I decided to freshen up and poured water from the ewer on the dresser into the floral-painted basin. Fresh water would become important, I thought, with a baby on the way. Now I was even more thankful that Papa had run a short piping system from the backyard well into the kitchen so a spigot could be installed at the sink. That luxury had been a wedding present. I wondered what he'd think when he learned the news that it would serve as a baby gift as well.

I chuckled, recalling Will's and my magnificent en-suite bathroom at the Havana hotel. Will had said that sooner or later—when electricity in the States reached beyond the cities—indoor plumbing would not be unusual. It couldn't come soon enough for me. Venturing out to an outhouse wasn't fun when it was pouring rain or worse, snowing.

While Will couldn't provide our home with a Havana-styled bathroom, he had made improvements. Weeks before, he came home after work with a big brown sack in hand, marched into the kitchen where I was in the last stages of preparing supper and plopped it in the middle of the table, already set with plates and utensils. He smiled like a Cheshire cat.

"What in the world are you doing, Will?" I had said with irritation. "You're messing up my table setting. What's in the bag?" He said nothing, but gestured for me to see for myself. "I don't have time. Your dinner is going to burn." He motioned again, his expression unchanged.

Rolling my eyes, I wiped my hands on my apron and opened the bag to lift out one of several five-inch rolls—of something—I didn't know what. "What are they?" I looked quizzically at Will and then the rolls. Black lettering on the paper covering read, "Scott Paper Company".

Will couldn't have been prouder. His was the first store in Rhea County to stock toilet paper. He'd presented it to me like a prize trout fished from Piney Creek. He was determined our fair town would remain on the leading edge of progress and our household among the first beneficiaries. So there, not seventy-five feet from our kitchen's backdoor in the corner of our two-hole out-house with a quarter-moon door, sat a basket piled with toilet paper rolls instead of the customary dried corncobs or occasional Sears and Roebuck catalog pages that provided nothing of the comfort offered by the rolls of soft paper.

Having these conveniences would now be even more valuable when caring for a baby added to keeping up the house and seeing after Will's needs. Walking into the kitchen, I spooned up a bowl of leftover beans and sat down to eat. My eyes fell on the dwindling row of glass jars on the wall shelves—green beans and corn—reminding me of Bertie's patient canning lessons before the wedding. Counting the remaining glass quarts, I knew I must can again before my size became an impediment.

I was already uncomfortable, but what was it going to be like? I'd felt twinges but guessed it was gas. But now? Was it the baby? How Mama would have chuckled if I told her that Will and I would not be going into the cabbage patch on a moonlit night to retrieve our firstborn. I dissolved into tears. How I missed Mama...and Gay. I sniveled and would have thrown something at Will if he had been present. But guilt sobered me. Gay? How could I complain that my husband was not near when my sister was fighting for her health, far away from any family? I sighed and wiped my wet cheeks with the hem of my skirt. Recalling the doctor's orders to drink copious amounts, I walked to the sink and cranked the well handle to fill a glass with water. Drinking it down, I wondered if Papa would loan Bertie out for a few days when canning season rolled around again.

CHAPTER 22

BLANCHE

Waiting on the train station platform, I felt the afternoon sun bearing down, its heat especially bothersome. Finally, the southbound train eased into the station. Through the steam belched by the idling engine, unfamiliar people filed out of the coach cars and walked past. The month of May would soon give way to summer when that stream would swell to the great migration of vacationers returning to Rhea Springs. I scanned the crowd of faces, fidgeting with the uncomfortable waistband of my skirt that reminded me of my changing condition. I wondered if Will had noticed. I had chosen to wear this outfit because Will often complimented my appearance when I wore it to church. I wouldn't be able to cinch the waistband in a few more weeks.

Where was Will? I had yet to spy him. I had worked all afternoon in the kitchen preparing his favorite meal, wanting to create a romantic atmosphere. I covered our small table with a pressed linen cloth and a pair of brass candlesticks at its center. I'd even polished the silverware. After I served him dessert—his favorite pound cake—I would tell him of our good fortune. On a full stomach and with such marvelous news, he would surely forget his fatigue.

There he was. "Over here, Will." I waved my hand high overhead, hoping he'd see me among those still milling on the platform. "Will, I'm here."

Spotting me, he flashed a quick smile and walked in my direction. What a handsome man he was, and always dapper in his fine three-piece suits. We'd soon offer a striking family photograph, he and I with children surrounding us.

I greeted him with a peck to his cheek. "Welcome home, dear."

"I'm glad to be home," he said, offering a token hug. "It's been a long few weeks." His voice was flat and his face drawn.

Taking my arm, he led us to the station area where trunks were unloaded and set aside for retrieval. He carried his satchel of clothing, but said he'd transported a crated parcel from Kentucky. When he identified the large wooden box among the other trunks, two railroad workers strained under the load to carry it to our wagon. I questioned Will as to its contents, but he mumbled it was going to the mercantile store and then changed the subject.

We climbed aboard the buckboard and Will took the reins. Every question I asked as we rode along—how his travel had been, how his parents were, how business dealings had gone—was answered in the briefest fashion, and he asked nothing of me. I nervously chattered the entire distance, trying to fill the void that hung heavy in the air. He drove directly to the house, saying he needed time to unwind, that he'd worry about the crate later. When we entered, the savory aroma of a pot roast greeted us that I'd left on the cook stove. I hoped it caught his attention, but he made no comment. Feeling a wave of nausea, I was uncertain whether the cause was the food or Will's mood. Meanwhile, he disappeared into the bedroom.

"Will, dinner is just about ready," I called from the kitchen. Donning an apron, I lit the candles and began to dish up the meal.

When he reappeared, Will had shed his coat and vest and rolled up his shirtsleeves. His face was still moist from washing, but his countenance was unchanged. My insides gurgled. I pretended not to notice and put on a cheerful mask. Will plopped down on a chair.

"I'm not very hungry," he said.

He paid little notice to the serving dishes I brought to the table filled with his favorites. As I moved between the stove and table, Will picked up his fork and mindlessly tapped on the table's edge. Through the window of his eyes staring into nothingness, I could see he was not with me. He was somewhere else.

I placed the platter of roast beef and potatoes at the table's center surrounding it with bowls of green beans and fried apples and removed my apron to take my seat opposite him. Checking my hair with one hand to reassure myself I looked my best, I cleared my throat, hoping to bring him back. I did. He stilled his fork, glanced at the spread before him, and then smiled. He bowed his head to offer a blessing. With the 'amen,' he lifted his eyes and served his plate. He did not comment on the bountiful table nor seem to notice the flickering candles. And he said nothing about my appearance.

"You're quiet tonight, Will. Exhausted from the trip?" Hoping to draw him out, I said, "Did you notice I cooked your favorites?"

Will nodded a silent acknowledgement as he chewed. My patience was wearing thin. I served my own plate, and said, "Will, what's wrong? You've hardly said anything since you arrived. Are you upset with me?" My confidence was waning.

"No, I'm not upset with you, Blanche. I'm tired."

"You may be tired, but there is something else. You're always like this when something's wrong. You turn to a pillar of salt."

Will's face morphed into a blank stare. I'd struck a nerve. But at that moment, I didn't care. He had ruined my preparations for a celebratory evening and I had no idea why. He had locked me out...again.

"Blanche, I have a lot on my mind. That's all." Will's tone grew impatient.

"Like what? Can't you talk to your wife? What is it?" I kept probing, knowing each new question riled him further.

"It's not your bother," he mumbled. "It's business—not something you need to fret over."

"If it's bothering you and affects us, then it *is* my bother. Tell me." Will ignored my pleading.

"It's not something I want to talk about right now. Don't you understand? Just let it go. I'm home, aren't I? What else do you want?" His eyes had grown large and round, his voice louder with each sentence, and his tone biting.

Before I knew it, words were spewing from my mouth. "Yes, you are home, but sometimes it's more peaceful when you're not." He had hurt my feelings and I struck back. "I'm alone here weeks at a time, while you're off tending to your other family's business. I'm the one keeping this household running while you're gone—chopping wood if we run low, seeing to things that break, feeding the horses, hauling water! And you don't even notice when you do come home! Why, I spent the whole day preparing this spread for you. Might as well have put a bowl of oatmeal in front of you. Should have!"

A dam had broken inside me and I couldn't stop the raging flood. I pushed my chair back and slammed my fork to the table. I stood up, putting both hands on my hips. Will had not tried to interrupt my tirade, but his face was red and his fists clenched, knuckle-white on his lap.

"Taking care of my 'other family' *is* taking care of us, Blanche," he said in a controlled voice, looking up at me. "What happens there helps us…or hurts us. Don't you understand? Success there means success here, but the opposite is also true."

Somewhere deep inside, I knew he was right. But Will's moodiness was difficult and I couldn't get past the fact that I was feeling neglected on the very night I would share that we were to become parents. Instead, I succumbed to my roiling emotions.

"I slaved over that stove for hours, William Day. I wanted to give you a homecoming you'd not forget." By then, I was sobbing, my words garbled. "Romantic candlelight, the pleasure of your company and warmth of our touch. But, no, I get silence and vacant stares. Would my informing you that you're going to be a father get your attention?"

The announcement was out of my mouth before I could reel it back. This wasn't what I'd envisioned, and this realization only made matters worse. I stomped from the kitchen through the parlor and out the front door, slamming it behind me. With no idea where I was going, escape was all I had on my mind. Sobbing uncontrollably, I realized that a neighbor might happen along as I headed up the road. It wasn't dark yet. Wiping at the stream of tears, I looked down to hide my face and emotions. I glanced over my shoulder to see if Will had followed. The road was empty. Whimpering, I walked on. It was thirty minutes before I reached the cemetery gate that was always unlocked. I found my way to Mama's headstone and slumped to the ground.

"Mama, what am I going to do?" I cried in the stillness, patting the chiseled ebony stone. "What have I done? How can I make everything right?" My body trembled as tears dripped to the grass. I was alone.

Eventually I quieted myself, finding solace near Mama. I heard the occasional call of cows as they grazed in the peace of the countryside. Darkness slowly gathered and when I could no longer ignore its advance, I stood up and kissed the granite marker before turning to drift in the direction of home. I did not know what to expect when I arrived. This was Will's and my first serious quarrel.

It was a starless night when I opened the picket fence gate and stepped along the flat rocks leading to the house. From the lamplight shining through the windows, I could make out Will's form sitting on the porch. I took a deep breath.

"It's a mild evening, Mrs. Day. Won't you come sit?" His voice was even and conciliatory as he patted the seat of the rocker next to him.

I joined him, but my anxiety was evident.

There was an early chorus of cicadas. We rocked and listened. Finally, Will calmly asked, "Where did you go?"

"To Mama...to her grave."

Silence returned and our rocking was like a lullaby that calmed my nerves.

"Blanche, I'm sorry I spoiled the evening. I had no idea it was a special occasion. My mind was on my own worries."

Will paused, but I offered no response. He went on.

"Three days ago Father got word that a large swath of our timber acreage is in jeopardy. Seems a beetle infestation is destroying many acres. If it goes unchecked, we could lose productivity. And that spells trouble. Cash flow is dependent on our timber sales and that's what keeps our grocery stores open without having to assume greater indebtedness to the banks."

I rocked as I listened. Then I asked, "What does that mean for you and me, for our family?" I didn't intend to pick up on my earlier theme of contention, but I didn't fully understand Will.

"What it means is that I will have no money to replenish the inventory at our mercantile store, nor funds to repay the bank in Spring City for the loans on my capital expansion of the store. The only collateral I have is this house."

"Does that mean we could lose our home?"

"No, it means I might have to borrow against its value in order to keep our shelves stocked, something I'd rather not do. It would further increase our indebtedness. Father and Uncle Winston's dilemmas are actually greater than ours. The timber business is the foundation of Father's wealth. It's a serious situation, Blanche."

"I see."

Silence returned. Was he going to say anything about our baby? Then I felt his touch. He reached across and put his hand on mine as it lay on the chair arm. He gently squeezed it. We looked at one another through the darkness and he lifted my hand to his lips. "I am the proudest man in Rhea Springs. When is our baby arriving?"

"In October sometime, the doctor said." A tear slipped to my cheek. Will reached over, tenderly brushing it aside and leaned in to kiss me.

He slid his rocker closer. Quiet conversation continued for what seemed hours. His hand never left mine. The moon inched across the blue darkness. The crickets and cicadas continued their chorus. When I began to yawn, Will squeezed my hand and suggested we turn in. A knowing smile passed between us. As we started inside, I said to Will, "I'm getting a glass of water first. The doctor said I should drink more." Will lowered the wick of the oil lamp in the parlor and headed to the bedroom. But then my loud scream brought him running to the kitchen.

"What's wrong? What is it?" His blanched face matched mine. I clutched at him, seeking protection and pointed across the dark room to a figure huddled in the corner.

"Over there, over there," I cried, pointing next to the stove.

Only then did Will begin to laugh. "Oh, I forgot." He started to step away from me, but I clung to him.

"Where are you going? Don't leave me," I said, totally confused.

"Just let me get the lamp out of the bedroom. It's all right; it won't hurt you." He quickly ducked around the corner and returned with the glowing lamp. It illuminated the kitchen, bringing everything out of the shadows. In the corner of the room between the stove and the wall was an oblong, slipper-shaped copper bathtub. About four or five feet in length and a couple of feet across and hip height, it completely filled the corner area.

Will set the lamp on the table. Clutching his sides, he began apologizing, or at least tried amidst his convulsive laughter. Relieved the intruder was not a man, I didn't know what to think—or whether to be angry that my husband was laughing.

"It's for us, Blanche," Will said, composing himself.

"How did it get here?" I asked, still dumbfounded.

"By train—from Kentucky. I brought it with me. The crate, remember?"

Then I did.

"When you raced out of the house earlier, I paced around outside trying to decide whether to go after you or just let you be. Then I noticed the wagon and team still tied up and decided to drive over to the stable to get some help. That boy, Charlie, was ready to leave for home, so I asked him to ride back here and help me uncrate the tub." Will chuckled, and added, "You should have seen his face when we unpacked it. He had no idea what it was until I explained. Probably thought it was a glorified water trough. I tossed him a dime for his time and muscle. Well, what do you think? Do you know what it is?"

"Of course, I know what it is," I said, still in disbelief. One was housed at Mother Day's home in Kentucky, and I had bathed in it when we visited over the holidays. The Days had even designated a special room in their large home just for its use.

"Given that the two of us are soon going to be three, I think my timing was serendipitous, no?" Will kissed my head as he stood behind me and we admired the copper vessel. "I absolutely forgot about it after Charlie left," he continued. "I decided to sit on the porch to wait for you. I was about to set out searching when you appeared out of the dark. I was so relieved that I forgot about the tub."

Will turned me to face him and looked into my eyes the way he did when we were courting. He kissed me, this time with passion. Holding my hand, he led us to our bed and I nestled in. Turning down the lamp's wick, he pulled me close. The better part of the day had been a nightmare. The only thing I wanted to remember was the sound of his voice saying, "I am the proudest man in Rhea Springs."

CHAPTER 23

CHARLIE

The year without Ida Mae had turned me into a different man. At first, I was filled with fury at Elijah Jenkins. Good thing for him I give up on churchgoing. Might've killed him if I got my hands on his scrawny neck. For certain, my hurt turned me sour on the Hickeys. How could they let Ida Mae go back where she was so miserable? I figured Mister Hickey was tired of young bucks like me circling his house ever Sunday and wanted some peace and quiet. When the flames of my anger died down, I turned inside myself. Mister Waterhouse thought his hired help had gone deaf and dumb. I'd go days without a word except "yes-sir" or "no-sir." Even Missus Blanche, who I didn't see often since she'd married, noticed my moping around. She'd asked Ma if I was sickly. Ma, on the other hand, busied herself scheming with Aunt America on ways to interest me in this girl or that. Their heart was in the right place, but if I wanted a gal, I could do that myself, thank you.

I just wanted to be left alone and stayed away from the house as much as I could. Down on the Piney at my fishing spot, I could think about whatever, and nobody bothered me. Pa was the only one who seemed to understand and wasn't a burr under my saddle. With a cane fishing pole in hand and a jar of worms in the other, he'd find me on Sunday afternoons after he and Ma got home from church.

We'd sit together with them poles stretched out over the lazy green water not saying a word. It helped.

I kept waiting to hear from Ida Mae. But after so many months, I gave up. Anyhow, she didn't know her letters that good. When the truth of it soaked in, I brooded more and thought some pretty unchristian things about that gal. Sometimes it spilled over on the folks around me.

"No, Mister Waterhouse, I don't wanna go with you. I've got five more stalls to muck before I leave out this evening, and you wanted those sorrel horses brushed and groomed." Searching for any excuse, I leaned on the pitchfork handle in the middle of the empty stall facing down my boss, his hard muscular frame filling the doorway in front of me.

He ignored my excuses and went on talking that he'd had an unexpected visit from Doctor Wasson earlier that morning while I was away from the stable on an errand. The doctor asked him to take a look at an ailing horse south of town. The owner, a preacher—name of Owens—needed his buggy to make calls on church members. Seemed the preacher was crippled years back in a farming accident and can't saddle ride no more. A horse-drawn buggy is his only transportation now.

The preacher and Doctor Wasson had been at the barbershop the day before; and from the barber's chair, the preacher worried aloud over his lame horse. When Doctor Wasson overheard, he offered up his stableman on the spot saying he could work miracles on horseflesh. The preacher reportedly had chuckled and said he was a man who believed in miracles.

Doctor Wasson's bragging on my boss man was nice and all, but I had no interest tagging along. Mister Waterhouse had barked back that he didn't know what he was gonna find and needed me to help steady the animal. I figured there were other reasons.

"Charlie, if you wants to do more than muck stalls, you better let me learn you a few things. Doctoring horses can bring you favor with folks around the county." He hushed and stared at me, like Pa did when he was twisting my arm.

I turned my eyes to the muddy floor to escape his stare. But it was no use, I knew, so I surrendered. "Let's go."

With a smug grin, Mister Waterhouse ordered me to grab the brown gunnysack of medicines out of the tack room whilst he gathered a few tools. We harnessed the sorrel horse to the buckboard, threw the things in the back, and headed south on Muddy Creek Road.

Didn't take long to reach the lone gray-framed house tucked alongside a church house, outside town. Out in a field on the opposite side of the road was the only other building around—a leaning, weather worn barn and across one side were big black painted letters, "Muddy Creek Saloon."

"Lookee there, Mister Waterhouse," I said, pointing. "Just a skip and a jump from the Baptist church and the preacher's house. It's a saloon. Sticks out like an ugly wart, don't it?"

"What'a you know," he mumbled, all the while scouting out the small house with covered porch and mess of cats lazing on its steps. "But it's not a place for the likes of you and me," he added, paying little mind to what stirred my curiosity. "Remember, we's here to see about an ailing animal." Handing me the reins, he climbed down. "Wait here while I round up the preacher."

Past the cats that skittered in all directions, Mister Waterhouse walked to the door and knocked. No one answered. Hollering to me he was going around back to rustle up someone, he disappeared and I settled in. Setting my sights on the barn, I thought about my frequenting that Chattanooga saloon in Negro town. Bet this place didn't have no purty women singing the blues. Then I heard laughing. Didn't white fellers have work to tend to? Two ambled out an open door, each with an arm over the other's shoulder, steadying each other. On a bender in the middle of a day, mid-week? About my age, both had yeller hair, one sporting a scraggly beard the same color. Then I remembered.

The creaking of a door opening up came from the direction of the house. Mister Waterhouse was nowhere to be seen, but a redheaded young feller had come out on the porch, his hand shading his eyes from the glare so he could see me.

"We's from the hotel stable," I answered his silent question. "My boss is looking for Preacher Owens. He walked around back. Is this the right place?"

"Who sent you?" the redhead asked while pulling his suspenders up over his shoulders like he'd just woke up.

"Doctor Wasson, the hotel owner," I said. "You the preacher?"

"No. That's my pa."

"You have a lame horse, right? We was sent to take a look."

About then Waterhouse and a short man with a bad leg rounded the side of the house. "Charlie, bring me that sack," Waterhouse called. "And the tools, too."

With the gunnysack of tools in hand, I followed the two men, watching the white man struggle to walk. Pale and slightly stooped, he didn't come shoulder-high to Mister Waterhouse. Even in his bibbed coveralls, I could tell the muscle in one leg was shriveled. Without that walking stick he leaned on, he couldn't get around.

Inside a shed behind the house was a muddy-colored horse, and I about gagged when we peered in. The place stunk to high heaven. I didn't say nothing. Neither did Waterhouse or the preacher, who explained the mare had started limping a week earlier.

Waterhouse looked around the stall before unlatching its half-door. "Let's get her out of here for a closer look," he said, frowning. About that time, the preacher's son walked up.

Mister Waterhouse led the mare outside to a fence post and I tied her off. He commenced to inspect all the horse's hooves. Then he said to me, "Charlie, hand me the hoof knife."

He lifted each leg again and cleaned the manure from the grooves of the sole and from around the iron shoes. When he got to the back right hoof, he motioned me over. "Come here. See this black jelly-like goo?"

"Yessir."

"That's not manure; that's thrush."

Then he looked up at the two men and said, "What you's smelling is thrush."

Waterhouse trimmed away the black gunk with the knife. "Thrush ain't too bad," he said to the two. "We'll clean it out good and pour some iodine in. But you're gonna have the problem again if you don't keep that stall clean. Looks like she's spending a lot of time standing in her own mess."

The preacher turned to his son with a scowl. "This is your fault, Daniel. If you'd kept that stall cleaned out—like the man says—we wouldn't have this problem."

I could see clear that Daniel didn't like his pa taking him down a notch in front of strangers, especially us. His pale face turned apple red. "If you'd let the horse out to pasture more..."

Before the son could finish, his father butted in, "And who's gonna fetch her when I need to make church calls? Not you."

They was going at each other like nobody was around.

"I'm home when I'm not working," Daniel protested. "I can't round up your horse from the pasture if I'm at work? Remember, you's the one that demanded I get a job or get out." He turned on his heels and walked off, but not before announcing, "And now I've got one."

Their feuding left me uneasy. It did Waterhouse as well, because he immediately told the preacher we had to get back, that no one was tending the stable while we was gone.

"His ma died when he was eleven," the preacher apologized, like he owed an explanation. "His anger at the Good Lord led him down some crooked paths. Got mixed up with some no account boys." The father sighed and shifted his weight, as he leaned on his stick. "But he's got hisself a job now working for the railroad, keeping him out of trouble, I hope."

He stopped short, like he realized he'd rambled on with strangers—colored ones—about his personal business. He changed the subject. "What do I owe you, Waterhouse? That's your name, right?"

"Yessir. Sam Waterhouse. You don't owe me nothing. We work for the Wassons."

After the preacher said he'd settle up later with the kind doctor, we took our leave. Out of earshot, I chuckled and said, "Well, you set them white men straight, didn't you? Barking at them that they didn't know how to care for their horse. Didn't you wonder how they'd react...with you talking so direct?"

"The man listened because Doctor Wasson vouched for my know-how. He was respecting the doc, not me—a Negro."

"I guess you're right. By the way, that red-headed son? He was one of the scrappers who beat me up years back, remember? And I think I spotted the other two staggering out of that saloon across the way."

"Could'a been," Waterhouse said.

"You know, those boys would have kicked in my ribs if that preacher's son hadn't called them off. He actually saved my hide."

"Must be some good in him then," Waterhouse mused.

"Good thing for me," I said, spitting off the side of the wagon as the stable appeared in the distance.

***

The weeks dragged on and my dark mood trailed me like a long shadow the noonday sun couldn't chase away. Mister Waterhouse must've taken pity on me or was just tired of my dragging around with a long face.

"Charlie, I want you to wear your Sunday duds to work tomorrow," he called down the hall to the stall where I was shoveling. When he got to me, the look on my face brought a doubled-over laugh from him. Didn't see that often.

Standing in manure and splattered with it up to my knees, I said, "If I wear my Sunday trousers, Ma will skin me alive, and it won't matter I'm a grown man and she's half my size."

"No, no," he said, chuckling. "You won't be mucking stalls or grooming horses. While you was out eating lunch earlier, Mister Wasson dropped by. Said his man who hauls luggage from the train station to the hotel is ailing. He wants you to drive the wagon tomorrow."

My first thought was to resist, but then I thought the better of it. Maybe Waterhouse and Pa and Mister Wasson had been scheming to buck up my spirits. And maybe it'd be good to get away from here, even if I had to bathe and wear Sunday clothes. So I said, "Yessir. Do I report to Mister Wasson?"

"No. Come here in the morning and we'll harness the team. Mister Owen will stop by as he heads to Spring City with his surrey. He has the list of arriving folks and train schedule. You can work on the leather tack while you wait for him. That won't dirty up your clothes."

Mister Waterhouse turned to leave, hesitated and said without looking my way, "And if you want, bring in those newspapers Mister Wasson gives you. I know you like to read them when you get the chance."

I smiled to myself. Mister Waterhouse had figured out years back that I had mastered my letters. He'd tease that my reading them city newspapers was nosing into a white man's world. But I think he was proud of me anyhow, even if he still signed his name with an "X".

The next afternoon when Mister Owen had slowed up at the stable for the third time and hollered my name, it was four o'clock. A train was coming in shortly from Chattanooga with a passel of folks headed to the hotel. Two families, he said. Laying aside the harness I was polishing, I climbed onto my wagon and followed the surrey.

Turning off Muddy Creek Road onto Old Stage Road, I loosened the reins in my hands, closed my eyes and lifted my face heavenward. The sun warmed my skin and the breeze felt fresh and clean. No smell of manure in my nose. It had been a good day, and the corners of my mouth turned up. I hadn't done much smiling in quite a spell.

When we reached the station, Mister Owen pulled his surrey to the usual place and tied the horses so he was free to welcome guests when they stepped from the train. I drove my buckboard to the other end of the station platform where railroad workers unloaded travel trunks from the baggage car. When the train pulled in and the snake of iron boxes came to a standstill, I climbed down and tied off the team. The men in blue uniforms were already swarming the last car like ants to carry out luggage that would quickly litter the platform. The train would head north again in minutes, as soon as travelers and belongings were safely off.

I moved among the trunks, searching out the travel tags reading, "Destination: Rhea Springs Hotel." It being my third trip of the day, the men in blue paid me little mind. I shortly found six large leather trunks marked for the hotel. As I shoved and pulled each to the side, I caught a glimpse of a dark-skinned woman out of the corner of my eye stepping out of the baggage car, directly behind a uniformed man. Colored folk coming off a train was rare. Not many could afford a ticket, but those that did were squeezed into the baggage car at the rear of the train. The woman was alone. Wearing a brown scarf over her head and holding a hand above her eyes to shield the sun's glare, she carried a single tote sack lumpy with belongings. Didn't appear to be anybody I knowed, but I couldn't see much of the face. Her dress was a purty yeller one, like what Ida Mae used to wear on Sundays.

The woman dropped her hand from her eyes and looked to pick her way around the luggage. When she caught sight of me, she stopped and gathered herself to her full height, like she'd turned to a statue. Then I knew, it *was* Ida Mae!

In a flash, every mean thing thought about her evaporated. Dropping the trunk I was dragging, I stared at the tall, slim figure and then walked toward her. Her face was smudged with soot from the train travel and her neck and brow was wet with heat, but her beauty showed through just as she had in my dreams. Standing dumb before her, I finally got out the words, "Ma'am, may I help you with your bag?" Her solemn, questioning face melted into a smile and she handed me her sack.

With the wagon stacked high with trunks and Ida Mae nestled close, her story spilled out as we headed toward the hotel. She had not wanted to leave the feller she had growed to love—me, but she had returned home to Alabama with hope that her and her ma could heal the hurt between them. But those hopes were soon dashed. The man her ma married resented her presence—saying she came between them as a newly wedded couple—and made trouble from the start.

Ida Mae said she landed a house job right off in Scottsboro and started saving ever penny she earned, socking it away under a loose board in the floor at the house of the man she grew to hate. Vowing to return to Rhea Springs was what kept her going, she said. When she finally saved the price of a ticket from Chattanooga to Spring City, she begged a ride with a neighboring sharecropping couple that carried their produce by wagon weekly to Chattanooga. She left out before dawn one morning without a word to her employer or her ma. Even the Hickeys had no idea of her planned return. By the time Ida Mae finished her tale, tears were slipping down her smudged cheeks. Her return had turned my world right side up again, and I determined right then I'd do the same for her. And it gave me great pleasure to start by brushing away the tears from her cheeks.

After work that evening, Ida Mae sat proud between Pa and me on our wagon as we traveled back to the Bend. When she walked through the door behind Pa, my ma was as surprised as I was at the train station.

"Land o' Goshen!" she exclaimed, and gave Ida Mae a welcoming hug.

Ruby scurried to put another tin plate on the table and by the time the last bite of cornbread was gone, we was all talking and laughing like Ida Mae was already family. Afterward, Ruby and Ida

Mae washed the plates while Ma walked up the road to Grandma Sulley's to ask a favor.

Grandma said she'd let Ida Mae stay at her place until she got settled into a job and could pay her way. Her one condition was that the gal help with the babies until then.

Next morning Pa questioned Mister Wasson whether there might be need for another hotel maid, now that the busy season had commenced. Within a week, Ida Mae was no longer tending babies, but changing bed linens and tidying rooms at the hotel, doing just what she'd become skillful at while working at the white household in Scottsboro. She folded and tucked sheets and left them beds looking like wrapped gifts. And Grandma Sulley appeared happy to have the company of a young woman at her supper table.

Now, when the four of us take the wagon into Rhea Springs each morning, the chickens are roused not by rattling lunch tins but by the talk and laughter of me and Ida Mae.

CHAPTER 24

BLANCHE

So heavy with child that my wool coat bulged and strained at its pearl buttons, I struggled to climb the narrow steps of the northbound train. Once Will and I settled into our seats, the train lurched and then crawled from the station in the direction of Winchester, Kentucky where I would receive the care of the Day family doctors. With no female family member in Rhea Springs and considering my delicate condition, Mother Day had determined that coming to them was the only reasonable course of action. So bewildered by the imminent prospect of childbirth, I was persuaded. Will thought it a fine idea and took comfort that I would be under his mother's watchful eye if he were traveling. Even Papa agreed with the wisdom of my in-laws.

Margaret Catherine Day was born October 26, 1912 with no complications. With the holidays approaching and wanting to convalesce in place, we stayed on for another Thanksgiving around the Day family table. To Will's delight, Margaret's first Christmas was celebrated in the Victorian home, surrounded by her Kentucky grandparents who spared no extravagance.

In early December, the help marched into the house with armfuls of winter greenery—pinecones the size of small melons, red-berried holly and Southern magnolia cuttings—to dress every fireplace mantel and tabletop. Evergreen roping wound the stair banisters and a twenty-foot fir tree, cut from one of the Days' timber forests, held a place of honor in the grand mahogany parlor. Dressed with gold and ruby red glass ornaments the size of oranges, the proud tree was lit by electric lights and filled the home with holiday fragrance.

Margaret Catherine was too young to appreciate it all but her doting grandparents nevertheless showered their first grandchild with extravagant gifts on Christmas morning, including a gaily-painted pink rocking horse that would make the trip back to Rhea Springs.

***

With the advent of 1913 and Margaret Catherine edging toward two months, I yearned to return home and was as excited as that fourteen-year-old schoolgirl leaving boarding school when the day arrived. Will did not share my enthusiasm and reminded me that I had had every accommodation in caring for Margaret since her birth and in going home it would now fall on my shoulders. He was right, but I was up to the task.

Our daughter managed her first train ride with flying colors, snug in my arms and wearing the buttercup yellow sweater and booties Gay had knitted and mailed from Arizona. When our train slowed into the Spring City station, Margaret roused from sleep, stretching her tiny arms above her head, already foreshadowing blonde hair. With the squeal of the train's braking wheels, her green eyes opened wide but she did not whimper.

Will strutted like a rooster as he shepherded us from the train and then offered a grand introduction of the first Wasson grandchild to Papa and Grandfather who waited on the platform. As we all departed the station, Papa insisted we join him and Grandfather for supper. Exhausted from our travels, I wanted only my bed in my own home and cringed at the invitation. But Papa promised that a surprise awaited us.

The music of Beethoven greeted us when we stepped into Papa's house. I smiled. Bertie must have been taught how to operate the gramophone. With that and the savory aromas wafting from the kitchen, I immediately felt better about accepting Papa's invitation. No doubt Will would be a happier husband pulling up to a table teeming with steaming food and drink rather than returning to our dark, cold house with empty cupboards. Even Margaret, after a meal of her own, contentedly slept on my childhood bed upstairs, pillows piled around her like fortress walls.

After a sumptuous meal and spirited conversation, Will spoke in oratory fashion as Bertie passed through the dining room, "Bertie, you've outdone yourself as usual." Like a conquering king, he pushed his chair back from the table still littered with half-empty china bowls. Papa and Grandfather grunted their agreement in unison, and we all laughed.

Bertie returned to the table with a silver-serving tray laden with pecan pie slices, each topped with a mound of fresh whipped cream. She ceremoniously placed a dessert plate before each of us. "I's saved the best 'til last, Mister Day."

"Bertie, you are one in a million," Will said before taking his first bite. There was no argument that in Rhea Springs there was no finer cook than Bertie Reynolds, even better than those who manned the hotel kitchen.

After Bertie emptied the dessert tray, Papa asked her to remain, so she took a step back and waited. Looking across the table at Will, Papa cleared his throat and said, "Now that you are a family man— not only a husband, but a new father as well—I'd like to present a gift fitting for a growing family." Papa cast a quick smile in my direction and turned his attention back to Will. I looked to Grandfather, who shrugged his shoulders in innocence.

"Chapman? A gift?" Will inquired, glancing at me and back to Papa.

"After you whisked away my youngest daughter," Papa began, winking at me, "And Owen left for college and with Gay in Arizona, poor Bertie has been somewhat idle around here—probably a bit bored." Papa cast an eye toward Bertie and proceeded. "I reckon I'm not as messy as the rest of you," he added, gesturing toward me. "So I've talked it over with Bertie, and she's agreeable…to spending some of her workdays at the Day household and a few here, keeping me straight."

Did I hear Papa correctly? I gasped, putting my hand to my mouth and looking to Will. His face was void of expression. After a long pause, he said to Papa, "That is generous, Chapman, mighty generous." Then Will's face softened. "Business does take me away more than I'd like…and Blanche is going to need some help now with Margaret and all…" He glanced at me and, I'm sure, saw my anticipation. Will turned in his seat to face Bertie. "What do you think of this arrangement?"

"Mister Day, I's watched Miss Blanche grow from a sprout in coveralls chasing after her ponies to a fine growed-up lady. I credit my good cooking over the years for some of that." Bertie smiled, showing off the space between her front teeth, and then pronounced, "I'd be proud to help out you folks. Tending to that beautiful baby would be a blessing."

When Will turned back to see me grinning, he looked to Papa and said, "What a welcome home gift!"

"Thank you, Papa—thank you so much." I jumped from my chair and ran to hug Papa and then Bertie.

"She'll be at your door first thing tomorrow?" Papa asked, looking first at me and then at Bertie.

***

No surprise, Bertie Reynolds quickly became indispensable to the Day household. With a pile of soiled diapers to greet her each day, an often-colicky Margaret to soothe, and meals to plan and prepare, she was like the arrival of a life raft to rescue me from raging waters. Hurrying through the backdoor shortly after sunup and Will's departure for work, she would take charge and her calm presence would reign as she managed the day. By the time my husband walked through the front door at dusk, Bertie was gone but our dinner table was set and a hearty meal waited on the stove, ready to be served. I would greet Will, holding his daughter who was always dressed in a fresh baby frock and smelling of sweet talcum powder. With wisps of curly blonde hair and sparkling eyes, little Margaret welcomed him with smiles and coos. Will knew nothing of the chaos before the calm, and I endeavored to keep it that way. I received the credit, but Bertie and I knew the truth.

During Will's long absences, Bertie's presence filled a void in other ways too. In our extended time together, she demonstrated in the most inoffensive manner how to soothe a fretful baby, remove ink stains from Will's white shirts or build a fire in the cook stove that would not smoke. I learned the secret of rolling the flakiest pie dough, though it never lived up to Bertie's perfection.

***

In February, Papa traveled to Arizona to find Gay's health greatly diminished. He did not return when planned. His telegraph message was ominous: "Staying until Gay shows improvement." However busy my days, my sister never left my thoughts and prayers.

On a cold, dreary March afternoon, Sam brought Will home from the train station after another extended absence. Greeting Will at the door with Margaret in my arms, I waved to Sam as he turned the horses, their nostrils flaring vapor in the winter air, to head the surrey back to the hotel stable. Margaret cooed in delight at the sight of her father and I was relieved to have him home.

Holding his satchel in one hand and a wadded paper in the other, Will's face looked pale and strained. "What is it, Will? Are you ill?" I inquired, my cheerful expression fading. Will shook his head 'no,' giving me a quick kiss on the forehead—and then Margaret—as we stepped into the house and closed the door to the cold.

"Come sit down," he said, motioning me to the sofa and the warmth of the crackling fire.

I complied, with growing apprehension. I passed Margaret into his arms, as he handed me a wrinkled telegram.

"This was given to me at the train station," he said. "It had just come off the telegraph. I'm so sorry, Blanche."

Addressed to me, I read it aloud, "Our dear Gay has succumbed to tuberculosis. Accompanying her body home for burial." The words on the paper blurred through my tears and my husband's voiced condolences faded into a black hole of grief. Bertie, who remained in the kitchen but had overheard, gasped in disbelief and her muted sobs were background to mine.

***

Owen trained home from school, Grandfather distracted himself with hotel repairs that had waited for the winter months, and Will postponed his business travels as we awaited Papa's return.

In burying my sister, I relived my worst nightmare. As with Mama, the Methodist church teemed with those wanting to show compassion and support. But Gay was my only sister. Nothing could fill the expanding hole in my soul. Pealing bells again alerted the countryside of the loss; but they would fall silent and people would go back to their lives. Mine would be forever changed. Our preacher read the same scriptures meant to comfort, and there was the long procession to the cemetery on the hill and final goodbyes. Again, Uncle Jack and Aunt Cinnie, Aunt Marian and Uncle Bill and my cousins all wore the same heavy garments of grief. Traveling from

Kentucky, Will's mother and father stood with us, sharing in our sorrow. We laid my sister to rest not far from Mama.

Margaret Catherine was oblivious to what life had wrought on the Wasson family. Just a baby, her needs demanded the same attention and care, but I resented the intrusions into my grief. Thank goodness for Bertie. Despite her own sadness, she took the baby from my arms and soothed her, changed her, and brought her to my bosom whenever it was time. My heart ached and nothing eased it, not even Margaret Catherine's sweet smiles.

***

April arrived, coaxing yellow tulips along our picket fence and greening fields everywhere, painting over the gray of winter. Margaret Catherine was sitting up now and giggled with delight to bang pots and wooden spoons on the kitchen floor at Bertie's feet whenever she cooked. Most days I walked the distance to the cemetery and lingered for hours, leaving Margaret in Bertie's care. At night I cried into my pillow and Will's comfort bore little effect. I rebelled at the thought of food and ate like a bird. It wasn't until the vomiting started that Will insisted I visit our Rhea Springs doctor. His findings complicated life even more. I was going to have another baby.

Neither of us celebrated what should have been a happy surprise. Will found escape in his work, and I dealt with the gradual changes in my body without much joy.

***

"Bertie, is that you?" I called from the bedroom, hearing the familiar squeak of the kitchen door as it opened. It was about time. Bertie was coming in later and later.

"Yes, Missus Blanche, it's me. Where's Little Miss Margaret this morning?"

Sitting on the bedside with my head hanging over a bucket, I could tell from her voice she was at the bedroom door. I blindly pointed to Margaret playing with my hairbrush and combs nearby. "Can you see to her? I'm sick again—breakfast came right up." I raised my head to see my daughter outstretch her little arms to Bertie.

"Are you late again this morning?" I asked, the question echoing from the bucket where my face had returned.

"No, ma'am, I's not late. The sun's just come up not more than thirty minutes ago."

Bertie's tone was defensive and a bit resentful, but there was disappointment also. I had accused her—as she saw it—falsely. "I need you here promptly every morning, especially when Mr. Day is traveling. Mornings are my worst time. You know that."

"Yes, Missus Blanche, I knows."

Bertie picked up Margaret and carried her to the kitchen without another word. Along with the clatter of dishes she was clearing from the table, she began humming "His Eye Is on the Sparrow."

"Would you mind not singing," I complained loudly, as I lay back on the bed, eyes closed, waiting for the nausea to pass.

"Yessum," Bertie called back, and the humming stopped.

I dozed off and awoke an hour later, feeling better. Surely these dreadful mornings would soon pass. Three months along, they should.

The house was quiet. After dressing, I ventured into the kitchen and heard Margaret outside the screen door squealing with delight. She was playing with the wooden clothespins beside the basket of wash Bertie was hanging on the line. The sun was cheerful and warm. Margaret's giggles brought an unexpected smile. Maybe a new baby coming will be a good thing, if she is as good-natured as our firstborn. But it dawned on me once more—as it did almost every day—that Mama and Gay would never hear their laughter, and my smile faded.

"Bertie, I'm leaving for the cemetery," I called through the screen. "I'll be home at lunchtime to nurse Margaret."

"Yes, ma'am," Bertie answered, as she picked up another sheet from the basket and tickled Margaret under her chin.

"Don't let her get into that wet laundry. All we need is a sick baby and a sick mama too."

"No, ma'am, I'll keep a close eye."

***

By mid-September, I had determined I would not leave Rhea Springs when my time came.

"I've made up my mind, Will. I'm staying right here in Rhea Springs," I announced, as we settled into the rockers on the porch, awaiting the night sky to unveil its splendor. A fall chill required our wearing wraps—a knit shawl snugly around my shoulders and covering my large girth, Will in his favorite navy cardigan. Margaret was fast asleep in her crib indoors.

"Don't you think you are taking unnecessary risks, Blanche?" he questioned.

"No, I don't. My doctor here is just as good as your family's costly specialists. I had no trouble birthing Margaret, did I?"

"But we don't know that will be the case with this one."

"Will, I'd appreciate your not patronizing me. Things could go differently, but the doctor says all looks fine. If you want to know what would calm my nerves, it would be your staying closer to home over these next months. There's already much I can't do around here because of my size. With my time nearing, I want you close, not two hundred miles away in a timber forest."

Will was silent, the only response his creaking rocker. "Well?" I pressed.

Without turning his gaze from the night sky, he said, "I'll do my best. It's not as easy as you might think. Discussions of a merger are underway now with a big grocery owner and Father is depending on me to be his eyes and ears when he can't be in two places at once."

I had heard that talk before, and frustrated outbursts insisting I was more important than his family's businesses had accomplished little. What hurt the worst was the sense that my husband felt far more passion for that part of his life than for me. Will said nothing else. The air grew rife with tension. The creaking of the rockers and the steely silence between us was deafening. When I could bear it no longer, I wiped the tear that had slipped down my cheek and went inside to check on Margaret and prepare for bed. I felt more alone at that moment than when Will was hundreds of miles away.

Over the next weeks, Will's travels tapered, but his mood darkened. When in Rhea Springs, he spent inordinate time at the mercantile store, claiming that Mr. Cobb needed help checking in merchandise or some such excuse. When around the house, he busied himself with whatever chores needed attention—splitting wood or sharpening tools out in the shed—anything to put distance between us. The only time I saw his countenance lighten was when he was bouncing Margaret on his knee or reading her a story as she lay playing with her bare feet on the rug beside him and giggling at his animated tales of Goldilocks.

***

On November 20, 1913 our second baby girl announced her arrival with lusty howls and red face. Will and I named her Gay

Wasson Day, in memory of my sister and to carry on my family name. Will was completely agreeable to honoring Gay, but he would have preferred a different middle name. I was adamant that too many Wassons had left this green earth and that the name must be carried on. Will relented.

The wiggling bundle was a mystery to her year-old sister. Having just learned to walk, Margaret would toddle to Little Gay's crib and stand as tall as she could, holding onto the rim. She peered over the edge with delighted eyes to watch the baby with the shock of dark hair and dark eyes that worked diligently to kick loose her swaddling blanket. Margaret would squeal and jabber on and on without an understandable word, only to go silent as if waiting for her sister to answer.

In the year following Gay's arrival, Will returned to his old self. His business travels resumed in earnest, but he seemed happy to come home to his girls. As for me, I was so busy with the demands of two children that I didn't have the time or energy to nurse the grief of losing two loved ones. The emotional hurt that Will had inflicted during those months of pregnancy, and my vitriol in return, was ignored but not forgotten by either of us. Life didn't allow for more than facing the day's demands. We were a busy family of four.

Thank goodness Bertie arrived daily, shortly after first light. I needed her more than ever. And the knock at the door from Papa and Grandfather at four thirty many afternoons when Will was out of town was also more than welcome.

"Papa, Grandfather, come in, come in. The girls will be up from their naps shortly." That was a fact because the men's voices, while unintentionally loud, were sure to rouse the little ones.

"Do I hear them, now?" Grandfather would put his arthritic hand to his ear in mock surprise.

"I believe so," I would say and then suggest they go into the girls' room.

An hour's play with doting elders was an hour's distraction, so I could retrieve clean sheets and towels from the clothesline and Bertie could finish the meal preparation without children under foot. By six o'clock, the house was filled with delicious aromas, and I would invite Papa and Grandfather to join the girls and me at the table. They would give each other a quick glance and agree in unison like a well-rehearsed play. An opportunity to enjoy Bertie's cooking was not to be passed up and it afforded an extended romp on the floor with the girls and time for Margaret to ride her pink rocking horse like it was a wild stallion.

CHAPTER 25

CHARLIE

After another Sunday supper with Ida Mae at our table and the dishes washed up, Ma had grabbed a bucket before herding Ruby and Ida Mae out the door and up the road to Grandma Sulley's. She called over her shoulder that they'd be picking some figs off the bushes behind Grandma's place and would be home later. With the place to ourselves, Pa had brought out his fiddle and we had settled on the wood steps to watch the sun play hide-and-seek behind the stand of trees beyond the field. Pa had pulled the bow across the strings, but then rested the well-worn instrument on his lap. I couldn't believe my ears when he suggested the idea.

"I want no part of working at the Day house," I blurted back and sprung to my feet. Folding my arms across my chest in defiance, I glared down at the man. What had brought this up? Go to work for Mister Day? What was Pa and Mister Wasson up to? Was Ma in on this? With the Day girls going on four and five years now, it seemed like Ma's work would be getting easier. Whatever the reason, I didn't want no part and said so.

"But Charlie, your ma's been working five years at their place, and she ain't had no problems with the mister. She's long gone by the time he comes in the door from the mercantile store ever evening, that is, if he's not off to Kentucky. With two growing young'uns tugging at Missus Blanche's skirts, your ma needs more help. She can't take on the man jobs, too. She ain't no spring chicken."

I hadn't seen much of Missus Blanche over the last few years, except ever so often around the hotel with her girls in tow. But Ma sometimes talked about her at the supper table. Just a couple of weeks back she was saying some disturbing things.

"I don't know what's going on in that house," Ma said, her forehead furrowed into crop rows. "Come in their back door this morning and didn't see hide nor hair of Missus Blanche. Little Gay was laying facedown on her bed squalling into her pillow and Miss Margaret was standing next to her all bewildered, not knowing how to calm her little sister. By the time I gathered Gay and got her riding on my hip and bounced into smiles, the kitchen screen door slammed and the missus come into the bedroom looking like she'd wrestled a big snake. Wild-eyed, her face was blotched and tear-streaked. Well, I asked what was the trouble and she snapped back that nothing was wrong, and wasn't a person allowed to go to the outhouse without accusations of neglecting her children? I hadn't accused her, but it was clear something had happened. She wouldn't look at me neither. Just spun around on her heels and marched into her room and closed the door, leaving me to tend the girls."

Pa said, "I'm guessing she and the mister had a spat, that's all. We know how women are when their feelings get stirred, don't we Charlie?" Pa rolled his eyes in my direction, and with a smirk I joined in on making light of women's ways.

Ma paid no attention. "I think there's more to it than that. Late morning Missus Blanche came in from tending her flower garden and rolled up her sleeves to wash at the sink where I was peeling some taters....and I saw dark bruises all up and down her arms---more than what you'd ever get from tending the soil."

I didn't know what to think, and Pa's face fell flat. "What are you saying, Bertie?" he asked in a worrisome tone.

"That house of theirs ain't much bigger than ours, so Missus Blanche is underfoot a great deal. And she talks; talks like a lonely woman needing company. But she never says nothing about Mister Day, good or bad. She's a proud woman, and if there's something gone sour between them, she'd not share it with the likes of me, even if I is the only growed-up listener around. But I can feel it in my bones. Something ain't right."

Ma said Missus Blanche had changed after becoming a mama and all that sorrow was piled on when her sister died. Said she'd lost her spark and growed demanding of everbody, especially Ma.

Maybe that was the reason Pa wanted me to work at the Day house—to lift some of the burden off Ma. But I stood like a stubborn mule in front of him. I didn't say nothing but he could tell by looking at me how I felt.

"Charlie, hear me out," Pa explained. "Mister Wasson's real concerned about Missus Blanche's welfare. He promised that you would work there only when Mister Day is traveling, and that might be two weeks at a time. The two of them has talked, and Mister Day is all right with that plan."

"What does Mister Day think about having a colored man at his house when he's not close by?"

"Charlie, you'll be right there under your Ma's nose. I can't imagine the man's worried over that or he wouldn't have agreed."

"That may be, but I don't figure Mister Day has much use for me and I shore don't like him—don't trust him neither."

"All I know, Charlie, is that it's a chance to better your lot. You complain you's tired of mucking stalls and washing down sweaty horses. And you don't have interest in learning horse doctoring from Waterhouse. Mister Wasson says when you're not at the Day household, you can work alongside me, learning my trade. You'd be completely free of stable work. Think on it. I promised Mister Wasson I'd talk it over with you."

I suspected working at the hotel and the Day house would give me a bigger payday. My saving to marry Ida Mae and get my own place was taking forever at the rate I was going. Maybe it wasn't a bad idea, but the thought of Mister Day as a boss made my stomach grip. I didn't cotton to him from the start—him in his fancy clothes and smart talk. Didn't like the way he looked at me neither—and I'm the one that saved his sorry self from drowning years back. I had steered clear of him and was surprised he remembered me.

"You'd scarcely see Mister Day," Pa said. "Like I said, he's at his store most days and out of town for weeks at a time. You'd answer to Missus Blanche, and you two has been friends a long time."

Pa was working hard to sell me. Maybe he worried Mister Wasson would not take it kindly if I refused. Pa was loyal to Chapman Wasson. From his point of view, the Wassons had given him and Ma more than work. They'd given them respect. My pa was proud he was seen as "indispensable" and Mister Wasson had said it for years, always with a slap to Pa's back. But I didn't see my folks getting ahead—a five-acre plot to till, paydays that kept a roof over our heads, and not much besides—excepting for a slap on the back. It was a subject Pa and I could not talk about without it turning ugly.

True enough Missus Blanche and me had known one another since we were young'uns. But if it was friendship, it was lopsided. I suspected her loaning me those readers was as much about doing her Christian good deeds. But I give her one thing, she never let others talk her down about helping me. She stuck to her guns, as did her ma and pa in their own private way. Maybe the Wasson family *was* an exception to what could be expected from white folks. I needed time to think on it and told Pa so.

***

"I'm glad to be here," I said to Missus Blanche a week later, with my straw hat in hand as I stood inside her back door on a bright Monday morning. Ma and me got to the Day house at her usual time, and she had already disappeared into Miss Margaret and Gay's room. Shifting my weight from one foot to the other, I could hear Ma talking with the girls as she helped them dress.

Missus Blanche smiled from her seat at the kitchen table and said, "Charlie, I am so pleased you are going to be our handyman. I've penciled a list of chores that need your attention."

"Yes, ma'am." I couldn't help but notice how grown up Missus Blanche looked sitting there as lady of the house. Been a long while since I'd seen her close up. Her braids was long gone, of course. Instead, her hair was pulled up into a bun the size of my fist, displaying a neck and face as smooth as a peach. The years had turned her into a handsome woman.

She laid the paper on the table and said, "Come sit, so we can go over this."

I hesitated, but she impatiently patted the chair seat closest to her. I sat and she handed me the list.

"You can read this for yourself—that is, if you can decipher my scribbles," she said with a grin, knowing I could read it all because of her. "But I need to explain a few things."

She went on, complaining the roof desperately needed attention—that a leak had sprung last month and water was seeping in around the fireplace when it rained. I could use the ladder in the back shed and her husband had brought home some pitch from the store to plug it. Missus Blanche went over that paper with the kind of excitement a child would a Christmas list for Kris Kringle. I reckon with so many unattended problems around the place, she was happy a willing, able-bodied man was finally gonna help.

"Yes, ma'am, I'll get started right away," I said, standing to leave.

"Oh, wait Charlie, I almost forgot."

A book lay on the table and she pushed it toward me.

"I thought you might like this. It's titled, *A Call of the Wild*. One of the books I brought home from school years back. I thought you'd enjoy it. It's an adventure…about a sled dog and a gold rush in the Great Yukon, a place where it's cold all the time."

I didn't know what to say. "Why, Missus Blanche, I'm appreciative. I really am, but wouldn't the mister have something to say about this?"

"It's my book, Charlie, and I'd be pleased to loan it…like old times. For that matter, when you're finished, you can look over the ones on the shelves in the next room and borrow another. Will and I have accumulated quite a few, and it seems a shame not to share with folks who love reading as much as we do."

I picked up the book and looked down at her. Her eyes sparkled with enthusiasm. I couldn't turn her down. "Thank you, kindly. I'll be real curious to find out about this 'Great Yukon.'"

Halfway out the back door with the book under my arm, she called after me that she appreciated my agreeing to come. "Yes, ma'am" I answered, but my mind had turned to Mister Day. I hoped I wouldn't see him any time soon and I sure wouldn't be bringing this book back when he was around.

***

As the weeks wore on, I had to admit my new day-to-day routine was a heap better than stable work. When Mister Day was off to Kentucky, I worked with Ma at the Day household. When the mister was in Rhea Springs, Ma was the only one to climb down from the buckboard just after sunup. Working at the hotel on those days, I would pass Ida Mae ever so often and always slipped her a wink. She'd giggle and disappear into the next guest room to clean. Pa kept me busy alongside him, learning what it took to keep a fine hotel running smooth, learning what it took to be indispensable.

On days I worked with Ma at the Day house, we hardly spoke once we climbed down from the wagon and waved to Pa and Ida Mae as they rolled off. We was both too busy. Ma would take the little ones outdoors after breakfast when she hung the clean wash or beat dust out of the rugs throwed over the clothesline. The girls seemed happiest when they was running around the fenced-in yard or chasing after the chickens. Whenever I chopped wood around the side of the house or worked in the shed out back, their squeals of laughter and chatter were constant company.

It didn't take me two weeks working there to see clear that Missus Blanche made up reasons sometimes to come around where I was. Maybe she was checking on me, but I figured her loneliness got the best of her. Losing a ma and sister and having a husband gone so much must have been hard.

One day when I was working in the shed, the house's screen door banged against its frame and Blanche's call was loud.

"Charlie, Charlie, where are you?"

"I'm in the shed, Missus Blanche," I called out, without slowing the rasp against the axe blade I was sharpening. It dulled after a few hours splitting firewood. A man could easily spend half a day swinging an axe, leaving little time to get much else done.

"There you are," she said, stepping inside the shed. "Mr. Day reminded me before he left for Kentucky that the tack needs some attention. Hasn't been cleaned and oiled in a spell. Could you put that on your list for today?"

"Yessum, I'll get right to it when I'm finished here. Nothing worse than a dull axe, Missus Blanche."

"Yes, I imagine."

She didn't turn to leave but lingered, leaning against the doorway. "Charlie, I've wanted to ask you something," she started, but hesitated. "I'm not sure if it's lady-like to let my curiosity get the best of me, but…"

I stopped and propped the axe against the workbench. What did she want? I had no idea where she was going with her talk, and my jaw tightened. She often asked Ma and me questions, personal ones about our family, about things I would never be allowed to ask her. "What is it, Missus Blanche?"

"When Will and I came out of church a couple of Sundays back, did I see you coming down the road in the back of a wagon…with a young woman sitting close to you?"

There she went getting into my business, but I answered, "Well, I don't know. Was she good looking?" Trying not to appear bothered, I grinned.

"She looked different from most of the young Negro women around here. She had reddish hair, and from a distance I could see a thick braid wrapped atop her head like a crown. She was wearing a dress the color of yellow buttercups and kept her head turned to that fellow at her side…like he was something special." Then she smiled coyly and waited.

"Yessum, that was me."

I was proud to be in the company of Ida Mae. I had no cause to be embarrassed. And if Missus Blanche thought Ida Mae was gazing on me with cow eyes, all the better.

"Well, well, Mister Reynolds. It's about time you were picking out a bride. Why, if you don't get busy, there won't be a Reynolds to work for my girls when they're grown. Your family has been with the Wassons so many years; it's a tradition…one I hope will continue."

Missus Blanche thought she was paying a compliment, but her words stung and hurt like gravel in my shoes. My children growing up to work for hers? That wasn't a tradition I cottoned to.

"Maybe, someday," I lied. "She's up from Alabama, outside Scottsboro. Ida Mae is her name. First came to Rhea Springs a few years back and stayed with kinfolk. Don't know if you remember, but you loaned me some primer books then so I could help her with her letters. She left for about a year, but she's back. Lives with Grandma Sulley now over in the Bend near me."

"Well, she's a smart gal if she returned because of you, Charlie Reynolds. As far as I'm concerned, there are no finer Negroes in Rhea County than the Reynolds family."

I felt my face warm. "Thank you kindly."

She turned and left me to my thoughts. On the one hand, I was proud of what she said about my family. On the other, it made me hotter than a flat rock left in the sun. She talked like we were part of her family's cherished possessions—like her mama's fine Kentucky-bred Thoroughbred horses. We didn't belong to the Wassons. It was high time I started my own traditions—and they wasn't gonna be hitched to Missus Blanche's.

I pulled the harness and leather tack from the pegs on the wall. Years working at the stable left me an expert at applying the elbow grease needed to soften leather to supple perfection. It didn't take long to work up a sweat and I was almost finished when a woman's shrieks shook me loose from daydreams of Ida Mae. Running out of the shed, I caught sight of Missus Blanche at the side of the house where the firewood was stacked. She was slinging wood logs in all directions.

Hearing the screams, Ma had come out of the house the same time as me and we both ran that way, only to find a little girl's body all but hidden underneath a pile of split wood. Missus Blanche was frantically slinging them off her.

"Help, Charlie, help me!" Missus Blanche hollered when she caught sight of me. "It's Little Gay."

Nearby Margaret Catherine stood whimpering, frozen in fear. Her little hands covered her pale face. Ma wrapped the five-year old in her arms and turned her away from the scene. I grabbed at the wood alongside Missus Blanche and in no time Little Gay was freed. She was cut and bleeding from the wood I had spent most of the morning splitting and stacking. The heap piled against the side of the house measured six feet high. The four-year-old, who had already earned the reputation as a mountain goat, must have tried to climb it and the logs had rolled out from under her.

Her mama scooped the limp, unmoving child into her arms. After what seemed minutes, we heard a whimper. Missus Blanche's fearful sobs turned to those of relief.

When I spied blood soaking through the little girl's leggings, I said, "Give her to me, quick. She's bleeding." Harnessing a wagon would take too long, so I lifted Little Gay into my arms and commenced to run toward the hotel where Doctor Wasson would be. I yelled to Ma and Missus Blanche to follow in the buckboard.

Two hours and five stitches later, the wagon—with me at the reins—returned the lot of us back to the Day house. Next to me a relieved Missus Blanche held Little Gay on her lap, as the child—in her dirty, blood-stained frock—licked the striped lollipop given her by her great-grandfather and paid little attention to the wounds he had tended and bandaged. Ma and Margaret Catherine sat in the back of the wagon where the five-year old went at her lollipop like a cow at a saltlick. Doctor Wasson had rewarded her pluck for running to find help when her little sister took that terrible tumble.

After unharnessing the team and putting the horses out to pasture, I returned to the side of the house and restacked the scattered wood, this time in a long, lower row that would not tempt a mountain goat. Afterward, I went into the shed to fetch a pick and shovel, having noticed when turning the horses out that one of the fence posts was pushed over. Rummaging in the back of the shed, I didn't hear Missus Blanche come in. When I turned, I saw her silent silhouette filling the doorway.

"I didn't hear you come in," I said, a bit spooked. "Is something wrong? Is Little Gay all right?"

"Oh, she's dirty, but fine. Nothing a little time at the washbasin and a change of clothes won't remedy. Your ma is tending to her, and Margaret is supervising."

When Missus Blanche stepped inside, I could clearly see her strained expression, and her eyes were intent on me, leaving me feeling uneasy.

"Charlie, I don't know what I would have done today without you." She dropped her head and fidgeted with her hands.

"Oh, it was nothing," I protested.

"Nothing?" she said, looking up. "If you hadn't been so quick, it could have been much worse. I went to pieces."

"Well, like I said, I'm glad..."

"Charlie, there's something I need to say, and I want you to hush and let me speak my mind."

"Yes, ma'am." She was emotional and I seldom saw her that way. I didn't know what to make of it.

"Since the babies came along, your ma's coming here has saved me. She's so smart about children—has better instincts than I. And now that the girls are getting older and not as easily corralled, it's a full-time job keeping up with them. And I couldn't manage without you either. This house has gone wanting with Mr. Day gone so much. There's always something breaking or wearing out."

"Well, Missus Blanche, I'm..."

"Let me finish." In the shed's dim light, I could see her chin quiver. Then her words rolled out like gathering thunder, "I don't think Mr. Day realizes how difficult it is to manage a family alone and keep up with its demands."

She stopped, folded her arms across her bosom—as if to shore up her courage—and stared across the room like I wasn't there. I kept quiet like she told me and turned my eyes to my own dusty boots. Finally, she sighed and spoke aloud as if she was talking to herself, "He comes home to a hot meal waiting on the table, clean children happy to see him, and a supply of wood stacked against the house. But porch slats do rot, the roof leaks sometimes, and fencing gets knocked over by grazing livestock. It doesn't fix itself. Somebody has to manage all that, someone stronger than me. I'm doing the best I can."

When I spoke up, her eyes shot back in my direction, as if she'd forgot I was there. "Well, Missus Blanche, maybe he's paying you a compliment because he knows you'll see to it."

I surprised myself saying something nice about a man that had never given me the time of day, but I was trying to make her feel better. It seemed that was what she was needing.

"Charlie, you've taken an enormous load off my shoulders. When Mr. Day is gone, I feel overwhelmed. Sometimes I'm not up to it, and he doesn't hesitate to remind me."

She was awful hard on herself, probably taking blame for Little Gay's accident. I was surprised she was telling me, and then I remembered Ma's talking about Missus Blanche's bruised arms.

"If you ask me, Mister Day should be more appreciative of what all his missus handles around this place," I offered. "With him being gone so much, I don't see how he thinks he has the right to criticize. You do a fine job---at least in my opinion---and you're always busy. Why your house is clean---neat as a pen. When Ma and me pull up in the wagon at the crack of dawn, you're already stirring around, feeding the chickens, watering the horses and putting them out to pasture, hoeing in that garden of yours. No moss grows on your north side. And repairs and man-work you're not strong enough to take on...Well, that's what you have me for." The more I talked, the more riled I felt. "Nope, I think he needs to pay his missus more attention, and I mean the right kind."

I came within a hair of asking if Mister Day had ever laid a hand on her. I wanted to, but bit my lip and quieted myself when I saw her cheeks was turning rosy. Was it embarrassment or surprise at my speaking my mind? I wasn't rightly sure.

An uncomfortable silence set in. Missus Blanche offered me a weak smile and turned to walk toward the house, appearing to wipe away a tear as she did.

That kind of personal talk coming from a white woman, even one I'd known a long time, left me awful uncomfortable. The more I learned about that Mister Day…He was a whole different breed. Apart from how he viewed my people, he didn't treat his own right. I wondered what else was going on in that house when he was home. Something wasn't right. As far as I was concerned, he was a sorry sort.

CHAPTER 26

BLANCHE

When Will walked through the door after three long weeks away, the children were ecstatic. They ran to their father with welcoming hugs. From the kitchen I could see him squatting to their level and opening his travel bag with a look of mischief on his face. He had brought them a surprise, which was not his usual practice when returning from Kentucky. He playfully pulled out a Raggedy-Ann doll for each, the perfect size for hugging, with red yarn hair and button-round eyes. The girls scampered into the kitchen to hold up their gifts for me to admire as they danced about in circles.

Busy at the stove stirring the simmering pot of greens, I had managed to scrape together a welcome-home meal in spite of the fact that Bertie had felt poorly and not come to work, leaving me to ride herd over the children. Had Charlie not come to my rescue, playing with Margaret and Little Gay the better part of the day, Will's homecoming would not have been as welcoming.

"Don't I get a proper welcome these days?" Will called into the kitchen.

"Not if you want a supper that isn't burned," I answered, hearing him walk into the bedroom and drop his travel satchel with a thud.

"Hmm...smells good," Will said, moments later.

I glanced over my shoulder to find him leaning against the kitchen doorway.

"What you smell is a pork roast that's been simmering for hours," I said with some pride, lifting the lid for the aroma to drift his way. "And we have greens, black-eyed peas and your favorite cornbread."

He offered a smile and turned to stroll into the parlor without so much as a peck to my cheek. The girls were calling, or at least that's the reason I wanted to attribute.

At supper Little Gay and Margaret were still wiggly with excitement, and their plates remained largely untouched. Their father had been away so long, it was like having Kris Kringle at the table. Both talked and chattered at the same time about this, that, and the other, with Margaret managing to override her four-year-old sister's attempts at center stage.

"Papa, Papa," Margaret said, jumping in before Little Gay had finished her tale of climbing the woodpile and earning a lollipop for her bravery after she was patched up. "Mama took us to Grandfather's strawberry fields last week, and we picked all morning. I earned enough to buy a jump rope at the store. It's red and white striped, with red handles. Wanna see?"

"No, Margaret," I answered. "We don't jump up from the table while we're eating. You can show your father later."

The children had found picking berries in their grandfather's strawberry field as much fun as an Easter egg hunt. Plump red berries peeked from under the bright green foliage, and I think the girls had eaten as many as they had placed in the shipping crates. Papa promised the same pay rate as his field pickers—by the flat—and the children swelled with pride when they presented their bounty for payment. Within the hour they were beaming once again as they plunked down their hard-earned coins on the store counter—for Margaret's jump rope and a set of jacks and red ball for Little Gay.

After supper, the party moved to the parlor. Will crawled about the floor like a horse on the loose, wrestled with the girls as if they were boys, and read a stack of books with a little girl nestled under each arm.

Silly as it was, I resented the children's pawing over their father and the undivided attention he paid in return. That gnawing feeling surfaced whenever he returned from another extended absence.

By the time the two were tucked into their beds, each clutching her Raggedy Ann, the hour had grown late and Will's exhaustion was unmistakable. He collapsed into his overstuffed chair, turned up the wick of the nearby oil lamp, and disappeared behind the Lexington Weekly newspaper that he'd brought home.

"Anything of great interest?" I asked, sinking onto the couch to share his company.

From behind the paper, Will answered, "No, just reading what's going on overseas. Since we declared war on Germany, who knows how many men have already been lost over there. You know the official casualty counts in the newspapers are probably not accurate. I'm afraid American blood will flow as freely in Europe as it did here fifty years ago."

"I'm ashamed to say I'm not current on world events," I said, talking in the direction of the newspaper separating us. I slipped a toss pillow under my head and stretched out. "Papa talks about it with Grandfather sometimes when they're here visiting. He always brings a newspaper or two that he's finished, but I'm too tired at the end of the day to bother. Not much energy left to think about world peace when my time is spent keeping the peace around here."

I chuckled, as did Will from behind the wall of newspaper.

"I'm thankful you aren't involved in that war," I mused.

"I confess I have mixed feelings sometimes," Will muttered.

"You'd really consider putting your life on the line thousands of miles away, and risk leaving your children fatherless? No, it doesn't leave me with mixed feelings," I stated emphatically.

Will lowered the paper and offered an indifferent glance. The newspaper wall rose again and silence returned. I repositioned my pillow and closed my eyes. Periodically, I heard pages turn.

I must have dozed off. Aroused by the crumpling of newspaper, I saw Will peering over it. "By the way," he said, "I know you're not going to be happy with me, but I have to leave again tomorrow, midday. I won't be gone but two nights."

Before I could speak, he hurriedly explained, "I need to be in Chattanooga to talk with several businessmen. Day Brothers may be opening a store there." Will's expression conveyed a positive, hopeful anticipation, but it was lost on me.

"What? You just got home today and you're gone again?" Before he could answer, I plunged ahead, fully awake. "Your children are going to forget they have a father. You're here so seldom, they already think you're Kris Kringle. You might as well start coming down the chimney."

My sarcastic comments were overblown. He would be away two nights, but he had been gone three of the last six weeks, and that had become the norm. But it was his attitude about it, an emotional absence that inferred far more, as if he cared not whether he was home with me or not.

I sat up and fluffed the pillow, returning it to the end of the sofa, all the while trying unsuccessfully to hide my sniveling. As a matter of fact, Will's family didn't seem to care either, not like I thought in the beginning. Since my sister's funeral three years earlier, they had made but one trip to Rhea Springs—for Little Gay's christening. And I had thought Mr. Day was a kind man who would support Will and his blossoming family. But no, he was more interested in keeping Will busy insuring his own prosperity. And Mrs. Day? Providing that extra bedroom—the girls' room—for her visits was a waste. She had never, ever slept there.

Will didn't console or try to reason with me, but rather sat with the crumpled paper in his lap staring at me. His face drained its color, and his only reaction was clearing his throat—in irritation, or maybe disgust.

I couldn't bear it so I left the room in a huff and shut the bedroom door. Changing into my nightdress, I climbed into bed and awaited his coming. He didn't.

The night was endless with tossing and turning. When I heard a rooster crow, it was barely light. I dreaded rising to face the day…and him. A low rustle came from the living room. It was probably Will. I dressed and went into the kitchen to find him at the table with a half-emptied glass of buttermilk in hand. He still wore yesterday's clothes, needed to shave and looked disheveled.

"Do you want me to fry some eggs for you?" I asked.

"No," he said.

He drained the glass, left it on the table and went to our room, presumably to change clothes. I pulled out a pot and set it on the stove and then opened the tin to measure out the oats needed for two generous bowls of hot cereal for the girls. Hopefully, they would sleep later, but knowing their father was home might rouse them earlier.

I placed several pieces of wood in the cook stove and lit it to make coffee for myself. While waiting for the water to heat, I sat at the table feeling barren. Will was in the bedroom longer than expected, but I resisted the temptation to call after him. Twenty minutes later, he walked into the room with bulging travel satchel in hand and set it by the back door.

"I didn't think you had to leave until noon," I said, sipping my coffee at the table, glancing at the bag.

"I don't, but I'm going to the store first to check in with Mr. Cobb and then I'll walk to the hotel so Sam can take me to the station. I'll not be back here before I leave, so I won't need the wagon."

"Aren't you going to wait until the girls are up?"

"No, it'll just upset them that I'm leaving. Maybe it's best I leave that for you to navigate."

"Yes, like you leave everything for me to navigate," I said under my breath, staring into my coffee cup.

Will leaned against the wall next to the door, staring at me. The tension was palpable. After a moment, he said, "You've asked me often what I want from you. Well, what I want is some maturity. How many times have we plowed this same ground, and how many times will it take to get through your head I have no choice concerning my responsibilities?"

I looked up from my coffee to glare at him. I would not dignify his verbal jab with an answer. But what hurt more than the words was his hardened visage, that all too familiar clinching of his jaw and hard angry eyes. To my way of judging, he didn't care a whit about me—maybe the children, but not me. I was nothing more than his housekeeper and occasional bed partner. Who knew, but maybe his long absences for family business were just a ruse for a more shameful purpose. What I did know without a doubt was that the shine had long since gone from his eyes. I rose from my chair and walked to the back door, needing some air to clear my head.

"Where are you going?" Will spat the words, taking my arm to prevent my opening the screen door. "The children will be up soon, won't they?"

"Yes, they may," I retorted, pulling loose. "So *you* deal with them." I walked out, but he was right behind me.

"Just leave me alone," I called over my shoulder, hastening my escape through the backyard gate and into the open field.

By then Will was red-faced and yelled for me to get back into the house, that I would wake the children, that I would alarm the whole countryside, and what kind of mother was I. When he caught up to me, he grabbed my arm and spun me around. I tried to pull loose, to no avail, so I hit him in the chest with my free hand. I'm not certain what happened next, but I found myself on the ground at his feet. He grabbed at my thrashing arms and cursed. Crumpled there, I kicked at his legs and pulled away from his reach the best I could, but then I felt excruciating pain to my head. In the tumult, my long hair had fallen from its bun and Will had grabbed hold, and was dragging me by my hair with one hand and holding fast to my arm with the other. I let out a shriek of agonizing pain.

"Shut up, bitch!" he yelled, glaring down at me. Then he lowered his voice and hissed, "You want the neighbors to come running?" With that, he turned loose. Standing above me, he brushed off his trousers and then stepped over me to return to the house.

Steps away, he called back, "You deal with the children."

I pulled myself to a sitting position, stunned as I watched him go through the yard gate toward the kitchen door. It was only then I caught sight of Charlie walking along the road nearing the house. Given the angle, he could clearly see both Will and me. Even from where I sat, the shock on his face was clearly evident. My eyes darted to Will. He had paused in the middle of the backyard and was staring at Charlie, probably contemplating what to do. But after hesitating, he resumed his retreat and disappeared into the house.

Shame filled me, even more than the rage over what had just occurred. I buried my face into my knees and whispered, "Lord, make me disappear." I wanted to die. Of all people, Charlie. He had always been an object of Will's disdain, and now this. What would Will do, knowing Charlie witnessed the scene in all its ugliness?

When I heard the screen door again, I raised my head to see Will coming out, leather satchel in hand. With a determined stride, he circled around the house to the road with not so much as a glance aside. Charlie was nowhere to be seen. The road was deserted except for Will heading in the direction of his mercantile store.

"Mama, Mama," the girls called. They were standing at the kitchen door in their nightdresses and appeared bewildered. What had they seen? What had they heard?

"I'm coming, girls." I stood to my feet and brushed the grass and dirt from my clothes. Trying in vain to rearrange my bedraggled hair, I wiped my face with my skirt hem and walked toward the house. They were wide-eyed, so I composed myself as best I could. "Now, let's get into the house. You don't want to be outside in your nightdresses for the neighbors to see."

"Where's Father?" they asked in unison and with trepidation, both clutching their Raggedy Ann dolls.

As I herded the children into the kitchen, pointing them to the table to sit, I tried desperately to clear my throat of emotion. Ignoring their question, I said, "Let's get your oatmeal going here. Neither of you ate very well last night. You must be hungry."

The children were no fools. It wasn't the first time they'd seen me after a heated argument with their father. Will's remedy was always to leave, so that I was left with the task of reassuring them, another job I had not mastered.

"Your Father left early to go by the mercantile store. The three of you were having such fun last night that he forgot to tell you he was going to Chattanooga today…where Great-Aunt Marian lives." Their little faces fell in disappointment.

Something took hold inside me and I heard myself say, "But we are going on a little trip ourselves today. How would you two like to visit Great-Uncle Jack and Great-Aunt Cinny at their farm? I bet Uncle Jack would take you for a ride on his white horse, and you could play in the barn with the cats and chickens, even climb the hay bales in the loft if you want. How does that sound?" Hearing my own words somehow roused my spirits.

"Can we fish in their pond, Mama?" Margaret asked, her frown already flipped into a grin—and Little Gay's, too.

"Of course, you can. And I bet Uncle Jack will have cane poles just the right length for two little girls to catch their supper." I turned to the stove to stir their oatmeal, and said over my shoulder that we'd have to pack our bags as soon as they finished breakfast.

I gathered the children's clothes into three satchels and two suitcases. I couldn't think beyond the moment and didn't try. Facing Papa to explain my family troubles was more than I could contemplate, so I jotted a short note and left it on the kitchen table, explaining that the girls and I had gone for a visit to Uncle Jack's farm. If he and Grandfather dropped by, they would easily spot it. I would bear my soul to Aunt Cinny. Maybe she would send Uncle Jack later to speak with Papa.

After packing our clothes, I walked out to the field in search of our horses. Peering down the road for any sign of Charlie, I sighed in relief that no one was around. After harnessing the team and loading the bags, I called the children from their perch on the back steps. "Let's go, girls. We're off on an adventure, and what a pretty day for one, " I said, seeking to encourage myself as much as excite them.

We settled onto the buckboard bench, and with a slap of the reins, we were off. The children seemed to have forgotten the earlier sight of their disheveled mother with tear-stained face and wild hair. They were smiling from ear to ear as we turned south in the direction of our escape.

***

At midday we reached the turnoff to the winding drive that led to the two-story, white farmhouse sitting atop a high knoll, surrounded by pasture. The girls clapped their hands with glee as we passed grazing cattle and sheep on either side of the rutted road on a landscape of green sprinkled with wild yellow buttercups. By the time I brought the wagon to a stop in front of the house, Uncle Jack and Aunt Cinny, who surely saw us coming, were waiting on the veranda.

They set quite a pose. Aunt Cinny's black hair had faded to silver gray over the years, and her lips had thinned. The smooth skin she had always shielded with farm bonnet or Sunday parasol had surrendered to age. Farming had taken its toll on Uncle Jack, but he still struck an impressive picture as the county's U.S. Deputy Marshall.

After hugs and smiles all around, Aunt Cinny served us a late lunch of cold fried chicken and potato salad. Later, Cinny and I settled onto the double swing on the veranda to enjoy its shade and catch the afternoon breezes as we watched the tall man with graying mustache and my two little girls no taller than the hip pocket of his bib coveralls stroll into the pasture. With cane fishing poles over their shoulders, the girls were looking up at their great uncle, one on either side of him, probably listening to him spin tall tales of giant fish living in his pond. When they caught sight of the emerald green water at the pasture's center, they raced ahead laughing and giggling, no doubt with every intention of catching their supper.

A smile slipped across my face, but my eyes were misty. I felt Aunt Cinny's arthritic hand on my knee and turned my eyes to hers. I could see in them love and acceptance that wielded no judgment. She had lived a long life as a practical farm wife and had no doubt weathered storms of her own. But most folks kept their problems to themselves and didn't hang them out for others to see. Aunt Cinny guessed I needed a mother's ear, and she was ready to listen.

I tiptoed around the reasons for our unexpected visit, but eventually gathered the courage to expose the ugly truth. Cinny's face betrayed no emotion. If I hesitated and fell silent, she patted my leg and waited. Her quiet presence was reassuring. When all was said and I wondered aloud if I had divulged too much, she reassured me.

"Now, Blanche, don't you worry. You and the girls are welcome here as long as you want. We're family and you need time to clear your head and think."

When a tear slipped down my cheek, she pulled a kerchief from her apron pocket and laid it on my lap. Dabbing my eyes, I gave her a grateful hug. "Thank you, Aunt Cinny. I know being here will be good for the girls, too." She nodded, and we surrendered to the peaceful surroundings and gazed out over the rolling acreage.

When the girls returned an hour later, they were beaming and pointing to the string of fish Uncle Jack held up—three brim and two sizeable catfish.

"Mama, look," said Margaret, as she scampered up the steps to the porch. "I caught the biggest one—the one with the long whiskers. See?"

Before I could answer, Little Gay echoed from behind her with equal pride, "I caught the two little ones."

Aunt Cinny was quick to say, "And what a delicious dinner we will have, thanks to you two."

***

We had a feast of fried fish at the farm table that night, finished off with pie made from apples gathered by the children from the twisted fruit tree next to the house. Afterward, the girls happily joined Uncle Jack on the sofa in the parlor and listened to more fish tales that had them in stitches of laughter. From what I could hear from the kitchen, Uncle Jack was having as much fun as my children.

229

After the dishes were washed and put away, Aunt Cinny settled into her rocker with her knitting basket and I took Uncle Jack's overstuffed chair. What a blessing it was to savor the sanctuary of my aunt and uncle's home.

It wasn't long before the girls began to yawn. It had been a long and eventful day. Aunt Cinny provided a kerosene lamp, and the children and I climbed the creaking steps to the spare bedroom upstairs where a welcoming feather bed offered plenty of wiggle room for the three of us.

Once changed into our nightclothes and with washed faces, we snuggled into the deep downy mattress. Snuffing the lamp's flame, I knew sleep would soon find me. It was all I could do to focus on bedtime prayers. But as soon as I whispered "Amen," Margaret spoke into the darkness, "Mama, how long are we going to stay?"

"I'm not certain. Why? Don't you like it here?"

"Oh, yes. I just wondered because Uncle Jack said we could hunt for his black mama cat tomorrow. She lives in one of the barn lofts and has a litter of kittens. He said we could give each one a proper name. And he promised we could ride on his white horse with him to check the fence lines." Then she added with the pride of knowing, "You ride the fence lines to make sure the cows and sheep can't escape through a broken rail."

I smiled in the darkness. "That's very nice of Uncle Jack to offer."

"Mama, did you know Uncle Jack's white horse was once in the circus?" Before I could answer, she rushed on. "It can dance on its hind legs. I didn't believe Uncle Jack. I thought he was pulling my leg, but he crossed his heart and said he'd show us tomorrow."

"I remember that," I said. "Your grandfather told me when I wasn't much older than you that Uncle Jack had just bought a horse that could do tricks."

"Well, can we stay?" Margaret's voice brimmed with anticipation. I turned my head and asked Little Gay if she'd like to stay on a few days, but there was no reply. She was fast asleep.

I whispered what Margaret wanted to hear. "I'm sure we'll be here long enough for Uncle Jack to keep his promises. Now close your eyes, and let's join your sister in dreamland."

CHAPTER 27

CHARLIE

The makeshift wooden cross smoldered, spitting sparks and sputtering flames as it loomed in the night at the far end of the fallow field across from the tumble-down houses along Piney Creek. Having burned through the kerosene-soaked feed sacks that wrapped it, the choking fumes sullied the country air. It all happened in minutes that passed like hours.

***

It was after midnight that the four of us were jolted awake by whoops and hollers and the ruckus of horses racing up the dirt road that ran between the two rows of look-alike houses. By the time Pa and I reached the window, a dozen men draped in white and wearing pointed hoods had already roared past to the far end of the road. With sheets swirling like a ghostly windstorm, the mob doubled back and then out into the field across from our place, circling the already-blazing cross that towered thirty feet into the black sky.

When Ma saw it, she gasped and clutched Ruby. Even in the darkened house, I could see Pa's wide-eyed stare. The horses raced 'round and 'round that evil thing, kicking up dirt and snorting with flared nostrils in the presence of the menacing flames. When gunshots rang out like firecrackers, Pa hollered to get down and pulled Ma to the floor. We crawled to the back door and under the cover of darkness ran to Piney Creek and the shelter of its trees. We weren't alone. Neighbors had done the same.

It all ended as quickly as it began, and the night fell quiet again. Hidden among the trees, no one dared move, but the men under the white sheets had vanished. Nothing remained but the burned-out cross, kerosene fumes and our fears.

A few folks started to creep back toward their houses. A few minutes later, Pa whispered we should too. Instead of following the family back to the house, I darted in the direction of Grandma Sulley's. I couldn't go home yet. Nothing would stop me till I knew Ida Mae and Grandma were safe.

Skirting behind the dark houses, I slipped from the cover of one to the next. No one was sure if any of the Klan had hung back, maybe to do something worse. When I reached Grandma's front door and pushed it open, screams greeted me. Rushing through the darkness into the back room, I found the two women huddled in the corner and when they saw it was me they ran crying into my arms, shaken but all right.

I don't think anyone along the Bend got back to sleep that night. Huddling in their homes with young'uns under their wings, the women bolted the doors while us men ventured to the field where the charred cross smoldered. We pondered what it all meant. One neighbor piped up that a couple of Negro men from up on Walden had been hanging around outside a Rhea Springs saloon. They hadn't gone in or nothing, but the owner suspected they was up to no good and chased them off with a double-barreled shotgun. Another wondered aloud if some young buck had gotten too friendly with one of the town's white women. He had heard rumors but hadn't put much stock in them...before now. Pa stood silent in the crowd, listening. I had my own thoughts, but kept my peace. After a spell, I walked back home alone...thinking, thinking.

Could this have come about because of what I saw at the Day house a week earlier? I couldn't get it out of my head and was afeared Mister Day hadn't either. He'd seen me gawking—I knew he had— after he dragged his wife by her hair and stood over her in that field, his face blood red, yelling down at her. I saw it all. When he left, he stepped over her body like she was nothing.

Now, this. When the hooded men lit up the night and barreled up our road terrorizing everthing that breathed, they had not yelled nothing. They were like ghosts on the prowl. Had Mister Day sent the men to scare me into silence? If he did, what had he told them? I wasn't the one who'd done wrong. Or did he think I was going to shame his family by talking?

I lay awake in my bed with no hope of sleep, my mind still racing. After seeing what happened to Missus Blanche, I recalled going straight to the hotel to find Pa. I told him everthing I'd seen, how Mister Day had manhandled his missus, leaving her in that field. After calming me down, Pa said to tell nobody, not even Ida Mae. The following morning we stopped off at the Day house to find it deserted. We had not been back since. Instead, I worked alongside Pa at the hotel and stayed out of Mister Wasson's sight.

The mister said nothing about his daughter to Pa, but he cornered Ma the next day. She was at the Wasson place, down on her hands and knees with a bucket and brush scrubbing his kitchen floor. With the house to herself—Mister Wasson spent most days at the hotel—she said she'd been surprised to hear the front door open and then footsteps. Stopping in the kitchen doorway, Mister Wasson had lit into Ma with rapid-fire questions about Missus Blanche without so much as a "Good day, Bertie." Not his usual mannerly self, he pulled a folded letter out of his back pocket and held it in the air saying Blanche had left it on her kitchen table. Asked Ma if she knew about any planned visit to the country. Ma reminded him that she had been ailing and hadn't worked at the Day or Wasson house on that day or the one before. That didn't seem to satisfy because he commenced to ask questions about the Day family's wellbeing that pried into a man and wife's personal ways together, questions that left Ma feeling mighty uncomfortable. When Ma told Pa and me later about that conversation, we had agreed I should keep my head down, mouth shut and wait for things to sort themselves out. As I turned again on my bed and smelled the charred wood and kerosene fumes from the burned-out cross, I wondered if life would ever sort itself out.

***

One evening a week after the cross burning and after Ruby had lit out for a friend's house, I asked Pa and Ma to linger at the supper table. I didn't know how best to start in, so I flat out said, "I've got to leave Rhea Springs, at least for a spell. From my way of looking at it, I don't have a choice."

Rumors were swirling as to why the KKK had started up again after years of quiet. No one knew, but everbody had their own ideas. Nobody in the Negro community, excepting Ma and Pa, knew what I did about Mister and Missus Day. With no way of knowing for certain, I figured Mister Day was scared I was gonna spread talk about what I seen happen in that field behind their place. I wouldn't, not because of him, because of Missus Blanche. But he didn't know that.

Pa tried hard to talk me out of leaving. Said not to be cowed, that it would all blow over sooner or later and we just had to be patient. Ma cried. Pa's thinking didn't calm my fears, fear as much for them and Ida Mae as for me. I spelled out my plans in detail so they'd know I wasn't going off half-cocked. I'd train to Cincinnati, Ohio and get in touch with Aunt America's relatives who lived there. I'd find some kind of work, but I had a strong feeling about joining the Army and serving my country. I'd read in several newspapers Mister Wasson gave me that in the North a Negro could sign up easy.

When I finished, Pa and Ma knew my mind was made up. Sitting there at the table, my folks had never looked so long-faced. When I couldn't stand it no longer, I stood and kissed Ma on the head and patted Pa's shoulder before heading out the door. I had to go up the road to talk to Ida Mae.

At Grandma Sulley's front door, I knocked and heard the old lady shuffling to answer. I often came by for a visit after supper and she opened the door with a knowing smile. But grandma knew something was up when I asked instead to take a walk with Ida Mae. It was already dark.

Unbeknownst to Grandma, Ida Mae had walked up right behind the stooped little woman and our eyes met over the top of her silver-haired head. When Grandma caught sight, her stern face melted like she remembered the ways of lovebirds.

"Now you two don't stay out long," she warned, her graying eyes danced and a hint of a grin appeared.

Walking hand-in-hand along the dirt road, I was not my usual talkative self. Instead, I savored the warmth of my gal's hand in mine, noticed the bounce in her barefoot steps and caught a whiff of that sweet talc powder. She must have guessed I would drop by and wanted to tickle my fancy by smelling purty. She chattered on about her day at the hotel, filling in my silence. I knew when I opened my mouth that everthing between us would change. In the dread of it, I shivered. Only when Ida Mae paused to ask if I felt all right did I finally say what I had to. Stopping in her tracks, she turned to face me through the darkness.

"No, Charlie. You can't go. Why do you have to leave? What if those ghost riders come back? Who's gonna protect Grandma and me?"

I told her it was because of them that I had to leave and she'd be safer if I was gone for a while. I couldn't say the whole truth so a few white lies filled in the blanks. We walked on, and she clutched my arm like I was gonna run away, maybe then and there. Wanting her to know I'd thought everthing through, I said, "I read in a newspaper that the Army is enlisting Negroes up North. I'm thinking on that, since I can read and write and figure that should put me in good standing."

Ida Mae should feel proud to have her man in uniform, but instead she sobbed. She cried that if I joined the Army I'd be killed in a faraway land and she'd never see me again. Trying to prop up her spirits, I said good wages goes to those in the service and when I was discharged, I'd send for her. But to Ida Mae that involved too many ifs and she boohooed even harder.

I held her close until her crying slowed and then steered us off the wagon road toward the creek. In the privacy of the trees along its banks, we lingered long. I swore my love and showed her as best I could how important she was to me. I'd come back, I promised. But she needed to be patient. Amidst her tears and sniffling, she forced a smile to her tear-streaked face and vowed she would.

***

Two nights later—on a Wednesday—was when an Ohio-bound Cincinnati Southern freight train out of Chattanooga always made a quick stop at the Spring City station to unload goods destined for Rhea Springs and Spring City stores. It rolled through around nine o'clock and idled in the station long enough for freight to be unloaded. My plan was to slip into one of the freight cars while the railroad men were busy.

"I appreciate your bringing me this far," I said to Pa when he pulled the buckboard wagon off the dirt road, a half-mile short of the station. It was deserted and we sat surrounded by the stillness.

Finally, Pa asked, "Your mind is made up?" Worry filled his words.

"Yes, Pa, this is best. I'll be fine; you know I will, so don't you worry."

I went over my plan with him one last time…to reassure him as much as me. I'd ride the train to Cincinnati. I wasn't sure how long that would take, but I was hoping it would be dark when the train slowed up on the outskirts of the city. After jumping off, I'd stay off the main roads so as not to draw attention. The address of Aunt America's people was scribbled on a scrap of paper, safe in my pocket, and Ma was sure I'd be received with open arms. What money I'd saved wouldn't buy a train ticket, but I had enough for my keep until I found where the Army was signing up folks like me. When things got squared away, I promised to get word back somehow to Ma and Pa and Ida Mae.

Pa listened without interruption. When I finished, the quiet spread between us and he struggled to find words.

"Charlie…I's been giving this whole situation a lot more thinking. As much as your ma and me ache that you're leaving, I's come around to your way of looking at it. Many believe times is changing and men in the white sheets are just a few mean scoundrels. But too often a morning sun casts a shadow off a noose at the bad end of a rope hanging over a tree limb. It ain't worth risking your life to see which is more true. Besides, I hear our people who are going North are finding life better there."

Pa and me sat a spell longer, with the nickering of the impatient horse the only interruption to the katydids' evening serenade. After a long sigh, Pa asked, "Charlie, did your ma put the biscuits and ham in your tote sack?"

He didn't want to turn me loose, and I was of the same mind. "Yes, Pa, I've got it right here." I patted my burlap sack and silence returned.

When I could stand it no longer, I reached around and hugged Pa. We held onto each other longer than anytime since my growing up. Finally, I climbed down from the wagon, and before heading into the inky night, I whispered aloud, "Take care of Ida Mae for me."

"We will, son. You take care of yourself."

I hurried my steps as much to put distance between Pa and my tears as to get to the station. In a few minutes, I heard the faint sound behind me of Pa's wagon turning and rattling away into the night. I was alone and felt it in a way I never had before. Grateful that no one was on the road and it was a cloudy, starless night, I wiped my eyes and walked on.

When I got to the station house and sneaked around the side to peer through the window, I was relieved to see the hands of the grandfather clock inside. It was eight-thirty. Only thirty minutes to wait. The station was dim and deserted inside its lobby, but I could hear voices of several men talking in the area behind the ticket window where there was a small glow of light. They was wiling away the time waiting for the train. When it did roll in, it would idle just long enough for the freight to be unloaded at the far end of the platform. Depending on the number of crates, the train could pull away in minutes.

Slipping to the opposite side of the tracks, I hung close to a nearby storage shed where I could hide and wait. I shivered in spite of the warm night as my mind pondered the places I was gonna see, places that I'd read about in Mister Wasson's big city newspapers. And maybe I'd find a better life, one where I had a greater say-so than any Negro did around these parts. But now that I was on the edge of it, I was scared. It took my breath away to think of being in a city with a hundred streets instead of these country roads, and among thousands of scurrying folks instead of a few hundred families spread across a whole county. It was scary, exhilarating and mysterious, all at the same time.

I felt the rumble underfoot of the nearing train and its loud whistle must have ended the card game inside the station. I peered around the shed to spot two men in blue uniforms stretching and yawning as they ambled out of the station and onto the platform, each with a lantern in hand.

The black hulk of the steam engine loomed large as it neared, its headlight tunneling through the darkness. I pressed my body close to the building to stay in its shadow. When the train came to a stop, I heard the squeal of the heavy doors that the men slid open. From where I stood, I couldn't see clear, but figured they'd gone inside the freight car because of the faint sounds of talking coming through the metal walls. A minute later they stepped out, balancing a bulky wood crate between them and walked it to the far side. After lowering it to the platform, they disappeared into the car again. Now was the time to make my move.

I slipped from the shed's protection and ran to the near side of the freight car, moving close to the gap between it and the train car ahead. From there, I could peer across the coupling. The men had left their lanterns close to the open doors. When I'd climb between the two cars onto the platform, I would pass through the lanterns' light to enter the freight car. I could be spotted right off.

I had to act fast. When the two men came out of the freight car the second time, they hauled an even larger wooden box and cussed under its weight as they headed in the direction of the first crate. I swung my body up onto the coupling and jumped to the platform right next to a lantern. If the men had not been struggling with that stubborn box, they would have caught me flat-footed. I darted inside the giant metal box and as far back as I could go. It wasn't as crowded as I'd hoped, but a pile of one-hundred-pound grain sacks offered a good-enough hiding place. I hunkered down behind them.

Both men entered again, loudly grumbling about the size of the boxes they were hauling out. Then it grew quiet again. A few minutes later a voice from the far side of the platform hollered, "Is that all?"

Someone just outside my boxcar answered, "I sure hope so. One more of them giant crates and my back will be done for."

I did not move a muscle. The man nearby called to his buddy that he was doing a final sweep with his cargo list, just to make sure. His footsteps across the metal flooring echoed like a giant walking and grew louder. When it stopped, I realized a light was circling me like a halo. I raised my head to see a form towering over me, holding the lantern high. I said nothing. I was frozen.

The man said, "Hey, boy, what do you think you're doing?"

When my eyes adjusted to the glare, I recognized his face at the second he recognized mine. He was the preacher's son, the one who had found a job working for the railroad, the red-haired, freckle-faced boy who had stopped his friends from breaking my ribs years back when I had wrecked their marble game.

I said, "I needs to get to Cincinnati," and then paused. "Please. It's important."

The man my age in the blue uniform stared down on me. He didn't say nothing. From outside the freight car, the other feller bellowed, "Come on, they's ready to get this train moving. Ain't nothing else to haul out, is there?"

The preacher's son hesitated and then called over his shoulder without taking his eyes off me, "No. Nothing else. I'm coming."

Without a word, without offering even a hint as to what he was thinking, the son who had lost his mother and once lost his way, turned on his heels and walked out of the freight car, calling out, "Help me close her up."

With the loud rumble of the metal doors closing me in blackness, I was left alone, alone to consider what lay ahead and, maybe more important, to think on what had just happened.

CHAPTER 28

BLANCHE

Cradled in the quiet of the rolling pastureland, soothed by its gentle breath and birdsong, with no gossip to be heard or uncomfortable questions to be answered, I savored the time on the remote farm. I greeted each new day with a hopeful heart, but when the fog of sleep lifted, the dilemmas I wasn't ready to address echoed anew inside my head. Was there any hope of an enduring union with the man I'd promised to spend a lifetime with, but who had gradually changed into someone entirely different?

My girls appeared carefree and unconcerned. They sprang from bed every morning anticipating new adventures. Hurriedly dressing themselves—finishing with pinafores and shoes—they could be heard throughout the house clattering down the steps, scurrying to the kitchen to pelt Uncle Jack with questions as he ate breakfast. What did he have in store for them—what would they see that day, what would they do? He was a magician at presenting farm chores as exciting escapades. Too bad he and Aunt Cinny had never had children of their own.

Despite the demands of a two hundred acre farm, Uncle Jack took the girls under his wing after breakfast and their happy little faces wouldn't be seen again until I stepped onto the front porch to ring the lunch bell. They returned with a skip in their step and choruses of "we're hungry!" as they bounded into the house with dirty hands and smudged faces. Only once—at bedtime—had they asked about home or their father and had been easily pacified by my evasive answers.

I spent the first few days working alongside Aunt Cinny, helping with tasks around the farmhouse. Whether we gathered eggs from the henhouse, harvested figs from nearby bushes to make preserves, or pinned wet coveralls to the long clothesline, she was ever a quiet presence and never intruded upon my thinking. Only if I sought conversation, did she oblige.

Self-questioning and gnawing guilt were my constant companions. What had I done to bring about this unfathomable heartache? What should I do? If I had been more understanding of the demands of Will's work in Kentucky, maybe he would not have become so intolerant and hurtful. But surely Will bore some responsibility. He was oblivious to my problems, keeping up the home place without his involvement or seeming interest. Yes, that's what hurt the most, his disinterest about anything in my world. He was cruel when I tried to reason with him. I had managed the way I thought Mama would, but circumstances were different. Papa's work never took him away for weeks on end and his family was always the center of his attention, the pride of his life.

By our third day on the farm, my worries had dragged me lower than ever. But that evening around the farm table, the children were anything but sad as they jabbered on about the day's exploits. Taking center stage, their spun tales brought Aunt Cinny and Uncle Jack to fits of laughter as I quietly watched.

After our meal, the cool summer night drew us to the porch where we were swaddled by a cloak of darkness, soothed by the stillness and awed by the limitless sky that teemed with winking stars on which to wish for good things. Surrounded by caring relatives and my children, my looming problems retreated at least for a spell. As we three adults swayed in our rocking chairs, the children scampered onto the grassy yard to lay side-by-side.

"I can count more stars than you," Margaret giggled and counted, her finger poking the night air toward each star. Little Gay wasn't to be outdone and sought to catch up, only to omit a number or two. Margaret counted on, undaunted.

Sighing as I listened, I said to Aunt Cinny, "I should be thinking about the girls' education. Won't be long before Margaret will begin formal schooling, and I'm not certain where we will be then."

Aunt Cinny reached across and patted my knee. "Blanche, that's a year down the road, correct? You needn't fret about that now. The puzzle pieces will fall into place. You'll see."

Nodding, I returned my gaze to the heavens, my fears quieted by the creaking rockers and giggling girls.

***

A week after our buckboard wound up the wagon road to our temporary sanctuary, Uncle Jack rode his white horse into Rhea Springs, personally carrying my letter to Papa, a letter that took hours to compose and left the wastebasket next to my bed filled with wadded attempts. Doing my best to be candid about the increasingly rocky life I had lived with Will over the last six years and begging for understanding as I pondered my future, I had finally sealed the letter, uttered a silent prayer and put it into Jack's hand. Would Papa accept that I might not return to Will? How would he react to the man to whom he had entrusted his daughter? The shame of a family's dissolution would ripple throughout our town and incite wagging tongues. I cringed at the thought.

When Uncle Jack returned late in the afternoon, we settled onto the shaded porch chairs to talk. Aunt Cinny was unpinning dry shirts from the clothesline at the side of the house and the children were nowhere to be seen. Pulling his rocker close, Uncle Jack avoided a direct gaze, obviously uncomfortable in his role as go-between. He cleared his throat as concern creased his forehead. "Your papa found the note you left on the kitchen table before you came here," he began. "He spoke with Bertie the next day, but she insisted she didn't know anything about a planned visit. That caused your Papa worry, so he had already planned to ride over this week to see about you."

Listening to Uncle Jack, I nervously tapped my foot and felt the prickle of tears as I looked to the fields and away from the bearer of unwanted news.

"I told your papa," he said, without noticing, "that your letter would clear up the mystery. And I also reassured him that the children and you were faring well and enjoying your stay here."

Uncle Jack paused but then described how Papa had turned away after reading my letter, apparently to compose himself, and then drew himself to his full height before instructing Uncle Jack to reassure me of his love and support for whatever decisions I would make, and then added his confidence that Grandfather would as well.

I felt Jack's eyes upon me. The sudden and welcome release of tension was replaced by sadness and my countenance surely showed it. He laid his work-calloused hand on my arm. "After reading your letter, your papa worried aloud that you were fretting too much about how this might hurt the family's reputation. He will put those worries to rest, I'm sure, when he sees you. His concern, Blanche, is for you and the girls. Before I left, he said that your mama would be proud of how you have cared for your family."

I bowed my head and then looked up through red-rimmed eyes and smiled. "Uncle Jack, I'm going for a walk. Tell Aunt Cinny I'll be back in an hour to help with supper." I needed to be alone to thank God for Papa, to think about Mama, to think about my future.

I drifted down the long, winding driveway and slipped through the split-rail fencing and across an open field. My mind wandered. How naïve I had been to think that marrying into a proud Kentucky family would guarantee a happy life. Would Mama have said I have made my bed, now I must lay in it?

The heat quickly caught up to me as the sun bore down despite the late afternoon hour. Seeing a grove of tall hickory trees in the distance, I headed in the direction of its shade. When I neared the wooded area, small voices drifted across the silence, but I saw no one. Then a cowbell clanged, followed by children's giggles. Quickening my pace through the trees, I made my way around thickets of vines and thorny shrubbery and was soon greeted by a most unexpected scene. Stopping short, I edged to the closest hickory to hide.

In a nearby small clearing was an old dairy cow—the color of my childhood, fawn-colored Lucinda—with an iron bell hanging from a rope collar around her neck. Tied to a sapling, she stood compliant with only an occasional flick of an ear or tail to repel a circling fly from her bony frame. Margaret and Little Gay busied themselves around her like attentive servants. Draping the animal's neck and head with green vines creating a regal robe, the girls had chosen the cow as the obvious starring actor in their make-believe play. Margaret was similarly adorned with vines about her head and neck, and she danced about in delight as Little Gay pulled more of them from the thicket to add to the costumes of cow and child.

"Now, you stand there next to the groom," Little Gay ordered her big sister, looking every bit the stage director as she took Margaret by both arms and placed her near the cow.

Margaret promptly disputed the roles. "The cow can't be a groom. She's a girl."

Little Gay didn't miss a beat. "We're pretending. Besides, you're a girl too. You don't want to be the groom, do you?"

"No," Margaret conceded. She shrugged and waited for Little Gay to take her position in front of the two.

"Wait a minute," Little Gay said aloud to herself. "If I'm the preacher, then I need a Bible."

As she searched about, I pressed close to the tree and listened to Gay's footsteps crunching across the floor of twigs. Then I heard her report, "This might work."

I peeked around to spot her pulling a chunk of loose bark about the size of a book from a rotting log. Examining it, she brushed it off and smiled with satisfaction as she ran back to her position in front of the bride and groom.

"It says here in the Bible that you two can marry and be husband and wife," she began in all earnestness, standing as straight as any preacher I'd seen before a congregation, holding the make-believe Bible in front of her. "Margaret, do you promise to love your groom always?" She waited for the bride to say 'I do.' Then she turned her attention to the cow and asked, "Groom, do you promise to love your bride?" The bony cow mutely chewed her cud. Waiting, Gay appeared impatient and after a few seconds reported aloud with some exasperation, "The groom says he will always love his bride and promises never to hurt her, ever."

I was stunned at my child's earnest tone. Margaret, embarrassed by her sister's words, bowed her head. Clearing her throat, she remained silent, awaiting her sister's next directive. Little Gay's words echoed in my head.

The cow suddenly let out a long beleaguered moo, having grown impatient with the children's play. Both girls erupted in laughter. The little preacher then uttered her pronouncement, "I now make you husband and wife." And she added, "You can kiss now." Both girls bent over giggling before Margaret turned to kiss the cow's velvet muzzle.

I stepped from behind the tree clapping. Surprised, the girls' laughter abruptly stopped as they stood stone still, not certain whether I would scold them or not.

"What a lovely wedding," I offered. "And the groom is so handsome."

The girls' faces melted in relief and we all had a great laugh, but not for long. As I neared, I saw the vines that served as wedding garments bore shiny jagged leaves. Wrapped around Margaret's head, neck and arms was none other than poison ivy. Even Little Gay, the preacher, had a fuzzy belt of the vine tied around her waist. The children had no idea of the itchy fate to which they had unwittingly doomed themselves. Slipping out of my petticoat and wrapping it around my hands for protection, I quickly unraveled the wedding garments. By the time we set the old cow free and hurried back to the farmhouse, both girls' hands, arms and necks were already swelling with pink and itchy blotches.

Stripped naked, the two sat shivering in the round tin tub in the corner of the farm kitchen as Aunt Cinny rushed back and forth from the well with a wooden bucket sloshing with water. With a paste of ground oatmeal and water, I kneeled beside the tub to plaster the girls' arms and necks with the soothing mixture. The sooner the oils were removed, the less damage to their skin.

***

After washing the supper dishes that evening, Aunt Cinny and I joined the girls in the parlor where they were nestled on the roomy sofa opposite Uncle Jack as he teased them about their afternoon bridal fashion choices. I joined the girls and Aunt Cinny took a seat in her favorite stuffed chair before clearing her throat to draw attention. She held up a brown glass bottle and rag that she pulled from her apron pocket and stated matter-of-factly that the bottle— filled with apple cider vinegar—was a magic potion that would wipe away all remaining itches. With every word spoken, the girls nestled closer to me, with eyes growing wide as an owl's on a dark night. Then their great aunt beckoned them with a weathered and knobby finger to come to her.

"Go ahead girls," I whispered. Already in their nightdresses, they stood and then inched in her direction. Aunt Cinny smothered a grin as she waited. The children stopped an arm's length away, their anxiety so great that their nightgowns trembled. Told to extend their arms like they were sleepwalking, they reluctantly obeyed. Aunt Cinny saturated the cloth with the concoction and—with an approving expression—wiped their arms and hands first and then their small faces and necks. The girls immediately pinched their noses and their faces puckered into wrinkled prunes as they cast questioning glances over their shoulders in my direction. I could not help but chuckle.

The Day children would never forget that wedding ceremony or its consequences, I thought as I lay in bed that night, the smell of vinegar still lingering. I wouldn't either, albeit for different reasons. In my naiveté, I had assumed the children had been sufficiently sheltered from the troubles that plagued Will and me. I realized—at their make-believe wedding—I had been mistaken.

***

Our brief visit had extended into July and the children were treating the place like a second home, with Aunt Cinny and Uncle Jack another set of doting grandparents. I, too, savored the comforts of the retreat but knew it couldn't last.

Aunt Cinny was in a livestock barn several acres away one morning, tending to an ailing calf. The girls had left with Uncle Jack to ride to a far pasture to check on the sheep, the children's favorite farm animals. In the side yard I was beating the dirt from the parlor rug hung over a line between two trees when I spotted the horse and buggy turning off the road in the distance. It moved up the winding wagon path like a small dark bug growing larger as it neared. I stopped to watch. Visitors were not a frequent occurrence and Papa had already visited the previous Sunday. The sun's glare made it impossible to identify the passengers in the covered black buggy. I smoothed the apron over my skirt and pulled the rebellious strands of hair away from my face. As the outline of a man and woman took definition, so did my shock and panic. It was Will, and his mother sat next to him.

My impulse was to run, as far and as fast as my legs would carry me across the field or into the house. Instead, I choked the rug beater in my grasp and my heart pounded like it would jump from my bosom. My legs turned to millstones, anchoring me to the spot.

I had promised Papa on his last visit that I would write Will, but my several attempts had failed. The words I had tried to lasso kept running in all directions, and I had not been able to tame any. Now he was here. I could hide from my husband no longer.

Will tugged hard on the reins, and his buggy came to an abrupt stop in front of the house, the horse whinnying its protest. I walked toward the two like I was going to the gallows. Not twenty feet away, Mrs. Day appeared as prim and proper as the day we met, but her demeanor was grim. The black bonnet tied tight under her chin shadowed her eyes, but her erect and rigid body spoke volumes. Her hands were quietly folded on the lap of her black dress. Given her appearance, she could have been en route to a funeral.

Will settled the horse and then trained his eyes on me. As I met his gaze, it struck me how handsome this man was that I had fallen in love with six years earlier. His dark hair was perfectly groomed, and he sported a starched white shirt with French cuffs and silver cufflinks that scattered the sun's rays. He wore a navy bowtie that sat properly leveled under his chiseled, clean-shaven chin. In the warmth of the day, I detected his musky cologne.

Will's dress always demonstrated how precise and particular he wished to be perceived. But his allure went much further with the impressionable young woman I had been when we met. His intellect and worldly sophistication was like a gateway to places new and unexplored, and that mysterious fascination had drawn me in. But looking upon this man now, I no longer swooned. Instead, my heart was hardened and my anger swelled like a gathering storm.

"Hello, Blanche," Will said in a controlled voice with a hint of a forced smile that quickly faded.

"Hello," I answered stiffly and offered Mrs. Day a nod.

She had no right to come. This was Will's and my business. Then again, maybe her presence would insure my husband's temper would remain in check.

"How are the girls?" Mrs. Day inquired.

With her chin held high, I could see her features beneath the bonnet, those prominent cheekbones and penetrating green eyes.

"They are fine, just fine," I answered, and turned my attention back to Will. Then I added without giving her eye contact, "They're off with their great uncle, riding the fence lines to check on his sheep."

After hesitating, Will asked, "Blanche, when are you coming home?"

"Home?" I asked, and then spouted, "Home is where the heart is. Isn't that how it goes? That being the case, I'm not certain where my home is."

Will's stare was like that of a cat before it pounced. "Blanche, I want you to come home, back to Rhea Springs. We can work through our problems. You belong there; you belong with me." His posture stiffened with each proud word and his eyes did not leave mine until he glanced aside to his mother when he finished. Was he expecting her to echo his demands? She offered only a silent nod.

"I belong where I am respected and valued," I retorted.

"I don't understand what you mean." Will's tone grew impatient. "Of course, I value you. You are the mother of my children...and my wife."

I cast my eyes upon Mrs. Day's stern visage and back to Will to say, "It appears that you place the greatest value on your other family and what they require of you." I was shocked that I had spoken freely, so bluntly in her presence. I knew I was burning bridges. But at the moment, there was ironic pleasure in flinging the words at her as well. She sat in silence, clutching her own hands.

Out of a wave of emotion, my words spilled. "Respect is shown in one's actions, and you know full well yours toward me have shown little respect and have hurt our marriage." My eyes darted from Will to Mrs. Day and back. Ashamed of how our disagreements had become physical, I would not be more direct in her presence. But he knew.

Will grimaced, his fists turning knuckle white as he squeezed the reins. His mother opened her mouth to intervene, but stopped short and glared her disapproval. Before Will could respond, I said flatly, "We will not be coming home with you, at least not now." There. I said it and felt strangely better.

"I don't know how long I will wait," Will replied, his face flushing.

The harsh response was expected, but it nevertheless plunged deep like a knife. Without his saying directly, Will implied he could live without me—that he wasn't willing to fight for our marriage, to make compromises.

He changed the subject to the children and said he wished to see them. I said they should be prepared for his visit and an agreed-upon date set. He argued the point briefly before stating he would return the next Sunday afternoon.

"I'm sorry you're being stubborn," he said. "Maybe with time you will see the folly of your self-centered ways." He repeated he would wait for my decision, but not indefinitely.

Mrs. Day then spoke up. "We are all hoping you'll return to your home." And then she fell silent again.

I held my peace, but raged inside. In the most controlled tone I could muster, I bade Mrs. Day a good day and then Will. As I turned toward the house, I heard Will slap the reins to the horse's back. His spoken words burned like a branding iron and my eyes stung with tears.

***

During July and August, Will made several visits to see the girls and they always looked forward to showing him their newest discoveries around the sprawling farm. Aunt Cinny and Uncle Jack were polite, but managed to remain scarce when he was spied traveling up the winding drive to their farmhouse. Other than his arrival and departure, there was scant exchange between us, except for an occasional curt remark or dead-eyed stare. The gulf grew between us, in large part because I never responded to a letter that Uncle Jack brought home from the postal mail shortly after Will and his mother's visit that July afternoon.

When I had seen the scribbled handwriting on the envelope, I knew immediately it was Will's. Seized with fear, I had pushed it deep into my apron pocket and rushed from the house. Finding my way to the seclusion of the familiar grove of trees, I found a mossy spot and sat. My hands trembled as I examined the unopened envelope on my lap. What would it say? Did he still love me? What amends would he make to salvage our crumbling union? Taking a deep breath, I found my courage and tore open the envelope:

Dear Blanche,
A letter allows the writer time to thoughtfully select the words to pen. A letter also allows the reader time to ponder a thoughtful response. A face-to-face conversation, on the other hand, often evokes immediate emotional reaction that might result in rash words one later regrets. My mother has always said that speaking one's mind, much like gossip, is like slicing a pillow

open in the wind. Its feathers fly to the four corners of the earth, impossible to recapture. I have spent hours considering. At the outset, I want to write that I love you and want our marriage to endure. We have been blessed with two beautiful girls that deserve no less. I believe that is what God wants as well...

Will's considered words scrawled across the page. Rereading them, I thought the strokes themselves resembled a spider's web woven to ensnare me in his logic. He stated I had misconstrued his responsibilities as husband and provider—that I expected him to confine his attentions to the mercantile store in Rhea Springs and neglect the opportunities awarded him by his father. Will complained that he was not like my father, content to confine his realm of influence to Rhea Springs. Will envisioned much more for himself and his family and that required his absence for extended periods. I should be mature enough to rise to that challenge. Will then clarified his view of my role as wife, mother and homemaker and how it should be borne and then concluded our family would thrive and experience harmony if we peered through the same magnifying glass. He wrote,

....my love for you is unchanged. I was smitten the night we circled the dance floor, your eyes—deep ponds of blue—looking up into mine. We both saw a promising and bright future together. It still can be.

Taking no responsibility for the angry, physical confrontations that had battered our marriage, Will used the letter to intimate that our problems had been caused by my discontent, my immaturity, and he concluded by writing:

Think long before making your decision, a decision that will determine the direction of four lives, not just yours alone.

The letter's tone brought me to my lowest. Any secret hope of a miracle evaporated. I slowly refolded the paper and tore it into pieces. I would not speak openly of the unspeakable damage our union had suffered. I could not bear the shame of condemning looks and whispers. But I would not subject myself any longer to a marriage in which I was demeaned, emotionally and physically, and one in which our children might also bear its curse. Tongues would no doubt wag unmercifully when they eventually learn of our divorce but I would not let that dictate my decision and I would not linger to listen. Then and there I determined that we three—Margaret, Gay and myself—would sort out our own futures, futures to be proud of.

***

On September 15, 1918 Will Day was not in Rhea Springs but as usual attending to business in Kentucky. Having spent little time in Rhea Springs over the remainder of the summer, he was the object of rumors that the mercantile store would soon be sold. I had no knowledge of the report's veracity.

But on the morning of that same day, one that predicted a day of azure skies, Papa and Grandfather escorted Margaret, Gay and me to the Spring City train station in the hotel's gleaming white surrey. My nervous chatter the entire four miles revealed my apprehension and excitement. I was lovingly indulged by the two men, and their unspoken support bolstered my resolve. The children's and my boarding the southbound train to Chattanooga would be my first giant step forward.

Papa promised to follow the next weekend by wagon with the remainder of our personal belongings and a few cherished family furnishings. I had refused to leave behind Mama's four oil paintings I had proudly hung in the parlor, my carved rosewood chairs and the rocking chair that had lulled my babies to sleep. The Cuban tile vase I abandoned on the fireplace mantel to gather dust.

As the five of us waited on the station platform, the air felt crisp and clean. This day was like a fresh white page, a new chapter ready to be penned. The possibilities were endless, I told myself, and inhaled my courage. As I admired the girls dressed in their Sunday-best yellow gingham dresses, they scampered around me like playful puppies, pausing only to peer up the track for the black giant that would belch gusts of steam when it neared.

Hours later the three of us would arrive at the Chattanooga terminal and be embraced by Aunt Marian and Uncle Bill, whose big house had echoed its emptiness since the marriages of cousins Sarah and Nancy. They had reassured me that the laughter and chatter of two little girls would breathe life into it again. My earnest prayer was that Chattanooga would bring life to me as well.

CHAPTER 29

BLANCHE - 1946

Thirty years since leaving my hometown, the Wasson Family Cemetery was now the only vestige of dry ground left from the 1941 destruction of Rhea Springs by the Tennessee Valley Authority. It was serendipitous the cemetery had survived because of its elevation, and I remained grateful for the opportunity to make the occasional visit.

Musing on life's now distant memories, I had lost all track of time. The summer sun had inched high overhead and erased the shade of the tall hickories. Because the place seldom entertained visitors, approaching footsteps and muffled voices startled me. Walking toward the cemetery entrance to identify the disturbance, I felt a trickle of perspiration meander down my back beneath my silk blouse. Glancing at my watch to find the hour hand pointing to eleven, I guessed it was not my brother Owen's voice I was hearing. Dropping me here on the way to his Spring City office this morning, he had promised to return at his lunch hour.

When I reached the gate, I spied two men snailing up the gravel drive. One was stooped, dark-skinned with a woolly white fringe around his head. The other was my age and smartly dressed in trousers and pressed white shirt. The old man had a rake in one hand. The younger provided a supporting arm as they navigated the washed-out ruts in the gravel. A beat-up black pickup was parked below.

As I stood staring, the elderly man lifted his eyes from his deliberate steps, paused and looked inquisitively in my direction. "Why, Missus Blanche, is that you?" he called in a halting voice.

In the sun's glare, I could not identify the man, but the voice was unmistakable. Could I believe my ears? The words warmed my heart with the hearing. "Sam, oh Sam, is it really you?"

"Yes, Missus Blanche, it's me, I reckon." As they neared, the two men exchanged a look of amazement, and only then did I recognize Charlie Reynolds at Sam's side. I hurried to them and embraced Sam without hesitation. His frame was bony beneath his faded plaid shirt. The muscular body, always fit for any task Papa had asked of him, had retreated over the decades. But that generosity of spirit I had known as a child still radiated in his eyes and broad smile.

And Charlie? I extended my hand and he clasped it warmly and embraced me with his eyes. Charlie—now the spitting image of his father back in the early 1900s—was tall, lean in stature and square-shouldered. But there was a different air about him, a greater self-assurance than I remembered from when we were young. I was taken aback by his confident gaze.

"It is so good to see you, Missus Blanche," Charlie said with perfect diction.

"And you, Charlie. What are you two doing out here in the heat of the day?"

"Didn't Mister Owen tell you?" Sam answered. "He's wantin' to keep this place neat and respectful for your mama and papa. I pick up trash and empty pop bottles, cut the grass and rake leaves when it's called for. Ruby usually drops me off on her way to work, but this feller brought me today. Down from Ohio for a long-awaited visit, right Charlie?"

Charlie smiled at his father and then explained that he hadn't often been south since his ma had passed away. With the demands of his work and family, he stayed a busy man.

"Papa wrote me about Bertie," I said. "I was sorry to receive that news. In many ways, Charlie, your ma was my lifeline during some difficult years. I'll always remember her with fondness."

He nodded and pointed behind me, saying, "She's right over there, Missus Blanche, in the colored section, the one your grandfather set aside years back."

I had completely forgotten. Grandfather Wasson had taken pity back in the day and provided a good-sized plot of ground, more than an acre, for the Negroes of Rhea Springs. Until then, there had been no proper burial site for colored people. They were forced to bury their deceased on the back ridges of Walden. The designated area Grandfather set aside was not close to our tended grassy cemetery with its cut and engraved headstones, but tucked among the trees, farther back on the hill. Instead of gravestones, I recalled small makeshift wooden crosses as markers. No doubt, over time, they had decayed and disappeared. With no fence around the area and no stone markers, few would know what lay underneath the blanket of decayed leaves and littered branches.

"When I come up here to clean," Sam said, "I always takes time to head back to our section and tidy up around Bertie's spot. Charlie bought a small stone marker for his ma's eternal resting place, and I keep the leaves raked and debris cleared. I know Bertie would come haunting me if I didn't."

We all smiled, remembering Bertie's ways. She was a stickler for neatness and scolded me as a child—who knows how many times— for leaving my bedclothes on the bedroom chair or not making my bed properly.

"We miss her, don't we Pa?" Charlie placed a reassuring arm across Sam's shoulder. Probably to distract his father, he asked me, "Did you know Ruby now has grandchildren of her own? They give their gramp here a run for his money when they're around. Isn't that so, Pa?"

As I listened to Charlie, his well-spoken words faded in my hearing and my mind drifted to when I was in this cemetery for Grandfather's funeral a decade ago. I'd learned then from Sam about Charlie's sudden departure from Rhea Springs. Will and I were the reason. The Ku Klux Klan had raised its ugly head after rumors began stirring, and Charlie was convinced he was the intended target. He had no idea what Will Day might have made up to bring down the wrath of those men. Charlie could have easily stained the Day and Wasson family names with gossip about what he witnessed that dreadful morning in the field behind the house or for other suspected offenses for that matter. Sam had said no one ever determined whether the cross burning had anything to do with my troubles, and the Klan went dormant shortly thereafter.

Since learning of that turn of events, my conscience had refused to remain quiet especially after hearing Charlie hopped a train to Ohio where the Army was accepting Negro recruits. They shipped him to France to fight in the Great War, and according to Sam, he was extraordinarily proud to serve. At the time, I had inquired with baited breath as to Charlie's well being, and Sam reassured me he never saw the front lines, a disappointment and frustration for his son, but a relief to his ma and pa. He was relegated to caring for a Cavalry platoon's horses several miles behind the fighting. I could still remember Sam laughing and saying that Charlie thought he'd escaped a life of grooming horses and mucking stalls, but he had made peace with it. He was doing a job for his country and lived to see the war's end. The sad turn for Sam and Bertie was that Charlie returned to Ohio instead of coming back to the South. My own departure from Rhea Springs had been equally traumatic. When Papa visited the girls and me in Chattanooga, I never inquired about what was happening in Rhea Springs. I didn't want to think about it. Starting fresh took every ounce of emotional energy and looking back was far too painful.

Charlie's voice ceased from tales of Ruby, and I forced myself back to the moment to ask, "How are you doing, Charlie? And Ida Mae?"

"Ida Mae? I haven't thought about that gal in ages. Aha, the one that got away!"

His comment was accompanied by an easy grin, as if a once momentous event was now trivial. Had my actions unintentionally driven those two apart?

Charlie saw my face drain its color, and he reached to pat my shoulder. "Don't feel bad, Missus Blanche. I'm a happy man, and so is Ida Mae, I would wager. She was convinced I was coming back from war in a pine box. And Elijah Jenkins took opportunity to comfort her at every turn. You can guess the outcome of that," he said with a chuckle.

Now was the time to say what I'd rehearsed for years. I took a deep breath and said, "Charlie, I'm sorry that Will's and my problems so disrupted your life. I was ashamed of what transpired before your eyes in that field and couldn't bear the thought of seeing you, let alone trying to explain...."

Charlie interrupted. "You needn't apologize. That was years ago, ancient history...for both of us. In the end, those terrible days drove me to places I would never have gone otherwise. I was one scared fellow then. But in retrospect, I'm actually grateful. After the war—back in Cincinnati—Aunt America's cousin dragged me to her church socials where I met the most beautiful gal north or south of the Mason Dixon line. Wilma's been the love of my life. She was as spunky a girl as you when we met—kind'a reminded me of you. Been a fine mama to our boy and two girls. And you might be especially interested to know that my boy grew up to become a teacher in the Cincinnati colored schools. He's taught hundreds to read and write and love books, so you see what you started Missus Blanche?"

I was speechless.

He laughed and said those books I had thrust upon him years back had turned the keys to his future. Not long after returning from France, Charlie said he applied for work on the New York Central Railroad. Because of his literacy and how well he presented himself, he had donned the official Pullman Porter Cap to travel as far west as St. Louis and back east to New York City. "And since then," Charlie said with a laugh, "the railroad has been *paying me* to ride the rails."

Sam added with a grin, "His ma carried around a picture of him in his tie and white coat and Pullman cap. Showed it to everbody that would give her the time of day. Wasn't one Negro in Rhea County who didn't know her son was traveling to fancy, faraway places on them luxury trains. And Charlie here," Sam said, slapping his son on the back, "played a part in the forming of the Pullman Porter's work union too."

"Oh, really?" I said, remembering that I'd read newspaper articles about those struggles.

Charlie shot his pa a side-glance like he wasn't too happy the subject had been raised. "Pa gives me a little too much credit, but I do belong. Yep, I thought when I went north, life would be better, and it is. The railroad has given me more than what I could have expected here, and I have been to places most folks, colored or white, don't experience in a lifetime."

Charlie spoke bluntly, however, that the slights he witnessed as a young'un in Rhea Springs were repeated everywhere. "Remember when I got hot under the collar over Sam Waterhouse's treatment by some out-of-towner?"

"Yes, I do remember. The father of my summer friend from Knoxville." My body tensed in discomfort from the subject we were wading into.

"Well, on the trains too many travelers see my nametag and call me 'George,' as in one of George Pullman's boys...just as demeaning. But I don't let them get away with it. Like Waterhouse said back in the day, you have to be smart in dealing with folks and not let them get the best of you. With a smile, I correct them. The Good Book says patience is a virtue, and I do get plenty of practice. But I'm not complaining too loud. My wages are good and I'm respected in my own community."

"Now, enough about me. I was sorry to hear of your papa's passing. With Rhea Springs being submerged and all, I guess you're grateful your papa didn't live to see that turn of events."

"So true," I said, relieved the topic of conversation had moved on.

Looking out over the lake, Charlie said, "Pa says he can paddle a rowboat out there and still make out the town's roadbeds underneath, and it's been five years. Isn't that what you said Pa?"

"That's the gospel truth," Sam said, slowly shaking his head as he gazed out over the water.

"I understand from Pa that your girls have enjoyed living in Chattanooga and are grown now... and married?" Charlie asked.

"Yes, living in Chattanooga was also a world away from Rhea Springs, but I regret they didn't experience the childhood I had in that magical place."

Charlie made no comment.

"I'm a grandmother myself now," I added. Wondering whether to speak of my personal life, I hesitated. But I guessed these men had a right to know since my life had cast long shadows across theirs.

"I also found another love...eventually. After some false starts with work that didn't suit me, I studied to become a legal secretary. I then met Carl Abernathy. He was a fine trial lawyer." I started to brag, but stopped short. "It was a good marriage, a happy one, but Carl passed last winter. Double pneumonia."

"I'm sorry, Missus Blanche," Charlie and Sam chorused.

"Me, too. That's really the reason I'm here, to see Owen. My inheritance from Carl has made it possible to make provision for my old age…with some wise investments, I hope."

As Sam and Charlie listened, the sound of an automobile horn interrupted from the bottom of the hill. Owen was waving from the rolled-down car window. It was time to leave. Knowing I might never again see Charlie or Sam, I hugged them—first Sam and then Charlie—and was almost brought to tears.

I looked first into Sam's graying eyes and then Charlie's and said in a halting voice, "Thank you both…so much." They nodded, yet their eyes were questioning me. I couldn't say more, so turned to leave. Their talk trailed me as I headed down the gravel drive.

"Missus Blanche looks mighty fine for a fifty-two year old woman," I overheard Charlie say. "She's tangled with life and appears to have come out on top."

"You know…She's had more than her share of struggles…just like the rest of us," Sam replied.

"Wish I could have done more back then for her," said Charlie, "but the Klan would certainly have had something to say about that. But like a good book, the ending's different than you might have expected from reading the early chapters…when all hell broke loose.

The last I heard was Sam chuckle, "You and your books!"

I wanted to turn around for one last wave, but settled on a smile to myself. The Reynolds' family had been more than hired help. I came to see them as friends. They had protected the Wasson family from far greater disgrace than a daughter's divorce. Whispers of abuse would have reaped consequences more devastating and far-reaching. Charlie had done more for me—and for himself—than he could have ever thought possible at the time. The altered paths of our lives had not led to dead ends after all.

By the time I reached the idling sedan and opened the door, the joy of the reunion had chased away my melancholy. Settling in my seat, I peered up the hill to see Charlie and Sam still talking.

"I see Sam and Charlie were keeping you company," Owen said, as he put the car into gear. "I didn't know Charlie was in town. Sorry to have kept you waiting. The trustee's office is never quiet and someone popped in unexpectedly…"

"Not a problem," I said. "It was a treat to see them. And Charlie, he's traveled a long way from his Rhea Springs roots, hasn't he?"

"As have you," Owen cast an approving glance and changed the subject. "Now what is it you wanted to discuss over dinner tonight?"

"Like I told you. A banker friend of Carl's has been counseling me on some investments to consider. Looking out for his old friend's widow, I guess. Anyhow, I'd like your advice."

"Why don't you give me some information so I can investigate—make a few phone calls this afternoon to the money people I respect," Owen said, as the car headed toward his bungalow in Spring City. "I'll drop you at the house to visit with Bessie, and I'll be along at suppertime."

"Well," I began. "Buying stock in Consolidation Coal Company is one possibility. We all know coal is powering the country these days. Even with more dams like the ones here on the Tennessee, water-powered electricity remains a small part of the country's power production. Coal-fired plants are here to stay, wouldn't you think? Am I impressing you with my knowledge?" I smiled coyly.

"Tell me more, little sister."

"The second is the Coca-Cola Bottling Company. They have agreed to supply all of America's fighting men overseas with the bottled drink and plans are in the works to make Coca-Cola available around the globe. My banker friend says his associates are already lining up to purchase shares. I know we're talking about soda pop, but I'm told it's gonna soar. Well, those are my choices to consider."

The car slowed to a stop in front of the modest fieldstone house. On the large covered front porch were a double swing and two rockers, just like we had at our old home place in Rhea Springs. When I closed the sedan door, I leaned down and said through the open window, "Thanks for giving me the morning with Mama and Papa. It was good to revisit the past. Helps me to keep the present in perspective."

Owen winked, and I turned to follow the stone walkway to the house. The door creaked as I stepped inside to be greeted by the familiar ticking of our family's old grandfather clock.

NOTE FROM THE AUTHOR

Rhea Springs, a small dot on a Tennessee map, was called home by many. As early as the 1700s, white pioneering families began settling the land that the Cherokee Nation had hunted and farmed before them. Known not only for its rich soil, proximity to the Tennessee River and abundant fishing, the area's numerous mineral springs promised cures and good health.

By the time my grandmother was born in Rhea Springs in1896, the Cherokees had been driven West and the small village and surrounding county, seventy miles north of Chattanooga, had swelled from a few farming families to a population of 14,000 countywide. At that time my grandmother's family owned and successfully operated Rhea Springs' only resort hotel as well as their gristmill and general store.

Fifty years later when as a child I sat at Grandmother's knee, she would wistfully sift through her box of curled and faded black-and-white photographs of Rhea Springs and reminisce about the joy of growing up in the shadow of the hotel that drew hundreds every summer. With a nostalgic twinkle in her eyes, she regaled me with stories of couples in ballroom finery circling the hotel dance floor on summer nights, of once chasing her pet cow onto the hotel's veranda, of Sunday afternoons listening to her father read Shakespeare aloud on their shaded front porch. To her, as a child, the place was a bit of Eden.

But others who made their homes there certainly had other perspectives. A number of families had resettled from Northern states, both before and after the Civil War, looking for new opportunity. But others, brought there against their wills as slaves well before the war, remained afterward for whatever reasons, experiencing servitude of a different form. Some sharecropped for white landowners; others worked as domestics for families; few prospered.

This novel seeks to capture not only the innocence of a young white girl like my grandmother who enjoyed a life of relative privilege but also to reveal another world existing in the same place and time with a far different reality, that of African-American families that shouldered the weight of cultural and legal bias and injustice that at the turn of the 20th Century was the norm, even in a fair-minded, peace-loving place like Rhea Springs. In the lives portrayed, I brought to the fore two children's growing awareness of the world and its stark realities, and how each sought to bridge the chasm to embrace change. It demanded a courageous response from both.

I have described the Rhea Springs locale as historically accurate as possible, using published resources as well as my grandmother's recollections. Although some character names are those of long-deceased relatives, the actions of those characters are fictional. The area experienced drastic change when the town saw its demise in 1941. Flooded over by the Tennessee Valley Authority, it is now the site of Watts Bar Lake.

Made in the USA
Middletown, DE
19 August 2017